AMANDA BELL

JEFF MINICK

ISBN: 1482390132
ISBN-13: 9781482390131

*Nobody has ever measured, not even poets,
how much the heart can hold.*

— ZELDA FITZGERALD

Dedication

To Kris

quae cantat cum angelis

PART I

Chapter One

nce upon a time....

When Amanda Bell was a girl, so small that the lilies in her mother's garden brushed her cheeks when she walked among them, these were the words she loved best in all the world. These were the heralds whose trumpets announced mist-locked mountains, rose-draped castles, endless caverns, dragons and goblins and trolls, witches and elves, orphans lost in a darkling wood, a maiden sleeping the sleep of the dead while awaiting the kiss of a handsome prince. For Amanda, these four little words were an incantation promising a life of magic, beauty, adventure, true love.

And then she grew up.

———

It was December of 2010, the Wednesday before Christmas, and by nightfall the storm had shut down the airport. Snowflakes big as quarters whirled from the night skies of Northern Virginia, slapping the windows like frozen gunshots. Beneath the glow of streetlamps a meringue of snow lay piled in folds, and farther away, out on the darkened runways, the running lights of snowplows and salt trucks flickered like holiday decorations.

Turning from the window and the blizzard, Amanda Bell studied the other stranded travelers with whom she would spend this wintry night. Some of them were reading the Post or paperback books. A few punched away at laptops, oblivious to their neighbors, intent on their screens as osprey on a fleet of trout. Others were eating, drinking, dozing, chatting with their neighbors, conversing, a little too loudly, on their cells. With the runways of Dulles heaped with snow and the nearby motels either inaccessible or booked to capacity, Amanda resigned herself to her fate. She was stuck with this motley crew of strangers until dawn.

She checked the time on her BlackBerry—10:23—returned the phone to her shoulder bag, and again scrutinized the room, this time with open disdain. Disorder, mess, and the unforeseen were Amanda's greatest enemies. They were wildfires threatening chaos and destruction, and she was the forester, ready at a moment's notice to stamp out the flames. But this tempest of snow and wind had ruined her plans for returning to work the next day. Worse still, the blizzard had condemned her to spend the night with this twitching press of raw humanity. Here in this terminal--how appropriate the word seemed!--were mess and disorder to burn: disgruntled creatures walking helter-skelter, some sleeping in chairs, a baby fussing, two children chasing each other in circles. Directly in front of her an elephantine man tilted back his head and poured a pack of peanuts into his mouth. Amanda shuddered as if someone had just run fingernails across a chalkboard.

Had some official bestowed on her charge of this cavernous room, given her a referee's whistle and the authority to use it, Amanda would have soon brought order to this ruck of humanity. She would have divided the room into sections: sleepers, readers, parents with children. She would have set aside a far corner of the lounge for those who wished to converse with one another or talk on their phones. Finally, she would have appointed guards to patrol the lounge in hourly shifts, thereby allowing their fellow passengers to sleep without fear of theft, assault, or molestation. An acrimonious few might rankle at such directives, but Amanda was confident she could persuade even the most seditious among them to embrace her arrangements. She had ways of getting people to obey her.

This was Amanda's special pride: she got the job done.

This management of people gave Amanda Bell a certain cool pleasure. Though a youngster in the world of corporate management--she had quietly celebrated her twenty-seventh birthday not two months earlier--arduous study and attention to lessons learned in the workplace had given Amanda the tools required for the maintenance of authority. She recognized, for instance, the importance of dress and carriage. Before leaving for the office in the mornings, she ordered her appearance to elicit respect from her superiors and obeisance from those she supervised. Every workday morning she plaited her long hair into braids or a tight, blonde bun. She limited her makeup to pale lipstick, a brush of blush, a touch of mascara. Generally she arrived at work an hour early dressed in a white blouse and powder-gray business jacket with matching skirt. Though of an average height—Amanda stood exactly five feet six inches in her stocking feet—her slender build, her dress, and her erect posture made her appear taller to most people. When faced with an especially daunting situation at work, and having once read that the towering veterans of Napoleon's Old Guard had worn bearskin hats to appear even more formidable to their enemies, Amanda would go into battle armored in a pair of black, stiletto heels and a matching black suit. Monochromatic colors, she knew, made her appear taller, thinner, and even more imposing than usual.

Many of the twenty-four employees under her supervision at Saxon and Henle despised her austere style of command, resented her cool demeanor, rankled at her blunt directions. Though none dared confront her face to face, Amanda had gotten wind of their gossip and ridicule. She knew well what they muttered behind her back, mocking her in their cubicles or in the break room, releasing their resentment through whispered monikers. The Iron Maiden. The Immaculate Perfection. Frau Storm Trooper. The Blonde Bitch. Occasionally their taunts and back-biting bruised Amanda's feelings, yet she understood the origins of their rancor. Fact One: Strong women, women who can push and shove and make things happen, are always despised, as much by other women as by men. Fact Two: Adults who behave like children will sulk or throw tantrums when treated like children. Tardiness, habitual mistakes, sloppy work, laziness, and a cavalier attitude were marks of the adolescent, deserving reprimand or in some cases dismissal. Consequently, Amanda had taught herself to slough off the maledictions of her underlings, to ignore their grumblings, to focus on the bigger picture. Respect and accomplishment, not love or friendship, were what she sought from her subordinates.

She got the job done.

Given no whistle, however, and possessed of no authority on this night of wind and snow, Amanda searched for a place to close her eyes until morning. Seeing that the quieter sections of the lounge, the rows of chairs by the window and along the wall, were occupied, she settled near the center of the room between a young woman wearing a Georgetown sweatshirt and a plump, softly snoring man in a red knit cap. She placed her luggage by her feet, held her shoulder bag in her lap, and debated reading a few passages from *Power Management* before undertaking the arduous task of falling asleep in the midst of such appalling anarchy.

As Amanda took her seat, Georgetown, who was holding a cell phone to her ear with both hands, twisted away from her. She was chewing a cud of gum and nodding frequently, her ponytail of red hair bobbing with each jerk of her head. Once she said, "Please," and then choked the word into the phone several more times. After another long moment, the girl took the phone from her ear and twisted round front again in her chair. Fixedly, she stared into space. Slowly, she closed her cell phone. Even more slowly, she bent forward, propped her elbows on her knees, hid her face in her hands, and wept.

Opening her bag, Amanda took out *Power Management*, which she'd already read twice, making notes in the margins the second time, and located as well a package of Kleenex. She tapped Georgetown's shoulder and offered a tissue. "Help yourself. Take several, if you wish."

While Georgetown wiped her eyes, Amanda resisted the urge to lecture the girl on the perils of weeping in public. Some men, she had observed, regarded weeping as a sign of female weakness while others viewed the act as a signal to commence sexual advances. Many women, though sympathetic on the surface, despised tears in another female, judging them an infantile shout for attention, usually from males. Outside the confines of one's home, all such lachrymose outbursts were best restricted to a stall in the ladies' room.

"A young man?"

The girl nodded, sniffling. "Caleb." She dabbed her eyes with the wadded tissue. "He's supposed to meet me in Atlanta, but now he says he loves Julia."

"Who's Julia?"

"My best friend."

"Your best friend?"

"Yes."

"Does Julia love Caleb?"

Georgetown turned her face toward Amanda, her eyes wide and perplexed. "Why, I guess she does…I don't know…I mean, I just assumed…."

"Assumptions are self-indulgent," Amanda said. "They can also be dangerous."

She studied Georgetown's face, seeking signs of strength and weakness. In the eyes and set of the mouth she could sometimes discover clues to a person's character. Liking what she found in Georgetown's firm chin, Amanda decided to offer assistance. "Here is what you must do. First, make a call to Julia. Tell her how disappointed you are in her. Tell her you can't believe she has betrayed you."

"But I'm not sure she has betrayed me."

"It doesn't matter—it only matters that Julia thinks that you think she has betrayed you. Whatever the circumstances, she will be shocked by your candor and will grow resentful of Caleb. Do you love him?"

"With all my heart." A fresh tributary of tears forced Amanda to dole out another tissue. "We've been seeing each other for years and years. I can't imagine life without him."

"You must learn to resist gross exaggeration." When Georgetown stared blankly at her, Amanda continued: "At any rate, after calling Julia, you will immediately telephone Caleb. You will tell Caleb you love him. You will tell Caleb you are going to fight for him. You will tell him— look here, are you going to remember my points or do you need to take notes?"

Georgetown stared at Amanda. Her mouth hung open. She might have posed as a caricature of a bug-eyed candidate for a lunatic asylum.

"Close your mouth," Amanda commanded her.

Georgetown closed her mouth.

"Well?"

"I'll remember everything you said," Georgetown whispered. "How do you know all this stuff? Are you a teacher?"

"Heavens, no," Amanda said. "My degree was in English literature. I minored in classics."

"How did you learn to talk so good?"

"So well," Amanda reprimanded absentmindedly while considering the girl's question. "I possess a strong natural will and a love of the English language. My father was an amateur actor who taught me the advantages of forceful speech. My mother was an inveterate reader who drilled me in the details of syntax and grammar."

"Are you married?"

"What does that have to do with anything?"

"I just wondered."

"I was almost engaged once. He broke off the relationship."

"What happened?"

"He said I was too controlling."

"Were you?"

"Probably. But if ever a man needed controlling, it was Steven."

"When—"

"Two years ago."

"I'm sorry."

"Don't be. It was, as they say, for the best."

"Is there anyone else in your life?"

Amanda pondered the girl's question. Joseph Grenier—he preferred the pedestrian Joe—popped to mind. A fellow manager at Saxon and Henle, Joseph had charge of the accounting staff. Two weeks ago he had suggested spending some time together over Christmas. Joseph possessed some intriguing features. He had, for example, directed the secretaries in his division to align their waste cans to the right and rear of their desks. He was adamant in his insistence on punctuality. Amanda had long admired men who favored order, though Joseph also struck her as somehow weak-willed by making friends of his underlings. Now, however, was no time for idle self-examination.

"We're not talking about me. We're discussing Caleb. What's his last name?"

"Davenport."

"You tell Caleb Davenport to meet you at the Atlanta airport or face the consequences."

"What are the consequences?"

"We'll invent those later, if we need them."

"Will he meet me, do you think? If I say all those things, will he meet me?"

"Wild horses couldn't keep him away." Amanda offered another tissue, but for a different reason. "Spit out your gum before you call. Conversing on the phone while smacking gum is unattractive."

Georgetown took the tissue, spat out the offending gum, and punched at her phone.

Amanda pointed to the nearest corner of the room. "Would you mind moving over there, please? I intend to read for a while."

Georgetown stood, clutching her phone like a weapon, and set off toward the designated corner and her showdown with Caleb Davenport.

———

Although she had learned many lessons from *Power Management,* Amanda disliked the chapter titled "The Manager as Cheerleader." Why on earth did people need so much encouragement nowadays? Didn't people already receive enough approval? Were there no grownups left in the world? People patted one another on the back so incessantly it was a wonder their shoulders didn't fall off. Amanda Bell was a firm believer in infrequent compliments and merited rewards.

Irritated by the thought of managers as cheerleaders, Amanda closed the book and turned her attention to the restive herd of fellow travelers. To her right, a handsome older man with one of those drooping Eastern European mustaches stood before a group of young people, waving his hands like a conductor as he tried to teach the teenagers a Christmas carol. His graying hair was curly and wild, and in the pocket of his long blue coat was the outline of a pint bottle. "Adeste Fideles," the man cried, swaying on his feet. "Sing vit me! Sing vit me!" He had a heavy accent, Polish or Russian, and he was singing in Latin, which revived in Amanda memories of Mrs. Donadio's ninth grade Latin class. Soon the man had the young people singing with him, some in English, some in French, and at least one in Latin. When they finished their polyglot carol, the students applauded. The man bowed, grinned at them, and wandered away.

Amanda returned to her book. In a quarter of an hour, a short, stout woman with dark hair and skin the color of an unpeeled kiwi wiggled her buttocks into the chair abandoned by Georgetown. Clinging to the woman's legs were two small girls who looked like twins. Four eyes brown as coffee beans stared at Amanda. Mechanically the woman bounced her third child, a fretful baby boy, on her knees. The two girls stepped a pace away when this reckless dandling commenced, watching their mother with their dark, solemn eyes and then looking again at Amanda. The woman crooned and bounced while the toddler, dressed, appropriately enough, in blue pajamas printed with cowboys and horses, bobbed up and down like a bronco buster. In a moment he was crying.

After a minute or so of this rodeo, Amanda marked her place in *Power Management* and turned to the woman. "Try a trot rather than a gallop."

The woman smiled weakly.

"Do you speak English?"

The woman shook her head.

The little boy's head waggled back and forth as if it might snap off at any moment. Amanda held out her arms. "Give him to me," she said. The woman stopped jiggling the baby to inspect her with narrowed eyes. "Come, come," Amanda said. She snapped her fingers, then opened her hands again. "Let me calm him. Then you must all be quiet and allow me to read."

Watching Amanda as if she were a scorpion, the woman handed over the baby. Amanda lay the child's head on her shoulder, gripped him firmly by the bottom, and patted his back. The baby burped, then spat up on her shoulder and down the front of her suit. Making noises of apology, the mother took a rag from her enormous purse and dabbed at the curdled milk, rubbing the mess deeper into the fabric of Amanda's outfit.

Amanda brushed aside the woman's hand. Quiet now, the baby in her arms gazed at her. Returning that stare, she wondered how her own offspring might look. Their physical features depended, of course, on her partner. Joseph Grenier? How would their progeny turn out should she someday marry him? Which of them, mother or father, would the children favor? Joseph possessed high cheekbones and a handsome mouth, but his nose was thin and long, and his ears were too large for his head. Were large ears hereditary? And what of her own contribution to their gene pool? Would their offspring be blonde? (Amanda was not a connoisseur of blonde jokes, which she considered racist. Suppose, she had once asked a startled friend, someone began telling kinky-haired jokes?) Blue eyes, a figure firm and shapely from years of exercise at local gyms and spas, a generous mouth, though perhaps overly-stern: Amanda was no Helen of Troy, but she wouldn't cloud the sun. Yet she was always honest in her self-appraisal, aware of her physical imperfections: her lips didn't exactly demand a kiss, and her eyes often frowned a warning at the world.

The little boy fell asleep, his mouth drooping open. Amanda handed him to his mother. The two girls watched everything with big, brown eyes.

"Well, what about the two of you? Are you like your mother or do you speak English?"

Their stare glimmered recognition. Otherwise, nothing.

Then one of the girls covered a yawn.

"You are tired." Removing the scarf from her neck, Amanda folded it around her hand into the shape of a rabbit with floppy ears, a trick taught to her by her father when she was seven. The side of her hand became the rabbit's mouth. "Hey, amigos," her hand said. She paused, then pitched her voice an octave higher. "I'm Squire Rabbit. You need sleep. It is getting late. Are you tired? You look very sleepy to me." The rabbit talked to the girls for five minutes, telling them about the snow, and their flight tomorrow, and why they must sleep. The girls kept their eyes on the rabbit and listened. When the rabbit said, "Let's go, little amigos. Let's get ready for bed," they nodded.

Leaving her coat and bag in the mother's care, Amanda escorted the girls to the women's room, where she washed their hands and faces. On their way back to mother and baby, Amanda paused by the assistance table set up by the airlines and asked to borrow three blankets. The uniformed boy manning the table, pimply and skinny as a stick, looked like an eighth grader in masquerade.

"What sweet little angels," he said.

"Children are not angels." Amanda took the blankets. "They are nuisances." Then she studied the girls. "Still, they do possess a certain charm."

Back at their seats, Amanda put the girls to bed beneath the chairs. She tucked each one into a blanket, piling up one end for a pillow, and patted each girl on the head. She wrapped the third blanket around the mother, who remained firmly ensconced in her chair. She resisted patting the woman's hair, but stroked the baby's forehead. She then gathered her travel bags and coat, and set off to discover quieter quarters.

Someone touched her arm, and she turned to find Georgetown smiling at her. "It went down just like you said," she said, blushing with excitement. "Julia never intended going out with Caleb. She never even knew about it. And Caleb's going to meet me at the airport after all."

"So it is working out for you."

"I can't thank you enough. You were such a help."

"And you are—"

"Mary Beth Miller."

"You must be pleased, Mary Beth. Promise me you'll get some sleep. You'll need your wits about you tomorrow."

"I promise." Happiness shone in her eyes. "What's your name?"

Amanda assessed Mary Beth's age—twenty was an outside guess—and declined familiarity. "I'm Ms. Bell."

Mary Beth hugged Amanda, then pecked her cheek. "Good-night, Ms. Bell."

"Sleep well, Mary Beth."

———

A chair among some potted ferns seemed suitable for sleep, but her neighbor on the far side of the ferns, an artificially tanned woman with tattoos on her forearms, was telephoning friends and relatives to tell them about the blizzard, as though she had never seen snow. "Unbelievable!" she said, repeatedly. "It's truly unbelievable!" Given the late hour, Amanda concluded that the woman's familiars kept wondrously strange schedules.

A short bench beckoned next, but as soon as Amanda had seated herself, Arctic breezes from the nearby hallway swept across the back of her neck. Near the water fountain, she secured a comfortable chair, but two men camped out beside her seemed prepared to talk all night about the price of real estate in Albuquerque. In their fascination with rates, points, and tax deductions, they remained oblivious to her exasperated stare.

Eventually she found a home beside a gray trash receptacle. Here she could lay her head against the wall, and the trash receptacle on her right meant that humanity could badger her only from the left.

And badger her it did. Beside her, at a chair's remove, a man in a loosely-knotted red tie and white shirt drank from a canned soda and conversed intently in whispers with the woman beside him. Both of them carried the telltale insignia of mediocre middle management: an absence of self-confidence, cheap clothing, scuffed shoes, harassed faces. After closing her eyes, Amanda remembered them quarreling earlier that evening, just after the airlines had announced the closure of the runways. Had they been going at each other this entire time?

Despite their low voices—the man in particular seemed concerned about confidentiality—Amanda was privy to enough of their conversation to feel both pity and contempt. She was just drifting away on the currents of their murmured words when the woman's rising voice reeled her back to the shores of wakefulness.

"—bastard!" she said. "You know damn well you've wanted me for months. And now that you've had me, you're scared! You know you want to leave her. You know it!"

"Vanessa, please," the man said, his voice low, pleading. "It was a party. We had too much to drink. It was wrong. I admit I—"

The woman slapped him, spinning him round in his chair. Dark liquid from his soda can flew onto Amanda's knees, shins, and shoes. The woman jerked to her feet, snatched up her travel bag, and marched across the room toward the rest room, where, Amanda thought, she would doubtless indulge in a healthy soliloquy of regrets and tears.

Amanda dug for more tissues in her purse while the man apologized. "Let me get you some paper towels. It won't take a minute."

"I'm fine." She patted her hose with the tissue, then removed her left shoe and wiped gingerly at her ankle and toes.

"I'm awfully sorry."

Amanda gave up the futile task of sopping cola from her stockings and contemplated the adulterer. He was green-eyed and freckled, tousled, a thirty-something Tom Sawyer whose memories of Indian Cave, Huck Finn, and Becky Thatcher lay long buried beneath obligation, debts, taxes, a mortgage. The blush on the left side of his face was about five shades deeper than the one on the right.

"Sorry for what?"

"I know what you're thinking."

"What am I thinking?"

"That I'm a stupid jerk."

"Why would I think you're stupid?"

The man missed the full import of her carefully chosen words. "Because of last night," he said. "What I did last night? With Vanessa? You must have heard."

"I heard too much."

He shook his head. "We've done it. We've really done it now. I never meant it to happen. Neither did Vanessa."

"Yes, she did."

"What?" He looked as if Amanda had just dumped one of the ice buckets from his company party onto his head. "What did you say?"

"Vanessa wanted it to happen. She made it happen."

"How could you possibly know that?"

"I heard it in her voice."

"Oh."

"You should have fended her off. She's in love with you—or thought she was."

"It was that open bar at the party. All that drinking. I don't usually drink—not the way we were drinking. Helen hardly drinks at all."

"Who's Helen?"

"My wife."

Amanda rebuked him with silence.

"All right," he said after a minute. "It was my fault, too." He turned the palms of his hands upward, a plea for understanding. "What do I do now? I'm so ashamed of myself. I love Helen. What if she leaves me when she finds out?"

"How will she find out? Will Vanessa tell her?"

"No, Vanessa won't tell her."

"Who else knows?"

"Just me. And you, I guess."

"So you're going to tell Helen?"

"I have to be honest with her, don't I? Don't I have to clear this thing up so we can get on with our lives?"

"Helen won't think of you as honest. She'll think of you as a fool. A drunk and a cheat. She'll never trust you again—not completely, not the way she does now. And you're right—she may leave you. Do you have children?"

"Two. Two little boys." The man choked. Amanda hoped he wouldn't begin crying. Her supply of tissues was dangerously low.

"You may lose them, too. And someday they'll find out what you did and hate you for it."

"So I shouldn't tell her?"

"I don't see the point in telling her."

"What should I do then?"

"You must take an oath. You must swear to yourself that you'll never betray Helen again. You must swear to yourself that you'll love her as ardently as possible."

"What if I break that oath?"

"You won't. You won't even be tempted."

"How do you know?"

"I can tell by looking at you."

"What do you mean?"

"You don't have the face for it."

"Are you a psychologist?"

Amanda was tempted to answer in the affirmative. It seemed the simpler explanation, and she was tired of explaining herself to people. Besides, wasn't everyone a psychologist today? There was Doctor Phil. Doctor Laura. Why not Doctor Amanda?

Sitting in that chair, her hose glued to her shins with cola, blouse smelling of baby barf, head buzzing with exhaustion, Amanda pictured her Atlanta apartment, that self-created haven where she could be alone and happy. Peach carpeting, white walls, and dimmed lights. Soft music--*Jazz for the Quiet Times* would be perfect--and a glass of dry white wine. A steaming bath, a favorite novel: *Pride and Prejudice, Sense and Sensibility, Emma.* After this night only the astringent prose of Jane Austen possessed the power to set life right again. "Yes," Amanda said, thinking of home. "Oh, yes."

The man mistook her affirmation and granted her a degree in psychology. "So, Doc, you think I shouldn't tell her?"

"Confessions other than those made to a priest or a psychiatrist are fraught with danger. Helen may be the nicest woman in the world, but telling her you had a drunken, one-night stand with a fellow employee will hurt her tremendously. Why would you do that to her? What good would come of it? People jabber too much these days. This idea that revelation necessarily brings healing is nonsense. We watch too many talk shows. Instead of looking for ways to exonerate yourself, why not do the right thing?"

"Yes," the man said. "The right thing." The slap mark on his face was fading, replaced by a pallor that was, no doubt, the result of last night's alcohol and the late hour. Bluish circles beneath the man's eyes and a stubble of beard further testified to his debauchery. Despite his cadaverous physiognomy, he was gazing at her with open admiration. He looked utterly ridiculous--a cartoon of gape-mouthed idiocy. "The right thing— yes, that's it. You've convinced me."

"Now I must sleep. You do the same. You look awful. Be sure to shave before you see Helen. And if Vanessa returns, please take your quarrel elsewhere."

"We will, Doc," the man said. "I mean—we shall."

He looked so puzzled by his own remark that Amanda helped him out. "Will or shall are both correct when used in the first person. Now good night."

——•——

Finally she slept. Throughout that short night she was often wakened by the annoyances common to such a room in such a place—sudden outbursts of talking, footsteps, people bumping chairs and luggage, snoring, the relentless overhead lights. She slept sitting straight as possible, head resting on the wall, coat folded in lap, travel bag under her feet.

Then she was dreaming. In her dream the man with the foreign accent and the wild hair swayed back and forth, snapping his fingers like Tevye in *Fiddler on the Roof.* "Sing vit me," the man commanded, and Amanda sang with him--not a Christmas carol this time, not in Latin, but fragments of "Run Through The Jungle" from the Creedence Clearwater Revival album so loved by her father. This dream segued into another in which Amanda was a girl again, sitting alone in her tidy room, her *Latin For Americans* textbook open, her desk immaculate as usual: three pens--two with black ink, one with blue-- on the left side, two Number Two pencils on the right, notebook ready and awaiting ink, Panasonic radio clock squared away beside the architect's lamp bought for her by her father at Goodwill. Beyond the door of her trim room her parents were hosting yet another of their interminable parties. In the dream, as was true in her earlier life, Amanda cobbled together the scene without the necessity of opening the door: her father, slender, built like a point guard, offering drinks round the room, here attacking the latest folly of the government, there quoting Yeats or Kerouac or whoever he was reading that week; her mother, fair, warm, soft, laughing in the dream as she had laughed on a hundred other Saturday get-togethers at some witty anecdote or rejoinder; the room itself unkempt, shelves dusty, furniture from a dozen yard sales and secondhand stores all higgledy-piggledy, a plaid shirt in want of a wash thrown in a corner, a stack of books beside the scarred and dented coffee table threatening an avalanche, walls bearing a hodge-podge of posters, family portraits and cheap reproductions in chipped wooden frames, the latest samples of her mother's textile art; the guests, customers from her father's used bookshop, actors from the community theater, professors from the university, poets, clients from her mother's studio at New Day Dance, friends now one and all, most of them besotted on the catchpenny wine, jabbering, laughing, singing. In the dream, as had happened in life, Amanda sat frowning and erect in her Spartan cell with its bare walls, vacuumed floors, and appointed closet--slacks to the left, blouses in the middle, school attire on the right--listening to this party with that conjunction of emotions, that mixture of pity, despair, disapproval, and bemusement, which a mother might extend to her wayward children.

When that dream slipped away, Amanda found herself hot, grungy, and dry-mouthed, lying in the sun on a beach. A bright light tugged at her closed eyelids, and a voice was calling her. All she wanted was to be left alone, but then the voice acquired a hand which was shaking her shoulder. "Señora! Señora!"

She woke. This part was no dream. The airport lights blazed in her eyes. The adulterer had disappeared. The plump, brown woman was holding her fussy baby in one arm while shaking Amanda with the other. "Señora!"

Half asleep, Amanda straightened in her chair, took the baby, put him to her shoulder, patted his back. He burped and regurgitated more undigested milk down her blouse and jacket. Groggily, she returned the baby to his beaming mother.

"Gracias, gracias, señora," she said. Beside her was one of the twins, holding out a small fist. Automatically Amanda extended her own hand and received a sticky pink jellybean from the little girl. Mother and daughter then departed, returning to their luggage and its tiny guardian.

Amanda wrapped the jellybean in a tissue and tucked it into her bag. Around her other travelers were stirring, grumbling and staggering about in that bleary daze acquired from a night spent sleeping on carpet-covered concrete. Teeth furred with sleep, limbs aching, she collected her belongings and walked toward the rest room. A line of haggard women, looking as if they stood at the gates of doom, awaited entrance. Switching direction, she walked to the window for a closer look at the weather. The snow had stopped; the sun was shining hard and bright; a runway glistened black beneath blue skies.

As she turned from the window, Amanda caught a glimpse of herself in the glass. Her braided hair had loosened during the night, blonde strands tumbling about her face. The smeared mascara about her puffy eyes gave her the look of a sorority girl the morning after a big dance. A lipstick kiss, plainly visible, compliments of Mary Beth Miller, decorated her right cheek. Two white stains, both malodorous and one of them shaped, Amanda noted dispassionately, like an upside-down Christmas tree, adorned her jacket. Her left shoe felt permanently stuck to her cola-soaked foot.

After joining the line of shuffling women waiting to enter the restroom, Amanda opened her BlackBerry. Using her pinky finger—it was the least begrimed—she punched in some numbers. In a moment he answered.

"Joseph?" Her vocal chords creaked. She coughed into her hand, and her voice cleared, became crisp, filled with purpose. "Yes, it's Amanda. Yes, I realize it's early. I wanted to catch you before you went to work. I'm calling from Dulles…yes, we were stuck here overnight…no, no, I'm fine…really, I'm fine. I need a favor, Joseph. Could you tell Mr. Martin I won't be at work today? Yes, that's right. Thank you, Joseph. Oh, and listen, Joseph. I wanted to ask you a question. About going out? Are you free this evening? Yes…yes…all right…seven-thirty would be perfect. Is Hannity's all right? No, I'll meet you there. No, I won't be too tired. I'm fine…just fine."

Chapter Two

"In an age of addled minds and deficient education," Amanda Bell had printed on the first page of her copy of *Elements of Style*, "the ability to write clearly and cogently grants its possessor power in the workplace."

Before placing herself once again under the capable tutelage of Mr. Strunk and Mr. White--her favorite adage of these two gentlemen was Rule Number 12: "Choose a suitable design and hold to it"--Amanda held the book unopened in her lap, pressed her forehead against the tiny window afforded by Seat 27-B, and perused the bustling airfield outside, bright now with snow and sunshine. The glittering landscape pleasurably stung her tired eyes, and the sunlight, comforting as a sauna, warmed her cheeks, offering respite from the commotion on the aircraft: the opening and shutting of overhead compartments, the babble of voices, the shuffling passengers and brisk flight attendants.

The seat beside her remained empty, but just as she'd begun hoping for the luxury of silence and privacy on the flight home, a lanky man in a black overcoat shambled down the aisle, cheerily counting off row numbers: "Twenty-four, twenty-five, twenty-six, and here we are."

He stopped beside the empty seat. Amanda's first impression was that of an owl she had seen at age eleven in the maple tree behind her childhood home in Charlottesville. The man's thinning salt-and-pepper hair was combed up and back; his ears were pointed; behind thick spectacles were large hazel eyes, pools of confidence and amiability. Amanda, who frequently miscalculated the ages of men over fifty, nevertheless judged this particular traveler with his liver-spotted hands and furrowed cheeks as past retirement, yet he energetically heaved a bulky paper bag into the overhead compartment. When he removed his overcoat, carefully folding it into the same compartment, she saw that he wore, in addition to a black coat, black shirt, and black trousers, the stiff white collar of a priest.

Holding onto a worn briefcase, he sat beside Amanda.

"Hello," he said. His voice was cheerful and spry. He offered an outstretched hand. "Father Joseph Krumpler."

Amanda returned his firm handshake with grudging cordiality. Though intrigued by his occupation, she had no desire for conversation. Her need for solitude and sleep was acute. "Amanda Bell."

"Well, Miss Bell, even a mess can look beautiful, eh?"

His comment startled Amanda. Had he actually dared chide her for her unkempt hair and abused clothing? She was on the brink of offering some snippy retort when she followed his gaze out the window and realized he was referring to the new-fallen snow. "Yes," she said, but without conviction. She was thinking of her day's absence from the office. "It's lovely."

The aircraft eased away from the loading gate. The priest sat stiffly, head against the seat cushion, eyes closed. Amanda's scalp itched; her sinuses and throat were stuffy and dry from the compartmentalized air. Whenever she blinked, her eyes felt raw and gritty. This priest, on the other hand—this Father Krumpler—looked fresh as new laundry. Had he spent the night in the airport?

His eyes popped open—had he been praying?—and as if reading Amanda's thoughts, he said, "That was a long night, wasn't it?"

"You were there?"

"Tucked away on the first row of chairs. I slept off and on until early this morning, when a wild young man wanted to make a confession. It was very odd--I think he was a Methodist."

"Gray suit? Red tie?"

"Why, yes. How did you know?"

"Just a lucky guess."

"At any rate, after talking with him I read my Office, and then it was time to board."

"I called my office, too," Amanda said. "I left a message with my boss, Mr. Henle."

The priest laughed. Amanda, who saw nothing humorous in her comment, wondered if he was giddy from his long night.

"I frequently leave messages for my boss," the priest said, as if that was some sort of explanation.

"I hope he's better at returning your calls than mine."

"In my case, it's more a question of understanding what he wants when he does return them."

"I don't have that problem, Mr. Henle always makes himself very clear." Amanda paused, thinking of Mr. Henle. "Since Thanksgiving he's been quieter with me than usual. Twice I've caught him staring at me. He's married with two grown children. He's short, and overweight, and has bulging eyes. I hope he's not getting ideas."

The plane, which had squatted these past moments at the end of a runway, eased into motion, gathered speed, and lifted off. The priest crossed himself. "A quick prayer," he said as they bucketed heavenward. "I'm not afraid of flying, you see, but just want to make sure the Lord knows I'm up here with the sparrows." They rose through cloudless heavens. "I'm sorry. You were saying—"

"My boss—Mr. Henle, that is—hasn't been himself around me the past few weeks. I'm starting to wonder if I've done something wrong."

"Have you? Done anything wrong, I mean?"

"Nothing that I know of." She thought about it. "No, nothing at all."

"Then that can't be it, can it?" The priest nodded to the Strunk and White on Amanda's lap. "That's an unusual book for a young lady to carry on a plane."

"I carry it everywhere I go. It helps me with work. Actually, I'm trying to memorize it. The rules from the first two chapters anyway."

"Really? That's remarkable."

"It's not that difficult."

"No, no, it's remarkable because I did the same thing years and years ago. Back when I taught high school and college classes in New Orleans. I memorized the rules and had my students buy the book. When I graded their essays, I'd put the rule number instead of a correction on their papers. I required them to go home, look up their mistakes, and then write the rule out above the mistake and give the paper back to me." He raised his eyes to the compartment above them. "'Rule Number 9: The number of the subject determines the number of the verb.'"

"How did they like it?"

"What's that?"

"How did the students like it?"

"Oh, they hated it, of course. Too much work, too much bother. But it forced them to be better writers. How about you? What sort of work do you do?"

Amanda explained her position at the office, her increasing responsibilities in management. Father Krumpler urged her on with quick nods or an occasional "Yes, yes, I see." As Amanda recounted her duties, she paid the priest a rarely tendered deference. Throughout her life she'd accorded all new acquaintances an initial respect, a habit traceable, like her posture and her manner of speaking, to her parents. Though Amanda did not always measure up to this parental standard--she lacked their gregarious grace and trust--she was aware of its value. In regard to this priest, however, this ingrained habit of courtesy lay on a different plane altogether. His interest and attention, combined with his age and the collar at his throat, made her feel like a schoolgirl, explaining situations and people while seeking approval for her opinions.

"You have many responsibilities," he said when she had finished. "Do you enjoy your work?"

Before Amanda could reply, a young flight attendant pushing a cart offered them juice, coffee, and packaged doughnuts. Amanda declined the juice; Father Krumpler passed her a doughnut and coffee, took the same and a juice for himself, made the sign of the cross, and apparently prayed again. Amanda sipped her coffee while she pondered his last question. She rarely considered her work in terms of feelings or emotions. Just as school had once been school, a part of life like air or food and so beyond debate, so work was work. It constituted neither a necessary evil nor a positive good. Work, her work, was beyond any judgment of good or ill. Work simply was.

"I wouldn't say I enjoy it," she replied at last. "I don't think of it that way."

The priest had patiently awaited her reply, munching on his doughnut. A tiny crumb clung to the corner of his lip, and Amanda reached out with one of the napkins supplied by the attendant and wiped away the sugary dot.

Father Krumpler smiled at her. "Why, thank you. Most people would be too embarrassed to do that, leaving me to walk around looking like a clown the rest of the day."

"It's a habit of mine, cleaning up messes," Amanda said vaguely. She was still pondering the question of work. "I do like things tidy at work. I like directing people."

"And now you're off for the holidays? Seeing relatives?"

Amanda paused again. She was floating on a river of fatigue, woozy and inebriated from her loss of sleep, so that focusing on his questions required all her efforts. Once—and only once in her life—she'd gotten drunk. She was a sophomore at college, and the rum she consumed that evening was masked by fruit and sugar. Though she hadn't enjoyed the consequences of her revelry—she had vomited in the back yard of the Chi Omega house and had woken in the morning beneath some dew-damp rhododendron bushes beside the front porch—Amanda always remembered the lovely, disembodied sensation wrought by the second strawberry daiquiri. "No. I work in Atlanta. I was in D.C. for a meeting with one of the firm's legal clients. I had to deliver some papers and securities to him, and then get him to sign a number of documents. He's new, so I also had to explain to his staff how our office worked."

The priest nodded. He finished his coffee and dabbed at his lips with the napkin. "I was visiting one of my nephews. He lives in Cheverly just outside D.C. Four boys and a lovely wife. Maria's just getting over a bout with pneumonia. She took a liking to me long ago at their wedding and we've become good friends." He smiled. "She's tough as a drill sergeant on those boys and on Bill, but their love for her is remarkable. You should have seen them falling all over themselves to take care of her. How about you? Any siblings?"

Amanda didn't reply. Siblings, cousins, aunts and uncles were creatures as strange to her as chambered nautili or giant isopods. She had neither brothers nor sisters, no generous uncles doling out sage advice and loose change, no tart aunts issuing admonitions about men and broken hearts, no cousins from whom she might seek congratulations in triumph or commiseration in defeat, no living relatives whatsoever other than her mother's sister, a Californian whom she had never seen, and a grandfather who had long ago disappeared in the maelstrom created by Woodstock, flower power, and free love, and who might or might not be among the living.

When Amanda didn't speak, the priest began backpedaling. "I didn't mean to pry. My curiosity often gets the best of caution."

"No, no siblings," Amanda blurted out. "No relatives at all. And my parents are dead." She caught her breath. What had come over her? Either her fatigue had eaten away at the foundations of the citadel she had erected around her personal life, collapsing those stout castle walls which protected her from such intrusions, or this man with his tufted hair, innocent hazel eyes, and white collar was a magician, some prestidigitator of the soul more adept at forcing confessions than a torturer. Amanda's cheeks blossomed like twin peonies--she couldn't remember the last time she had blushed--yet even so, stricken as she was by her broken defenses, by this unforeseen raising of the portcullis guarding her interior life, more revelations tumbled from her lips. "They died in a car crash the summer before my junior year at the university. Up on the Skyline Drive. Dad was driving--he was a careless driver, fiddling with the radio, looking everywhere but the road--and he was probably talking to my mother or laughing at something she'd said, and they drove straight off the highway and two hundred feet down a slope."

Here at last Amanda regained control: here this exotic urge to disclose herself smashed against the castle keep, her final protection, and was defeated. By force of will she restrained the tears threatening to slip from her eyes to her cheeks, loosened the knots in her throat by pinching her left forearm, and restored her defenses by staring fixedly into the back of the seat in front of her.

"My parents were careless people," she said flatly.

She then steeled herself against the inevitable expressions of sympathy and pity, twin entities which she sometimes extended to others but which she despised when they were offered to her. Pity was the banner of the weak, the standard flying above the undisciplined and the debilitated, the flag of the therapeutic society in which everyone laid claim to the rank of victim. In an age which celebrated the emotionally crippled, which declared weakness rather than fortitude a virtue, which honored wild revelation while denigrating self-control, Amanda Bell prided herself on her powers of self-government.

But the priest gave no sign of empathy. Instead, he veered onto a different path.

"Did you finish college?"

"Yes. The University of Virginia."

"A fine school. And you majored in--"

"English literature with a minor in classics."

Amanda yawned. The airlines coffee, rather than reviving her, had acted like a soporific, pushing her toward sleep. Resting her head against the back of the seat, she stifled a second yawn.

"You're exhausted," Father Krumpler said. He gathered her coffee cup and napkin, then pushed up the plastic table to allow her more room. "Close your eyes. See if you can catch a snooze."

———•———

Within seconds of closing her eyes, Amanda whooshed off into sleep, as if she herself had become an aircraft, a winged apparition whose destination was the cave of Morpheus. She slept dreamless until Mr. Henle appeared, sitting behind his massive, clean desk—what was the point in owning a desk the size of a bed if you never put papers on it?—glaring at her with his bulging eyes as he repeated her name: "Ms. Bell....Ms. Bell...Ms. Bell...."

"...Ms. Bell....."

Amanda opened her eyes, boggled by the light and blinking into the priest's lean face.

"We're landing in Atlanta."

"We are?"

Even as she spoke, the aircraft touched the earth. Runways and other aircraft raced past her window.

"I'm sorry I had to wake you."

Amanda yawned, then remembered to cover her mouth. "I'm fine."

"You know, my friends tell me that sometimes I can look at a person and see certain promises in them."

"In him or her," Amanda emended.

"How's that?"

"Person is singular. It must take a singular pronoun."

Father Krumpler laughed. "All right. All right then. Sometimes I am told that I can look at people and see certain promises in them."

"Yes," Amanda said, but she was only half-listening to the priest. A deeper compartment of her mind was already printing off the preparatory list of details of her return—the collection of baggage, the ride to the long-term parking lot, the drive home, a nap, a bath, Joseph.

"You strike me as more a teacher than an office manager. Has any-one ever told you that?"

"No...I mean yes." Mary Beth's question--*Are you a teacher?*--echoed dimly from last evening. Meanwhile the clacking printer inside her skull reminded Amanda that she must shape her conference notes into a more formal report for Mr. Henle.

"You'd make a good teacher. You've never taught?"

"Never. I don't have a teaching certificate."

The plane rolled to a stop. Gripped again by the earth and the business of the earth, passengers loosened seat belts, groaned, yawned, stretched. Amanda herself went on full alert, back straight, shoulders squared, already planning the race through the concourse.

Father Krumpler extended a small card. Amanda took it, glanced at the engraved name—how odd, a priest with business cards—and dropped it into her shoulder bag.

"If you're ever interested in a teaching job....if I can ever help you...."

"I don't have the proper credentials." What would the blizzard in D.C. have done to the airport traffic here? Perhaps she could arrive home even faster than anticipated.

"You wouldn't need state teaching credentials for this school. It's private. Catholic, of course. I think you'd handle the students well." He smiled at her. "And you certainly possess a rare command of the English language."

A steaming bath scented with lavender bath gel had become Aman-da's holy grail. If she hurried, she could make her way quickly to the concourse, grab her bags, zip to the parking lot, and be home an hour from now, tucked into her apartment, shed of the stained clothing and the touch and bother of people--clean, safe, alone. She stood, ducking her head under the overhead compartment, and squeezed past Father Krumpler into the aisle. "I've enjoyed talking."

"Keep in mind what I said. Feel free to call me anytime if you wish. You have a certain quality...a certain...."

"Yes...yes...." She yanked down her coat, tucked it under her arm. "Yes." People crowded the aisle. Amanda faced front, joined the shuffling procession, baby-stepping her way toward the exit.

"Amanda...."

She turned impatiently to the old priest, annoyed by the delay, adrenalin pumping, ready for the run through the airport. Three rows back, Father Krumpler was still sitting, calm and collected, staring as if he could see right through her. The man in front of her was sidling down the aisle toward the doorway. "What is it?" Amanda said, sidling as well.

He gave her a peculiar little wave, his right hand moving up, down, then left and right. "Merry Christmas."

"Merry Christmas to you," Amanda said, and made her escape.

———

Shortly after noon, Amanda arrived at the Gardens. In the car her vision of the bath had faded away, replaced by the need for sleep. On entering her apartment, she went straight to her bedroom, dropped her luggage on the floor by the closet, stripped to her underwear, climbed beneath the quilt, and slept dreamless for nearly five hours. On rising, she peeled and ate an apple, followed by two pieces of unbuttered toast, and drank a cup of hot green tea while filling the bathtub with steaming, sudsy water. The tub was too small, too plastic, too poorly designed for real bathing comfort, but the lavender bath pellets and three candles defrayed these short-comings. For half an hour Amanda soaked in these warm, perfumed waters, washing away her night in the airport, an ordeal which had left her arms and legs aching as if she'd spent hours in violent exercise.

Pleasantly weak with the heat of the bath, Amanda stood up, pulled the stopper, and watched the water run out of the tub. Suds dripped like melted frosting from her thighs as she inspected her flight-battered flesh. Normally, Amanda treated her body like a machine. She vigorously exercised at the Y four times per week, Thursdays through Sundays, she did sit-ups, leg-lifts, and weights while watching television, and she frequently took long walks on weekends. Her body was as trim and muscled as that of a middle-distance runner. She pinched her left thigh, then drew the shower curtains closed, turned on the tap, and let the hot spray pummel away the last vestiges of her stiffness while she washed her face and hair. After drying off, she twisted the towel about her hair, pulled on her terrycloth robe, and sat before the bedroom mirror to apply her makeup. She studied her face as impartially and critically as a beautician, then commenced her ministrations.

The dialogue began while she applied a light blush to her cheeks:

This evening is a mistake. Joseph is a mistake.

You need to get out.

I want to stay home. Read. Watch a movie.

You watch too many movies. Go out. Find someone. Do something besides work.

Who says? Who says I need someone? I'm fine the way I am.

You have no real friends.

I want to read.

Aren't you a little tired of Jane Austen and the Brontë sisters?

I'm tired thinking about tonight. I've made a mistake. I should call it off.

Part of you is dying.

Why am I dating someone from work?

Because you don't know anyone else.

"Oh hush," Amanda said, and the interior debate shut down as quickly as if she'd pushed the "Stop" button on a recorder.

That point about friends, however, lingered in Amanda's mind. It was a point she readily conceded. As she rubbed lotion into her hands and then, slipping the robe to her waist, onto her throat, breasts, and arms, she examined her life in terms of friendship and love. The truth? She had no real friends. What she had were acquaintances. Over the years she had maintained contact with several sorority sisters—just last week she had mailed their Christmas cards—but they were far away, and their correspondences and telephone calls had mutated into obligations rather than pleasures. Until recently, she'd gotten together for supper every few weeks with Tracy Clark, with whom she'd shared an apartment on Rio Road her senior year at the university and who now worked as an accountant with a software firm in Buckhead. Like Amanda, Tracy hadn't married, and they shared the conviviality of like circumstances, but Tracy's engagement in August to Sam, a physician's assistant, had blunted the edges of their friendship. In the fall Amanda had twice gone for drinks with Mollie Fletcher, a nurse she'd met at the gym. They had bantered in a casual way, mostly about men and work, and since then would often converse as they burned up calories on the cross-trainers. And last summer, at the apartment association's swimming pool, where Amanda, having read that most Americans were deficient in Vitamin D, sunbathed occasionally in the evenings after work, she had met Justin Hobbes, a gay legal assistant from Apartment 3A. Justin loved to cook, particularly seafood, and had several times invited Amanda to supper, where he teased her about her lack of friends and lovers. "No boyfriends, no close girlfriends. Not even a dog or cat, which are the usual comforts of women living alone." He'd laughed. "Warm hands, cold heart," he said, and touched Amanda's fingertips. "Hot as a stove in July, sweetheart."

These relationships comprised the extent of any claim Amanda made on human camaraderie.

Despite occasional yearnings for companionship, despite the rare pangs of envy she felt when she saw other young women laughing with their friends or walking hand in hand with a man, despite the fact that some parts of her solitary life which had so long born pleasure—trips to the library or used bookstores, exercise, watching movies made before the sixties—now at times bored and even irritated her, despite all these absences of affection and delectation, a black dread nevertheless metastasized in Amanda's heart as she contemplated her date with Joseph. By allowing a ridiculous outburst of euphoria brought on by the holidays and a lack of sleep to override her habitual prudence, she had broken not one but two of the cardinal rules gleaned from her management books: Do not mix business with pleasure. Do not become romantically involved with office personnel.

Amanda was going on a date with Joseph Grenier. Worse--so humiliatingly worse--she herself had made the date.

Not that she felt romantically inclined toward Joseph—not yet, anyway. Her pulse didn't race at the sound of his name, her breath didn't quicken when she caught sight of him at work, his face and lanky form didn't haunt her dreams. As she arranged her hair into a braid that would fall down her back three inches shy of her waist, Amanda wondered whether she even liked Joseph. Why had she arranged this evening with him? Had she taken him up on his standing invitation from desperation? Is this what happened to women—and to men, she supposed—who approached the age of thirty alone? Did they simply lose all sense of decorum and reason?

This evening will be a disaster.

Only if you make it so.

Too late, too late: speculation and regret were wasted at this point. It was nearly seven o'clock—too late for misgivings, too late for cancellation. Amanda opted for casual dress: white blouse, pink sweater, jeans, loafers. She shrugged on her long blue overcoat, checked her shoulder bag for her phone, spare key, and billfold, locked the door, and marched to her car.

———

A wave of clattering flatware, loud voices and laughter, and louder stereophonic music broke over Amanda as she entered the restaurant. In the last few years she had patronized Hannity's four times, perhaps five, to meet an acquaintance for a drink or meal. Waiting to be seated, she realized with a tiny shock that the restaurant slightly disgusted her— the Tiffany lamps and mirrors, the sports memorabilia, the music and crowded tables, the odors of beer and cooking grease. The last time she had dined here, she recollected, the quesadillas had tasted like oiled cheese on cardboard. Why had she selected such a place to meet Joseph?

An overworked hostess, beaming with cheer and carrying a menu clutched to her breasts like some holy writ, led Amanda to the booth where Joseph Grenier waited. Quickly she noted that he, too, had dressed down for their evening together. Gone were the white shirts, the suit jacket, matching ties, the cordovan shoes. This evening Joseph wore a plaid shirt and jeans. He looked, Amanda thought, a little like a pee-wee lumberjack. As they greeted each other, she glanced at the nearby tables to observe that nearly everyone, young or old, was wearing jeans. The sight of uniform denim depressed her, though she couldn't think why.

"Sleeping in airports must agree with you," Joseph said. "You look fabulous."

Compliments, especially references to her appearance, made Amanda uncomfortable. For one, she never knew what to say in return. For another, since the age of fifteen she had daily felt the eyes of men-- and sometimes women-- sliding over her, appraising her face and figure as if she were a sports car or a steak. Though some women possessed the personality and the ability to employ their beauty as either a weapon or a lure, Amanda did not count herself among them. Her beauty had more often seemed handicap than help.

She smiled at Joseph. "You look nice too."

They ordered drinks, studied the menu, gave their order to a harried waitress. Amanda settled on a salad with chicken strips. Joseph ordered wings and salad.

Amanda sipped her chardonnay while Joseph told her what she'd missed at the office these last three days. The new water coolers had arrived. Emily Bates had returned from her pregnancy leave ("I hope she's ready to work," Amanda said, a comment which brought a frown from Joseph). In a memo to the office staff Mr. Henle had mentioned the strong possibility of a major Miami importer coming aboard as a legal client after Christmas.

"That would affect our work load quite a bit—at least in the short run," Amanda said. "I'll need to look into that tomorrow."

"You're going to work tomorrow?"

"Certainly."

"But it's Christmas weekend. It's Friday. The day before Christmas. No one will be there."

"Have they closed the building?"

"No," Joseph said slowly.

"Will Mr. Samson allow me inside?"

"Of course."

"Don't businesses normally continue operations on Friday?"

"Yes."

Amanda sipped her wine, looking at him above the rim of the glass. Case closed. Joseph shook his head and looked away, muttering.

"I'm sorry. I couldn't quite hear you."

"It doesn't matter."

"No. Tell me."

"Someone called you Scrooge yesterday."

He was examining her with what she interpreted as fascination and pity.

"Scrooge?"

"You know. Like *The Christmas Carol.*"

"Scrooge?"

Joseph nodded.

"Why? Because I want to work?"

"I'm not sure why."

Joseph had ordered a Heineken for himself and had told the waitress to keep the glass. Now, when he tilted the bottle upward to drink, Amanda saw that he had missed shaving the underside of his chin. She also noticed how his neck bobbed as he drank and that the plaid shirt was all wrong for him; he should be wearing a solid color, stripes at best, a dark blue perhaps. She had made a mistake; she shouldn't be here; all she wanted was the comfort and quiet of her apartment.

Joseph seemed to read her criticisms. "Something wrong?"

"No." She faked a smile and changed the topic. "So what are your plans for Christmas?"

"Tomorrow I'm driving up to Greensboro to my brother's place. My folks are coming down this weekend to join us. We used to get together for Christmas at our house in Baltimore, but Steve has kids of his own, so now we go to his place." He smiled. "It means getting up at dawn on Christmas, but it's fun watching the kids run around. My sister's coming too—she's a nurse at Johns Hopkins."

"How many children does your brother have?"

"Three. The oldest is seven."

"That should be fun for you."

"How about you? Any big plans?"

"Not really."

"Family coming in?"

"No."

"You're spending Christmas alone?" After asking the questions, Joseph left his mouth hanging open his mouth as if Amanda had just thrust a knife into his belly.

His shock surprised her. Was spending Christmas alone truly so strange? "Yes," she said. "Alone."

Joseph stared as if she'd just turned green and grown knobs out of her head. "What about your folks?"

Though that topic was broached earlier than she expected, Amanda had anticipated it. She kept her voice cool and controlled. "They died when I was twenty. A car accident."

"I'm so sorry." His eyes scanned her, rearranging her personality, as if this bald fact might explain so many levels of her behavior. "Good grief, if I had known that, I would have said something. I would have...."

His voice trailed away. Amanda refused his pity, mentally taking Joseph's legs out from under him. Much later, in one of those odd moments when a snatch of conversation will drift from the unconscious, Amanda realized that Joseph had gotten wind of some information, some small piece of the fate awaiting her in the near future. But now she noted only his jumbled confusion, the guilt like a signboard on his long face.

"It was a long time ago."

Joseph studied her. Amanda replied with The Stare. At work she used The Stare when confronted by argumentative employees. The Stare was an unblinking appraisal meant for intimidation, aimed at the other's forehead.

"Your mom and dad…Jesus, I didn't know…."

Their waitress brought the salads and Joseph's wings. With the arrival of the food the mood between them again changed. It was clear to Amanda that their meal together had run its course before they had taken their first bite, that their evening had reached its denouement, that their friendship, such as it was, was finished before it had begun. Though she acknowledged the necessity of salvaging their relationship so that they might continue working comfortably together, Joseph was making the job tough. He continued probing her with the same dumb-founded misery in his pitying brown eyes.

"Wasn't your dad a Marine?"

"A what?"

"A colonel in the Marines."

"My dad wasn't a colonel in the Marines."

"All that traveling—that must have been tough."

"What traveling?"

"In the Marines."

"My dad was never in the Marines."

"Never?"

"Never. Why would you think so?"

"Someone at work told me he was a colonel in the Marines. Real gung-ho."

"You mustn't believe everything you hear, Joseph."

"Well, what did he do then?"

"My father was a bookseller. He ran a second-hand bookshop. He liked the stage and sometimes acted or directed with the community theater."

"Oh." He consumed a wing, licked the barbecue sauce from his fingertips, and chewed. His Adam's apple danced up and down when he swallowed. "So what will you do for Christmas?"

"Read," Amanda said. "Watch a movie. Eat a meal. Last year I went to church."

"You're a believer?"

"I don't know. I don't think so. I don't practice any faith, if that's what you mean."

"So why did you go to church?"

"On a whim," Amanda said, though this wasn't quite the truth. She had gone for the same reason that she had invited Joseph Grenier to Hannity's: a momentary lapse in her willpower. On Christmas Eve last year she had watched *White Christmas*, read four chapters from *Northanger Abbey*, and was drinking her third cup of hot chocolate when the same urge that had brought her to this noisy restaurant struck her. Remembering that Catholics usually had some sort of late-night service on Christmas Eve, she had dressed and driven to Saint Ann's only a few blocks away. She had gone hoping for something she couldn't put into words, some connection or comfort, but had instead spent most of the Mass distracted by the wiggling eight-year-old boy at her side, the tawdry clothes of two women in front of her, and the whispered Spanish prayers of a young couple behind her.

"We're Episcopalians," Joseph said. "My family. My dad still helps out with the youth group and my mom's sung in the choir for years."

The evening dragged. After supper, though she desperately longed for home and bed, Amanda nodded her assent when Joseph suggested they go to Barnes and Noble. Once inside the store, they drifted apart. Joseph left her to wander through the compact discs, to listen, as he told her, to country music. Amanda trolled the bookshelves until she arrived at the section on management, where she selected a copy of *You're The Boss: A Primer on Instant Obedience*. She sat in a nearby stuffed chair and read until her eyelids grew heavy. Closing the book on her lap, she gave way to sleep, commanding herself to awaken in ten more minutes.

Although her interior clock usually roused her at the directed time, her alarm this evening failed. She opened her eyes to find Joseph poking at her arm and calling her name. For one instant she imagined she was on the airplane and the priest was beside her. She sat up stiff-necked, blinking, then woke so fast she felt dizzy. She had drooled in her sleep and wiped her lips with her fingers. Joseph's own fingers thumped the cover of the book in her lap. "Still working, eh, Iron Maiden?" he said. The contempt in his eyes belied his jesting voice. Clearly he despised her.

Amanda came out of the chair so fast that the top of her head just missed smacking Joseph's chin. She deposited the book on its proper shelf and gathered her bag and coat. She struggled putting on the coat, snagging her arm, but pulled away when Joseph tried to help her. She hoisted her bag to her shoulder, faced Joseph, and stuck out her hand. Joseph returned her grip before he realized she was leaving. "Merry Christmas, Joseph. I'll see myself to my car."

"Come on, Amanda. Don't—"

"I'll see you in the office Tuesday."

"Let me get my things. I need to tell you something. You need to know that—"

"Go back to your music," Amanda said in a withering voice. "I'll walk myself to my car."

Religion, Self-Help, Journals, Calendars, Sale Books and Best-Sellers sailed past her in a blur. In the crowded parking lot she joined a line of vehicles loaded with Christmas presents creeping toward the exit. On the radio she punched the scan button, but kept getting Christmas music. Finally she found a sports talk station and let the empty words carry her home.

———

The trick to surviving holidays alone, particularly Christmas, was to avoid the sentimental or lugubrious. Rote activity and practical thinking offered the antidotes to these poisons.

On Friday, Christmas Eve, Amanda woke fifteen minutes earlier than her usual hour of 5:30, showered, dressed, ate a bagel and banana, and drove to work. Her 2006 Accord, purchased secondhand two years earlier, a luxurious extravagance with its heated leather seats, sunroof, and V6 engine, purred along the expressway. Amanda listened to a daily news and traffic report, switched off the radio at the first appearance of the inevitable seasonal music, and drove for the remaining fourteen minutes in silence. Traffic was so light—schools were out, of course, and half the city had apparently decided to make an extra-long holiday of the weekend—that Amanda was in her cubicle shortly after seven o'clock. No one else from her staff darkened the corridors of the firm that day, a circumstance of solitary calm which Amanda used to write her semiannual employee efficiency reports.

Amanda regarded herself as an insightful and stern, but not harsh, judge of character. For Marissa Mellencamp she checked off various boxes, then wrote under comments: "A giddy young woman whose love of bangles and ear apparel distracts the male members of our staff. Takes direction poorly. A fine typist." Jason Green was "a nine to fiver who is primarily interested in his home, his wife, and his children. He puts in his hours, but begs off projects requiring extra time or effort." Of Rachel Thomas, the newest addition to the staff, an Emory graduate clearly running in place while making up her mind about law school, Amanda noted: "A hard worker. Cheerful. Expresses few personal opinions. Too easy-going for any consideration of management position."

After finishing these reports, a task broken by a lunch consisting of an egg-salad sandwich with lettuce on eight-grain bread, half a dill pickle, an apple, and a vita-water, Amanda devoted another sixty-five minutes to personal maintenance. She cleared out the drawers of her desk, wiped down her desktop and keyboard, sharpened pencils, deleted messages from her computer, consolidated the machine's disk space, and emptied the can of papers beside her desk into the large shredder in the copier room. Around three o'clock she inspected the cubicles of her staff and noted with satisfaction that everyone but Abby

Yates had left their workspaces tidy for the weekend. Cookie crumbs and candy wrappers littered Abby's desk, and she had forgotten to turn off her computer monitor. Amanda made a mental note to have a word with Abby when the office reopened on Tuesday.

Amanda left the office by 3:40 that afternoon, an hour earlier than usual, and drove back down the expressway to her exit. She stopped at the Piggly-Wiggly where she bought eggs, milk, a loaf of wheat bread, and four rolls of paper towels. She then detoured to Rosebud Video, where she rented *True Grit*, the older version starring John Wayne as Rooster Cogburn. Amanda loved the movie for its character Addie, with her careful diction and brave heart. Then, when she arrived home, she found in her mail-box the red-and-white envelope containing *Twelve-Point Management*, the instructional CD she'd ordered from Netflix. With this treasure in hand–the two disc set contained six hours of viewing time–Amanda was now assured that she would carry this weekend before her, that she would triumph over loneliness and the bathetic spell of the Yuletide. Wreaths of holly, twinkling lights on a fir tree, and ten thousand Saint Nicks would count for nothing against her level-headed demarche. She would skate through this holiday like blades on a newly-glazed rink.

And so it happened. For the next three days, one nearly indistinguishable from the other, Amanda allowed herself the luxury of sleeping late. She rose and exercised, jogging three miles on Saturday, when the gym was closed for Christmas, and returned to the gym on Sunday and Monday, where she rode the machines, pumped iron, and sat for twenty minutes in the sauna. She prepared a special brunch each day of two eggs, a bagel, hot tea, and orange juice. Sunday and Monday afternoons found her at Barnes and Noble, reading magazines, jotting down notes about the office, and drinking iced Café Americano. On Saturday, Christmas Day, when the bookstore was closed, she devoted the early afternoon to the preparation of a chicken and rice soup livened by peas, corn, and tomatoes with green chili, and then spent the fading hours of daylight organizing documents and bills for her January tax preparation.

Evenings brought her the pleasure of her Sanctuary.

The few visitors to Amanda's apartment these last three years had noted its Spartan austerity. The bedroom, bath, kitchen, and part of the living room had none of those knick-knacks common to the apartments of young women: the teddy bear or favorite doll from childhood, the posters left over from college days, the framed photographs of an exotic vacation to Spain or the Antilles, refrigerator drawings from favorite nieces and nephews, glass figurines of dolphins and ballerinas, potted plants, painted coffee cups flowering with pens, pencils, and a pair of scissors, clay vases from third-world factories, Mardi Gras masks, odd wooden boxes filled with paper clips, rubber bands, loose change, and stamps, oriental rugs, a wine bottle from a special birthday.

No--Amanda's apartment with its off-white walls and peach carpeting displayed few outward personal touches. Her bedroom was as devoid of ownership as any room at the Holiday Inn. Beside the bed, which she'd covered with a quilt purchased on sale at Sears, was a nightstand with an alarm clock and a small neat stack of books. The vanity was covered with a bare sheet of glass, its tools--make-up, hair dryer, emery boards, and brushes--all tucked neatly into drawers. On the opposite wall a metal table held a flat-screen computer and printer. Hanging clothes and a chest of drawers were concealed inside the large closet. The kitchen with its tile counters and wooden cabinets gleamed when lit, without even a stray shred of lettuce to remind the observer that someone used this space for chopping vegetables or washing cutlery. The bathroom did contain towels on a rack, soap in a dish, and candles on the side shelf of the tub, but otherwise it too showed no signs whatsoever of Amanda.

To the right of the front door of the apartment, however, was the living room, and here, in the corner opposite the door, was the Sanctuary, Amanda's castle keep, that fortress which offered protection and certitude after a hard day's work, that eight by ten foot chapel which restored her soul and gave her sustenance. This space, which covered little more than half of the room, contained four bookshelves purchased from K-Mart and assembled by Amanda herself, two large comfortable matching chairs, one of which reclined, bought from a salvage store, an end table placed between the chairs for drinks and books, one supper tray, a standing lamp on the left side of each chair, and a small television on a low shelf whose sliding panels concealed Amanda's small collection of DVDs.

The bookshelf to the left of the chairs contained a Shorter Oxford English Dictionary, two thesauri, a Webster's Collegiate Dictionary, compact discs, several books on grammar and business writing, a small Emerson CD player and radio, and a keepsake of her mother, the ceramic statue of an angel watching over two children about to cross a broken bridge. The shelf to the right of this eclectic collection held Amanda's books on self-improvement, exercise, diet, and management, ranging from her mother's copy of *The Moosewood Cookbook* to last year's best-selling *Shape Up!* In the corner between the shelves were the television and the DVD player. Hanging on the wall above these machines was a framed photograph of Amanda, age ten, standing with her parents in front of a rose bush outside their home. That was the last year of her childhood, the last time in her life when she had regarded the man and woman standing on either side of her as her parents rather than her own erstwhile children.

But the key to Amanda Bell's joy in this rectangular barbican, the well from which she drew the greatest pleasure, stood on the two shelves to the right of the television. For here were the writings of Amanda's beloved nineteenth century authors. Here were her fat, ragged Norton anthologies of Victorian poetry and prose, here were worn and tattered copies of Austen's *Emma* and *Pride and Prejudice*, Bronte's *Wuthering Heights*, George Eliot's *Adam Bede* and *Silas Marner*. Here were the other Brontes, Anne and Charlotte, with their accounts of governesses, strong women, and passionate men. Here was Maria Edgeworth's *Castle Rackrent*, Mary Hays's *Memoirs of Emma Courtney*, Fanny Birney's *Cecilia*, *Camilla*, and *The Wanderer*. Here was Susan Ferrier's *Marriage*, another tale of a responsible heroine commanding her own life despite all adversity; Elizabeth Inchbald's *A Simple Story*; Edith Wharton's glittering accounts of New York society. Like spice added to a stew, some few male authors mingled with the ladies on these shelves: Trollope, several volumes by Dickens, including her favorite, *Great Expectations*, and William Thackeray's *Vanity Fair*. Here were collections of her favorite Victorian poets--Henty, Tennyson, Elizabeth Browning, Christina Rossetti.

With the exceptions of *Gone With The Wind*, which Amanda had read at age eleven and had reread five times since, and which probably accounted as much as any other factor for her residence in Atlanta, and of *A Tree Grows In Brooklyn*, which had helped her first understand that not all adults were grownups, there were no modern or post-modern writers on Amanda's shelves. She had studied many such authors at the university, and after a brief infatuation, had finally come to dislike them, more for their general philosophy than for their style. The Victorians whom she admired lived and wrote by a standard, however much they might protest it: they played a game with rules and referees.

Modern and post-modern writers, on the other hand, were playing what Robert Frost had once called "tennis without a net." They made their own rules, true, but they also abused the sense and sensibilities of their readers. Joyce, Hemingway, Mailer, the Beats, the magical realists, the minimalists, the new journalists: these and others whom Amanda had studied were, in her eyes, weak as water when compared to their predecessors. Writers of the last forty years, many of them women, also roused her disdain, for they all seemed to share the same values, the same view of the world, even the same style of writing.

On this particular Monday evening, Amanda read from *Idylls of the King*. Sometimes she murmured the lines to herself, letting the words drip from her tongue, savoring their sound, their taste, their shape on the page. She sat in the chair closest to the Victorians, already dressed for bed in her white flannel gown with the pink roses around the collar, her hair loosened and falling like spun gold around her neck, shoulders, and breasts, her feet tucked beneath her, her cup of chamomile tea on a coaster on the table beside her. Presently she stood, restored the anthology to its shelf, carried the cup and saucer to the kitchen, washed and dried them, and put them in the cupboard.

In the bathroom she flossed her teeth, then brushed them the usual three minutes. When she finished, she tapped the brush on the sink, placed it in the medicine cabinet, rinsed her mouth, looked approvingly at her fingernails, and turned out the light. In the bedroom she switched off the computer, then slipped between the quilt and white sheets. She turned onto her right side, clicked off the lamp beside the bed, glanced at the red numbers on the face of the digital alarm--it was 10:49, just four minutes past her usual bedtime on work-day evenings-- set the alarm, and cuddled into the warming sheets.

All was well. Everything was as she wished it. Amanda closed her eyes, thought briefly and gladly of the challenges the next day would bring, and slept.

Chapter Three

The weatherman had promised cold temperatures and dark skies for Tuesday, but Amanda had missed any mention of the brisk wind now tugging at her coat and stinging her eyes with grit from the street. She waited on the crossing light, shifting from foot to foot, moving the briefcase from one hand to the other, shaking out her fingers like a runner ready to set herself in the blocks. Before her rose her battleground and cathedral, the arched windows and brick walls of Saxon and Henle.

In the lobby Jake Samson stood at the security desk, looking as much a part of the imposing decor as the Edwardian chairs or the tall, green ferns. "Good morning, Miss Bell."

"Good morning, Mr. Samson." Many employees addressed the security guard by his first name, Jake, but Amanda had never availed herself of that familiarity. If she was to be Miss Bell, then he must be Mr. Samson.

"Raw weather this morning."

"The weatherman is predicting rain. We may get hit with a freeze."

Mr. Samson handed her an envelope. "Message for you from Mr. Henle. He said to make sure you got it soon as you came through the door."

"Thank you, Mr. Samson."

On her elevator ride to the sixth floor Amanda opened the envelope and read the handwritten note: "Ms. Bell—Please come directly to my office on your arrival. A. Henle."

This crisp summons sounded urgent. Had some crisis in personnel occurred during her trip to D.C.? Had one of her charges committed some horrendous gaffe, some grievous error in judgment? It was a rare morning indeed when Mr. Henle arrived earlier at work than she, and this particular morning Amanda was fifteen minutes ahead of her own early-bird schedule.

She stepped from the elevator. The carpeted hallway, empty and quiet, greeted her like a friend. Amanda always found it remarkable that on a normal business day this same corridor would by nine o'clock swarm with realtors, clients, attorneys, and secretaries. Sixteen other legal and insurance firms rented office space in this building, with Saxon and Henle quartered here on the fourth, fifth, and sixth floors. John Lee Saxon, one of the founders of the firm now fifty years dead, had purchased the building new in 1930 when everyone else was selling. He had selected these three upper floors as home to the firm both for the views and for quick access to the roof, where he had built himself a tennis court.

Amanda stopped at her own tiny office to deposit her thermos and purse. When she turned the knob, however, she found the door locked. Like all employees of the firm who weren't attorneys or top accountants, Amanda never locked the office. She didn't even possess a key to the door. Had the door somehow locked when she'd closed it last on Christmas Eve Day? Was that the reason Mr. Henle wished to see her? She rattled the knob again, then stepped back, feeling foolish, to make certain she had the correct office.

It was then she noticed her nameplate missing from its place on the dark oaken door. That blue nameplate with its letters graven in three white lines--Amanda Bell/ Director of Personnel/Legal Department-- was gone, leaving only a faint outline against the dark wood as proof of its former existence.

With unbelieving fingers Amanda touched the empty rectangle. What did it mean? Had the firm moved her office over the weekend? Surely someone would have notified her. She jiggled the doorknob once more, and the metallic clicks echoed coldly off the cream-colored walls. As her hand dropped away, a tension ran through her, touching every nerve with a needle of apprehension.

The walk down the corridor this morning became an excursion into a grotesque dream. Though familiar to Amanda as her own apartment, the wide hallway with its photographs of Atlanta landmarks, its paintings and ferns, now seemed surreal and menacing beneath the florescent lights, metamorphosing into the maw of a chimerical beast. The closed doors became columns of brown teeth, the elegant red carpet a throat swallowing her with each step.

The door to Mr. Henle's office stood ajar. Amanda shifted her briefcase to knock, but in doing so fumbled her purse, which thumped open when it struck the floor, dumping out change, pencils, a mascara tube, a cylinder of lip gloss. *Power Management* stuck out of the top of the brown leather bag. Putting her thermos to the floor, Amanda stooped to pick up the scattered contents.

"Ah, Ms. Bell," Mr. Henle said from above her. He looked efficient and brisk this morning, crisp in his gray suit, white shirt, and striped tie, his face round and rubicund as a grocery-store tomato. He didn't offer to help her. As she gathered up a last few things, which included the jellybean from the little girl in the airport, Amanda noticed how small Mr. Henle's feet were, even for a short man. He was wearing black wingtips, highly polished, and his right foot tapped the carpet like an impatient metronome, as if keeping time on her.

She stood. "Good morning, Mr. Henle."

"Yes, well as to that—" Brusquely he turned from her and crossed the room, which, in addition to his immense desk, contained a blue sofa and chair, a wet bar, and a baby grand piano. Instead of going behind his desk, Mr. Henle sat at the piano. He motioned to Amanda to sit in the chair beside him. He took a sip from a tall black coffee mug while

Amanda sat, briefcase on the floor beside her chair, purse on her lap. Mr. Henle stretched out his arms, wiggled his fingers, and ran them gently across the keys.

"Do you know this tune, Ms. Bell?"

"'Put on a Happy Face.'" She had the recording at home on Rod Stewart's "American Songbag."

"Gray skies are going to clear up, Put on a happy face," Mr. Henle sang. He dropped the singing after the first line, but continued playing the music. "Gray skies today, I'm afraid."

"The weatherman thinks it will clear up by the weekend."

"I hope so. I certainly hope so." Amanda watched his short, blunt fingers caressing the keyboard. "You're here early as usual. Extra early today, I'd say."

The grandfather clock at the end of the corridor chimed the hour as if at his command. Seven o'clock.

"I wanted to get some work off my desk before the others arrived."

"Mighty early. Admirable, of course."

Amanda was silent, waiting for him. She had no idea how to respond, what he wanted from her, where he was taking the conversation. "Gray skies are going to clear up…." Mr. Henle sang again, closing his eyes, swaying to the music. His warm baritone was a surprise. But what did he want? Was she receiving a promotion? Had he suffered some sort of terrible breakdown? Or was he really trying to seduce her?

Just then Mr. Henle opened his eyes, shifted his weight on the piano bench, and stared at her. "Here's the thing," he said. "Ms. Bell, as of today you're terminated."

Amanda sat cold and still.

"Pardon me….what was that you said, Mr. Henle?"

"We're firing you." Mr. Henle slowed his playing, as if providing background music for their little drama. "We're letting you go. Officially, you're being released because of shifts in our corporate structure. We're doing that to allow you to collect unemployment. But unofficially I'm firing you."

Some of the characters in Amanda's reading, confronted by some similar frank revelation, swooned, or at the least, experienced a rush of blood to the head. Amanda had found their reactions overblown, but now blood was in fact rushing into her head, so much so that she reached up and touched her right temple with her fingertips. Had she been standing, she might well have fainted dead away. A physician presenting her with news of a terminal cancer would have roused less reaction.

"You're firing me?"

"Firing you, yes," Mr. Henle confirmed.

She lowered her hand to her lap. Her fingers didn't seem to belong to her. She noticed how still they lay against her black woolen skirt, how thin and pale they looked. "May I ask why, sir?"

"I thought you would." Mr. Henle paused, then began playing 'Night and Day.' "Otherwise, I would have stuck to the official story and let you go. But I wanted you to know why you can't work here anymore." Amanda looked up and found him looking dispassionately at her with his bulging eyes. "Many of your fellow workers despise you. I have a file full of complaints about you. They look at you as the Scrooge of this place, the Captain Hook, the Malvolio, Machiavelli, the Nurse Ratchet, the...." Apparently unable to dig out another literary comparison, Mr. Henle ceased. "In short, Ms. Bell, you are disliked."

"Don't I get the job done?"

"You get the work done, yes. But you haven't learned to balance the people with the job."

Amanda looked just beyond Mr. Henle's left shoulder, at the wall and the glass case containing his pocket knife collection. When she had first come to work here six years ago as a mere secretary, Mr. Henle had invited her into this office, stood with her before the glass case, and explained the name of each knife, the unique qualities that made it a collector's item, and why he had first become interested in amassing such a collection, but right now Amanda couldn't recollect a word of that long-ago conversation. Right now, in fact, she could hardly think of anything. The unreality of Mr. Henle's words--had she misunderstood him?--pecked at her mind, tore at her with hallucinatory talons, so that she didn't know what to think, what to do, how to behave.

From girlhood, Amanda had grown adept at giving and taking orders, at assuming control of any situation or solving any problem, but she had never acquired the ability to ask for favors. Had she known how to do so, had she possessed the vocabulary and even the smallest talent for entreaty, she might have begged Mr. Henle to reconsider his decision, to take another look at her, to allow her to continue working while on probation, anything other than lose her job. But words like mercy, pity, and forgiveness when applied to herself were as foreign and incomprehensible to Amanda as Swahili. No one had taught her how to ask for forgiveness, how to plead for a second chance, how to play the beggar when fate rides roughshod over dreams and ambition. In dealing with the difficulties of others, Amanda could at times dispense valuable advice or necessary favors, but she had never learned the art of asking for forgiveness or mercy.

"Someone should have said something to me. Someone should have told me how to do the job better, how to do what the firm wanted."

"People tried. You ignored them. What do you think of Alicia Fernandez?"

Alicia Fernandez had come to work for the firm a year ago as a file clerk. She generally completed her assigned tasks, but was late at least two mornings a week. "She isn't dependable in terms of her hours," Amanda said.

"Why is that, do you think?"

"She says her son is sick."

"Sick from what?"

"I don't know."

"He has asthma and allergies, bad lungs, and a weak heart. She's a single mom who didn't go on welfare or food stamps, who decided to work instead. She's late because he has asthma attacks and the sitter, her sister, doesn't always know what to do."

"I'm sorry, but she doesn't get the job done."

"Ms. Bell, you are impenetrable."

Before she could offer a reply, Mr. Henle swung his large head toward her, gazing like a toad at her face with his cold brown eyes. "Normally at this time we send employees accompanied by a security guard to their desk or office to pack up their personal items. You know the sort of things I mean--pictures of the family, some little knick-knacks or trophies, candy in a box, cigarettes, a book. But I checked your office yesterday, Ms. Bell. You have no personal items. Not one solitary thing. Not even a stick of gum. Do you know how unusual that is?" He shook his head. "But then, you're an unusual woman."

Into that last flat pronouncement Mr. Henle heaped all the disdain, all the contempt he so clearly felt toward her. To hear such a verdict delivered by this ugly, unctuous man, who was himself cold as a dead fish, who treated clients like bank vaults and employees like balance sheets, this man whom Amanda had admired for his frosty leadership and refrigerator heart, to hear this king of icy reserve now proclaim her a cold-hearted bitch cracked into her like an executioner's pistol shot. Unaccustomed tears welled in her eyes, and her lower lip trembled. She took a deep breath, willing herself not to reveal her pain. "You wouldn't fire me this way if I were a man."

Mr. Henle paused, his fingers hovering just above the keyboard. "That's true," he said. "If you'd been a man, and if I'd had these same problems with you, I would have fired you two years ago. I was waiting to see if you might change."

His face was implacable, smooth as stone. Amanda gathered her briefcase, purse, and thermos, stood, and stumbled from the room.

"Night and day...you are the one...."

The music followed her all the way to the elevator.

———

Amanda hadn't cried since she was a child--not even for her parents' funeral--but an earthquake had just shattered her world, destroying everything familiar to her, rendering her a survivor whose thoughts and dreams were as smashed up and unrecognizable as the broken streets and fallen buildings of such a horrendous calamity. Tears trickled from her eyes before she'd left the parking lot, and by the time she'd driven two blocks, the tears had swollen to sobs, grotesque animal noises that came from a place so deep inside her that she was unaware until this moment of its existence. Her chest heaving, nearly blinded by tears, her mouth tasting of salt undercut by shame and fear, she pulled into a Quik-Mart. Parking beside the store, she bent her forehead to the steering wheel, hands covering her face, elbows digging sharply through her coat into her ribs. She felt twisted up inside, compressed somehow, a spring being pushed down and down into itself, and then her stomach churned, and she just managed to throw open the door and lean out of the car before she threw up. The watery bile splattered and steamed briefly on the cold pavement.

Leaving the car door splayed open, Amanda sucked in a lungful of the frigid, gritty air, another, another. When she had caught her breath, she reached into the glove compartment, pulled out the travel package of Kleenex she kept there for winter sniffles, and dabbed at her eyes with a tissue. Still crying--the escaped tears blazed cold trails down her cheeks--she reached again into the glove compartment for the tiny bottle of mouthwash she had picked up from some hotel long ago, twisted off the cap, and swished the mint-flavored wash around her mouth. She rinsed her mouth again, then closed the car door, returned the bottle and the Kleenex to the glove compartment, drove out of the lot, and rejoined the traffic. Fragments of her conversation with Mr. Henle, still barely comprehensible to her, ran again and again through her mind. Behind their words the piano music echoed, the soft, hideous notes sounding a motif for her humiliation.

And humiliation it was. With a dull start Amanda realized that Joseph had gotten wind of her dismissal before today, that he had heard hints of her termination. "If I had known that," he'd said when he heard that her parents were dead. The entire office must have known about her firing—not in a direct way, not with certainty, but by way of rumor and office gossip. Weirdly, she thought of her long-ago Latin class, of Mrs. Donadio lecturing about Allecto in the *Aeneid*, the demigod of gossip and strife flying about the city of Carthage spreading dangerous rumors. That her co-workers had possessed this insight into her life— how amusing they must have thought it, Amanda Bell, the Ice Queen, the Iron Maiden herself, dismissed, discharged, discarded like a sack of garbage—made Amanda feel naked, branded with shame. Even if some means existed by which she could now persuade Mr. Henle to restore her to her post, she could never go back. Not now. She had lost too much face, too much dignity; she would be pitied rather than respected.

On the expressway she drove mechanically as a robot through the morning traffic, seeing neither the other cars nor the familiar buildings, intent only on reaching her apartment, her refuge, that redoubt of books, tea, hot baths, and security where she had so often regained her strength and where she might now pick through the wreckage of her life. By the time she entered the Gardens--with many of the tenants still away for Christmas or already departed for work, the apartment complex was bleak and bare as a deserted prison yard--Amanda had entered into a state of shock. Automatically, she parked the Accord in its assigned slot. Oblivious to the cold, the leaden sky, the sprinkle of rain born sideways in the stiff wind, she gathered her things, locked the car, and walked to her apartment.

———

Still lost within herself, seeing nothing but Mr. Henle's face—What was he thinking? How could he fire her?—Amanda turned the key in the lock, opened the door, and stepped into the living room. Flipping the lock closed, she followed the path of her usual post-work trajectory, heading left into the kitchen to rinse out the thermos, though today's catastrophe had stripped even this small task of its meaning. The thermos was unopened, still full of French roast coffee.

She felt rather than saw a shadow gliding behind her. She swung round, her reddened eyes taking in her Sanctuary across the carpet, the rolling table that held the television yanked now from the wall, the DVD player missing, the cushion of the far chair lying on the floor, her books pushed and shoved from their usual neat ranks.

Continuing her pivot, she found a small brown man in a knit stocking cap and green Army jacket standing in front of the door. He was grinning at her, but his eyes were black ice. With her thoughts numbed by the piano-playing Mr. Henle, Amanda couldn't make any sense of the man, why he was here, why he was smiling at her. Was he some sort of maintenance man? She froze, fixed in place by the sight of him. "Señorita," the man said, holding out both arms as if welcoming her home.

She was still trying to fathom the meaning of his presence, to connect him with the mess in her living room, when she was jerked up and backwards off her feet. Her shoes tapped at the air, and she dropped the thermos and clawed at the arm that had snaked around her neck, but her fingernails found no purchase against the slick nylon coat. The arm was clamped like a vise against her throat, yanking her up, choking her, and the man strangling her was cursing in her ear, his breath hot against her cheek, stinking of coffee and cigarettes. Squeezing her against his chest, he jerked hard with his free hand on her long braid, dragging her backwards down the hallway. Amanda twisted against him, kicked at his shins, tore at the thick arm crushing her throat. The swarthy man followed them down the hall to the bedroom, laughing and saying something, but Amanda couldn't understand him, couldn't hear anything but the sudden roaring in her head. Then the short man stopped smiling and slapped her hard across the face, and the man choking her spun and flung her onto her bed. Amanda bounced hard off the covers, and gasping for breath, looked up to see him looming above her. She twisted up from the bed, scrambling onto all fours, telling herself to fight, to scream, but before she could make a noise or lift an arm the big man punched her in the face, slamming her backwards against the pillows and into the headboard. She kicked out with both feet, heard a grunt, and kicked again, but then the big man was crawling on her, tearing her bag from her shoulder. He threw the bag to the shorter man, then grabbed her with a thick, meaty hand around the back of the head, forcing her to sit up while he tore at her coat. "Slut!" he whispered. "Cheap bitch. You got nothing in this place. Where's your money? Your jewelry?" "I got the cards," the other man said. "Only money's twenty dollars and change."

The big man--his eyes were green and raging, his cheeks pocked, his large teeth stained the color of corn--was jerking at the sleeve of her coat. Amanda clawed at his face with her fingers, and he pulled back and backhanded her hard across the face. She slumped sideways, and he jerked off the coat. "No one lives this way," he said. "Where's your money? Your stuff?" She opened her mouth to cry for help, but nothing, no words at all, came out, and she shook her head. He slapped her again, then shoved her head onto the pillows and sat astride her chest. Her hands lay unmoving on his thighs. "You give us that goddamned pin number to the card, bitch," he said. She worked her mouth, tasting blood and salt. "Four two six one," she said. "It's four two six one. Now--" "Four two six one," the man whispered. "Four two six one. Four two six one." He scooted backwards, walking on his knees down her body, and Amanda thought he might stop here, might leave her alone, but he ripped at her blouse, buttons popping away, tearing it open to her waist. She caught him round the wrist with both hands, but he broke free, slapped her again in the face, pinned her hands above her head against the pillow. Then both of them were working on her, rolling her back and forth, tugging and pulling at her torn blouse and skirt. The big man lay on top of her still cursing while the other grabbed her ankles and pulled her legs apart. "Please," she said. "Please--" "That's better, bitch," he whispered. She opened her mouth to scream, and he released her hands and slapped her again, and then again, and then again, and then clamped his own hand over her mouth. The short man had crawled onto the bed and sat beside her shoulders, laughing and holding her arms, and then something loosened within her, and Amanda Bell closed her eyes and went away and was never the same again.

Chapter Four

. . . h *elp me…please…help me…help me….*
Sometimes the words ran in a ticker tape across the back of her mind. Sometimes they drifted lazily above her, like one of those signs pulled by a small plane above a beach. Sometimes she heard them in her sleep. Sometimes when she woke the words lay like dirt and grime on her tongue. *Help me…help me….*

Sometimes days passed when she hardly slept, when her eyes refused to close, when raw nerves prickled every inch of her skin. Once she drove twenty-four hours straight, dawn to dawn, before parking at a rest stop off I-10 and crashing into a deep, dreamless sleep. In cheap motels with names like Sleepy-Time, Stop-In, and Creek-Side, where she rented rooms for the express purpose of rest and recuperation, she might instead find herself unable to close her eyes, sitting on the bed until the sun rose, staring in dull incomprehension at the images on the television screen.

Then came other days when all she seemed to do was sleep. In the week she spent near Bay St. Louis, driving along the Gulf, she frequently pulled her car to the side of the road, into the parking lot of a church, grocery store, or a casino, and slept, waking every hour or so to turn on the engine and reheat the car. In some nameless rest stop in Kentucky she once crashed for ten hours straight, roused only when a policeman tapped on the window and directed her to move along.

When she tired of sleeping on the road or in run-down motels, she would settle for a few days in one of the generic establishments of the interstate—a Holiday Inn Express, a Best Western, a Quality Inn. There she lived off the continental fare included in the room rate, filching bananas, apples, and croissants from the breakfast bar and eating them later in her room. Often she spent hours and hours, day and night, reading books purchased from shops with names like the Trading Post or the Book Exchange. She passed entire days in libraries, reading, napping, gazing out a window. She read the weird adolescent novels of Steven Millhauser, William Styron's horrific accounts of slave revolts and concentration camps, Susan Howatch's psychological novels about the sexes, God, and the Anglican Church. Once she lingered all day in a children's room at a branch library in Montgomery, opening book after book beneath the cold suspicious gaze of the librarian. Sometimes, too, after driving through the night, she would use the libraries as a place for sleeping. She was clean and quiet, and the librarians left her alone.

———————

Help me…help me….

She had prayed those words while the men were on her, while they were doing the things they did to her, but no help came. After a while they had stopped, and pushed themselves from the bed, and she had pulled up the covers, curled onto her side, and waited for them to kill her. She could feel them walking around the bed, stomping into their shoes, zipping their trousers, whispering. She didn't know how much longer they stayed in the apartment or what time they left. She heard them raise the window in the bedroom, still cursing her, and then the window slid closed. She lay for a long time curled on her side on the bed, waiting for them to come back. The smell of them, their sweat and the stink of their cigarettes, was in the bedcovers and clung like a film to her flesh. Her face ached. Her left eye was swollen shut, and her lips cleaved together, sticky with blood. She had separated into parts as they attacked her, hitting her, doing what they did to her, and now her mind was disconnected from her body, from her self. Her mind floated away, hovering above the bed. *Poor thing*, her mind whispered. *Poor, poor thing*.

She breathed through blood-clotted nostrils. She stared at the wall. Sometimes her eyes closed, and she drifted in and out of consciousness. The room was gray with the light of afternoon when she pushed herself from the twisted sheets and walked naked and splay-legged to the broken window, stepping around the glass on the floor, and pushed a pillow from the bed into the broken pane. She walked into the living room, bolted the front door, and secured the chain lock. She had trouble making her arms and legs work. Her loins, hips, arms, and legs ached, and she went to the bathroom, avoiding the mirror over the sink, and locked the door and turned on the shower. She ran the water so hot that it nearly scalded her as she stood beneath it, her flesh reddening, the spray pounding into her. She washed herself twice with soap and a cloth, scrubbing her flesh until it hurt, then turned off the water, dropped the washcloth and soap into the waste basket, and dried herself with a towel.

She didn't dry her hair or put deodorant on her underarms or lotion on her body. She brushed her teeth without looking in the mirror. She put on the robe which hung from the back of the bathroom door, shuffled into the kitchen, opened a can of beans, and heated them on the stove. When the beans bubbled in the pan, she poured them into a bowl, dug a spoon from the drawer, sat stiffly in the chair in the breakfast nook, and took a bite. Her stomach rebelled at the taste and the odor, and she hurried to the sink and vomited into the garbage disposal. With both hands she clung to the sink while her stomach boiled and churned. Afterwards, she wiped her lips with a paper towel, rinsed her mouth with water from the spigot, spat into the sink, and went into her bedroom. She pulled fresh sheets, a pillow, and a blanket from the closet. She didn't look at the bed. She closed the bedroom door, went to the living room, and made up a pallet on the floor beneath her bookcase of novels and poems.

In the kitchen she opened the cabinet beneath the sink, pulled a small saw from her tool-kit, got the broom from its place beside the refrigerator, then carried the saw and broom back to the bedroom. She held the broom up to the window, measured the space from the top of the lower window to the upper casement, and then, holding the mark with her left hand, propped the broom on the windowsill and sawed it in two at that spot. She took the wooden handle back to the window and wedged it into place on top of the lower window. After testing this homemade bolt--the window rose only an inch or so before meeting the broom handle, and anyone reaching through the window from the out-side would have trouble dislodging the handle--she dropped the saw on the floor, returned to the kitchen, removed six glasses from the cabinet, put two forks into each glass, went again to the bedroom, placed three glasses on the window ledge and three on the floor below for a primitive alarm system. Then she opened her bureau, took out a t-shirt and some flannel pajama bottoms, and left the room, shutting the door behind her.

It was growing dark outside, with only the streetlight in the parking lot illumining the windows of the living room, and she moved through the shadows like a ghost into the kitchen, where she snapped on the light above the stove. Beneath that warm glow she rummaged through the drawer beside the dishwasher where she kept her cutlery, spatulas, and measuring cups, until she found the Cutco carving knife with its six-inch blade, the blade that the salesman had rightly promised would never dull. She carried the knife into the living room, put it on the makeshift bed, loosened and dropped her robe to the floor, wiggled into the t-shirt, and pulled on the flannel pajama bottoms. Dropping to her knees, she crawled into the bed, gripped the knife in her right hand, and curled onto her side.

Sleep brought a parade of nightmares. Mr. Henle with his frog face lay naked on top of her, breathing into her ear, his short fingers digging into her neck, choking her, and then the small brown man appeared, stroking her cheek, laughing at her, his teeth flashing. Hovering over her, grunting as he took her, the big man asked her why she was such an icy witch, and backhanded her face. Mary Beth appeared from the airport and squatted beside her, no longer weeping, no longer seeking advice, asking her whether she was happy now that she had a boyfriend. In still another moment the knife in her hand turned into jelly beans, and she heard someone shouting "Sing vit me! Sing vit me!" On and on these hallucinations flashed in her mind, threaded together by a motif of piano music. *Gray skies are gonna clear up...put on a happy face....*

Daylight splashed on her face. Gripping the knife in her right hand, she rolled to her back and stared with her one good eye at the ceiling. After a while she pushed herself from the floor, every muscle a bundle of pain, and carrying the knife went into the kitchen and drank two glasses of water. With each swallow her throat ached where the big man had choked her. She put the empty glass into the sink, limped back to the living room--her left thigh throbbed, bruised from a punch she hadn't remembered or even felt--and got between the covers of the pallet. In the sun-lit room she closed her eyes and slept, dreamless this time, a heavy sinking sleep that covered her like a shroud.

When she woke again, the apartment was all shadows. She crawled across the floor on her hands and knees, found the remote control, and turned on the television. She hadn't watched anything for months, had used the screen for her Netflix rentals only, and she stared at the screen for a few minutes in a dull stupor. A woman was winning money by answering questions. Click. A man was singing about his beautiful day in the neighborhood. Click. A man lay in a hospital bed with a woman kissing his ear. Click. A black woman was talking with two white women about sex and gang violence. Click. A woman was selling used cars.

She pushed herself off the floor, went into the kitchen, and took the hammer from the tool-kit. Back in the living room, she turned off the television, dropped the remote to the floor, and smashed in the television screen with the hammer. She hit the screen too hard and cut her thumb on the glass. Leaning the hammer against the television, she sucked at her wound and lay down again.

Time moved without her. Seconds, minutes, and hours lost their meaning. She slept, she stared at the ceiling, she forced herself to eat. When she used up the last of the milk, she ate her oatmeal with water. The phone rang at some point, and she unplugged it. She kept her cell phone turned off. One morning she went into the bedroom and turned on the computer. She looked at the list of e-mails, mostly work related or advertisements, and deleted them. She deleted addresses, programs, favorite sites, then shut down and unplugged the machine.

She slept as if she hadn't slept in years, dropping into dreams and darkness whenever she lay down and closed her eyes. Always she drifted off with the knife gripped in her fingers, its hard black plastic handle familiar to her now, a comfort she grasped in her sleep like a lover's hand, never losing the blade in the long hours of unconsciousness when so much else was thankfully lost.

On her fourth night she jerked alert, sitting straight up with the knife at the ready. From the apartment above her came loud cries, thuds, shouting. Then a voice cried, "Happy New Year!" and slowly her shoulders relaxed, and she lay back, breathing hard, while her neighbors laughed and a stereo thumped hard bass notes. *Auld lang syne, baby... auld lang syne....*

"I have to get out of here," she said. This was the first time she had spoken aloud since she had said "Please" to the big man, and her grating whisper vibrated in the room with a strange resonance, disconnected from her, the voice of a stranger.

Her mind, once so quick to pounce on a problem, gnawed at this prospect of departure for two more days before a plan began taking shape. At two a.m. on Tuesday January 4th--she needed a weekday for what she was about to do, and the banks were closed on Monday for New Year's--she gathered up her dirty laundry, leaving only the bed sheets and torn clothing from the bedroom, and went outside and down the sidewalk to the laundry room, carrying the knife atop her basket of clothing. She started the load of wash, walked to her mailbox holding the knife at her side, gathered up the accumulation of letters and fliers, and returned to her apartment, where she threw away all the mail except for the envelope which she knew she would find, her two weeks' severance check from Saxon and Henle. Dispassionately she noted the postmark--Tuesday December 28th, the same day of her catastrophes: they'd clearly wanted to be rid of her. She put the check into her shoulder bag. From the hallway closet she selected two suitcases and filled the smaller one with some of her books, Austen, two Norton anthologies, a collection of poetry, her mother's copy of *Gone With The Wind*, turning each one over in her hands as if she'd never seen them before in her life. She returned to the laundry, put the clothes in the dryer, and sat waiting with the knife in her hands. When the clothes were dry, she took them back to the apartment, folded some of them in the larger suitcase, pulled more clothing, mostly socks and underwear, from the bedroom bureau, and added these to the suitcase. Into a small duffel she packed basic toiletries.

By five a.m. she had loaded the bags into the trunk of the Accord. She made a final trip carrying two bath towels, a wash cloth, two blankets, and a pillow. Lights were coming on in some of the apartments as people stirred and rose for work, but the car was packed and no one would see her or speak to her now as long as she stayed inside. She showered, brushed her teeth, braided her hair, and dressed in a white blouse, dark grey sweater, and jeans.

For the first time in a week she examined herself in the bathroom mirror. The high collar of her blouse hid most of the bruises on her throat. Her left eye was fully opened, though still yellow and bloodshot, and the swelling in her lips had disappeared, but the left side of her cheek was a welter of yellow and green bruises. The sunglasses which she kept in the Accord might partially hide these injuries, but she knew she must steel herself in anticipation of some stares.

In the kitchen, standing at the counter, she wrote a note to her landlord: "I have gone away." She left it on the counter with one of the apartment keys. She put the other key in an envelope, addressed it to her neighbor Justin, and wrote to him: "I have gone away. Please take what you want of my belongings. If you have the time, please pack my novels and put them in the storage room. I need you to collect my mail. You can throw away anything that isn't personal. Don't worry. I'm all right."

———

She waited until half past nine when those going to work that day would have left the Gardens, then shouldered her bag, tucked the knife inside, locked the apartment door, returned the key to the envelope, inserted the note and key into Justin's mailbox, walked to the Accord, placed her long, black coat and her shoulder bag on the passenger seat, and drove toward the highway without a backward look.

As she entered the bank, her insides felt wobbly and she thought for a moment she might be sick. Pausing by the customer counter, she drew out her severance check and checkbook from her purse, and pretended to study them until her equilibrium returned. After a few deep breaths, she stepped into the line of people waiting to see a teller. Feeling suddenly foolish in the sunglasses, she removed them and folded them into her bag.

"May I help you?"

"I'd like to cash this check, please, and then close my checking account."

The teller, an older woman with short grey hair and baggy eyes who recognized her from her previous visits, nodded. The woman's eyes stopped only a moment on her face before she took the check, glancing at it to get her name. "No problem, Ms. Bell."

"And could you tell me how much is left in my checking account, please?"

"Sure thing."

The clerk punched some keys on her computer, frowned, looked down at the screen again, and said slowly and in a low voice: "Your account is nearly depleted, Ms. Bell. In fact, you have eighty three dollars and forty-three cents left."

"I need to close the account."

"You'll need to see a rep." She pushed the air with her chin. "Mrs. Dowling's open."

Taking her check and banking books, she crossed the room and entered Mrs. Dowling's office. "Good morning. I'm Dorothy Dowling. May I help you?"

"I'm Amanda Bell," she said automatically, thinking: *No, you're not. She's gone. You're nothing. Nobody. Nobody at all.* "I need to close my account." She opened the check book and placed it on the desk.

"Any trouble?"

"Someone is using my card."

"You're sure?"

"My money's all gone. Almost two thousand dollars. They got it."

"Do you know who is using the card?"

"No. No, I don't." She shook her head, her voice trembling. Lying was not a habit with her. "They've apparently taken everything."

"When did you notice it was missing?"

This time she didn't lie. "Last week."

"You're supposed to report the card as stolen or missing as soon as you know."

She said nothing. Mrs. Dowling, who wore that thrown-together look of most workers on their first day back to work after the holidays, sighed after a moment, then located Amanda's account on the computer screen. "All the purchases were made a week ago. Six hundred dollars in cash withdrawals, a four hundred dollar purchase from Best Buy, two hundred and change from three different liquor stores, smaller purchases for gas and groceries. These aren't yours?"

"No."

"Give me a few moments."

While Mrs. Dowling worked on the computer, took a phone call, and left to check some piece of information with one of the tellers, she sat stiffly in the chair in the trim office, unaware of her surroundings, seeing nothing but the two men in her mind. She should have given them the wrong pin number, pulling random numbers from the air, but she had been so frightened, so afraid of being killed, that she had blurted out the real numbers. She thought of them going into stores, using her card right after what they had done to her, and she felt violated all over again. At this very moment they were eating her food, drinking liquor which she had paid for, driving their cars on her gasoline.

The severance check in her hand made her feel stained and dirty--twelve hundred and twenty-six dollars and ninety-one cents--and she placed it on Mrs. Dowling's desk on top of her savings book. In her mind piano music played again and Mr. Henle was saying her name. She bent her head forward and touched her forehead with her fingertips, closing her eyes, wanting everything and everyone to go away and leave her alone.

In the next few minutes Mrs. Dowling closed her checking account, put the Saxon and Henle check into her savings, and withdrew from that account forty-five hundred dollars, leaving the severance check and a matching amount in that account. She counted out the forty-five hundred dollar bills twice before tucking the bills into a banking envelope and sliding it across the table.

She put the envelope into her purse and rose to go.

"Ms. Bell. Amanda. Is everything all right?"

"Yes."

"I have a daughter about your age. Stacie. She works for a bank in Charlotte. I know how hard it is being on your own these days. Being young."

"Yes."

"Sometimes Stacie gets lonely. She has friends, of course, and her boyfriend Ned, but even so she feels alone sometimes. She calls me and we talk it out."

"Yes." She stood rigid as a statue, the fingers of her left hand gripping her shoulder bag.

Mrs. Dowling dropped all pretense of ignoring her bruises and stared with compassion at her face. "I just thought--"

"Everything is fine. Thank you for your help."

———

By three o'clock that afternoon Atlanta was a memory two hundred miles behind her. She hit I-95 above Savannah and headed south in heavy traffic. Near Jacksonville she stopped for gas and a restroom, and looked at her AAA map of the Southeastern States. She thought of heading for the Keys, but they would be crowded and expensive this time of the year, and she opted instead to drive west on I-10. She stopped late that night at an Econo-Lodge near Panama City. When he handed her a room key, the man behind the desk said, "Quite a shiner," saying "quat" for "quite" so that she took a few moments unraveling his meaning. The dressing room lights of the bathroom revealed the ugly extent of the dappled bruises--the left side of her face from her eyebrow to her mouth was still discolored, as if someone had whacked her with a two by four. She looked at the eyes in the mirror, flat blue sapphires cloudy and wild with confusion, and saw the eyes of a stranger.

She slept until almost noon that second day on the road. That evening, driving in Mississippi, she found a K-Mart where she bought a pair of scissors and a pregnancy test. In the bathroom of a MacDonald's, she took the pregnancy test and found negative results. Late that evening in a Best Western near Memphis, she took out the scissors, looked into the bathroom mirror, reached behind her head, chopped off her long braid, and dropped the hair, which felt lighter than she'd anticipated, into the trash basket. She trimmed her remaining hair, showered, and sat in a chair in front of her window, watching the night and the winking lights of a truck plaza.

On her fifth day on the road she found a women's care center in Tuscaloosa, noted the hours of operation posted on the door, and took a room in a nearby Quality Inn. In the morning, freshly showered, she drove to the center and sat in the parking lot for five minutes with the car engine running, watching the front door, steeling herself for her inquisition. After switching off the engine, her fingers resting on the steering wheel, she watched the door another five minutes. Finally, she took a deep breath, removed the knife from her shoulder bag, put it in the side pocket of the front door, and crossed the parking lot beneath the sparkling winter sun.

Inside, she asked about an appointment. The receptionist, a heavy woman with a soft country voice, informed her that the office was booked for the day. "Please," she said. "I think I'm in trouble." The woman studied her a moment, then reached beneath the desk and pulled out some papers attached to a clipboard. "Fill these out," she said. "I'll get you in."

She filled out forms. One section, colored in blue, asked questions about her previous sexual activity. She marked "Past month" and left the rest blank. Probably no one here would believe that she was--that she had been, less than two weeks ago--a virgin. Twenty-seven year old virgins were a joke nowadays, or else a phenomenon to be wondered at, rare in Atlanta, or anywhere else in America for that matter, as a herd of wildebeest, yet that was the truth. She had never given herself over to a man--not in that final physical sense. She'd had plenty of opportunities in college, and a few at work, but that "final surrender of flesh," a phrase she'd read somewhere in one of her Victorian novels, had never occurred. Once last year, she had joined an internet dating service for a month in hopes of finding someone to love. Though she was impressed by how many thousands of lonely people inhabited a fifty mile radius of Atlanta, she had never gone out with a single one of the men who had written her. Late at night she would parse their photographs and profiles--"Loves dogs," "Looking for someone to love," "Motorcycles a passion"--but found herself unmoved by their comments, their electronic winks, their letters explaining themselves and why they might be perfect for her.

Half an hour after she returned the form to the receptionist, a nurse emerged from another door, called her name, and escorted her to an examination room. She was weighed, was asked more questions, was ordered to urinate into a sterile bottle and return it to the nurse. She sat numbly in a cold room dressed in a hospital gown. While the doctor, a man of middle age who smelled of coffee and soap, examined her, she lay on the table blinking into the overhead light, rigid, braced against his touch. When he had completed the examination, he smiled at her with kind eyes and asked a few more questions. "I'm told you're not from around here," he said when he had finished.

"No."

"Normally we'd call you back for another visit to discuss lab results." He saw her hesitation and brushed the air with a large hand. "I'll tell the lab to speed it up. Do you want to wait for the results?"

"Please."

"Should be less than an hour."

She waited on the sofa near a magazine rack, looking at pictures of women and girls, mothers and babies. The nurse came out, called her name, and took her back into the examining room. "You have Chlamydia," she said. "Do you understand what that means?"

"An STD?"

"Yes. It's easily cured. You'll need to take doxycycline two times a day for a week. Dr. Stanford already made out the prescription." The nurse handed her a slip of paper. "You'll also need to tell your partner. Otherwise, you'll just be re-infected."

"I see."

"Don't do anything together until he's treated. And don't do anything with anyone else until your treatment is over."

"No," she said. "I won't."

———

Early February found her sitting in the Accord on the narrow street outside her girlhood home in Charlottesville. The large magnolia tree which she had climbed as girl was still there, green and somehow more stately than the house itself. There were no toys in the front yard. She wondered if a girl lived there who was as tidy as she once was. She thought of her parents. She knew in her heart what she had always known and recognized, that her mother and father had loved her but that they had loved each other even more, loved each other so much that she and everyone else were always on the outside of that love, onlookers watching through impregnable glass. Allie and Sam she had called them, ever since she could remember. Her friends from school thought this replacement of Mom and Dad by first names was cool, but she hadn't liked it. She had always wanted the grounding that came with Mom and Dad, the recognition of being special, of belonging to them.

She watched the white frame house for nearly an hour that late afternoon, wanting someone to come outside. Some dry leaves skittered on the street, and candy-cotton clouds tumbled across the vast sky. Once from down the street she heard a car door slam and the thin shouts of children. When the street lamps came on, she started the engine, left the dark house behind, and drove east toward Richmond.

She had begun early on to conserve her money by staying only every other night, and then every third night, in motels, and then searching out the cheapest accommodations she could find, those busted-up places shunted aside by motel chains and interstate highways. By March she occasionally sought food and sometimes a bed from public shelters. These rough quarters cost her little in privacy, for by then she had withdrawn into the citadel built deep within herself. The people around her talked and ate and walked back and forth, but she rarely saw or heard them. She could live in a book or in the blank space of her mind, and so could live without people. Once at a soup kitchen in Winston-Salem a skinny man with a rubicund nose sat at the table beside her and, ignoring her, began digging through her shoulder bag. She was eating a baked potato, and as she brought the fork from her mouth, she stabbed him in the hand with it. The man jumped, fell backwards, and knocked a glass of water into the lap of the large man beside him, who hit him under the chin with his fist and then fell on top of him. While they were wrestling, she picked up the potato and her purse, and walked calmly toward the door past the cooks and servers who were running to stop the fight. In a city whose name she later forgot a demented woman wearing a red sweat suit and white canvas shoes had followed her down a street of secondhand shops and broken windows, imploring her first for money and then cursing her. "I'm a-gonna kill you, I'm a-gonna kill you," the woman chanted. She rounded a building, then turned on the woman and slapped her so fast as she came around the corner that none of the people walking past them noticed what had happened. The woman staggered backwards, sat down hard on the pavement, leaned against the building, and began to weep.

After her first few days on the road, she abandoned the interstates and traveled the secondary highways through countryside and small towns. Here even in winter were distractions, sights and sounds that afforded cheap amusement and took her away for a moment or two from her interior self--yard sales, flea markets, children at play, forests, fields, farms. The week she spent traveling up and down the coastline of North and South Carolina brought her the solace of long walks on empty beaches, smelling the sea-spray and watching the gulls.

Often she dreamed in the night. Mr. Henle or the two rapists invaded her, taunting, touching, grabbing at her as she tried to flee them through dark, strange rooms. Added to these nightmares were other twisted shapes: the faces and voices of strangers she'd met on the road, jungles choking her with their foliage, weird reptilian creatures and brittle anthropoids tearing and scratching at her. When she was able to yank herself from these vision and awake, she found her fingers stiff from clenching the knife.

Only once had she attempted writing in her journal. She had pulled the ledger from the bag when she was cleaning out her car at a Wash-and-Go in Northern Alabama. That afternoon she carried the journal with her toiletries into her motel room, sat before the window, opened it, and wrote at the top of the page: *I am not I.* Until twilight darkened the room she sat there staring at the four words, but could find nothing else to say to the blank paper. She closed the journal, returned it to the bag in the car, and carried into the room the copy of Delderfield's *God is an Englishman,* purchased at a Salvation Army store for fifty cents.

In early April she checked into the Star-Brite Motel in Front Royal, Virginia. She took a long walk through the small historic downtown and through a neighborhood of shabby homes, many of them in need of paint, with small yards enclosed by metal fences. She browsed in the Royal Oak Bookshop and then wandered down Royal Avenue. For the first time she noticed that the grass was turning green again, that the limbs of the maples and oaks were heavy with buds.

I have slept through the winter.

She had left her apartment and Atlanta without giving any thought to the future. She had wanted to escape the wreckage of that wounded creature which she had once claimed as herself. As the miles, places, and days had piled up, she kept telling herself she must find a job, must make some money, must uncover some means to retrieve herself and return to the pathway of her life, yet nothing had happened. She had never recaptured the citadel of her old self, and the shell that remained still awaited habitation.

———

Back at the Star-Brite, she went into the bathroom and looked at the stranger before her in the yellow light of the mirror. She had lost weight these past few months, and her face was lean and grim. Her eyes were cold, flat as blue coins, and her blonde hair, once a secret pride, was chopped and windblown. Her eyebrows needed plucking. She looked at her hands, which had become dry and chapped from the weather. She tried to open her mouth and speak the name of the image in the mirror, but no words, not even a sound, emerged.

She went to her car, took out her large shoulder bag--she already knew the contents of the library bag which she carried with her every-where, the Cutco knife, her driver's license, a cellophane pack of peanut butter crackers--and went into the room and emptied the shoulder bag onto the bed. She counted out the money remaining in the bank enve-lope and the loose change, and laid three hundred and thirty-seven dollars and sixty- two cents in a neat pile. She threw away gum wrappers and gasoline receipts, some odd bits of paper, three paper clips, a rubber band, a pink jelly bean fuzzy with lint. She picked up a book called *Power Management*, looked at the black-and-yellow cover, and dropped it in the trash can. She threw away business cards, a few movie stubs, a sheet of blue paper listing the hours and amenities of a YMCA in Knoxville.

Three hundred and thirty-seven dollars and sixty-cents. She might live another ten days, perhaps two weeks, before running out of funds. There was always her savings, of course, but what was the point of spending that? Another few months of aimless driving seemed unlikely to bring her any closer to an explication of her tangled self.

She opened the bag wide, turned it upside down, and shook it. Some lint, a candy wrapper, and another business card floated to the bed. She picked up the card. One corner was torn, and a pink stain, perhaps from the loose jelly bean, dotted the graven print:

Father John A. Krumpler
Basilica of Saint Lawrence
97 Haywood Street
Asheville, NC 28801

She read the name several times. Each time the shape of a man's face and the sound of his voice became clearer in her mind.

"*I can help you…if I can ever help you….*"

She went to the car, opened the glove compartment, and found the map.

PART II

Chapter Five

The church's bells were tolling ten times when she approached the Basilica of Saint Lawrence. The light rain that had fallen the previous day had given way to cloudless skies and shining streets. A stocky middle-aged man with a goatee and a pipe clamped between his teeth was pulling weeds from the rose garden in front of the basilica. He stood when she asked him where she could find Father Krumpler.

"He went for coffee with some of the ladies—he celebrated the early mass today." The gardener's reply baffled her. What was there to celebrate today? What holiday fell on a Tuesday in April?

The man took a box of wooden matches from his shirt pocket, lit his pipe, shook out the match, and returned it to the matchbox and the matchbox to his pocket. "He'll be back soon if you want to wait." He nodded toward the church door. "You could wait inside the church." He sucked at his pipe, exhaled a cloud of smoke, and pointed with the pipe toward the doorway in the adjoining building. "Or in the rectory. Just ring the bell—Beth will let you inside."

She thanked him, crossed the small courtyard, and pushed open the heavy wooden door of the church. The interior was cool, dark, and vast, and she paused in the tiny side vestibule to allow her eyes to grow accustomed to the dim room. The air smelled of candle wax and flowers. At the front of the church a group of tourists, cameras hanging from their necks, backpacks and satchels strapped in place, stood before the main altar. To the right of the altar, in a smaller chamber, three women knelt in prayer.

She walked down the left side of the church and slipped into one of the pews. Directly ahead of her in the other side chapel stood the statue of a woman. Her white body was twisted, her marble gown whipped and torn as if by the wind. The woman's face was lifted to heaven. A bank of candles guttered along the wall to the left of the statue.

She slipped her bag from her shoulder, found Father Krumpler's card, read it again, then closed her eyes, holding onto the card as if to a talisman. She felt rested after her night in the Sheraton on Woodfin Street, upping her usual place of accommodation by several notches in anticipation of meeting the priest, feeling somehow that she might make a better impression if she treated herself to such a luxury. Early that morning, fearing that she might not immediately locate Father Krumpler, she had requested a late check-out from her room. She now reminded herself that she would need to return there no later than one o'clock.

After checking into the motel yesterday, and hoping to make a better impression than if she had appeared in one of her travel-worn outfits, she had bought this green and yellow sundress at the Goodwill Store on Patton Avenue. The dress fit her loosely--she'd lost more weight than she'd realized these past few months--but she liked the way the material felt brushing against her thighs and knees. She had spent part of the previous evening snipping her hair until she achieved a reasonable looking bob. This morning she had showered again, eaten her fill at the breakfast bar, taken two bananas and a muffin for lunch, put them in her room, brushed her teeth, and then walked the four blocks to the church, which she had located the previous afternoon.

She heard a noise and opened her eyes. The tour group was shuffling past her toward the door. Above all of them was a high, domed ceiling, and she lifted her chin and looked at it when the tourists stopped to crane their own necks upward. They left with whispers and a squeaking of shoes on the marble floor, and she was alone again except for the three women in the chapel. On either side of the church as well as behind the altar were more statues. An enormous crucifix hung above the altar. Stained glass windows down both walls of the church offered pictures from the life of Christ.

In this place of shadows and quiet she felt protected, the way she felt when she was driving in her car, as if no one could hurt her. It wasn't God who made her feel safe; she knew little of God and cared little about religion. No--she was comforted by the silence of the place, a silence so deep she could hear herself breathing, the fabric of the dress rustling against her body, the sonorous and throbbing silence of silence itself.

She had just closed her eyes again, giving way to the peace, when she heard footsteps. They stopped beside her. She stood, bumping her knees against the pew in front of her.

"Yes?"

It was him. He was dressed exactly as he'd been on the aircraft but without the black coat. He still resembled an owl; his hair stuck out in tufts, and his eyes were bright and gleaming. "Nick said you wanted to see me."

"Nick?"

"Our sacristan. The man outside."

"We met once."

"You and Nick?"

"Nick and I?"

"You're saying you met Nick once?"

Unaccustomed to talk, she was clearly snarling up the conversation. "No," she said with effort. "You and I--we met once."

"We did?"

That Father Krumpler remembered nothing of her didn't surprise her. She knew how she looked with her dress and her hair. She knew as well how strange her voice must sound, unaccustomed as it was to usage. Just thinking of words to speak, much less uttering them, was painful.

"We met on a plane."

"On a plane?"

"On a plane. Just before Christmas. You were flying to Atlanta from D.C."

He stared at her. Recognition slowly grew behind his face, as if someone was flicking on one of those three-way lamps. "It's you?"

"Yes."

"Forgive me for not recognizing you. You look different. Your hair, maybe. No, something else."

"Yes," she said. "Something else."

"I'm sorry. I've forgotten your name."

"Amanda. Amanda Bell." There: she had said it, her name, the badge by which the world had once identified her. When she had given her name to him on the plane, she knew exactly what her name meant. Now it meant nothing to her. She remembered the card in her hand and held it toward him as if handing a ticket to an usher. "You gave me this card."

"Yes." With a puzzled look he took the card from her, examined it, and returned it. "I remember you now, Amanda. You were reading Strunk and White." His eyes probed her face, touching her like fingers, and she looked beyond him to an invisible spot on the wall. "I remember how you were, but you've changed. Something's happened to you, hasn't it?"

She nodded. "Something has happened to me."

Both were silent for a moment, standing there in the shadows.

"On the plane you offered to help me. You said you could help me. Can you help me?"

"I can try."

"First, I need a place to talk. Alone. I need to tell you things. I need to tell you things you won't ever tell anyone else."

"You want confession?"

"Yes. I think so anyway. Yes."

"You aren't Catholic, are you? I don't think you said you were Catholic."

"A long time ago I was Episcopalian. At least I think we were Episcopalian. We never went to church. I really don't know what I am. I don't think I'm anything."

"Everyone is something."

"I don't think I am."

"I can hear your confession and I can give you a blessing, but I can't give you absolution."

Here was the foreign talk again, like the man in the rose garden with his talk of celebration. "I need to say some things."

"Privately?"

"Yes. Privately."

"Wait here one minute."

He walked quickly down the side aisle and into the chapel where the marble lady stood, and disappeared into a doorway. A moment later he strode back down the aisle draping some sort of purple cloth about his shoulders. "Follow me," he whispered.

———

Carrying her shoulder bag, she followed Father Krumpler down the aisle and across the back of the church. Here were three wooden boxes side by side, two of them with hanging cloth for doors. "We can use the confessional if you like. Or we can go to my office."

"I don't want you to look at me when I'm talking."

"I won't be able to see you in here."

"And you can't tell anyone, can you? Not ever? No matter what?"

"That's right."

"All right then."

He entered the middle box and she chose the one on the right. She slipped past the curtain, drew it closed, and knelt on a tiny bench beside a little grilled window. "You'll need to talk softly," Father Krumpler said. Then he murmured a prayer and was silent.

Staring into the grill, her hands clasped not in prayer but from fear, she told the priest everything: the scene with Mr. Henle, the men in her apartment, her time on the road since then. Despite her whispering, her throat ached before she was two minutes into her narrative; she hadn't talked this much at any one time since December. She didn't cry, and though she needed to pause several times to think and to gather herself, her voice remained emotionless. She tried to sound as if she were describing the misfortunes of someone else. Oddly enough, this recitation pained her less than anticipated. Each spoken word was like a sparrow lifting a crumb or two from the horrors of the last four months.

Then she was finished.

Father Krumpler remained silent.

"What are you doing?"

"I'm praying for you. And for me."

The silence from the other side of the grill wrapped itself around her.

"I don't know who I am anymore. I used to be someone else. Someone safe who knew her life. But I don't think I could go back to that person."

"No, you can't."

His comment jolted her. She was expecting consolation, not agreement. "Really?"

"I don't see how."

"What then?"

"For now you must continue to suffer." His whisper became urgent, fierce. "Today you've taken the first step toward a new life. You've made your first attempt to reconnect with a life outside yourself. All these months you have drifted on a strange river. Whether you realize it or not, you have suffered a severe breakdown. This is your first step toward recovery, toward your self, maybe to a new self. But it's only one step-- one tiny step. You must use your will—and I remember how you were on the plane, you have a strong will—to push yourself back into the world."

"But I don't want to suffer anymore. I want to find myself now. It's why I came to you."

The priest said nothing.

"I'm tired. I'm tired of everything. I don't know what to do with myself."

"You have a right to be tired, to be lost, but you can't quit now. And look at yourself--you've taken the first step. You've gotten past the moment when so many people quit, when so many people give up. Those poor lost souls stay lost. The fortunate ones settle for dreaming instead of doing. They exist but don't really live. The unfortunate ones turn inward, become obsessed with themselves, give way to self-pity, and slowly kill the remaining good inside their souls." She heard him shift on the other side of the screen. "Now bow your head and pray for God's mercy and blessing."

She bowed her head, though she believed in no God, and listened as the priest murmured: "May the Lord bless you and keep you, may He make His face to shine upon you and bring you peace."

———

When she heard him moving, she pushed herself to her feet and stepped outside the curtained booth. He smiled at her.

"Let's go to my office for a few minutes."

Amanda followed him to a side door of the rectory, which he unlocked, and into a pleasant hallway that led past offices and meeting rooms and then up a flight of stairs to his office. Here sunlight glowed on bookshelves and on a large wooden desk. Behind the desk was a framed poster of the popes and an illuminated copy of a prayer. Through the windows on the other side of the room she could see hills and blue mountains.

Father Krumpler motioned her toward the chairs in front of the desk. "Anything to drink? Tea? Coffee?"

"A cup of coffee would be nice."

He busied himself at a side table beneath the windows, measuring water from a carafe into the pot, scooping teaspoons of coffee into the basket. "Are you up for some conversation?"

"I don't think I'll be much good at it. The last few months--I haven't spoken much to anyone."

"What about your friends? Didn't you call them? I'm sure they've wondered how you're doing."

"I--" She thought of lying to him. Who, after all, didn't have friends, people in whom to confide, with whom to share broken dreams as well as triumphs? But she couldn't lie--not now, not after the confessional. "I don't have friends."

He took her admission as if she'd just commented on the weather. "Family? You told me on the plane that your mother and father had died. There's no one else?"

His recollection of their conversation from the flight surprised her. "No."

"Cream or sugar?"

"What?"

"In your coffee."

"Black is fine."

She had spent the morning tense as a cat, all muscle and emotional bone. Now the confession, the smell of the coffee, the pleasant clean office, and Father Krumpler's regard and kindness calmed Amanda. She took the cup he offered her with steady fingers.

Father Krumpler settled himself in the chair beside her, blowing steam from his coffee. "It's decaffeinated, I'm afraid. My system doesn't tolerate caffeine the way it once did."

"It's fine."

He sipped his coffee, then placed the cup on his desk. "I'm curious about your time at Saxon and Henle. May we talk about that for a bit?"

"All right."

"You worked for this Henle fellow. Your main duty was to manage some of the staff?"

"Yes."

"How were you with your coworkers?"

"How do you mean?"

"What sort of relationship did you have with them? How did you treat them? Did you get along with them?"

"They thought I was tough. Hard. But I always tried to be fair." Amanda shook her head, looked at her hands. She tried picking out other thoughts, but strained at the effort. "The truth is they didn't like me very much."

"Leadership and management can be tough propositions."

"I read books. I went to workshops. I was harder on myself than I was on them."

"Too hard?"

"I needed them to perform. I needed to get the job done."

"That's not what I meant. Were you too hard on yourself?"

"I don't know what you mean."

"We'll let that go for now. Your fellow workers--might you have managed them in some other way?"

"I don't know any other way."

"Human beings require different incentives to perform any job. The old carrot-and-stick, you know."

"Carrot-and-stick?"

Father Krumpler laughed. Amanda recalled his laughter on the flight that day, merry and bright, filled with fellowship rather than derision. "I'm showing my age," he said. "The carrot-and-stick refers to mules working in the fields. Some mules work best with a carrot dangling in front of them while they plow, while others need a thumping with a stick. Some require both." He reflected a moment. "Mules...I haven't seen one of those in years. We used to see them all the time down in Louisiana."

"What sort of carrots do people need?"

"Rewards of some kind. Incentives. Reasons to excel in their work."

"I always thought the work was enough in itself. That they should do the jobs they were hired for."

"In an ideal world, perhaps, but most of us need more. Perks, positive recognition. They don't have to be financial. I know a manager at Staples who takes candy to his employees every day. Goofy, right, but they love him. A little bit of charity goes a long way."

"I don't know how to do that sort of thing."

"You can learn. People need tending and help. They're exotic, like the creatures in Hopkins' poetry--"'original, spare, strange.'"

"'Whatever is fickle, freckled (who knows how?),'" Amanda said, adding the next line.

Father Krumpler's face glowed with delight. "You know Hopkins!" He wiggled like a boy in his chair. "Amanda Bell, you surprise me."

"The Victorians were always my favorites. The poets and the novelists."

"I'm more partial to the poets of that era. When I read fiction, I reach for twentieth century writers, the ones in the first half of the century. Waugh, Faulkner, Fitzgerald, even poor old Thomas Wolfe, who isn't a favorite with critics these days. Last year I read that book about the young college girl by the other Tom Wolfe."

"*Charlotte Simmons?*"

"You know the book?"

"I read it last month in a library in Tennessee. I wouldn't think priests were allowed to read books so full of--."

"--sex," he finished for her.

"And other things."

"Priests need to know as much about the human heart as they possibly can, and fiction is a grand gateway into that heart. Stories allow us to comprehend the pain of others without confronting them in the flesh. Reading about Charlotte Simmons, for example, is much easier on me than hearing your own story. She is a book I can put down. It's the books you can't put down that make life so tough."

She wasn't sure what he meant, though his last words frightened her. Did he intend to put her down, to lay her aside, to leave her now to make her way again on her own? She lifted her head, and looked at him.

"You've changed," he said simply. "You're very different than when we met."

His kind, inquisitive eyes bore into her. The abyss above which she had hung all winter yawned beneath her, tempting her to let go, to break her last precarious hold on her self, her independence and will. The dark powers of this pit buzzed inside her, urging her to ignore this priest with his cheap advice. *What could he know anyway? How could some priest understand your troubles? What does he know of rape and ruin?* She was tempted to leave this office and this man with his white collar, to strike out on her own again, yet no one in her entire life had ever looked at her this way. His steady gaze touched her face as it had in the church, a look so filled with love for her, with such hope and compassion, that her own eyes blurred with tears.

Father Krumpler reached to the desk and offered her a box of Kleenex. Clumsily, she pulled out a handful of tissues, ducked her head, and pressed them to her eyes. The darkness inside her receded, and she began weeping, crying as if she were falling apart inside, and all the time she could feel him watching her, could feel him waiting beside her unperturbed and patient as a stone.

———

He let her cry as if he had all the time in the world, as if he had nothing better to do this morning than to sit, drink coffee, and listen to her sobbing. Yet all the time she was aware that he was praying for her, that he had discerned the awful darkness gathered inside her, and was offering her a lifeline to keep her from tumbling away.

"I hate what's happened to me," she managed at last in a choked voice. "I hate change."

"Most people hate change," Father Krumpler said easily. "Especially when it brings us pain or grief. In fact, when you think about it, our attitude toward change is a damned odd thing. We eat food, and our body changes its composition for our nourishment. We change our clothes. The news changes daily, the weather changes every hour, and yet deep down most of us wish for our lives to be happy and unchanging."

"I want my old life back," Amanda said, though she wasn't sure this was true. "I don't know who I am anymore." She patted her eyes with the tissue, but the tears kept welling up. "I don't know what I should do or be."

"You need to be patient with yourself. You've undergone a terrible trauma. You lost your job and your place in the world. You were burglarized and raped. You suffered a terrible wound of the soul. Since then you've followed a path--a rather strange path, if you don't mind my saying so--through a dreadful time of loneliness and despair. Now you've come to the end of the path and all you can see is darkness and a cliff. You're stuck between leaping off the cliff or turning back and retracing your steps until you find the right path. Today, I think, you decided to step away from the cliff."

The wadded tissues had at last staunched her tears. "But I don't know where to go next."

"I would advise some counseling."

"Counseling? With a psychiatrist, you mean?"

"With someone who will listen to you. Someone who will know how to guide you back to your self. We have a parishioner here, a psychologist, who does that sort of work. She might--"

"I don't want a psychologist," Amanda said, and for the first time in months she knew precisely what she did want. "I want you."

"Me?"

"Yes, you. You must have helped lots of people in your time. You could help me." When he didn't reply, she added: "I can pay. I still have a little money in Atlanta."

"It isn't the money. I wouldn't take money. I--"

"You can help me. You've already started. And I promise not to be too much trouble. I won't take much of your time. If I could just talk with you every once in a while, if you could meet with me once or twice a week, I'd have some sort of map to my life again." The rising panic within her had put a stop to her tears. She was pulling at the tissue in her hand, tearing it, and put it on the desk top, then stuffed it instead into her purse, talking all the while to him. "You know about me now. You know what happened to me. I don't want to have to tell that again to anyone. You--"

He raised one hand. "Shhhh," he said. "Just a moment."

She was babbling. First the confession, now the well of tears: she was pathetic. He must think her a complete fool. But if he didn't help her, if she didn't allow him to help her, then she was most assuredly lost.

"It's my fault," he said. "We need to take small steps, and I forgot that. I was looking too far into the future. Let's go back a step and concentrate on the here and now, on the basics. Tell me, Amanda, what you are looking for right now."

"Right now I could use a mirror and a washroom."

He laughed. "At least your sense of humor is intact."

"I was being serious." She had never regarded herself as possessed of a sense of humor. Life hadn't allowed for a sense of humor in a long time.

"You look fine. But if you like, there's a restroom at the end of the hallway."

She started from her chair, to take him up on the offer, but sank down again, afraid that if she left him, the bonds between them, the line he had cast out to her, might be snapped.

"Let me redirect the conversation," he said. "What do you need?"

What did she need? The list shaped by that question appalled her by its length. After considering his question for a moment, however, her mind automatically performed as it had at Saxon and Henle, setting priorities, putting the most important tasks first. "I need a place to settle for a while. I don't want to go back to the apartment or to Atlanta, and I can't go on driving all over the countryside. I want a place to rest and catch my breath. I'm tired. Worn out." She hesitated, uncertain how far she might trespass on his generosity. "And I need something to do. A job. I'm running out of money."

"Two more steps in the right direction. A place to stay--a haven of sorts. And work--the right kind of work-- might be good for you. It might take you out of your self and give you a different perspective."

"I know I can't go back to the way I was. I can't go back to an office or manage people. Not right away."

"No."

"On the plane you said I'd make a good teacher."

"What do you think of that idea?"

"I don't know. I…" She groped for words, fatigued by the conversation, by the thinking it entailed. She tried to call up a picture of herself in a classroom, and failed miserably. "I don't think I'd be very good at it right now."

"Bad timing, anyway," Father Krumpler said. "School's nearly over for the year. You don't have a teaching license, I suppose?"

"No."

"You don't need one for private schools. Maybe we could find a place for you at Asheville Catholic this fall. But right now we have to find something for the summer."

"I'll take any sort of job. Wash dishes. Bag groceries."

Father Krumpler frowned. "I'm not sure that would be wise. Of course, you could work a register at a grocery store or as a clerk in an office, but I see you needing work that would speed your recovery. Something challenging without being overwhelming, something that involves helping others more directly. You've heard the old adage 'God helps those who help themselves?'"

"Yes."

"Well, he's even better at helping those who help others."

"I'll take any job where I'm needed. If I can stay here in Asheville."

"Why here?"

"Because—" She stopped. He was the reason, of course--not because he was a priest, not because he was a good man, compassionate and honest. Other than Joseph, he was the last person to see her before she was violated, the last witness to what she once was. He was a piece of her past. She tried to speak, but could only shake her head.

He waved a hand toward the door, removing her need to reply. "You go freshen up. Give me a few minutes--I'll make a call."

"All right." He stood when she did, and escorted her to the door. As she walked down the hallway, she heard a voice from one of the rooms she passed, a woman talking on the telephone about the schedule for the choir. Another woman stepped from a doorway, nodded to her, smiled, and headed in the direction of the stairwell.

———

The bathroom was tiny and old fashioned with a tiled floor and black and white tiled walls. She bolted the door, ran the spigot, cupped her hands, splashed water on her face. When she had patted her cheeks dry with a paper towel, she examined the hardened eyes in the mirror, the cropped hair, the roughened cheeks. Her face had the washed-out look of someone ill--or crazy.

When she went back down the hall, the door to Father Krumpler's office was ajar. She could hear him talking and so remained in the hallway away from the door, allowing him his privacy. Soon the door opened, and he gestured her back inside. He nodded toward the window as they sat again. "Beautiful spring. Easter should be lovely."

"I thought Easter would be over by now."

"No, it's later than usual this year. April 24th. More coffee?"

"No, thank you."

"All right. Now, Amanda, I'll get straight to the point. There is a man. A very special man. I was just speaking with him on the phone. He has four children. His wife Anne was murdered a little more than a year ago. Anne and I were friends--close friends." The priest's voice become husky, and he hurried on: "Nathan's had some assistance with the children from parishioners and friends, and one special young woman, but that situation has changed. The woman, Katie, is married and gone away, and friends can only do so much. Nathan needs help with the children so that he can continue to earn a living. Have you ever worked as a nanny?"

"You mean like Mary Poppins?"

Father Krumpler seemed mystified by her question, but then a light bulb went on and he nodded. "Like Mary Poppins."

"No, I haven't."

"Are you good with children?"

Now it was Amanda's turn to look mystified. Women who confessed to a dislike of children or who felt inept in their company were often regarded by others, men and women alike, as deficit in some special female gene. She wasn't sure how she felt about children. "I don't know whether I'm good with them," she said honestly. "I haven't spent much time with them." A chill came over her like a warning. "You talked to this man Nathan. What does he say?"

"He could offer you room, board, and a small salary. You'd be responsible for a good bit of the cooking and housekeeping as well as taking care of the children. He has the money--he's an architect and a builder, and even with the housing collapse he's done well. So money's no object."

"You mean I would live there with him?" It seemed a funny idea coming from a priest.

"It's a large house. You'd be in the bedroom on the first floor where Katie and her baby stayed."

"She had a baby?"

"It's a long story. We'll save it until later. Anyway, Nathan is trustworthy. He's a good man, but he's also been badly hurt. Like you, he's not the person he once was. He's retreated in upon himself. He didn't say so directly just now, but I could tell he was concerned about letting a stranger into his life."

"That worries me too. I haven't lived with anyone since college. I'm not good that way with people. I told you—"

"You're on a different path now." Father Krumpler leaned forward. "Amanda, you and I hardly know each other. You've told me a tiny part of your story, and I can understand only some of what you've suffered. I really don't know much about you, but I do know that you must break out of what you are, what you are becoming. Somehow you must find love. These four children not only need someone to watch over them and love them, but they can give love in return. I know them. As I said, I loved their mother, a saint of a woman, and I saw what she infused in each one of them. You can help them by keeping them safe and healthy through the summer, and there's a good chance they can help you."

She tried to imagine directing the lives of four children--visualizing a situation before tackling it had played a part in her tactics at work--but no images came to her. She saw only a solitary face in a mirror, pale, grim, graven with pain, haunted by ghosts. "When did he want to see me?"

"This evening at seven-thirty. I'll meet you in the lot behind the church and run you to the house. It's in Montford--only a few blocks from here. Better yet, meet me here at six and we'll have supper together."

"You don't need to do that."

He ignored her. "Where did you stay last night?"

"I splurged and got a room at the Sheraton."

"The one near here?"

"Yes."

"And where will you stay tonight?"

She waited a beat too long in her reply.

"We'll get you a motel," he said.

"I have some money left. And some savings."

"I don't mind paying for a room for a night or two. If this works out with Nathan, the cost would be negligible. As I said, Anne was special to me. A wonderful wife and mother. A wonderful friend. In a way, a saint. If I could find someone to watch her children, it would mean the world to me."

"I don't want charity."

"Then we'll call it a loan. Now—"

"I need to be on my own. I need to make it by myself." It was her old mantra, the mantra taught to all females nowadays: a woman should be independent. On the other hand, she had spent six of the last ten nights in her car. The thought of a bed with sheets, of a bath, of a locked door undermined her sense of independence.

"None of us are on our own," Father Krumpler said firmly, "and no one makes it alone. We all have help along the way."

"I didn't."

He was silent, leaving her to listen to her own words and all that they implied.

Chapter Six

Amanda's confession and subsequent conversation with Father Krumpler so exhausted her that by the time she reached Woodfin Street and the Sheraton, she felt as if she hadn't slept in a week. Entering the lobby, she congratulated herself on possessing the foresight to request late-departure checkout. She could sleep for an hour before packing and finding some place to stay while she awaited her supper with the priest and her interview with Nathan Christopher. Dragging herself toward the elevator, she suddenly became aware of the clerk calling--"Ms. Bell! Ms. Bell!"--and waving to her. Hearing her name spoken aloud in a public place, even an empty lobby, was strange, and she approached the desk with trepidation.

The clerk, a college-aged boy with close-clipped hair and large ears, nodded to her. "You are Ms. Amanda Bell?"

She nodded back at him. How strange after so much time to claim that name again.

"I thought so. He said you were wearing a green and yellow dress."

"Who said?"

The clerk glanced at the pad of paper before him. "A Father Krumpler from the Basilica of Saint Lawrence called not five minutes ago, Ms. Bell. He said I was to catch you before you checked out and to tell you that he had reserved your room for you for another two nights."

"Pardon me?"

"He's reserved the room for the next two nights. He said to tell you to relax and enjoy yourself." When she didn't respond, the clerk asked, "I hope the room is satisfactory?"

"Oh, yes. It's fine. Everything is fine. It's just that--"

She shook her head, unable to offer any further protest. Father Krumpler was obviously a man of determination. Dazed both by the priest's generosity and too worn out even to question whether she ought to accept it, whether such a gift might not entail some obligation on her part, Amanda left the desk and the smiling clerk, and took the elevator to her room. Here, after latching the door, dropping her shoulder bag onto a low-cut bureau, setting the bedside alarm for four p.m., and carefully hanging up the sundress, she fell into the bed and slept away the afternoon.

On rising at four, Amanda ran water for a bath while eating the muffin and one of the bananas she'd taken from the breakfast bar that morning. Though she had often preferred showers to baths--they took less time--she knew that for draining away tensions a shower could in no way compare to the luxury of a steaming tub. After half an hour in the tub, a shower and a shampoo left the scent of raspberries in her hair, and the tiny bottle of body lotion provided by the motel perfumed her arms, shoulders, breasts, and legs with a faint aroma of flowers and sunshine.

Dressed, and carrying a pink sweater, she went to the lobby and into the alcove offering computers to guests. No one was on either computer, and she sat in one of the plastic chairs, switched on the screen, and entered the word "governess." One site examined famous literary governesses--Becky Sharpe, Jane Eyre, and others--and Amanda realized that she might know more than she had given herself credit for about the art of governing and teaching children. She had read the books containing these characters, some of them several times, and the stories arose again in her consciousness. Perhaps her literary interests might prove practical, after all. She ran through several sites, then typed "nanny" and read a few minutes more. Twenty minutes allowed her little time to prepare for her interview, but reading even these brief descriptions gave her some confidence that she might not appear a total fool in the eyes of her prospective employer, and even more importantly, in the eyes of Father Krumpler.

He was waiting for her in the church courtyard. Amanda immediately thanked him for the room and promised to repay him, but the priest waved both appreciation and pledge aside, and took her by the elbow. They crossed the street in front of the church, cut through the parking lot, and went to the Grove Arcade, a low building with ornate carvings and two concrete griffins guarding the north entryway. "A monument to the Depression," Father Krumpler said. "The architect originally planned a much taller structure, but ran out of money. So it was left like this."

He led her to a Cajun café, Fireflies, in the arcade. The evening had turned chilly, and they ate inside at a table beside the window. If he had intended supper and some small talk as a way of loosening her up for the interview, Amanda severely disappointed him. Idle conversation was never her forte, and her long winter of silence had further crippled her small talent for chitchat. She replied in monosyllables to his comments about the weather, the restaurant décor, the offerings on the menu.

"Shall we pray?" he asked when their waitress brought the food.

Amanda bowed her head while he asked the Lord to bless their food, though she was confused as usual by such offerings of thanksgiving and gratitude. Why thank some unseen being for what was clearly the work of human hands?

Father Krumpler had ordered a house salad with a vinaigrette dressing, a cup of gumbo soup, and a glass of beer. Amanda had selected a po' boy sandwich with shrimp and iced tea. "That's the ticket," Father Krumpler said on the arrival of her thick sandwich. "Put some meat on those bones."

Eating was a relief not only because she was hungry, but also because it required less talk. As they were finishing up, he asked what she liked to do for fun, for relaxation.

"Now, you mean?" she asked him. "Or before?"

"Either. Now, I suppose."

"Pull-offs. Especially in the mountains."

"Pull-offs?"

"You know. Those places alongside highways where you pull off the road and take in the sights."

"Ah."

"There's one just north of here. Off Interstate-26 going toward Virginia. Gorgeous views. I like to sit and look at the mountains."

"I see."

Having decided that she sounded like a simpleton, Amanda finished the rest of her supper in silence. Around them rose the noise of the restaurant: the conversations of the other diners, the clatter of plates and silverware.

"You don't talk much, do you?"

"I'm afraid I'm not used to talking anymore."

"You'll be in good company. Anne's death shook Nathan to the core. He's withdrawn, from what I can tell, though he tries hard with the children."

"You said she was murdered?"

"There was an intruder, a small-time burglar and street person named Curtis Mauney. Apparently he thought no one was home. Katie--that's the girl who lived with the Christophers, they helped her with her newborn--was there with Anne and told the police that Mauney seemed to fire his gun by accident."

"What happened to him?"

"He ran. The police caught up with him on the bridge over the bypass beside the church. He panicked, jumped from the bridge, and was killed by a truck. One of the policeman later speculated that he'd watched too many action movies."

"And the children? What about them? Did they see their mother get shot?"

"They were away, thanks be to God. Tessa--that's Anne's mother, she was living with them then--had taken them to the library."

"Does Tessa still live here in town?"

"She lived with Nathan for a while. Last summer her sister in Colorado became ill. Tessa has lived with her since then."

"And Katie--where's she now?"

"She's married and living in D.C. Her husband's a writer. A biographer and historian. A man named Scully. He was there the night Katie had her baby in the church."

"She had the baby in church?"

"Christmas Eve. Midnight Mass. Her water broke right after the Mass ended, and the little boy popped out before the medics could get there."

"So the baby wasn't his?"

"No. Katie had gotten pregnant her last year in high school in Virginia. She ran away from home and came here. Scully was close to thirty--a good bit older. Anyway, the pair of them fell in love and ended up marrying." He smiled at her. "You remind me a little of Katie. Like you, she was a runaway. And like you she was lost when she came to Asheville. Staying with the Christophers helped her find her way."

"Meaning it may help me find mine?"

"Not necessarily. You won't have Anne to help you. She was an incredibly strong woman emotionally and spiritually. A convert with all the convert's zeal for the faith. She had a way about her that made people love her."

The strong emotion in his voice touched Amanda. "I can tell you miss her."

"More than I would have thought possible. At the hospital the doctors found she was two months pregnant. She hadn't told Nathan the news yet. Probably she didn't want to worry him. They were having financial struggles. The building trades crashed here, the same as most other places, and for about a year Nathan barely managed to make ends meet. Business is better for him now, some design work coming to him, running a regular crew again, new construction, painting, repair work. Whatever he can find."

"I don't want to be a burden."

"What do you mean?"

"I don't want him to pay me if he can't afford it. I don't want any more charity."

"I wouldn't worry about that. Nathan does all right, as you'll soon see. The idea here is that you can help the Christopher family out while you get yourself up and running again."

Amanda fell silent again. Could she really help anyone right now? And even if she could, how could helping someone else bring her any sort of inner peace or security? Wouldn't involvement in the lives of five other people stack even more mess and trouble on her disordered life? Suddenly her confidence, already thin, dissipated, and she dreaded the coming interview. This was a mistake. She tried to picture herself living with a real family, directing the children, helping them dress, preparing meals, but drew a complete blank. Who was the priest kidding? She could hardly take care of herself, much less four children and their grieving father. To stand proxy for mother and wife was ludicrous; she lacked the experience, the temperament, the desire; she had not a solitary ounce of familial instinct. She--

"We should go," he said. "Are you nervous?"

"Yes."

"Everything will be all right."

"And how do you know that?"

"It generally is, isn't it, in the end? More than we suspect."

She started to disagree with him, but Father Krumpler was already on his feet, shrugging on his coat and looking toward the door.

———

After they had crossed the bridge separating Montford from Asheville's Downtown--this was the Flint Street bridge, Father Krumpler said, from which Curtis Mauney had jumped after shooting Anne--the priest explained that Montford was an old historic neighborhood which in the 1960s had fallen onto hard times, but was now fast becoming a desirable place to raise a family. They passed large homes, some of them clearly divided into apartments, set down on green lawns and budding trees. Nearly every block contained at least one house under renovation, and the spacious yards did indeed give evidence of children: wagons, bicycles, swing-sets in the back.

The Christophers lived on Cumberland Avenue in an old, white-trimmed, brick house. A pickup truck with tools sticking from the bed stood in the street in front of the house, and a white picket fence enclosed a broad green lawn. Along the walkway leading to the house were azalea bushes in full bloom. "Anne's work," Father Krumpler said, parking behind the pickup and pointing to the bushes. "She loved to garden. Katie tried to keep the yard up after she died. How about you? Do you like gardening?"

"I don't know. I've never gardened."

On the lawn by the small porch, neatly aligned, were two bikes, a tricycle, and a wagon. Father Krumpler pushed the doorbell, and a moment later the door opened and a little girl whose eyes were on a level with the doorknob looked up at them and said, "Daddy's nearly done with the dishes, Father. He said to come inside."

"Ah, Teresa, you look lovely tonight. And what a beautiful outfit."

"I just took my bath. Now I'm a ballerina." She was wearing a black leotard, a pink tutu, and white tennis shoes with pink trim. Someone had tried to shape her hair into a French braid, but the braid wasn't quite working, and strands of hair fell across her neck and about her face. Teresa closed the door and turned to look at Amanda. "I want to take lessons next year, if Daddy will let me."

"I'm sure you'll make a fine dancer."

"Thank you."

"Teresa, this is Miss Bell."

"Hello."

"Hello," Amanda replied.

"Daddy said you should wait here in the living room."

"All right."

Amanda's fingers itched to restore Teresa's hair, but she restrained that impulse and followed Teresa into a large open room. "Tim's giving Mikey his bath, and Bridget's helping Daddy with the dishes. Daddy said to have a seat and he'll be right out."

"Maybe I can give him a hand," Father Krumpler said. He peeled away from them and disappeared in the hallway.

Amanda at once became acutely conscious of the child standing in front of her and found herself tongue-tied and awkward.

"This is our living room," Teresa said, turning from her and sweeping her hand around the room.

In the far corner, set off from the rest of the room by a sofa and three chairs, was a television set, a compact disc player, and a built-in hutch holding a collection of discs and electronic equipment. Along the walls were hutches and casements of various heights holding books, wicker baskets, candles, statuettes, photographs, a globe. Between the windows of the long outside wall was a gas fireplace, glowing with a low blue flame to knock the April chill from the air. Before the fireplace was another sitting area consisting of more chairs and a comfortable-looking green sofa. A pile of children's books, topped by a math book with a pencil tucked inside, lay on the coffee table in front of this sofa. Ferns and several plants which Amanda couldn't identify stood on a glass-topped table before the large window on the other side of the fireplace. Attracted by the fire, Amanda drifted in that direction, followed by Teresa. The girl stopped before the ornately carved fireplace mantle, above which hung a crucifix, and pointed to a picture of the family.

"That's us," Teresa said, following her gaze, "before Mommy died. You can see how little I was there."

"You were little. I see you liked ballet even then."

In the photograph, taken before this same fireplace, Teresa was wearing a pink tutu and matching ballet slippers, and was holding hands with an older boy, but it was Anne whom Amanda secretly studied. Seated in a straight chair, holding a baby in her lap and surrounded by three other children, she appeared younger than Amanda had imagined her. Her hair, roughly the color of Amanda's, hung in a braid across one shoulder. From the smile and the wide eyes came a sense of serenity, the feeling that here was a woman at home with herself, her family, her life. Standing behind her was a man whom Amanda took to be Nathan. He was darker in aspect--black hair and heavy eyebrows, dark eyes-- yet he too was smiling, impishly, more comfortable in front of a camera than his wife. He looked as if he was ready to burst into laughter at some joke told by the photographer or by one of the children.

"That's Daddy and Tim and Bridget and Michael, but we call him Mikey. He was a baby then, but he's three now."

Just then a hand-held bell clanged from somewhere in the house. From the second floor came a shout, "Coming!" followed by the sound of feet thumping down the stairs. In the next moment a black-haired boy in blue jeans and a yellow t-shirt, the lower part dark with water, jumped down the last two steps. He was carrying on his back a little boy dressed in pajamas. The pair of them skidded to a stop in front of Amanda.

"I'm Tim," he said, panting and readjusting the toddler on his back, who regarded Amanda with that blank stare three year olds accord adults to whom they are totally oblivious. "Isn't Dad here?"

"I am," said a voice behind them, and the four of them turned to face Nathan Christopher. To his right and left stood Father Krumpler and Bridget, a larger image of her sister wearing white pajamas and pink slippers, her hair gathered in the same loose braid.

"Miss Bell," Nathan Christopher said.

Amanda's throat constricted, dry as sand. She nodded. "Mr. Christopher."

He said: "Everyone take a seat."

He had apparently assigned the children their seats, for they scrambled around the room hunting specific chairs. He himself took the Lazy-Boy chair in the middle of the room, the chair just in front of the television, while Father Krumpler and Amanda sat side by side on the sofa. The soft cushions of the sofa sank under Amanda's weight, leaving her looking up at Nathan Christopher, who swung his chair round to face her.

"Miss Bell?" he said, his eyes on her like twin accusations. "Or do you prefer Ms.?"

Which did she prefer? Once she was called Ms., but she wasn't sure whether she had preferred it. But that title belonged to the past, to the office. A governess required the more traditional form of address. "Miss is fine."

"These are the children, Miss Bell. You've met Teresa. This is Tim. He's ten and has just finished fifth grade. This is Bridget, aged seven--"

"I'm almost eight," Bridget said.

"--almost eight," Nathan said. "And Teresa's six and will be in second grade, and Mikey's three as of last month."

The eyes of all the children rested on Amanda. Even Mikey, who was wriggling in his brother's arms, stopped his twisting to stare at her. It was time to speak, or to retreat defeated, and Amanda could almost feel Father Krumpler's prayers for her as she croaked, "Pleased to meet all of you."

"Would you care for anything to drink? Tea? Water? A cup of coffee?"

"No. Thank you, no."

"Father? A glass of wine?"

"A glass of wine would be nice. Red, if you have it."

"Tim," Mr. Christopher commanded, and the boy deposited his brother on the chair and left the room. Amanda immediately regretted her refusal, for a glass of water might have washed the cotton from her throat.

Mr. Christopher sank lower in his chair and appeared to glower at her, though his dark features may have helped create that effect. "Father Krumpler says you've been traveling these last few months."

"Yes."

"And that you've worked as an office manager."

"Yes. In Atlanta."

"I never cared much for Atlanta. Too much traffic. Too many people."

"It's a big city."

Dull. Inane. Why couldn't she think?

"Were you from there?"

"No, I grew up in Virginia."

"Why'd you move there?"

"For the work. And I wanted a big city."

"And now you've come here."

"Yes."

"Have you ever worked with children?"

"A long time ago." Thomas Leahy came to mind, the bratty son of a neighbor, an adjunct professor at the university who lived down the street. The last time Amanda had babysat him—he was eleven and already a hulking lout of a boy, so babysat was hardly the appropriate word—Thomas had flushed his goldfish down the toilet, and had then locked himself in his parents' bedroom, watching MTV at full blast on their television. By the time Amanda had found a nail and popped the lock, he'd scattered his mother's underwear across the bed and scented himself with her perfume. Last reports had placed Thomas in an art school in Savannah.

Another silence. Everyone clearly expected her to speak, but her mind, like her throat, was closed. Tim returned with Father Krumpler's wine. "Thank you, Tim," Father said. And then more silence: Amanda could hear the ticking of a clock down the hall and the swishing of automobile tires from the street.

Teresa was swinging her legs back and forth in her chair, looking at her ballet slippers. "You'd have your own room. It's just down the hall. It's where Katie and the baby lived."

"Can you cook?" Bridget asked. "I can make soup and pizzas, but I can't really cook."

"I—"

"Katie took us uptown a lot. She liked walks," Teresa said. "Do you like walks? And sometimes she danced with me. Do you ever dance?"

"Katie," Mikey repeated, smiling with pleasure at the name.

"She was teaching me to read," Teresa said. "Can you do that?"

"She read us lots of stories," Bridget said. "And sometimes Scully told us stories."

"About history," said Tim, livening up. "He knew lots about history. He wrote books. He majored in history in college. I think I might like majoring in history, too."

"Scully was Katie's boyfriend. Now they're married," Bridget said.

"Did you go to college?" Teresa asked.

"I want to study plants in college," Bridget said.

"College," Michael repeated.

"Do you like any sports? I play soccer," Tim said.

"I like soccer too," Bridget said, "but Teresa doesn't. She doesn't like the ball."

"I don't like chasing the ball, you mean," Teresa said. "It's silly. I like dancing. Do you like dancing, Miss Bell?"

She tried again to form a reply. "I—"

Father Krumpler laughed, that warm, low laugh which invited all who heard it to join him in his amusement. "All right, all right," he said. "You've terrified Miss Bell, and you've put your father to shame as an interviewer. Tim, why don't you troop everyone upstairs for a bit?"

Carrying Michael, Tim led Teresa and Bridget up the stairs. Teresa paused to smile and wave at Amanda. She tried smiling back at the little girl, but felt as if her face was breaking.

Father Krumpler sat back in his chair, still chuckling. "Can you answer all those questions, my dear?"

"I'm an adequate cook," Amanda said. "I like reading. I graduated from the University of Virginia. I like walks. I haven't danced in a long, long time. I can kick a soccer ball."

That burst of words left her ragged-out. Perspiring from nerves and the heat of the fireplace, she unbuttoned her sweater, slipped it off her shoulders and arms, and bundled it in her lap. Mr. Christopher stared at her, and she was immediately aware of how she must look: the bare shoulders, the ill-fitting and slightly low-cut bodice. What was she thinking, wearing a sundress to an interview? Leaning forward in his chair, he thrust out his chin at her as if in challenge. "Do you practice any religious faith?"

The intensity in his voice told Amanda that truth in her answer was important to him. "No," she said. "Not regularly."

"Tell me what's important to you."

"Now?" she asked.

"Yes. What's important to you now."

"I'm not quite sure. I once thought I knew, but I've gone off track. If I could just—" But there her voice got stuck again. To utter one syllable more would bring tears.

But Mr. Christopher was satisfied. "Father told you what I need? What you'll be doing? What I can offer you by way of room, board, and salary?"

"A little."

"You'll be responsible for the care of my children on the weekdays from the time I leave home until I return. You'll also need to teach them lessons. You can work into that part slowly. You can cook, you say?"

"Yes."

"It would be a service to me if you could prepare suppers. The children will be glad to help you." He looked at Father Krumpler, then back at her. "I can't give you much--room and board and two hundred a week. You'll have evenings and Sundays off. Saturdays, too, unless I have to work, in which case we'll negotiate extra pay. As Teresa said, your room would be down the hall; the children and I sleep upstairs. In spite of what happened here"--and here his voice lost its harsh edge and became flat, neutral--"you're perfectly safe in this house. Finally--you aren't married, are you?" and when she shook her head, he continued: "Finally, I think it's best if you call me Mr. Christopher and I'll call you Miss Bell."

His request for formality lifted Amanda's spirits. They didn't rise much--on a scale of one to ten, they may have hit a two--but they rose nonetheless. In a decade characterized by informality, slovenly dress, vulgar manners, and meretricious language, such a consideration offered so forthrightly watered Amanda's budding respect for him.

"My children need stability, Miss Bell. They need someone in their lives who will teach them things, who will take them out for swimming or walks, who can bandage up their cuts and bruises. Most of all, they need someone paying attention to them. Someone who respects them. They have their flaws—Teresa whines when she's tired, for example, and Tim sometimes gives me fits with his tree-climbing—but they're good kids and not at all terrors or difficult. I want someone who will help them develop in a positive way. Someone who will serve as an example to them."

Offering Mr. Christopher reassurances might have buttressed her hope for employment, but Amanda could only nod again.

"Are you that person?" he asked, looking for more of an answer.

"I'll try to be."

"Did Father explain that my children are educated at home?"

"No."

"I forgot," Father Krumpler said.

Nathan gave him a dark look. "More likely you didn't want to scare her off."

"I was a good student," Amanda said. "I think I can do what you need in terms of teaching."

"Some other things we'll have to work out as we go along. I'd rather you didn't talk on the phone with friends while you're working."

"That won't be a problem."

"You'll have use of the van. Within reason."

"I have a car."

"I demand punctuality. This household runs on a schedule."

"Schedules are important."

"One more thing," he said. "Do you have any objections if I run a background check on you?"

"None at all."

"Your turn now. Any questions?"

"Do you know how long you'll need someone?"

"Not exactly. Depends on how it works out. How you and I get along together, if I hire you."

"Of course." She glanced at the math book on the table. "I want you to know I've never taught school."

"You don't need a teaching certificate. You do need enthusiasm and patience. I'll be glad to show you how the schooling works and get you started. It's really pretty basic. Do you know CPR? The Heimlich Maneuver? Basic first aid?"

"I had the Red Cross come to our firm and train the office staff every two years."

Mr. Christopher scrutinized her as if running some sort of inventory check. His eyes paused briefly again on her bare shoulders, and he seemed about to say something further, but then shrugged and turned instead to Father Krumpler.

"I suppose you want a thank you," he said.

"You might serve up a better brand of wine," Father Krumpler said, dead-pan.

"You'd only drink more of it."

"Whiskey would be even better."

"Krumpler's German, but his mother was Irish," Mr. Christopher said, abruptly shifting his attention to her again.

"As was his own mother," Father Krumpler said, also to Amanda. "Can you imagine it? A decent Irish lass marrying an Englishman. It's little wonder you're the mess you are."

"Me?" said Mr. Christopher. "I'm the product of two noble races of men. You're a mixed-up confused mess with that German and Irish. The Kraut's always plotting and planning while the Irish blood keeps screaming the charge."

The two men were communicating in some sort of code. Then both of them smiled at her.

"Can you start Thursday morning? Day after tomorrow?" Mr. Christopher asked. "Get here around eight-thirty and the children and I can help you move your things to your room."

"Yes, sir. There's not much."

Mr. Christopher pulled the hand-bell from the floor by his chair and rang it. Footsteps patted across the floor overhead. The children appeared on the stairwell, Timmy and Teresa first, then Bridget with Mikey holding her hand.

"Miss Bell will be staying with us for a while. She'll be your governess."

"What's a governess?" asked Teresa.

"Don't you mean nanny, Daddy?" asked Bridget.

"I don't know," Mr. Christopher said, and turned to Amanda. "What's the difference, Miss Bell?"

"A governess is charged with the education, care, and supervision of children in a private household," Amanda replied crisply, thankful that she had taken the trouble to look up the two definitions online. "A nanny is more of a nursemaid."

"You're a governess," said Tim, with a look of relief on his face.

"But Mary Poppins was a nanny," Teresa said. "Can't you be like Mary Poppins?"

"I don't know—"

"She could fly. Mary Poppins could fly, and Father Krumpler said you were flying when he met you."

Tim, Bridget, and Father Krumpler laughed.

"A governess is like a nanny," Amanda said.

"Should we call you Nanny Bell?" Bridget asked.

"You'll call her Miss Bell," Mr. Christopher said. "Now let's show Miss Bell her room and the rest of the first floor."

"What about showing her our rooms?"

"You can show her those on Thursday."

——

With the children trailing them, except for Teresa, who pirouet-ted ahead, Mr. Christopher took Amanda to a brightly-lit kitchen, long and narrow, which adjoined the dining room. One side of the kitchen was windows, below which was a long counter with cabinets. On the other side were glass cabinets containing cups and dishes, a sink and dishwasher, a stove, another counter. It was a clean and tidy place, with some pots and pans washed and drying on the drain board. The children pulled open cabinets and drawers, showing Amanda where they kept everything from canned goods to cutlery. They walked through the dining room without turning on the lights, and in the shadows she could see that someone, presumably Tim or Bridget, had already set the table for breakfast. The door at the end of the dining room opened onto a small hall that hooked back toward the living room, but they crossed the hall rather than following the hook and went into a bedroom.

"This will be yours," Bridget said.

In the room were two windows overlooking the side yard. There was a double bed with a brightly-colored quilt, a large wooden bureau flanked by a small empty bookshelf, a small desk, and a cushioned chair made for reading and relaxing. On a stand beside the enormous claw-foot tub in the adjoining bathroom someone had arranged a bowlful of dried petals, giving the room the scent of rosebushes in moonlight. "Where does that door lead?" Amanda asked.

"It goes to the parlor," Tim said. He opened the door, revealing a square room with bookcases, tables, lamps, and chairs. Through the parlor windows she could see the street and Father Krumpler's car.

"You're welcome to use the parlor for reading," Mr. Christopher said.

"And the living room," Teresa added.

"It's lovely." She turned back to the bedroom, trying to imagine herself sleeping in the bed, sitting in the bulky cushioned chair beside the window of the side porch, soaking in the tub.

"We took the books off the shelves in the bedroom this afternoon," Bridget said. "Father told us you liked to read, and we wanted you to have room for your own books."

"Thank you."

Then they were in the living room again, and Father Krumpler was on his feet, hugging the children and shaking hands with Mr. Christopher.

"Say goodnight to Miss Bell," Mr. Christopher told the children.

They chorused a good-night to Amanda, then trooped up the stairs. "I'll be right up," Mr. Christopher called after them. "Brush your teeth."

———

Outside the evening was pleasantly cool, scented with mown grass and Anne's azaleas. After bidding Mr. Christopher good-bye and thanking him for the position, Amanda walked to the car. Father Krumpler hung back, talking earnestly with Mr. Christopher on the porch, gripping his shoulder. Beside the taller priest, Mr. Christopher resembled a boy being either reassured or reprimanded. To Amanda's quiet amusement, Teresa knocked on the glass of a window above the porch and waved to her. She returned the wave with a nod of her head.

"You let a piece of your old self out tonight," Father Krumpler commented as he pulled the car away from the curb. "That part about the governess—that's the tone of voice I remember hearing on the plane."

"I'm not sure that's a good thing."

"You can't completely erase your past. None of us can--not entirely."

"I don't much like my old self any more. And even if I did, I'm not sure I could reconstruct myself the way I was." Despite her nap, Amanda was edgy and exhausted. The long day had focused a hot bright lens on her past, and sleep offered her the only escape. "What were you saying to Mr. Christopher on the porch?"

"Like you, tonight is a sort of turning point for him. It's a big step for him, entrusting his children to a stranger. He and Anne knew Katie before Anne was killed--she was living with them--and the sitters he's hired since Katie left in November have all come from families he's known for years. He's not totally enthused about having a stranger underfoot, but he knows he can't keep up the juggling act." They were approaching the Flint Street Bridge below the church. Father Krumpler said: "I'm counting on you, my dear. He needs your help."

Amanda had rarely considered the trials and travails of the lives of others. For years, her world had revolved around her own ambitions, her own desires. Only through her books and movies had she considered the difficulties of another's life. She thought of Mr. Christopher and how lonely he had looked standing on the porch, and a twinge of pity for him rose in her. But then thoughts of her own past intruded, and the brief surge of her commiseration receded.

"We all have a cross to bear. Isn't that what your church says?"

"I do say that. The Church says that." He gave her a glance. "But we usually say it with a bit more pity."

Even before he spoke, Amanda realized how supercilious and snotty she sounded. There was a time, not so long ago, when she would have masked such a remark with silence, but the strange day had finally caught up with her, exposing the raw nerve of pain throbbing inside her.

"He seems like a tough boss."

"He wants the best for his children."

They drove the last few blocks to the Sheraton in silence. When he pulled the car up to the doors of the motel, Father Krumpler turned in his seat toward her.

"Look here," he said. "You don't see it right now. But you and Nathan are two of a kind. You're both lost at this point in your lives. You're both looking for meaning. You've both been dreadfully wounded. You're like two soldiers in a convalescent ward, shattered by your wounds and not knowing what to do or how to go on. You could go on alone, but you could also be a tremendous help to each other."

"I'm not sure I can help anyone right now." She reconsidered her remark. "His children, maybe."

"You have tomorrow off. Do some shopping. Take some time to relax, to enjoy yourself if you can. As your counselor, I would also suggest you spend an hour sitting in the church. The Basilica is usually quiet in the late afternoons, and the Blessed Sacrament chapel is a good place for thought and meditation. If you'd like, come and see me around four. I'm normally in my office until five. Just ring the bell, and ask Mrs. Barnes to let you in. Tell her I'm expecting you."

"All right."

Amanda pushed open the car door. "So I'll see you tomorrow?" he asked, leaning toward her from the driver's seat.

"Yes. Around four."

"Sleep well."

"Thank you, Father," Amanda said, and closed the door. Only when she was on the elevator did she calculate the debt she owed him and how little appreciation she had shown.

Twice that night she woke from dreams to lie staring at the ceiling. She couldn't remember the first dream, but in the second she was in the office building of Saxon and Henle. It was nighttime: she had stayed late for work and was searching for some document--a contract, a letter--moving from room to room down the dim corridor when she sensed a man behind her. She began running down the hallway, stumbling, falling, picking herself up again, until at last she sprinted, breathless, into the safety of her own office, where she locked the door. Someone was outside her door, scratching at the wood and glass, and then the lock was turning. Sobbing to catch her breath, she hid beneath the desk even as she heard Joseph Grenier laughing and saw Mr. Henle leering at her from the shadows. Then hands were grabbing her, dragging her from the desk, from safety, pulling her back into the past.

In the morning she slept until nearly nine, showered, and ate oatmeal, an orange, and toast at the breakfast bar. For once, an entire day lay before her like a gift rather than a trial. She needn't think of where to spend the coming night or where to drive next. She had time to ready herself for her ordeal on Thursday, to prepare in some way to govern the lives of four children. While finishing breakfast, she decided to make her preparations in the public library.

First, however, she needed to do some more shopping. She returned to the Goodwill Store on Tunnel Road, keeping in mind the gimlet eye Mr. Christopher had cast on her sundress. Thirty minutes of picking through the racks produced two blouses, a dark knee-length peasant skirt, and a summer dress, brighter and gaudier than her usual tastes, but whose flowery pattern might attract the children, particularly Teresa, while hiding the stains and spills that would surely be a part of the job.

By noon she had returned to the motel, deposited the two bags of clothing in her room, and was walking on Haywood Road to Pack Library, which was less than a block from the Basilica.

What churches were for some, what bars were for others, public libraries were for Amanda. When she was just a week old, her father had carried her in a geri-pack to the library off Court Square in Charlottesville, where he introduced her to the librarians, held books to her tiny fingers, and allowed her, as he later said, "to breathe in the fragrance of great thoughts." From that time on, he escorted her to the library at least once a week until she was in her teens, helping her select books, showing her the ones he remembered from his boyhood or those which had received enticing reviews. In addition to her father's bookshop, libraries became for her a sort of magic kingdom, a place where books could whisk her off into another time or land, where her circumstances, however irregular or confusing, could be shunted aside while she absorbed another's personality and problems.

Pack Library offered all that she required. It was quiet, the librarians were helpful, and though she wasn't allowed on the computers without a library card, the shelves of books contained a plentitude of advice about child care and development. She read intently for nearly two hours, jotting down observations in a Jumbo Note-Book she had purchased for a quarter at Goodwill, rising only for a drink of water from the fountain or for additional books.

When she had finished her reading, she raised her head from the books and took note of the people around her. Most of them, like Americans everywhere, were casual and slipshod in their dress: shirt-tails hanging out, t-shirts with various logos, sweat-suits as if they planned doing some push-ups while reading. One girl wore army boots with a blue skirt and a purple sweater, and an older man entered wearing a t-shirt so small that the bottom of his hairy belly protruded over his pants. The librarians were dressed more professionally, yet none of the men sported a tie, and two of the women wore jeans.

At one point a man walked into the library. He looked about Amanda's age, perhaps three or four years older, yet of all the people in the room he alone was dressed like an adult. He wore a dark gray suit, white shirt, a dark tie, and black wing-tip shoes, shoes identical to those worn by one of her college professors, shoes that looked as if the wearer meant business. This man's hair was conservatively cut; he stood erect; he looked directly into the eyes of the librarian, who treated him with a deference she hadn't shown to other patrons, laughing with him and listening intently to whatever he was saying.

Amanda began writing:

Guidelines For A Governess

1. *Appearance is important. It separates the grownup from children of all ages. A governess therefore must dress like an adult, dress the way adults dressed forty years ago. The clothing of a governess indicates that she is a person of intent who clearly intends business. Vestes virum facit: clothes make the man--and the governess as well. We define ourselves and our purpose by our clothing. Dress as if dress mattered.*

Her next two points appeared just as swiftly on the paper:

2. *Carry yourself as if you mattered. Good posture gives off a sense that all is well and under control. Do not slouch. Avoid waving the hands too much. Children, like many adults, respond favorably to people who carry themselves with dignity and authority.*

3. *Modulate the voice. Speak slowly and deliberately. Don't drag your words, but don't rush them either. Practice slow, correct breathing. When speaking to the young people in your charge, do as Winston Churchill once did: speak as if your words were on sheets of paper, with only three or four words per line. "The jaws of another Russian winter///are closing on Hitler's armies." Speak distinctly. Distinct speech will sound eccentric to others, but it will also inspire obedience.*

4. *Look the children directly in the eye.*

5. *Expect obedience. Take charge immediately. Remember that all initial acts and commands set precedents.*

6.*Note to myself: practice giving compliments and small rewards when deserved.*

Around three o'clock, Amanda left the library and walked down Haywood Street to the Basilica. In the small chapel to the right of the altar a man knelt in silence before what appeared to be a silver starburst. After settling into a pew near the front of the church, Amanda stared straight ahead. She didn't know what it was to pray or how to do it in a church, but she had long practiced the disciplines of stillness and silence, and so had no difficulty with this exercise. She used the first minutes imagining herself tomorrow with the four children, trying to visualize her duties, anticipate their needs, and face the demands of dealing with others than herself. Eventually her mind wandered, as it so often did, to the turn her life had taken. She forced herself not to think of her last day at work or the men in her apartment, but to reflect instead on her old life. Was she happy then? Had she been meant to be a manager? And what did it mean, "to have been meant to be" anything? After college she had set her goals without establishing her motives, had focused on means rather than ends, or at any rate, final ends, and so had failed in her endeavors. She applied this analysis to her present situation with the Christopher family, and saw that not only was her motive clear--she must have a job, and according to Father Krumpler, the job should have the purpose of serving others--but her goal was clear as well: to offer service to the Christopher children and their father, to make their lives better and more secure. It was a relief, in a way, to consider herself and her own ends as only a secondary part of this equation.

Nearly the full hour had passed when she rose and crossed the courtyard to the rectory, where she rang the bell. Mrs. Barnes, a heavy-set woman with glasses and curly hair, admitted her and escorted her to Father Krumpler's office.

"Amanda, it's a pleasure," he said, tucking away some paperwork, then half-rising and beckoning her to a chair. "Or is it Miss Bell now?"

She sat. "Only to Mr. Christopher."

"Is that Miss or Ms.?"

"It's still Miss, of course," she replied, then got down to the first point of business. "I want to apologize for last night. I felt overwhelmed and tired, but that's still no excuse for my remarks."

"No bother."

He waited for her to say something more, but her gratitude remained stuck inside her. She couldn't work the necessary words. Not yet.

"You've had a good day? Shopping? Relaxing a bit?"

"Yes."

"And the church?"

"I sat for an hour."

"And what did you do?"

"I thought about things."

"What sort of things?"

"Mostly about tomorrow and what I need to do."

"Did you pray?"

"I don't know. Mostly I talked to myself."

"That's no matter. I was just curious. Anything else?"

"I was surprised Mr. Christopher would hire me without knowing more."

"He knows me and I recommended you."

"But you don't know me that well either."

"True. I don't have a resume or recommendations. But I know what you told me on the plane and what you told me in the confessional. I know you better than you might think." He paused, held up one finger to her, and sneezed. He sneezed again, took a Kleenex from the box, and dabbed at his nose. "Allergies. Every spring and fall."

One other question had eaten at Amanda most of the day. She had kept it under wraps, wanting to focus her thoughts and energy on the task before her, but now felt free to raise her concern with Father Krumpler. "I did wonder how much Mr. Christopher knew about me. About my past."

"He knows that you are a young woman who lost her job and who has spent the last few months traveling."

"Does he know why I lost my job?"

"He knows you were a manager whose employer didn't agree with her style of management."

"Does he know--"

"I told him you had suffered another sort of trauma in your life as well."

"And he didn't ask any questions?"

"Most people would, wouldn't they? They'd want all the gory details. But you have to remember that Nathan's suffered his own share of trauma. He's still self-focused rather than looking outward."

"It's been more than a year, hasn't it?"

"It has. But he loved Anne. And keep in mind he's had little time for real grief. He keeps up a front with the children, he works long hours, and until recently he's been beset by money woes. Having you in the house may help him come to terms with his grief. Certainly it will give him a measure of relief in his care for the children."

"So he doesn't know?" She was repeating herself, but sought reassurance.

"As I say, he only knows you suffered some sort of terrible wound."

"Is it really wise to have two wounded people trying to heal each other? Wouldn't it be better if they saw a doctor?"

"Not necessarily. People who have suffered, people who are broken, are often much more understanding of others than those who haven't. And Nathan Christopher, as you'll soon discover, is not the type to go to a physician of any kind. Like someone else I know."

"Meaning me, I suppose?"

"Yes. You said you didn't want counseling."

"I said I wanted you."

"Why, you have me," Father Krumpler said, somewhat surprised.

The relief that rose in her took her by surprise. He was not going to abandon her, leave her to cope on her own with a stranger and his children, or worse, leave her to stand alone and hopeless above the abyss.

"You'll help me then?"

"Whenever you need it. You call, and I'll be there. Still, I think it would be best if we scheduled some time for you. How about Tuesday evenings? We could talk over supper if you like or we could meet somewhere afterwards."

"I can't have you paying for my meals all the time."

"How about if I buy the food and you do the cooking and the washing up?"

"What do you mean?"

"You can come to my apartment and cook supper. I live in the priest's apartment upstairs. We'll eat and then we'll talk."

"Isn't that--" She couldn't find the appropriate word.

"Scandalous?"

She nodded. She had taught many seminars to employees on sexual conduct and the workplace.

"I won't tell if you won't," Father Krumpler said. When she didn't laugh, he smiled ruefully. "I'm seventy-one years old. I'm both celibate and chaste. The people who know me, the people of this parish, may consider me eccentric but not dangerous. Besides, committing to you helps me avoid all sorts of more tiresome obligations--meetings in which I typically doze off, invitations from the old ladies of the parish to dine with them. You'll be doing me a sort of favor. We'll get to know each other, and you can talk about whatever you like. You did say you could cook?"

"Yes. Actually, I'm better than I let on to Mr. Christopher. I'm an excellent cook."

"And there you have it. Not only do I get the pleasure of your company, but I also get a gourmet meal. And what could be better than that?"

Chapter Seven

Thursday morning, D-Day, Amanda woke shortly before five. Except for her toiletries, she had packed her bags Wednesday evening after laying out an outfit both functional and dignified—the navy blue skirt, a short-sleeved white blouse, some Docker shoes from her old life. She had decided against hose--the April day promised to be unseasonably warm, and working with children seemed to preclude hose anyway.

The difficult stage of her preparations--hair and makeup--came after her shower. Little could be done with her hair, which was still cut too short to pull back and hung limply about her jaws and neck. Finally she combed it straight back and kept it in place with the copper-colored headband she'd bought at Goodwill.

This morning the face in the mirror had lost some of its tension. Her lips appeared fuller, less drawn and thin, and her cheeks after the massage of the hot shower had lost some of their rigidity. The reflection still seemed that of a stranger, but with more attractive features. The mask hiding fear and darkness had gentled. Amanda had read somewhere that people wear the faces they deserve: if that was true, then surely, she thought, she deserved a lower, meaner visage than the one in the mirror.

After a moment of consideration, she added a trace of color to her lips and a hint of blush in her cheeks, and plucked a few stray hairs from her eyebrows. She then rubbed some of the hotel body lotion with its scent of flowers on her neck, arms, and hands.

The hotel served up its continental breakfast at six, and Amanda was among the first to arrive in the dining room, where she fortified herself with a bowl of oatmeal, an orange, an English muffin, and coffee. By six forty-five she had returned to her room, where she brushed her teeth, packed her bag, and then sat before the big window, watching as the lights of the city vanished under the coming dawn.

———

She rang the bell beside the front door. From inside the house, ablaze with light, she heard someone running down the hall, and then the lock of the door clicked open, and Teresa was there, tousle-headed, still in her pajamas. Mr. Christopher walked down the hall behind her. Dressed in black trousers, a white shirt, and red tie, and holding a large blue mug of coffee, he wore on his face the sleepy expectation of a man preparing for work. He nodded to Amanda.

"Good morning, Miss Bell."

"Good morning, sir."

That "sir," a remnant from her office days, gave him pause. Then he said: "You're early."

"I hope that's all right?"

"It's fine. Should we get your things?"

"The children can help me later." She put down the shoulder bag and small duffel she had carried with her. "I thought I could help you right now."

"Let's go to the kitchen."

Down the hallway they went, Teresa bouncing at Amanda's side, and into the dining room, where the other three children were sitting at the table. Clearly under earlier instructions from his father, Tim said in a firm voice, "Good morning, Miss Bell," and Michael waved a spoon at her, glopping milk onto the table. Bridget said nothing, but bent instead closer to her bowl, as if she intended to stick her face directly into her cereal.

Teresa scrambled into her chair. Amanda followed Mr. Christopher into the kitchen.

"Coffee?"

"Please."

He poured coffee into a white mug. "Cream? Sugar?"

"Just black, please."

He handed her the mug, replenished his own cup, and said, "Let me show you the upstairs before I go."

They left the kitchen and went up the back staircase to the second floor. He gave her a quick tour: the girls' room, where both beds, already made up, swarmed with dolls and stuffed animals; Tim's room, tidy with a small bookcase, sports equipment--a basketball, a baseball bat, gloves, soccer shoes--piled in a corner, a poster of Gandalf and Frodo over the bed; a sunroom built over the back porch with a large table and a smaller child's table--"It's the schoolroom," Mr. Christopher told her. He showed her his own bedroom from the doorway--queen-sized bed, bureaus, pictures on the wall, everything tidy and clean--and then Mikey's small adjoining room, with playthings scattered across the floor and his bed in one corner. "Sometimes he still takes a nap after lunch," Mr. Christopher said, "and for some reason, he likes napping in Tim's room. Soon we'll move him in with Tim. Bridget's good about putting him down for the nap, if you need some help with that."

They descended the front staircase into the living room where they'd conducted the interview. Here Mr. Christopher placed his coffee on top of the newel post of the staircase, picked up her bags, and placed them in her room. He retrieved his coffee, and they walked down the hall.

Back in the kitchen, he opened cabinets and drawers, pointing out to Amanda cutlery, knives, plates, and cups, and then showed her a small pantry, saying, "There's lots to eat—soups, pasta, tuna fish, though Teresa doesn't much care for that, bread in this box. In here," he said, swinging open the refrigerator door, "are fresh fruit, butter, milk, the usual things. There's a lasagna in the freezer. If you'll unthaw that later and put it in the oven around five, we'll have it for supper."

While he spoke of supper, leaning against the refrigerator, Amanda glanced past his shoulder and noted a shelf with cookbooks, an assortment of vases, pitchers, and drinking mugs. On one corner of the shelf was a picture of Anne, surrounded by what looked like stringed beads, some wilted flowers, an unlit candle. Suddenly she realized Mr. Christopher was watching her as she studied the picture. The pain on his face was like looking into a mirror.

Stepping around her, he moved into the dining room and circled the table, giving each of the children a kiss on the head. "Tim, you know the routine. I expect you to show Miss Bell how we do things here. I want all of you to help each other, especially today." He paused, looking at them. "I love you."

"We love you too, Daddy," the children said in return. He took his silver-colored lunch box from the counter, gave Amanda a solemn nod, and was gone.

———

And there she was, left alone with four pair of eyes watching her. As she walked closer to the table--she had hovered in the doorway while Mr. Christopher made his goodbyes--Amanda had the sensation of walking out of a dream and into reality. She had played out this moment a hundred times in the last twenty-four hours, had visualized herself stepping into place and taking command, dispensing love and order. Now the moment had arrived, and she stood frozen in panic.

Tim broke the silence. "Do you want anything to eat, Miss Bell?"

"No, thank you, Tim." She consciously used his name, a bond to him. "I've eaten."

More silence followed, a stillness so loud that every small noise--Teresa wiggling in her chair, Mikey tapping his spoon on his bowl--was magnified. Then she remembered the hour and asked them if an early rising was part of their usual routine.

"On school days, it is," Tim said.

She was completely unprepared for that response. "Is today a school day?"

Bridget muttered under her breath after she asked this question, but she kept looking at Tim.

"Yes."

"What do you do on school days?"

"We do our lessons. We read and write and do math. Sometimes we do art projects or go on special trips." He paused. "Dad said I could explain it to you as we go."

"And religion," Teresa said. "I'm getting ready for first communion in May."

"Who were your teachers before me?"

"Mom was and then Katie. And then some other moms."

"Mom and Katie were the best," Bridget said. She lifted her face from her bowl and glared at Amanda.

"Katie left before Christmas," Tim said. "To get married. Since then we've gone to the Moore's house on Mondays, Wednesdays, and Fridays. On Tuesdays and Thursday Mrs. Smitherman was here. She helped a little, but mostly she cooked and cleaned."

"She goes to Mass at Saint Lawrence," Bridget said. "She used to teach a long time ago in the public school."

"Tim helps me with my reading," Teresa said. "And sometimes Bridget."

A third bout of silence threatened when Amanda remembered her car. "Would you like to help me move my things to my room? We could do that and then start your lessons."

"It's Katie's room," Bridget said. Scowling, she stood and took her spoon and plastic cereal bowl into the kitchen and dropped them with a clatter into the sink.

Tim sighed. "Katie's gone, Bridget."

"It's her room," Bridget called back from the other room. "It will always be her room."

"Dad says we need to get used to change."

"I don't like change," Bridget called back again. Amanda could hear the scowl in her voice and wondered if she herself had sounded so angry when she had spoken those same words to Father Krumpler.

"Where did Katie go?" Amanda asked, but Bridget wouldn't answer.

"She's in a place called D.C.," Teresa said. "With Mr. Scully and Jake. Mr. Scully's her husband. He's a writer. This summer they're going to France for a year. He got a bright scholarship."

"A Fulbright," Tim said.

"Who's Jake?"

"Her baby boy," Bridget said, pityingly, as if Amanda were the thickest individual on the planet. She was standing in the doorway.

"You must miss her."

"*She* was nice," Bridget said, pointedly.

"I'm sure she was." Amanda remained calm. At work, she would have attacked such impertinence with a chilly stare, but here she had the sense to offer bland indifference to Bridget's wrath. It was time, she thought, to take charge. "Pop into some clothes and brush your teeth, and we'll get my things."

While the children were upstairs, Amanda wiped up the table with a sponge from the sink, rinsed the breakfast dishes, and put them in the dishwasher. After picking up a few bits of cereal from the kitchen floor, she peeked into the refrigerator to make plans for her lunch menu. Fruit--apples, oranges, grapes--was readily available, but what else? Sandwiches? Vegetable soup from the pantry? She could ask the children what they preferred, but didn't want to set a precedent or lose control.

All the while she felt the woman in the photograph watching her. When she came out of the pantry, having decided on peanut butter sandwiches for lunch, she walked closer to examine the face of the dead woman. She wore her hair as she had in the picture in the living room, braided and pulled over one shoulder. Her eyes were honest and friendly, her lips curled in a slight smile. Something in that gentle face steadied Amanda, promised comfort if she needed it.

"That's my mom."

Amanda started at the sound of Tim's voice, twisted to see him, and catching her feet together, nearly fell backwards into the shelf and the picture. Tim was carrying Mikey on his back and looked frightened. "I didn't mean to scare you."

Her heart walloped away inside her chest. "It's all right. I just didn't hear you."

He shifted Mikey on his back. "I wanted to tell you about Bridget," he said, coloring a little in the face. "She's not mean. She doesn't usually behave this way."

"I'm sure I'll take some getting used to."

"Yes, but it's not that. It's my mom. Her birthday would be this Sunday. Bridget's been upset about that all week. Last year we didn't even talk about it, we were so sad, but this year Bridget's even sadder. And having you here makes her miss Katie too."

Just then the girls came down the stairs. Teresa was laughing and chattering, but Bridget was quiet. In the girl's silence Amanda now heard a great sadness. Being dropped into this household of children and emotions suddenly daunted her, so that she wondered again whether she was capable of doing this job, whether indeed she could make it through the day. Father Krumpler had patched her up, but the glue wasn't holding. She felt as if she was coming apart in pieces.

"Don't tell her I told you," Tim said.

"Of course not."

They met the girls at the front door. Outside, a lacework of dew glimmered on the grass of the yard, and the day was already bright and blue with sunshine. Teresa took Amanda by the hand as they descended the porch steps, and she felt herself jolted by the child's touch, its innocence, its trust. On the sidewalk Teresa jerked to an abrupt halt and inhaled a great gulp of air. A moment later she released her breath--"Ahhhhhhh!"--like a delighted connoisseur. "I love morning air. It's the best air in the world." She looked up at Amanda, her golden-brown hair wispy around her face. "Can you smell it?"

"It's very nice."

"Could you show me how you smell the air, Miss Bell?"

Imitating her, Amanda sniffed the air while Teresa watched her. The others stood off to the side by a patch of jonquils, observing her just as seriously. "No, no, that's not right," Teresa said. "Like this," and she again took a breath as if sucking up all the air in neighborhood. She held the breath, then whooshed it out again.

"Now you do it," she said, watching Amanda intently.

Under other conditions, Amanda might have considered Teresa's command a breakdown in order, the private dictating to the captain, but the eager insistence in her face and voice was so filled with wonder and delight that Amanda took in an enormous breath of air, aware as she did so of the scent of grass and damp soil, of azaleas and a perfume of cool breeze. The scent thrust her back twenty-five years to her own childhood, to mornings when she had risen before her mother and father to sit in splendid solitude in the garden behind her own house.

When she released the breath, the tremendous rush seemed to carry all the tension of the morning from her body.

Teresa laughed. "Doesn't that feel good, Miss Bell? Doesn't it?"

"It does indeed."

At the car the children were surprised to find only two packs, a small box of books, and a few hanging clothes needed to be carried into the house. "There are a few things in the trunk," Amanda said, thinking of the sleeping bag, the library-sized handbag of books, a box of odds and ends acquired on the road, "but we can bring those in some other time."

Tim slipped into one of the back packs, Teresa stoutly took the other, and Bridget followed them up the sidewalk, staggering with the books. Amanda took out the dresses, and with Mikey beside her, followed the other children back to the house. At the front steps, Mikey held out his hand; she looked at him a moment, then took his hand, which was warm and slightly sticky. Having gotten up the stairs, he released her hand and trotted into the house to Amanda's room.

Those who have suffered and survived a loss or a violation--the death of a loved one, serious illness, violent assault, rape, the natural catastrophes of fire, flood, or storm--know well the meaning of the word refuge. Their old familiar sanctuary is torn from them, smashed beyond recognition by whatever cataclysm has overtaken them, and they drift, forlorn and gloomy, uncertain whether they will again find a port for themselves. But often there follows that magical day when, with the blink of an eye, they slip into a bay of peaceful waters, drop sail and anchor, and find safe harbor.

So Amanda felt as she entered her room on this particular morning. Here indeed was a refuge, however temporary, a harbor, a home.

The room was bright with sunshine. Light falling through the eastward window bounced off furniture, puddled in the corners of the room, gleamed on the polished hardwood floor. Someone had brought in a large, white rocking chair, which matched the wrought-iron headboard of the bed whose yellow coverlet in turn complimented the pinewood bedside tables and bureau. A small crucifix hung above the bed, and on the walls were a few pictures she hadn't noticed earlier: a reproduction of Van Gogh's bedroom in Arles; matched chalks of a house in snow and in moonlight; a framed calligraphic copy of Frost's "The Road Less Traveled." The small, empty bookshelf and the desk and chair completed the décor.

Without invitation the children were already opening bags and putting away her belongings. Bridget arranged her socks, undergarments, and blouses in the bureau drawers; Teresa set out her books, lining each volume up with the end of the shelf; Tim carried her toiletries to the bathroom, saying gallantly, as he left, "I'll just put these by the tub, Miss Bell, and leave the unpacking to you." Mikey stood with his hands on his hips, watching his siblings like a crew boss looking over road repairs.

In less than five minutes they had finished, a project to which she had allotted half an hour, and were standing at the foot of the bed, lined up like little troopers watching her. Scarcely an hour had passed since Amanda's arrival, and the rest of the day loomed like some sort of insurmountable mountain. She fought hard against the urge to retreat, to give up; she had to struggle forward; she had built some momentum and if she slipped back, it would mean losing them. Even Bridget had given up her frown and was looking at her as steadily and expectantly as the others.

"School next," Amanda said briskly. "Your books are upstairs?"

"Yes," Tim and Bridget said in unison.

"All right then. Let's go have a look. You can show me what you've been doing."

Upstairs, she placed Teresa in temporary charge of Mikey while Bridget and Tim explained their daily routine and pulled out the books they were using. In math Tim had reached long division and word problems, in history both he and Bridget were reading about the Civil War, in science he was studying electricity with his father two nights a week and was spending a good deal of time with an electric kit he had received at Christmas. Bridget was on a similar track for her grade level. Both children were splendid readers--they adored the Narnia series and the Harry Potter books, neither of which Amanda had read--and both children typically spent some time each afternoon reading to Teresa and Mikey.

Amanda started Tim reading to Mikey and Bridget reading to herself from an elementary school edition of *Anne of Green Gables*, and spent nearly an hour helping Teresa with subtraction problems, reading from a book called *Little Angels*, and practicing her capital letters. From time to time Mikey would leave his pile of blocks to sit in her lap and pretend to read aloud. When Amanda had begun her lessons with Teresa, Tim had told her that Mikey sometimes needed lots of attention. "You'll have to be patient with him," he said. "I think he feels left out." For the most part, however, the dark, little boy--he was a miniature copy of his father-

-spent nearly the entire time playing with a set of blocks, glancing now and then at Amanda. While Teresa was writing, Mikey came and stood beside Amanda's chair and laid his hands on her knees. "I'm hungry," he said.

She was surprised to see from the wall clock that it was nearly eleven thirty. "Suppose you come with me and we'll make lunch together."

He nodded.

The others looked to her for their own instructions. "Keep going with your reading," she said to Tim and Bridget. "Teresa, see if you can write another five rows of letters." Again she considered asking them what they wanted to eat, but decided such a choice might set a precedent she would come to regret. "I'll call you when lunch is ready."

———

In the kitchen she lifted Mikey into his high chair at the table, rummaged around until she had collected peanut butter, strawberry jam, bread, carrot sticks, and bananas. She found two table knives and had Mikey help her slice bananas and spread peanut butter. He squished one of the ends of a banana, and managed to get peanut butter on his nose and in his hair, and seemed perfectly delighted by it all. "Do Tim and your sisters like milk?"

"Teresa likes water," Mikey said. "She only likes milk on her cereal."

When the sandwiches were ready, Amanda called the children. "Be sure to wash your hands," she reminded them.

In a minute they were downstairs. "Daddy uses the bell to call us," Teresa said. She went to the counter and shook the bell. "You can use it too."

"All right."

When they were seated, they didn't eat but watched her instead. She thought they were being polite, waiting for her to take the first bite. She picked up half a peanut butter sandwich.

"We need to pray first," Bridget said. The contempt which had earlier dripped from her voice had returned. She regarded Amanda as she might have stared at a heathen in the middle of a jungle.

Amanda returned the sandwich to her plate. "Of course. Bridget, why don't you lead us?"

"It's Mikey's turn."

"All right. Mikey?"

The boy and his siblings all made the sign of the cross. "Bless us O Lord, in these thy gifts which we are about to receive from thy bounty through Christ our Lord. Amen." Amanda lifted her head, assuming the ritual was over, but the children continued. "May the Divine Assistance remain with us always and may the souls of the faithful departed through the mercy of God rest in peace."

"What do you do in the afternoons?" she asked once everyone had eaten for a few moments.

"We used to go to Mass every Friday at noon with Mom," Tim said.

"And with Katie," Bridget added.

"And what about the other afternoons?"

"We do all sorts of things. Sometimes we go on field trips. Sometimes to the park. Sometimes we get together with friends. If the weather's nice, we play outside a lot."

Amanda wanted to ask them what part Katie had played in these activities, but was afraid of goading Bridget. Instead she asked: "What did your mother do?"

Then Bridget spoke. "She took us on the field trips and to the Saint Maria Goretti group."

"What's the Saint Maria Goretti group?"

"It's our home school co-op," Tim said. "We still go sometimes. It meets once a week."

"Who's Maria Goretti?"

"She was an Italian girl," said Teresa.

"She was attacked by a man," Tim said, "and when she wouldn't do what he wanted, he stabbed her. She died from her wounds."

"Ah." Her fingers tightened on the water glass she was bringing to her lips, but she moved smoothly into her next question. "Anything else?"

"Mom loved to be outside in the afternoons. She loved gardening," Bridget said.

"Do you like gardening, Miss Bell?" Teresa asked.

"I'm not sure. I've never really tried it."

"Mom taught us a poem once," Bridget said. "It's about gardening and how good it is for you. I think the man who wrote it was named Steven something or other."

"Robert Louis Stevenson," Amanda said.

"Yes. It was all about gardening and how not to be frumpy."

"Well, it's a fine day. Why don't we go outside?"

Without instruction, the children tidied up the kitchen. Bridget cleared and wiped the table while Tim stood at the sink, rinsing the plates and cups, and handing them to Teresa, who put them in the dishwasher. Amanda was puzzled by their efficiency, their lack of complaints, and their clear affection for one another as they worked. Knowing what she did of children, which was little, and having read of the many problems encountered in their raising, she marveled at their good behavior. She had expected depression, defiance, arrogance, but instead found four remarkably well-behaved young people. Only Bridget with her angry eyes and stern mouth worried her.

They had wiped down the table and were outside while she was still upstairs helping Mikey put on a favorite pair of cowboy boots. When she came into the yard, Teresa immediately left Tim and Bridget, who were kicking a soccer ball back and forth, and ran to her. "Don't you want to change clothes, Miss Bell?"

Amanda had not considered changing, though jeans and her plaid shirt were more appropriate for gardening. "I'll change next time," she said. She looked over the yard. Two old apple trees were in blossom, and several flower beds, one of which contained a statue of Mary, were bursting with various green shoots. Toward the back of the yard a great oak tree held a rope swing. A brick walkway separated two broad expanses of lawn.

Teresa ran to play with her brother and sister. Carrying Mikey on her hip, Amanda strolled down the brick path to a trellis with roses climbing up it. Beneath the trellis was a bench. After seating Mikey on the bench, she bent to pick a weed from the nearest plot, a bed planted thickly with peonies. One weed led her to the next, and she was about a quarter of the way down the plot when Bridget tapped her on the shoulder and held up a pair of gardening gloves. "These were Katie's. She said they helped to keep her hands soft."

"Thank you, Bridget." She slipped the gloves over her fingers. "They fit perfectly."

"She was a little shorter than you."

"You liked Katie a lot, didn't you?"

"My mom did, too," Bridget said, as if explaining. Amanda began pulling weeds again. Meanwhile, Mikey had slipped off the bench and toddled alongside her, poking his fingers into the dirt. "Make sure you get up the roots," Bridget said. "Otherwise, the weeds grow back. You have to reach into the dirt and then pull real slow."

"Did Katie teach you that?"

Bridget shook her head. "Mom."

A key clicked, a door opened: for the first time that day Amanda connected Katie and Anne as they appeared to Bridget, one mother murdered, the substitute mother gone now too, five hundred miles away. No wonder she mistrusted and resisted Amanda: she didn't want to be hurt a third time. For once, watching the willowy girl trudging across the lawn to her brother, the breeze touching her long hair, Amanda felt as if she knew the pain of someone other than herself.

Around three they went into the kitchen, where Amanda poured glasses of water and milk, and opened a package of cinnamon Graham crackers. They ate in the living room, sitting on the floor around the large coffee table, nibbling their crackers and sipping their drinks while she read to them the opening chapters of *James and the Giant Peach*.

"We saw the movie once," Tim said, "but I like the book better."

"You've read it before?"

"Three times. And Katie read it to us too."

"Oh, I'm sorry. I would have picked a different book--"

"No, it's all right. We've read a lot of the books here. Maybe we could go to the library again soon and get some more."

"We'll go tomorrow," Amanda said, thinking: *I'll need to ask for the van.* "After Mass."

"We're going to Mass?" Tim asked.

"Tomorrow's Friday, isn't it?"

"Yes."

"And you said you go to Mass on Friday?"

"Yes."

"We could go to Mass and then the library. Do you eat lunch before Mass?"

"No, we can't eat for an hour before Mass."

"Maybe I could pack some sandwiches and we could have a picnic."

"Where would we eat?" Bridget asked.

"There's a lawn behind the church with the statue of the Blessed Mother," Teresa said. "We could eat there, Miss Bell."

"Grandma Tessa took us to the library a lot," Bridget said.

"Grandma Tessa from Colorado?"

"She's our mom's mom," Tim said. "She lived with us and then she moved out west again."

"Sometimes she read us stories," said Bridget. "And sometimes she took us swimming."

"Where did you go swimming?"

"At the Y."

This was comforting. "You have a membership?"

"I think so."

"All right, then," Amanda said. One part of her brain was thinking: *You have to stay alert. You have to stay in touch. You have to talk. You can't let go or float away.* "I think I'd better start that lasagna now."

———

After putting *Shrek* on the television, Amanda preheated the oven, prepared a simple salad of greens, tomatoes, and mushrooms, and slid the lasagna onto the rack on the stove. She set up five places in the dining room--she wasn't sure if she was expected to eat with the family--found a candle in the dining room hutch for a centerpiece on the table, and tidied up the kitchen once more. She was removing the lasagna from the stove when Bridget drifted into the kitchen and asked if she could help by pouring water in the glasses on the table.

Then Mikey cried out, "Daddy!" and she looked out the kitchen door and down the hallway, but had only a glimpse of Mr. Christopher's trouser legs as he headed upstairs.

"He likes to wash up and change his clothes right away when he gets home," Bridget explained. "Sometimes he gets really dirty."

Mr. Christopher soon appeared in the kitchen, showered, his dark hair already beginning to curl again, wearing khakis and a white shirt. Bridget gave him a hug. "May I help you with anything?" he asked, hesitating at the kitchen door.

"I think we're fine."

Bridget pulled her father's sleeve, and he bent and she whispered in his ear.

"Set a place at the end of the table," Amanda heard him say.

He opened the refrigerator door, and took out a Heineken. "Would you care for one, Miss Bell?"

"Just iced tea for me."

He started to ask Amanda how her day had gone and what she had done with the children, but by then Teresa and Bridget were telling him about what they had learned in school and about lunch and how tomorrow they were going to Mass and the library.

"I was going to ask you about the van," Amanda said, afraid that she might have promised too much without first obtaining his permission. "We can walk if the weather is good."

"I'll give you the spare keys to the van."

There was never a question of where Amanda would dine. The children and Mr. Christopher carried six plates of lasagna to the table, and the salad was passed and a prayer said. While eating, Nathan listened to the children's accounts of their day. He sat at the head of the table, with the children on either side, and Amanda at the other end. Amanda wondered whether the children noticed how sunken in on himself their father was, how a part of him seemed to be missing. He did ask if her room suited her and if the day had gone well, and she smiled to herself to see the children stop eating and listen intently as she told him how helpful the children were moving her belongings into the room and that as far as she was concerned everything was satisfactory.

When he had finished eating, Nathan asked each of the children what they had learned that day in school. He had them describe their arithmetic lessons and the stories and poems they had read and what they had studied in their history books. "And how did catechism go?"

"We didn't do catechism," Teresa said.

"Don't talk with food in your mouth. Tim?"

"We forgot to do it today," Tim said.

"You forgot?"

"We went outside right after lunch."

Something was clearly wrong, though Amanda also thought she detected a hint of a smile beneath Nathan's frown.

"I'm sorry," she said. "Catechism?"

"Religious instruction. They put in fifteen minutes a day right after lunch."

"It's my fault. I didn't know."

"They were supposed to help you follow their routine. Tim?"

"I just forgot, Dad."

"Next time remember."

"Yes sir."

From his tone Amanda was reasonably sure Mr. Christopher was teasing Tim, but she nonetheless added: "We'll be sure to include catechism from now on." This word, another part of the Code, sounded strange and foreign to her when she said it.

"We'll make up the lesson. Mikey," Mr. Christopher said, "Who made us?"

"God made us," Mikey said, looking at his father. He had a moustache of tomato sauce which his father wiped away with a napkin.

"Teresa," he said. "Who is God?"

"God is the Supreme Being who made all things."

"Bridget, why did God make us?"

"God made us to know, love, and serve Him in this world, and to be happy with Him in the next."

"Tim, what is a sacrament?"

"A sacrament is an outward sign instituted by Christ to give grace."

"There," Mr. Christopher said. "That was short, but it will do. Now let's clear this table and start getting you ready for bed. But first a thank you to Miss Bell for all her help today."

The children, even Mikey, said in one voice, "Thank you, Miss Bell."

Their words and voices worked like tiny flames against the ice in Amanda's heart.

———

By nine o'clock, the house was quiet. Though it wasn't part of her contract, Amanda had done the dishes and cleaned up the kitchen, and had then put on her sweater and gone for a stroll around the neighborhood to give Mr. Christopher some time alone with the children.

When she returned, slipping into the house, he was in the large chair in the living room with a beer in his hand.

"Thank you for taking kitchen detail."

"You're welcome."

"You don't need to wash up the dishes, you know."

"It gave me something to do."

"So? It went all right today?"

"It went fine, I think."

He motioned her to a chair. "Please. Let's talk a minute."

She sat opposite him, wondering whether she had met his standards. Undoubtedly he and the children had talked upstairs, and Amanda felt the fear of the last winter gnawing inside her. "Today was different from what I expected."

"How so?"

"I expected more problems. You have wonderful children."

He nodded toward the fireplace mantle behind her and the photograph there. "The credit goes to Anne. She raised them well." He looked at Amanda appraisingly, his face dark and unsmiling. "The children had nothing but good to say of you. Except that you're not Katie."

"She must have been a tremendous help."

"I don't know what we would have done without Katie." He drank from the beer, then continued looking at her. She broke contact by staring into her lap. She imagined him with his clients or with competitors, and saw that he would be a tough man in negotiations.

"You'll stay then, Miss Bell?"

She had passed a test, and felt a surge of pride and relief. "If it suits you, Mr. Christopher."

"It does."

"I thought I'd use Tuesdays and Fridays as cleaning days. Would that be all right?"

He nodded. "I see you pulled some of the weeds today. I appreciate that. Anne was proud of her garden."

"I'm curious about one thing. Do you mind?"

"Not at all."

"Why do you teach the children at home?"

"Anne's idea. She heard about it before Tim was born and thought it made a lot of sense. I thought she was nuts at first. She was also a convert--I was raised Catholic, but she was a Methodist--and I think she saw schooling the children at home as a way to pass the faith along to her children. She was crazy about the Church--not a fanatic, she could ask some tough questions-- but she was in love. Sometimes I even used to be jealous."

"I didn't mean to pry."

"No, it's okay. Anyway, after she died I knew home schooling was one thing Anne would want me to do. It's been hard--since Katie left, some other moms have stepped in and helped quite a bit--but it meant a lot to Anne."

"I see." When he didn't say anything more, she asked: "Was there anything else?"

"Tomorrow you should take the van to church for Mass. Park in the lower lot behind the basilica--there's less traffic and it's easier to leave. You know where the library is?"

"Yes, sir. May I use your address as my home to obtain a library card?"

"Of course. By the way, we go meatless on Fridays. There's some shrimp in the freezer for supper."

"Yes, sir."

"Good night, then, Miss Bell."

"Good night, sir."

She went to her room, where she spent the next few minutes rearranging her belongings. She opened *Pride and Prejudice*, simply to read at random and pass the time, but all of a sudden a deep exhaustion bore into her, reminding her how unaccustomed to company she was, to conversation, to any sort of higher decision making. Her early awakening, the day with its burdens and commitments, the stuff of normalcy in most people's lives, pushed down on her eyelids like a set of barbells. Quietly, she went to the bathroom, brushed her teeth, returned to her room, slipped out of her clothing, and put on the extra-large T-shirt that served as her nightgown. From her handbag she pulled the carving knife with which she had slept all these months. She put the knife beside the clock on the nightstand, reminding herself that she must hide it again in the morning. Switching off the light, she stretched out beneath the covers of the bed, curled up on her side facing the nightstand, and fell at once into sleep.

———

Shortly after three in the morning, she woke and lay very still in the bed, getting her bearings. The big house was quiet, and though a blade of moonlight sliced through the window, the room itself seemed freighted with a heavy darkness. The restless urge that came to her during her nights on the road was with her now; had she been traveling, she might have packed her car and left the premises. There was no leaving these premises, of course, but finally, feeling claustrophobic and oppressed by the darkness, she opened the door of her room and walked to the kitchen for some water.

From the kitchen she saw a light and heard whispery voices coming from the living room. Wondering if one of the children had slipped downstairs in the night, she tiptoed down the long hallway and peeked around the corner. Still wearing his white shirt and khakis, Mr. Christopher lay sprawled back in his adjustable chair, his eyes closed, his hands folded on his chest, his dark heavy face gloomy and pensive even in sleep. On the carpet at his feet, like stiff, green shoots, several empty beer bottles flickered in the light of the television. With one of those revelations that came to her from time to time, she recognized in him a fellow traveler in the realms of pain, a pain different from her own, but nevertheless real and deep, traumatic as a battle wound. On the mantle Anne's portrait stared down at him, and in the lambent glow Amanda could almost feel the woman in the room, a gentle phantasm keeping watch over the sleeping man.

She debated creeping across the room and turning off the television, or at least throwing one of the sofa's afghans over him—the room was chilly—but then remained where she was. Not only was she afraid she might wake him, but she also feared inadvertently interfering in his war; Mr. Christopher might resent her entrance onto his own battlefield just as she had resented some who had tried to help her. She backed away and returned to her room, where soon she slept again.

Chapter Eight

Meaningful activity, order, structure, routine: these were the building blocks Amanda had once used as the foundation for her grand plans. She had cut and placed these stones as the bedrock for the superstructure of her success.

Beginning that April in the Christopher household, these same stones provided a wall against pain and doubt. Just as flight and solitude had that winter offered Amanda a means of escape from her suffering, now the order and routine of her days threw up a defense against the most powerful of her enemies--her thoughts, her past, her nightmares. These still disturbed her sleep, jerking her upright in bed and snatching away her breath, and she still wept sometimes when she woke, wept with shame and anger at what had befallen her and how miserably she had handled the consequences, wept even during the daylight hours when she was alone, mourning the blasted landscape of her life and her ambitions.

Mr. Henle, robbers, and rapists were not the only specters who haunted these nightmares. No--she was now hounded as well by the faces of those injured by her decisions: Mary McElroy, the older woman whom Amanda had once chastised in front of the staff for her failure to finish her daily work; Nick Webster, whom she had fired on the spot when she'd caught him texting his girlfriend for the third time that day;

the young woman, scarcely more than a girl whose name Amanda could not even remember, who had burst into tears when Amanda told her she was incompetent and of no use to anyone.

For the most part, however, the routine of her days in the Christopher home allowed Amanda to push aside her past, at least during her waking hours. In the mornings after breakfast they'd see Nathan off to his truck, the children waving to him from the large back porch while Amanda stood behind them. Then the children would help with the breakfast dishes, get dressed, and brush their teeth—Amanda had to oversee Teresa on this detail every day—at which point school would commence. Tim and Bridget would read to themselves while Amanda helped Teresa with her phonics and Mikey played blocks or trucks. Throughout the morning Amanda would go from student to student every few minutes, checking Tim's long division, assisting Bridget with her spelling, listening to Teresa read, playing with Mikey to keep him entertained and busy. After lunch and catechism, if the weather was agreeable, the children played in the yard or helped Amanda while she pulled weeds or fertilized the flower beds. Sometimes they swam at the YMCA or walked to the small park two blocks away. Once in May they drove in the van to the Arboretum, where Mr. Christopher had a pass, and picnicked and hiked a trail shimmering with spring foliage.

The children weren't perfect. As they became more deeply acquainted with Amanda, as they realized their new governess was not the cruel step-mother of fairy-tale fame or some wicked crone fattening them up for a trip to the oven, they dropped their guard with her and revealed more of themselves. There were spats, roughened feelings, arguments. Though Amanda had originally anticipated trouble from Bridget, it was Teresa who proved the most challenging. Teresa had a stubborn, independent streak to her personality, but was also easily moved to tears. She often resented both Tim and Bridget when they helped her with her lessons or directed her during the housekeeping chores. In contrast, Bridget, once she saw that Amanda had no intention of taking the place of her mother or Katie, became friendlier and more cooperative. The boys were easier; Tim was mature for his age, and more serious than his sisters, while Mikey was a docile child contented with whatever gifts the day carried to him.

Their book of days, then, was healthy, not only for Amanda but also for the children, who were still recovering from their mother's death. Not that they would ever fully recover; a wound so immense left scars. How, Amanda wondered, does a six-year-old replace her mother?

Weekends broke their routine. Mr. Christopher was home then, for the most part, having made a commitment after Anne's death never to work Saturdays or Sundays, to spend this time with the children. This was a worthy and noble goal, but he was self-employed, charged by the nature of his work with the management of construction crews and the needs of clients. To take off weekends left him at an enormous disadvantage in regard to his competitors. Often, after putting the children to bed, he spent Saturday and Sunday evenings on the phone with clients or crew members, and even Amanda, self-absorbed as she was in her own battles, could see his anxieties eating away at him. Playing soccer with the children in the back yard or supervising some household chores, he frequently broke off to look at a text message or the number of a phone call, and with a stony face would shake his head.

For Amanda, these same weekends also proved unexpectedly miserable. Though the children relished her company, she felt like an intruder during those hours when she was not formally employed. To give the family its privacy, she took long listless walks or spent hours in the library reading books, or simply sat in her room. She enjoyed the YMCA pass which Nathan had obtained for her, but her time in the gym brought less pleasure than the trips with the children to the pool or to the grocery store.

Downtown Asheville might have entertained her. Less than a ten minute walk from the house, the city was known across the South for its communities of artists, homosexuals, and nature-worshippers, a mecca for the young, the entrepreneurial, and tourists. Hundreds of people swarmed the sidewalks on any weekend between April and January; dozens of restaurants and outdoor cafes were brightly lit and filled with diners. On Friday evenings the Drum Circle, amateurs beating various drums with their fists and palms, filled Pritchard Park with hypnotic primitive music. Malaprops Bookshop, the Battery Park Bookshop and Champagne Bar, the Orange Peel, the Fine Arts Theater, the Asheville Reparatory Theater, Jack in the Woods, and dozens of bars and clubs offered a varied nightlife.

These attractions held few charms for Amanda. The throngs of people made her claustrophobic--or worse, made her feel still more alone. The drumming on Friday evenings was tribal, repetitious, and somehow ridiculous. Most of the artwork in the galleries on Lexington Avenue and Haywood Street struck her as trivial, and the writers and artists who held forth in the bookstores and cafes seemed pretentious in their dreadlocks, tattoos, and body jewelry, like actors playing a part. On her first free Saturday evening, she wandered into Malaprops during a poetry reading. The poet, a tall, bony, black-haired woman--she reminded Amanda of a Brothers Grimm witch-- seemed angry about having a vagina. After becoming annoyed, Amanda browsed the bookshelves, purchased a copy of Parini's *The Art of Teaching,* and ordered a coffee at the outdoor café across the street. She tried to read, but two men at the next table kept staring at her. When one of them asked her if she'd like to join them, she shook her head, closed her book, left some dollar bills under the coffee saucer, and walked home, glancing over her shoulder every so often to make sure they weren't following her.

After her third foray into this nightlife she decided to restrict her evening walks to the neighborhood of Montford with its gardens and Victorian homes. Here she was not particularly safe either, for the streets were dark in many places, and pockets of the large neighborhood were home to drug dealers and prostitutes. Amanda thought often of Anne when she took her nightly walks, and how awful she must have felt, as Amanda herself had felt, when her home was violated. Always on these walks she carried her shoulder bag with the Cutco knife.

Holy Week, which she learned was the name given by Catholics to the week before Easter, was miserable for her. On Monday of that week Mr. Christopher informed Amanda that she might take Good Friday off, that he planned on being home with the children all day. While the children anticipated the events of the upcoming weekend--they explained to her about Holy Thursday, the quiet hours of Good Friday, the great Vigil Mass of Saturday, followed by Easter baskets on Sunday--a gray dread of time spent alone grew in Amanda.

That Saturday evening, while the family was at Mass, she sat in her room reading Susan Howatch's novel *Glittering Images*, but after a few minutes closed the book, looked out the window at the spring twilight, and tried to identify the source of her dread. Not a month earlier, she had possessed the ability to sit in a motel room, television off, for hours at a time. She had gone for days without conversing with another human being, had thought nothing of solitude and silent. Now fifteen minutes alone had her pacing the floor. Friday had crept past at a snail-like pace, and Saturday was even worse, with every hour an agony of leaden minutes. What, she asked herself, had happened to her capacity for solitude?

It was the children, she concluded: she had developed a need for them. They were a drug for her pain, a medication for her loneliness. The irony of her situation was not lost on her, namely, that she, unmarried, childless, a modern independent woman, now needed four children to validate her existence.

One Sunday evening in May, Amanda heard Mr. Christopher coming down the stairs after putting the children to bed. Deciding to take action--Sundays had become insufferable with boredom and anxiety--Amanda put her book aside and met him at the foot of the stairs. "Sir, I wondered if I might have a moment of your time."

"Funny, but I was just coming to talk with you." His words sent her heart plummeting. "I'd like to pour a glass of wine first. Would you care to join me?"

"That would be nice," Amanda said, thinking that, given her nerves, he might want to bring the entire bottle. The suggestion of wine increased her apprehension: he had sometimes offered it at supper, but never when they were alone.

"It's a fine evening. How about sitting on the back porch? I'll meet you there."

She took one of the rockers on the porch. She and the children had hosed off the porch furniture that week, removing the yellow pollen of spring and a winter's worth of dust, and the rocking chairs gleamed white in the evening's soft light. In a moment Mr. Christopher came out, handed her a glass of red wine, and sat in the chair beside her. Faintly from a house up the street they could hear a television and the excited voice of a broadcaster.

"Sounds like baseball," Mr. Christopher commented. He clicked his glass against hers. "Here's to--what? What should we drink to, Miss Bell?"

She couldn't think of a single thing. Weakly, she said: "To the children."

"To the children. Tonight Teresa must have asked God to bless everyone she's ever known. I think it took about five minutes just to finish her prayers."

A breeze stirred the blue dusk of the yard.

"I've wanted to talk with you for a while now," Amanda said.

"I've been meaning to talk to you all week."

To Amanda, Mr. Christopher was often pensive to the point of melancholy, but this evening he looked so grim and wary about the mouth that she wondered whether he intended to reprimand her, or even to send her packing, though she could think of no cause for remonstrance or dismissal. Abruptly, he turned his entire chair to her and looked straight into her face with his dark eyes. Amanda felt her heart twist from that look. Discomfited, she pretended a sudden interest in her glass of wine, unnerved by the pain behind his eyes. She felt rather than saw his face swivel away.

"Did you want to go first?"

"No, you go ahead."

"All right. First, I want to commend you on your work. The kids have taken to you—they tell me great things about you and what you do with them. You've set a routine for them. They feel comfortable with you. Tim and Bridget especially have loved the trips to the Y--"

"Teresa's happier on land than in a swimming pool," Amanda said, trying to deflect with a small joke the coming blow. It was clear now: he was going to fire her.

He gave a stiff smile in return. "At any rate, you've captured them. They're happier again now, happier than they've been since Katie was here. You're doing a marvelous job."

"They make it easy."

"I understand everything is new to you here and you've had to make a big adjustment. I also know this isn't exactly what you want to do with your life. But I wish you'd stay on--at least until the end of the summer. Or until I can find someone else. You've been an immense help." He stopped rocking and swung his face toward her again, his eyes probing her in the shadows. "Please," he said. "Don't go."

After waiting for a sledgehammer of dismissal to fall, his entreaty came as such a relief that Amanda laughed aloud--a jagged laugh, rough with disuse. "Why would you think I was going away?"

"You've been quieter than usual all week," he said. "And then the look on your face when I handed you the wine."

"I thought you were going to fire me."

"I thought you were going to quit."

His expression was so dumfounded that she again laughed aloud, more naturally this time.

"Why would you think I was going to fire you?"

"The same reason. You had this look on your face when you asked if we could talk. And you seemed even more serious than you usually do."

Now it was his turn to laugh. She had heard him laughing with the children, but never in her presence. The laughter and smile brightened his face, and she had a glimpse of another man buried behind the grim façade. "All right," he said, "we've played out our comedy of errors. Now, what was it you wanted?"

"I want to help out on weekends," she said, and her voice picked up its pace. "I know it's your time with the children and I know how important that is to you, but I could free you up if you needed to work and I promise I wouldn't get in the way. I could do some extra housework--wash the curtains in the living room, spring-clean the closets--or garden or cook, and I could still leave you plenty of time alone with the children by going to the library or the Y."

"Don't you want your weekends off? Most people would."

"True," Amanda said, thinking *Most normal people would.* Unwilling to explain too much of herself, she continued: "But I'm new in town and don't really have much else to do. Besides, I like being with the children."

"I can only pay you a little more. I--"

"You don't need to pay me more. My salary is more than sufficient for my needs. I really want to do it. Besides, I'll still take some time off for the gym and the library."

"You'll tell me if you want more time off? No guilt--you'll just tell me?"

"Yes," she said. "I'll tell you. I promise."

———

She treasured her sessions with Father Krumpler. Tonight was their third Tuesday evening together--they had not met during Holy Week-- and the tall priest was in an expansive mood. He had greeted her with two large stemmed glasses of chardonnay, and while Amanda fried pieces of chicken in olive oil, boiled red beans and dirty rice, chopped and fried in a separate pan mushrooms, a green and a red pepper, and an onion, he lounged in the corner of his tiny kitchen, sipping the wine and pumping her for information about Mr. Christopher and the children. "You're an enormous help to all of them," he concluded after Amanda had delivered her answers. "Three weeks in, and you're already making a difference in their lives."

His praise brought a rush of blood to her cheeks. "Amanda Bell! You're blushing."

"It's the heat of the stove, you old owl."

"You're feisty, too. A good sign. Do I really look like an owl?"

"Has no one ever told you that before?"

"Never."

"Then let me be the first. You look like one of those wise old birds in the Disney cartoons."

When the rice had cooked, she scurried around the kitchen gathering up plates, napkins, and cutlery, and set the table. After Father Krumpler had blessed the food, they ate. He brought his usual hearty appetite to the table this evening, praising her cooking and taking seconds on the rice and vegetables. They didn't discuss her past during the meal as they had in previous weeks, nor her future plans, but instead talked over the day, the weather, and the news of the world: the upheavals in the Middle East, the battles in Congress over the budget, the crippling effects of oil prices on the economy. Amanda had once kept up with such topics through the headlines on her computer and by watching television news in the mornings before work, but had lost track during her winter's hegira. Father Krumpler filled her in on the revolutions in Egypt and Libya, the rising costs of groceries, a preacher in Florida who had caused riots among Arabic peoples by burning a Koran and another who had earned a place in the media by predicting the end of the world.

"He's foolish to prophesize. The date is going to roll around in another two weeks and the world will go on and he'll look imbecilic."

"I feel like Rip Van Winkle," Amanda said. She focused on the last thing he'd told her. "What would you do if you knew the world was going to end?"

"I hope I'd carry on with my life in a normal way. Pray. Drink a glass of wine in the evenings. Read. More likely, though, I'd spend my last moments comforting Mrs. Turpin."

From previous conversations, Amanda knew Mrs. Turpin was the protagonist in one of Father Krumpler's favorite Flannery O'Connor short stories. Mrs. Turpin was also his code-word for all the old ladies of the church. These were the women, he said, who helped make the church run, serving on everything from the parish council to the altar society. They were also the women whose supper invitations, unsolicited advice, and nagging complaints proved the bane of his existence.

"And you--what would you do if you believed the world was about to end?"

Amanda shrugged. "I don't know."

But of course she knew precisely what she would do if she saw her world coming to an end. She had already done it.

———

After the meal she washed the dishes, packed the leftovers into plastic containers for his lunch the next day, and joined him in the sitting room. Father Krumpler sat listening to some music, and she thought he had fallen asleep, but he raised his head when she took the chair beside him.

"Henryk Gorecki of Poland." The orchestral music with voices had a deep mournful tone. "Symphony Number Three. It's an homage to the victims of the Second World War. What do you think?"

"It's sad."

"True, true, but if you listen carefully there's a wonderfully triumphant note, don't you think? A very human note of triumph over catastrophe." He paused a long moment, listening. "For me, this is his best. He took the tragedy of his people--all the dead of that terrible war, all the hardships heaped upon the Poles by the Nazis and Communists alike--and by his art transformed rape and ruination into an elegy."

"Like me, I suppose."

He smiled. "Perhaps."

"I'm not sure I want to be an elegy."

"First blushing and now a sense of humor. I'd say the patient is making excellent progress."

The music played around them. Outside the big window the spring evening had reached that point Amanda had always loved both as a child and adult, that time of deepening shadows when quiet came and she would read by the window in her room, obligations at an end, her hour of delight.

"I've thought of you many times these last three weeks," Father Krumpler said, and by now she knew him well enough to realize the priest used the word "thought" as a euphemism for prayer. "I wondered why you reacted as you did after the rape."

"Why I didn't go to the police?"

"Or get medical help."

"I did get some later. I went in for some tests." She told him of her visit to the clinic and of the results.

"That was wise. But why didn't you go to the police?"

She picked her way back through that awful day, trying to remember what that other Amanda had felt, what that Amanda had been thinking. "I don't remember the idea ever occurring to me."

"I'm surprised. Most women would have at least considered calling the law."

"I don't know how most women feel." She tried to remember her feelings, her thoughts, her motives, but *she* blocked the way, that persona left behind in the wreckage. That Amanda she had become for three months, that Amanda still so much a part of her, that beaten, bruised self which had reared what defenses it could muster against indignity, terror, and violation: that Amanda was still inside her, calling her even now to shut down, to raise up the gates of protection. "I did what I could to survive. Mr. Henle and then those…they…it was too much. I couldn't see where to go or what to do, I couldn't think, I don't remember thinking at all. I just did what was necessary."

"You got the job done."

He infuriated her, even though she understood what he was saying. "All right then. That's right. I got the job done. I did what I had to do. I know what you're thinking. You're thinking I ran. All right--I ran. I ran until I ran out of myself and now here I am." By then she scarcely knew what she was saying, and there were tears rising in her throat.

"My dear girl," Father Krumpler said, ever so softly. "You're wrong about what I'm thinking. I'm thinking you had to endure far more than anyone should have to endure in one day. I'm thinking your entire life shut down that morning. I'm thinking of a young woman with an extraordinary power of will who had laid out a plan for her life, a plan which contained only a single flaw."

"What flaw?"

"You didn't allow for the unexpected. You were blindsided by the unforeseen. It's the awful surprises in life--the sudden death of a loved one, the bankruptcy, the utter disaster--that sooner or later test every human being. Worse, you didn't allow anyone into your life. You lived in a fortress, and you kept the drawbridge up and the portcullis lowered. You probably began building that fortress long ago, when you were a child--we'll need to talk about your parents sooner or later--and at some point when the walls surrounded you and were high enough you were safe, but you were also alone. You couldn't be rescued because you couldn't figure out how to let anyone into the castle. Worst of all, you couldn't figure out how to escape from the castle."

She held the wine glass in her fingers, but had forgotten to drink from it. Had someone taken a snapshot of her just then, Amanda had no doubt but that she would have appeared in the photo as a gape-mouthed idiot, for the old owl had bored straight into her, drilling like some sort of psychic machine into the rock inside her, splitting it open and turning over its contents for examination. And he wasn't finished yet.

"You disassociated your self from what was happening to you--not only from your boss, not only from the men who tore what was left of your life to pieces, but from nearly everything you were. You told me last time we met that while you were traveling you hardly spoke to anyone. You said, in fact, there were times you could hardly stand being around other human beings. More than ever before in your life, you separated your inward and outward self, but the mask you had always put on for the world had slipped, and you weren't sure what mask might replace it. We're all built that way, to a degree--we give one face to the world, and another to our loved ones, and keep another just for ourselves, but the mask you'd built over the years wasn't working anymore. I'll wager you didn't like looking in mirrors, did you?"

Every word he spoke drove the drill deeper. To his last statement Amanda could only murmur: "I never liked looking in mirrors."

"Many people don't. They can't reconcile themselves with the image in the glass."

"How do you know these things? How can you--"

"You told me yourself. You started telling me the minute we first met on that plane before Christmas, and you told me much more in the confessional and in our last two meetings. Not everyone has suffered a double calamity like you, but many people have moments and days and weeks--and sometimes a lifetime--when they feel disassociated from those around them, when they feel like aliens, when they can't connect with anyone or anything. They plod through their days wondering whether they're crazy or whether it's the world that has lost its mind. Those poor souls you see on the streets of Asheville and in every other city, the ones who lump about all hunch-backed and talking to themselves--some of them are so lost that they can't even lift a finger to raise the gate to their castles. They're stuck, buried in the dungeon. And they're the visible ones. Hordes of people feel the same, but they don't know how to connect."

——◆——

He spoke matter-of-factly, as if they were discussing the actions of a third party--which, in some respects, they were.

"Do you think I can be rescued?"

He took aim slantways at her question. "See that book over there? The one with the green binding?"

She looked at the bookshelf and was puzzled. "Grimm's Fairy Tales?"

"That's the one. Have you read those?"

"My dad read some of them to me when I was little."

"I doubt he read you the originals. They're grimmer--if you'll pardon the pun--than most people know. Still, those and other fairy tales have a lot to teach us. We live more than we know in fairy tales, especially as adults. We get lost in the forest, like Hansel and Gretel; we're forced to solve riddles, as in Rumplestiltskin; there are even some princesses"--and here the corners of his mouth curved upward--"who are shut away in castles and need rescuing. All of us face hobgoblins and trolls. But if we can find the right path, if we can answer the riddles correctly, if we can escape from the castles, we just might, as the fairy tales tell us, live 'happily ever after.'"

"You're talking about heaven, aren't you?" Amanda asked, with suspicion and faint disdain. "But I've told you I don't believe that stuff. I don't know how anyone does. It's not from dislike; I just don't understand how anyone can believe it. I--"

He cut her off. "Happily ever after could mean heaven, yes, but I am talking about the here-and-now. Find the right path, solve the riddles, break down walls, and you move away from disintegration and toward your true self. The self you were intended to be. The self Christ and every good shrink in the world wants you to be."

He was inserting God into the picture again, but Amanda ignored that fact. "I just don't know what to do. Practically speaking, I mean. I don't know where to go. I'm tired of thinking so much."

"You have a right to be tired. It's time to think less and to do more."

"But what do I do?"

"You could begin by taking a sip of that wine."

Dutifully she obeyed, and the chardonnay ran cool and sharp over her tongue and down her throat. Father Krumpler continued: "You do as you are doing. You connect with the people around you. You allow them to wrap you up in their lives. You start figuring out a way to take the bars off the windows and lower the gate of the castle. You already have helpers--me, the Christophers. Tell me, Amanda, have you met anyone else outside of the Christophers since you started working there?"

"Only some of the other home school families. I see them Fridays at Mass, and the children know them. Apparently there are scheduled play-dates after Mass on Fridays when the weather is good, and Mr. Christopher wants me to take the children, but with Good Friday that didn't work. We'll probably start next week."

"And how did those conversations go for you?"

"They were awkward. There was one woman who's nice to me. Mary Celeste--I can't remember her last name. She has red hair. We've talked a couple of times."

The priest smiled. "Mary Celeste Moore. A good woman."

Amanda nodded. "Mary Celeste Moore. But I don't fit as well with the others. I'm not a mother, I don't have children, and I don't really know what to say to them. It's awkward. And one of them doesn't like me at all, for whatever reason."

"Barb Brinkman."

"Yes. How did you know?"

"A lucky guess," Father Krumpler said. He kept his tone of voice neutral, but a cloud passed across his face. "You may or may not know that Mary Celeste was Anne's best friend, and she's like a sister to Nathan. After Anne's death, she was a god-send to him and the children in terms of morale. When Katie left in December, Mary Celeste was the one who stepped up and helped Nathan get through until you came on the scene. She organized some of the other moms to take a day during the week to go to Nathan's home and help with the schoolwork, teaching the Christopher children along with their own. She and others delivered meals several times a week, did some cleaning, and kept the household running. She's also one of the few people who can get Nathan to laugh."

"She does have a sharp sense of humor."

"And a tongue that could cut steel. You say you can talk to her?"

"I should rephrase that. She talks to me. Mostly, I just nod and listen. It's not Mrs. Moore who's at fault, though--it's me. I never was good at small talk."

Father Krumpler stretched, lifting his feet off the floor and extending his long, thin arms toward the ceiling. "Cramps. Too much sitting." Then he grinned at her. "Let me point out that you talk with me well enough."

"This is different." She tried to inject a lighter note to deflect the turn of the conversation. "We're trying to breech those castle walls."

"But at supper and in the kitchen we spoke of other things, and you seemed completely relaxed."

It was true: she had gotten better this last month at simply emitting words, a condition she attributed to her time spent with the children, who took her as she was, who didn't mind if she fell into long silences, who met her with uncritical eyes. "When I was a girl," she said slowly, "I was sometimes ashamed of my parents and of how we lived. My friends lived in nice houses and had mothers and fathers who had money and worked normal jobs and seemed like grown-ups instead of children. And I was bookish, too, and didn't need people around as much."

"The foundation walls of the castle?"

"Maybe. And even though I joined a sorority at the university I never really felt I belonged. Not like some of the other girls. I always felt like someone looking through a window. Then I discovered I had a knack for managing people, that they would listen to me, that I could command them and they would do what I told them to do. And about that same time I formed my plan for my life."

"Which brings us back to what I just said. How is it you can converse so easily with me and not with Mary Celeste?"

Now that shyness of which he had spoken did indeed make an appearance. She had placed her wine glass on the coaster on the end table by the chair, but picked it up to have something to hold between her fingers, an object on which to focus rather than on him. "Maybe men are easier to talk with than women."

"So you had male friends before you came here?"

"No, not really." She thought of poor Justin, who probably thought she had vanished from the face of the earth, and winced. "I think I like men better than a lot of women. Women want so many things and are confused, and they often turn domineering or even sadistic. Sometimes they seem to enjoy crushing a man."

"Weren't you that way a little bit?"

"Maybe. All right--yes, I was. I ordered men about just the way I did the women. But I always felt sorrier for the men. They were easier and had a better sense of humor."

"So you can talk with me, make small talk as you call it, because I'm a man."

"Well, not just any man. You're old enough to be my grandfather. Besides, you're a priest."

He waggled his eyebrows at her. "Dear child, you don't want to let those two minor details get in the way."

She laughed along with him. "Surely you don't go around lusting after women."

"Old men lust just as heartily as young ones. And a priest's collar chokes the neck, not the imagination."

"So you're nothing but a dirty old man."

"Guilty, dear girl. Guilty as charged."

"Should I change your nickname from Old Owl to Old Goat?"

They both laughed again, but then he smiled tenderly at her. "Granted that you can talk with me because you consider me safe. Take away thirty years from me--better make that forty--and I might not qualify. So you feel safe. But you see, safety is one of the tenets of friendship. I want you to be on the lookout for people who can make you feel that way. The children make you feel safe, and you can talk with them. Mary Celeste may have the same effect on you. She's a woman with an immense capacity for joy and for comforting others. What about Nathan?"

"Oh no," she said. "No--Mr. Christopher's my boss. I don't feel safe around him."

"He has a kind heart. He's suffered. He might make a good friend."

Amanda pondered this suggestion. Though she had promised to observe Mr. Christopher for Father Krumpler and give him updates on his condition, she didn't want to tell him what she was thinking right then, that Mr. Christopher was, like her, buried inside his own castle, that only his children kept him from becoming what she had become these last few months.

"Amanda?"

"I don't think a friendship with him would work."

"Well, we'll let it go then. Had enough for one night? You look tired."

She agreed that they had reached the end of their session and thanked him. He walked her to the door downstairs, where impulsively she gave him a hug. He returned her squeeze, patted her shoulder, and reminded her again to keep her eyes open for friendship.

———

As Nathan and the children slowly absorbed her into their lives that spring, so also did the home in which they lived. Though its dark, brooding quality never quite left her—due, she thought, less to the looming maples of the yard than to the murder committed within its walls—she soon came to love the old brick house.

Built just after the First World War, the house was solid as a good ship. The floors did not creak, the thick plaster walls absorbed noise, the doors swung silent and true on their hinges. Each room offered its own small architectural treasure. The living room boasted the large fireplace and the built-in bookshelves; the dining room offered an enormous window—what Nathan called a "picture window"—opening onto a quiet side yard and an ivy-covered wall; the upstairs bedrooms had window seats or cupolas; the playroom, its original purpose lost, contained both a window seat and a cupola as well as a working fireplace. Like an old-fashioned bank, or like her beloved libraries, this house offered reassurance and a sense of safety to its occupants and its visitors.

Purchased originally by Mr. Christopher's great-grandfather, a broker, and then passed to different members of the family, the house also reflected the character of its current owner, for Nathan Christopher emanated the same sturdiness as the house both in his physical characteristics and in his emotional character. Like the house, he was built solidly; like the house, he wore a mantle of old-fashioned dignity. Though they spent a good amount of time together on the weekends--Amanda tried to keep out of the way after supper so that he might spend time alone with the children--Nathan was reserved and polite in his dealings with her. From what she observed, he was a quiet man, though she suspected that Anne's murder had driven him more deeply into that last tangled wilderness of the modern world: the self.

As for Amanda, this house, her place in it, and her new responsibilities acted like a drug upon her battered self. Her frozen heart unthawed with each new spring day, and by June she was sleeping through most nights, tortured less and less by the unremitting nightmares of her wintertime. For the children's sake, and then for her own, she prepared tasty, nutritious meals. She paid more attention to her appearance, not from vanity nor from old habit but simply as a reflection of a reawakened interest in the world. Her hair, which she tied loosely behind her head, was growing out, and for the first time in her life she worked in slacks and blouse, finding them more practical than skirts or dresses in the kitchen and schoolroom. The memories stemming from her discharge from Saxon and Henle and her rape remained strong, but gradually took on a crepuscular tone, shadows at twilight rather than the glittering images of daytime. Given the restorative conditions of this life, she managed to deal with those dark dreams in both the day and the night more adequately than she had on the road.

Throughout May and the first days of June, Amanda began to perceive that she had spent her years in Atlanta as a captive within her own self, an incarceration which made her simultaneously guard and prisoner. Father Krumpler was correct: the fortress which she had constructed with such care and which she had designed with the idea of self-protection had in fact become her prison. While she still dwelt inside that prison--she felt most comfortable, aside from her time with the children and with Father Krumpler, in solitary silence--she was more aware of the light shining through the barred windows, of a whole world vibrant and teeming with life beyond the thick walls.

The children were Amanda's lifeline to this shining world. Children, she was discovering, live more intimately with the here-and-now than do adults; they carry less baggage into each new day, and are less concerned with the heavy weight of the past or the uncertain winds of the future than they are with the pleasures and pains of the moment. Each of them presented to Amanda a different personality with singular gifts. Tim, though only ten, possessed his father's patience with his younger siblings and with Amanda's own mistakes and hesitancy. Whether his quiet good nature and sense of ease were the result of his mother's death she did not know, but she observed that after the Friday Masses, while other children were running about the rose garden and the Marian statue behind the church, Tim stood with a few of the older boys, hands on his hips in an imitation of his father, watching the activity and talking and laughing quietly with the others, looking as much like a man as a boy.

Of all the children, Bridget, Amanda sensed, most closely resembled Anne in her personality. The girl Amanda had known her first few days in the house--hard-nosed, recalcitrant, suspicious--was not the true Bridget. No--the real Bridget quietly helped wash the dishes and the laundry, set the table for meals, knelt with her eyes closed in the schoolroom for the morning prayer, looked at her father with a face full of trust and love. She lacked Tim's confidence in herself, and she was far less lively and volatile than Teresa, but she offered a gift of quiet love rare not only among children but among human beings in general. In the touch of her fingers, in the tone of her voice, in her slow gentle smile were the makings of a woman who would offer compassion to all who crossed her path and who would be harder on herself than on others.

Teresa was the Roman candle of the family, wild, adventurous, willful, explosive. One rainy Thursday afternoon, bored at being indoors, she decided to scale one of the bookshelves in the classroom "to see if things looked different from up there." Amanda was marinating chicken for supper when she heard a screech and a tremendous crash which rattled the cups in the kitchen cabinets. Racing upstairs–she could hear the other children running from different parts of the house–she threw open the door to the schoolroom and stopped short, with the others poking their heads around her into the room. There lay the bookshelf, its contents scattered across the rug all the way to the other wall, with Teresa standing in the corner. She was smiling until she saw their faces, and then burst into tears of remorse at her foolish daring.

Yet despite her stubbornness (Teresa fought with Bridget about everything from brushing her teeth to which story she wished read to her) and her wild antics (less than a week after the bookshelf incident Amanda caught her slipping out the schoolhouse window to sit on the roof and "see how things looked"), Teresa's mercurial temperament could also transform her into a sugarplum princess whose looks and generosity of spirit would have brought a smile to the lips of a lifelong curmudgeon. She was the one who ran to her friends after Friday Mass, who told her nighttime dreams, often obviously concocted, at the breakfast table, who changed clothes six and seven times a day, dashing from cowgirl to ballerina, from pirate to soccer player. Her daring and wild schemes endeared her to her siblings and to Amanda even while they were scrambling to prevent another accident.

And Mikey--Mikey also was sui generis, a singular personality. Clearly bright, stocky and strong as a little bull, he contentedly follow his brother and sisters about the house and yard, allowed himself to be bossed by Teresa and mothered by Bridget, loved looking at books while the others were in school, and delighted in learning songs from a series of discs titled *Wee Sing*. Of all the children, Mikey was least affected by his mother's death; he didn't pause the way the others did sometimes to look at Anne's photograph on the mantle or have moments where a shadow seemed to pass over him. He was an easy child who watched the world with his round dark eyes as if taking constant delight in its amusements.

Aeneas had the Sybil to lead him from the Underworld; Amanda had the four children. They brought her out of herself, shaking awake emotions that had slumbered far too long in her: compassion, tenderness, an ability to respond happily to needs other than her own, even love. Soon she was responding strongly to their affections, matching their acceptance of this stranger in their house with powerful feelings of her own. Every day the ease with which this exchange of emotions occurred surprised her, and she regretted having willfully neglected for so long this shining realm of simple pleasures.

Once when they had just finished their schooling for the morning and were discussing the activities for the afternoon--Amanda wanted to dust the downstairs furniture and vacuum the carpets, and Tim promised to keep an eye on everyone in the back yard--Teresa left her picture book and stood gazing out the window. "I miss Mommy," she said, suddenly.

They sat watching her. Even Mikey turned away from his blocks. Amanda got up from the carpet where she was sitting with the other children and went and put her hand on Teresa's shoulder. She looked up, tearless but sad. "Where do your Mommy and Daddy live?"

None of the children had asked about her parents until now, and the unexpected question threw Amanda into a tangle of emotions. After a moment or two she knelt beside Teresa and said, "My mother and father are dead."

She could feel Tim and Bridget watching behind her, as quiet as if they were holding their breath.

"Were you seven when they died?"

"No. I was twenty."

"Do you ever get sad about them?"

"Sometimes," Amanda said, and realized with a sense of wonder that it was true.

"I think it's okay to be sad sometimes," Teresa said.

"I think so, too."

—·—

The unseen presence in the house was, of course, Anne. The longer Amanda stayed with the Christophers, the more enmeshed in their lives she became, the more she wanted to know about Anne. She never initiated a discussion of their mother with the children, and they revealed little, except to say at times "Remember how Mommy used to swing Teresa by the arm and leg in a merry-go-round?" or "Once when I was sick Mom planted those daffodils. I watched her through my window."

Mr. Christopher, Amanda had observed, also lived in the presence of his wife, particularly after the children had gone to bed and he was alone in the living room, quiet and still, yet he never mentioned Anne unless one of the children brought her up or asked about her in conversation. Even then, though he responded authentically and with love to their questions, he kept his grief locked within himself.

Except once.

It was just past ten, and Amanda walked quietly from her room to the kitchen for a glass of water and some ice. From the living room at the other end of the hallway she could hear the whispering of the television and could see the flickering of its light. From the apparatus on the front of the refrigerator she got crushed ice and water, and turned and found herself facing the photograph of Anne on the small cabinet in the corner by the back door.

Illuminated by the light of the security lamp in the yard, Anne's face appeared softer and more mysterious than during the daylight hours. Whether it was the light or the angle from which Amanda viewed the photo, Anne seemed to be smiling directly at her, and Amanda noted once again that her eyes smiled along with her lips, as if, unlike so many people, she was truly delighted to have her picture snapped. A vigil candle, its wick blackened from use, stood in front of the picture along with a piled string of rosary beads. The corner seemed an odd, remote place for such a shrine. She touched the beads and was bending closer to the picture when she heard a noise behind her and jerked backwards, bumping against the refrigerator and spilling a dollop of water on the floor.

Mr. Christopher was leaning in the kitchen doorway.

"I'm sorry." She got a dish towel from the sink and began dabbing up the water.

"I didn't mean to startle you. I was after another beer."

He waited until she had wiped the floor, then stepped around her, opened the refrigerator, pulled out a Heineken, and popped the top with the magnetized bottle opener from the refrigerator. In the meantime, Amanda had maneuvered past him. She leaned against the sink, her arms over her breasts, awkward in the long t-shirt which she had put on for sleeping. They were rarely together without the children, and certainly he had never seen her as she was now--barefooted, bare-legged, bra-less. It felt strange to be dressed this way and to be so alone with him at this hour of the night, and she was looking for the words to take her leave from him without seeming rude or frightened when he gestured with the lip of the bottle toward the photograph. He had taken off the tie he'd worn that day and loosened his collar, and she could see by the reddish hue of his neck and face that he had worked long hours in the sun these past few weeks.

"I keep that picture there for a reason," he said, as if he'd earlier deciphered her puzzled face. "Anne was shot in this room. She died here."

His calm, matter-of-fact voice pinned her in place. She struggled to think of something to say, but no words came to her, no condolences, nothing. It struck her how much farther she had to go to reach liberty and that fullness of herself which Farther Krumpler had addressed in their last evening together.

"The children don't know," he said. "They think she was shot in the yard. They'd gone to the library with their grandmother for the morning, and the police said the man who killed Anne must have seen them leaving and thought the house was empty. Katie was here with her baby. She said the man seemed shocked when the gun went off."

He stopped talking, and Amanda could hear the low, dull humming of the refrigerator in the silence between them. "Anyway," he said at last, "that's why I keep her picture there."

He didn't wait for the silence to continue this time, but instead walked past her and through the doorway. "Good night, Miss Bell."

"Good night, sir," she replied, and then whispered, though by then he was gone: "I'm sorry."

PART III

Chapter Nine

Religion as practiced in the Christopher household, and among many of the other home-schooling families, baffled Amanda. Her own parents, so far as she could discern, had adhered to no particular religious faith other than those vague beliefs advocated by so many in the nation's post-Christian society. No one offered up prayers in the Bell home, not even for meals, and though they celebrated Christmas with a tree, presents from Santa Claus, and some electric candles in the windows, they didn't darken the door of any church even during that season. Baptism, sacraments, salvation, redemption: these were as foreign to the Bell household as the great silver canopies of Jahangir. Occasionally her father might talk about God as a sort of force in the universe, removed from human affairs, impersonal as quarks or quasars. Once a Presbyterian neighbor girl, Priscilla, had tried to explain predestination to her. When Amanda had asked her mother about the discussion, she had dismissed the girl's beliefs, saying with a wave of her hand: "Oh, that stuff's just mind games. It's the heart that counts."

Though she took the children to Friday Mass, met once or twice a week with a dear old owl who was Catholic to the bone, bowed her head for mealtime prayers, helped instruct the children in their catechism, and heard them at night reciting the rosary, Amanda was unmoved spiritually. Often she felt like an anthropologist in the midst of some remote primitive tribe, studying the habits of the natives, noting their exotic customs, puzzled by their beliefs. At first, the children appeared curious when they noted her absence from Sunday Mass, but counseled, as she discovered much later, by their father to avoid the topic of religion with her, they never asked Amanda why she remained at home while they marched off to church at 8:35 on Sunday mornings.

The families whom she met at the Friday Masses also kept their silence, though they obviously knew that she did not make the sign of the cross, receive communion, or kneel during the consecration. She could feel their eyes on her, some curious, some digging into her like surgical tools. Following these Masses, while the children played or conversed with their friends, Amanda held herself apart as much as possible from the adults, following Mikey and Teresa to the tidy garden behind the church and watching them from the periphery of the lawn while the mothers of other children remained in the upper courtyard. When forced to speak with them, she stumbled over her words and clumsily deflected questions about her past.

One Monday evening in early June Mr. Christopher announced that the home-school group's annual covered dish picnic was the next Saturday evening. "I got a reminder today by email. It starts at four."

"Can we go, Dad?" Tim asked.

"Of course we can. We'll have a great time. We just need to think of some dish to take with us."

That afternoon Amanda had prepared for supper a ham and broccoli quiche, a spinach salad, homemade muffins, and a raspberry yogurt pie. She was curious to know what Mr. Christopher thought of the quiche, but right now he seemed more interested in the upcoming picnic than in her cooking. He dangled his fork above the quiche.

"We could bring hamburgers," he said, "but that means I'd have to grill them there."

"Or hot dogs and bratwurst," Tim said. "They're easier."

"I like potato chips," Teresa said.

"You can't just bring potato chips," Bridget told her.

Mr. Christopher picked at his food with his fork, but still hadn't tasted it. Afraid the quiche would get cold, Amanda wanted to reach across the table with her own fork, cut off a bite, and plop it into his mouth.

"I make a great Mexican bean dip," she said, to speed the decision along so that everyone could eat. "You could take that and some chips and salsa, and have a feast."

Mr. Christopher looked at her in surprise. "I thought you'd be coming too."

"Me?" She was disoriented by this unforeseen invitation. Dread and panic set up their fearsome armies on her borders, raising the black flag, preparing an invasion. She forgot all about the cooling quiche. "Me?"

"Sure."

"But I don't know anyone. I think--"

"You know the Moores."

"You know Mrs. Brinkman," Bridget said, "and the Andersons and the Bevilacquas and the Surbers."

"Catherine really likes you," Teresa said. Catherine Bevilacqua was her current best friend. "She thinks you're pretty."

All of them were looking expectantly at Amanda.

"But I'm not even Catholic."

"You don't have to be Catholic," Mr. Christopher said. "A few of the spouses aren't."

"I'm not really a part of the group." She tiptoed past her real objection, that she wasn't fit company for anyone other than an elderly priest and children under the age of twelve.

"You're our teacher," Tim said. "You should come."

"I don't mind staying home. Really. I'll be fine." She looked for help to Mr. Christopher, but he regarded her blandly.

"We'd love to have you," he said. "And you could meet some people. I'm sure some of them would like to get to know you."

What Amanda gathered from this remark was that a small number of female busybodies were curious to meet the woman who had the care of Anne Christopher's children and was living in her house. Part of her understood this curiosity, part of her was offended, but mostly she was afraid. They would have questions, which meant she would have to explain herself, and she lacked both the willpower and the inclination to do so.

"The weather's supposed to be perfect this weekend," Tim said. He was doing a unit study on meteorology and was following the local weather reports on the computer.

"Yes, but you see, I don't really fit in." Her excuse sounded weak and phony, and even she could hear the rising panic in her tone.

Then Bridget, who was sitting beside her, tapped Amanda on the shoulder. "Please come, Miss Bell," she said when Amanda turned to her. "Please come with us."

The pleading in her voice matched Amanda's panic. She looked at Bridget and was shocked to see the girl on the verge of tears. With a yank at her heart Amanda realized how close the two of them had become these past few weeks, how it was Bridget who hung about the kitchen after a meal helping with the dishes, Bridget who encouraged Teresa to obey "Miss Bell" whenever Amanda was having trouble with her, Bridget who wanted to sit on the sofa beside her during their reading lessons and who would lean on her shoulder while Amanda explained the construction or meaning of some word or phrase.

"It would be nice if you came," Mr. Christopher said. "I'd like you to come too."

What else could she do but assent?

"All right," she said. "I'll go."

The children, who to this point were watching her, began eating.

"It's settled then," Mr. Christopher said. "And I'll take you up on that bean dish. This quiche is good, too. Delicious."

Amanda scarcely heard him. The last thing on her mind now was cold quiche.

———

It rained in the night before the picnic, but by mid-morning the storm clouds had tumbled away to the east, and the rest of the day lay before them like a gift--mild temperatures, a ceiling of blue sky, sunshine glinting on the pavements and drying the rain from the green lawns of Montford.

They had never all ridden together anywhere in the family van, and the fifteen minute drive to the park on Patton Avenue passed awkwardly for Amanda. Though she had volunteered to sit in the back of the van beside Teresa, Mr. Christopher shook his head and instructed Tim to take that place. During the drive Amanda developed a slight crick in her neck craning around to talk with the children in the back seats, finding that conversation more comfortable than having to face Mr. Christopher. Sitting beside him, though they were a foot apart and separated by a console, seemed too intimate somehow, as if she had bumped a ghost from her rightful place in the car.

When they arrived at the park, Bridget and Teresa jumped from the car and ran toward the playground and picnic shelters, which were already swarming with people. Tim helped Mr. Christopher carry the bean dish, salsa, and chips while Amanda followed, holding Mikey by one hand and with the other pushing his stroller, the seat of which was filled with a bottle of iced tea and some juice boxes. Having chosen to wear sandals and the sundress which she'd bought her first day in Asheville, she was relieved to see the other women in casual dress as well.

The table slotted for food was in the middle shelter. Amanda wedged the bean dish between some potato chips and biscuits, loosened the bottle-cap on the salsa, and was tugging open a bag of tortilla chips when Mary Celeste Moore appeared beside her.

"Need any help?"

She gave Amanda a little hug, a surprise--when was the last time anyone had demonstrated such spontaneous affection, physical or otherwise, for her?--and then knelt to say hello to Mikey face to face. Glowing like a rose in the late afternoon heat, Mikey beamed back at her. All the children loved the Moore family. Erin, a teenager and the oldest of the Moore's five children, was their favorite sitter, and Erin's siblings were their close friends.

Mary Celeste brushed a wisp of scarlet hair from her cheek. "Hey, Nathan," she said. He was endeavoring to open the other bag of chips with his teeth. "You ready to do a little work here?"

He popped the bag open and propped it on the table. "We're not in your kitchen, vixen. Opening this bag of chips is all the work I intend to do the rest of the evening. Besides, I don't take orders from sassy Irish redheads with Napoleonic complexes."

"You do if you know what's good for you."

"And when on earth did I ever know that?"

Mary Celeste threw back her head and laughed. She wasn't what anyone would call beautiful, but the vigorous spirit in so thin and pale a body gave her a magic of attraction. She pulled Nathan to her in a sisterly hug.

"Where's Tom?"

"Over there with the other guys." She gestured toward the men standing near the grill. "It's like a city work crew. One grills the burgers and ten others stand around and watch him."

"I'll go say hello." He turned to Amanda. "I'd be glad to take Mikey."

"No, I'll watch him." Mikey was key to Amanda's plan, her buffer against this sea of strangers. She would follow him about the playground, push him on the swings, and so avoid the busybodies.

"You're sure?"

When Amanda nodded, Mr. Christopher walked across the strip of lawn toward the grills, waving to Tom. "Look at them," Mary Celeste said. "Why is it that men who wouldn't be caught dead in a kitchen are so natural around a grill?"

Amanda didn't know how to respond, but Mary Celeste didn't notice. She was watching Nathan as he joined the men around the grill. "How is he these days?"

"Mr. Christopher?"

Mary Celeste laughed. "Is that what you call him?"

"Yes."

Amanda didn't see the joke, and Mary Celeste's laughter quickly faded in the face of her solemnity. She gathered Amanda to her with her eyes, offering comfort, as if she had some insight into the strain she was under. "It was sweet of you to come this evening. And I'm glad for a moment alone with you. I truly am curious about Nathan. Is he doing all right?"

"He goes to work early every morning and comes home between five and six. He plays with the children quite a bit, reads them stories, puts them to bed. He's painting a side of the house this summer."

Amanda felt silly giving such a bland description, but lacked no standard of comparison by which to render any real judgment.

"Does he laugh much?"

"No. Well, sometimes. With the children."

Mary Celeste leaned one hip against the picnic table and regarded Amanda earnestly, again pushing the strand of red hair from her flushed face. "He's different, Amanda. If you had known him before--he used to laugh a lot, tell stories. He and Anne would throw this New Year's Day party that was always a hoot. Lots of people, good times."

She might have said more, but her son David, who was about Teresa's age, ran up with mud on his face and arms, and Mary Celeste took him by the arm and marched him toward the restrooms.

Amanda picked up Mikey and carried him down the grassy slope to the sandbox below the picnic shelters. An enormous oak threw its shadows over this spot, and Amanda sat in the shade of the tree on one of the railroad ties holding back the sand and watched while Mikey patted together what were apparently meant to be houses. He had worked intently for a few minutes when someone behind them called out in a bright voice, "Mikey!" and then Barb Brinkman was standing above them, holding the hand of a little girl about the same age as Mikey.

"Debbie's come to play with you, sweetie," she said, and the little girl released her mother's hand and clambered over the ties and squatted down beside Mikey. Amanda stood, dusting sand from her fingers.

"How are you, Amanda?" Barb Brinkman's voice was husky, twined with the honeysuckle of a deeper part of the South. Her white skirt showed off a country club tan, and her soft red blouse collected the sunlight and made her hair shine like black velvet. The tiny gold crucifix about her neck fell just above her breasts. She appraised Amanda with a smooth cool face while she squeezed her hand. "How is life in the nanny lane?"

"Everything is fine." Just as she was wondering how long Barb intended shaking her hand, the woman released her fingers, took a step back, and pretended to eye her approvingly.

"It's a long way from a black dress and an apron, isn't it?"

"Pardon me?"

"You know--the way nannies used to dress? You nannies are a popular bunch right now--movies, television shows. Don't you ever watch *The Nanny*?"

Watch it? Amanda had never heard of it. Later that week, after searching out *The Nanny* on one of the library computers, she found it was one of those reality television shows which had hit their peak and were now waning in popularity with the public.

"What exactly do nannies do all day?" Barb asked without bothering to wait for an answer to her first question. "I mean, I know you help teach the children, don't you, but what else? Do you cook and clean? Shop for groceries? Do you get some time off? It must be difficult for someone like you--you're what? Twenty-three, twenty-four?-- having to spend so much time with someone else's children when you could be off with people like yourself having fun."

Amanda had seen attorneys avail themselves of this bombardment of inquisition and twisted syntax to badger their adversaries. She had utilized it herself at Saxon and Henle as a weapon to intimidate new members of the staff. Only this time she was the new employee.

"I'm twenty-seven," she stammered. "And I do have some time to myself. I--"

"Twenty-seven," Barb drawled. "Goodness, you're older than I thought. Of course, it's children that age a woman, isn't it? I'm thirty-four myself, and Nathan's thirty-six. It must be hard on you being around all these old married folk and children." Without turning round, she jerked her head back toward the picnic tables. "You must be bored out of your mind."

"No," Amanda said, miserably. "It's nice being here. Besides, Mr. Christopher and the children wanted me to come."

"Mr. Christopher? How quaint. And how is our Nathan?"

Her lazy drawl with its stress on 'our Nathan' sounded a loud alarm. They were now in a contest, hissing and circling each other, backs raised and claws bared. Only Amanda felt more a mouse than a cat.

Barb was already striking from another direction. "Nathan's a busy man, isn't he? What with work and the kids and all. I've asked him to supper three times in May, and he's always tied up with work or children. That man must work every day of the week. And the kids, poor things, he has to keep up with them. It's so sad what happened to them. Anyone can see they need a mother."

"Mr. Christopher stays busy, and he's a good father."

"But it's so much harder meeting people, isn't it, when you have children. Of course, not a lot of single people are willing to take on an entire family."

"Pardon me?" The convoluted conversation was draining her energy, and she wished Barb Brinkman would go away and leave her alone. The woman was attacking her in some way, but she couldn't understand how or why. A great fatigue flooded her; she was an invalid who had wandered far beyond the limits of her illness. If she could just think--

"Some women don't find a man with children attractive in the long run. Especially when they don't have little ones of their own. Oh, don't worry, I don't mean you, for heaven's sakes, I'm just talking in general. I'm assuming you don't have any children, of course. No? That's what I thought. Anyway, I was talking with Father Krumpler after Mass the other day. He said you might make a good English teacher."

Amanda surrendered. She was defeated. The jumbled remarks and questions had left her baffled, depleted, empty of any real reply, and the warm air suddenly weighed on her as oppressively as chains. She detected the cruelty at work in the other woman--the false encouragement of her smile, the tilt of her sun-browned face--but Amanda was powerless. She could only nod.

"I see you at Mass, but you're not Catholic, are you?"

"No. I--"

"I've watched you at Mass and wondered who you were and where you came from and how Nathan was ever lucky enough to find you. You're pretty, by the way, as I'm sure you know, but you haven't worked much with children, have you? Have you ever taught anywhere? No? How did you become a nanny? Do you work for an agency or did you just wander in off the streets?"

Once again the smiling woman's shifting barrage of inquiry and innuendo rained down on Amanda. She felt trapped and powerless. In her old life that power over the weak and the terrified, that aptitude for domination, had belonged to her, a useful tool for commanding obedience, but she was the weak one now, and Barb Brinkman had the big guns. All Amanda could do was stand transfixed, waiting for the next blows to fall. "Father Krumpler introduced us. He said--"

"Ah, Father Krumpler. You'll want to keep an eye on that one. My family knew him when he lived in New Orleans, when he taught at Tulane. He caused quite a stir there, twenty years ago. A scandal, really, involving one of his students. She left school one afternoon and the next day she committed suicide. The family never filed any formal charges, but the school let him go a short time later." Her upper lip rose contemptuously over perfectly white teeth. "Well, at least he wasn't chasing boys."

Her scornful accusation seared Amanda's heart. Could there be any truth to this tale? She thought of her suppers with Father Krumpler and the counseling, and then of the woman named Maggie, tattooed, eyes glazed, wearing a tank top and high platform shoes, who had come to the rectory door last week as Amanda was leaving. What was a woman like that doing in a priest's apartment at that time of the evening? Surely by then it was too late for counseling, and she couldn't imagine them as friends.

Yet she had no time to waste on such musing; Barb Brinkman, splendid strategist that she was, pounded away at her from another direction.

"I worry a lot about Nathan. What's he do with his evenings these days?"

"He spends his time with the children."

"No, I mean after he's put them to bed."

With this query one of Amanda's old work adages--never ever discuss the boss--kicked into play. She shrugged. "The usual things."

Perspiration trickled down her back.

"He misses Anne so terribly much. You can see it in him. She was a convert. Did you know that? And like so many converts, she became incredibly devout. A lot of people thought she was a saint. I wonder what it's like, though, living with a saint."

"I can understand your wonderment."

Holding her youngest in her arms--the toddler of the Moore crew, Jack--Mary Celeste had approached them unseen and was studying Barb Brinkman with the wide-eyed innocence of a Macy's clerk who has just told a size fourteen matron that she looks splendid in a size twelve dress.

Barb pulled her sunglasses to the tip of her nose and eyed Mary Celeste. "You have a strange sense of humor, Mary Celeste."

"Yes, but I do have one. Besides, I like a little barb." She winked at Amanda, who wouldn't catch the pun herself until the following day.

"I never quite know what you mean by anything."

"That's because I practice confusion. I work hard to tangle up the minds of teenagers, arrogant men, and stringy old ladies. Which places you in a category all your own. And now if you'll excuse us, I promised Bridget I'd find Amanda. She's saving you a seat, Amanda."

"We were discussing Anne and sainthood," Barb said.

Mary Celeste shifted Jack in her arms, turned to Barb Brinkman, and said quietly, "You are just amazing."

"In fact, Amanda, if you have any questions about Catholicism, you can ask me. I help teach the adult catechumens at church. The Creed. The sacraments. The Ten Commandments."

"Those commandments can be pretty heavy lifting," Mary Celeste said to Amanda. "Take number eight. And number six. That one's a real bear."

Beneath her tan a red stain spread from the throat of Barb Brinkman to her cheeks. Pushing her sunglasses back into place, she got to her feet, said good-bye to Amanda, and walked toward the shelters.

"Good riddance to bad rubbish, as the old line goes." Mary Celeste looked like a mischievous pixie. "She was ready to pounce when I came up, wasn't she?"

"Yes."

"It's Nathan. She wants him, but she's not his type, and he's just too nice of a guy to tell her to get lost. And she's jealous of you, plain and simple."

"How do you know?"

"It's written on every sun-bleached line in her face."

"Why would she be jealous of me?"

"Well, for one thing, she knows the children adore you. She hears them talking after Mass--'Miss Bell this' and 'Miss Bell that.' And for another, she's terrified that Nathan's going to fall in love with you instead of running after her. You're with him every evening, and you're beautiful to boot. What a witch."

Her casual observation horrified Amanda. "How do you know she's thinking all those things?"

"As I said, it's written in her face."

"What's a catechumen?"

"Someone seeking instruction for the purpose of coming into the Church."

"Why'd she get so upset about the sixth and eighth commandments?"

"Thou shalt not bear false witness against thy neighbor--that's number eight. And then there's number six--adultery. I just took a shot on that one." Mary Celeste squinted, facing the sun and the other picnickers. "Gossip's a sin, and suffice it to say that Barb brings it to a new level.

Now let's go find out what devilry my children have committed in the last five minutes and have some supper."

————

That picnic brought another revelation involving Mary Celeste.

The Moores and the Christophers had been friends for years, and the eighteen months since Anne Christopher's murder had drawn the two families even more tightly together. Though aware of this friendship by the time of the picnic, Amanda had not understood until now the special bond between Mary Celeste and Mr. Christopher. They were more sister and brother than friends.

"Good grief, Tom," Mary Celeste said when they had settled themselves at the table, "are you really going to eat all that?"

Tom Moore was a real-estate attorney who had played soccer at the local university and had retained his athletic build despite his hours behind a desk. He had thinning sandy hair, bright eyes, and a face that transmitted every passing thought. After Mary Celeste's comment, he stared guiltily at the pile of food on his plate.

Mr. Christopher spoke for him. "Pay no attention to her, Tom. You've earned it." He cocked his head at Mary Celeste. "You should go easy on him--he helped with the cooking."

"Helped with the cooking?" Mary Celeste laughed and nodded toward the smoke of the grills. "Why do so many men equate flipping burgers over a fire with cooking?"

"All the great chefs were men."

"Not true. All the great blowhard chefs were men. Women don't need to brag on their cooking." She pointed her fork at his plate, also heaped high with food. "And look at that. What's your excuse for gluttony?"

"I worked up a sweat getting your brood settled with their meals."

"You worked up a sweat doing something I do three times a day every day of the week?"

"Is that why you're so skinny and mean?"

"I eat a healthy diet."

"Then maybe you should eat more and put some meat on those thin Irish bones."

"If I ate like you boys, I'd be making the Guinness Book as the fattest mother on the planet. You'd never get portions like this from my kitchen."

"We're not in your kitchen, vixen."

"Tommy Moore," Mary Celeste said, shifting her attention to her third child, who had inherited, like the other children, their mother's red hair, "quit shoveling those chips into your gob. You're worse than the men."

"Shovel away, Tom," Mr. Christopher said. "We're at a picnic, not the Grove Park Inn."

"Grove Park, Shmove Park," Mary Celeste retorted. "Take a look at your fathers, children. They're fat and sassy now but in twenty years they'll be hauling their bellies around in wheelbarrows."

"It was the wheelbarrow," Mr. Christopher said, "that brought the Irish up off all fours and onto two legs."

"Erin go bragh."

"What's Erin go bragh mean?" Tim asked.

"Ireland forever," Mary Celeste replied.

"Bog-trotters galore," Mr. Christopher said.

Mary Celeste balanced a salad crouton on the back of her thumb and shot it straight at Mr. Christopher. It bounced off his chest. "Take that, English dog."

The children, though apparently accustomed to this verbal play, now raised their heads and looked at Mr. Christopher for his response. He in turn looked at Tom Moore. "Tom? What about it? Potato chips at five feet?"

"No way, man. I have to go home with her."

Mr. Christopher threw up his hands. "I'm too much a gentleman to return fire anyway."

"You a gentleman?" Mary Celeste said. "Then pigs can fly."

"Notice my fine manners, children," Mr. Christopher said. "My exquisite sense of etiquette. When some boorish bog-trotter throws food at me or offends my savoir-faire, I smile back politely."

He put on such a look of offended propriety that Mary Celeste threw back her head and burst into laughter.

———

As supper was winding down, Mary Celeste turned the care of the children over to her husband and Mr. Christopher, and taking Amanda under her wing, conducted her to the other tables and introduced her to some of the parents. About half of them she had already encountered, however briefly, at Saint Lawrence; the others attended different parishes in the area. Two of the couples--the Berquists from Haywood County and the Parinis from Greenville--were complete strangers to Amanda, but the others had clearly heard of her through a grapevine cultivated, Amanda guessed, by Barb Brinkman. From their guarded looks and comments she could tell that her reputation had not only preceded her but was under rigorous scrutiny.

By the time they had finished this stiff debut of smiles and hand-shaking, Amanda's face glowed with perspiration and she felt wrung out as a rag. "You're new to them," Mary Celeste said as they drifted down the hill below the shelters. Even Mary Celeste, with all her bantering and easy ways, had lost some of the quickness and fire of her spirit. "And they're definitely not used to the idea of a governess. This is Asheville, not Park Avenue."

"But wasn't Katie a nanny for nearly a year?"

"That was different. It was Anne who took her and the baby in when they had no other place to go. And by the time of Anne's death Katie was dating John Scully. She was also ten years younger than you--closer to Erin's age than to ours. There was no question of what her place was in the life of the Christopher family."

"But why would they care a whit about me?"

"I imagine the Wicked Witch of the West has put some poison out about you," Mary Celeste said. They had drifted away from the shelter and were standing in the shade of a pine tree. Twilight was approaching in the long shadows. Mary Celeste had put Jack in his stroller, and he was sleeping with sunlight dappling his face. "Barb has some good points--she does a fine job with the adult education at church, she's a good mother, and her life isn't easy--but you have to dig deep to find her likeable. But it's more than Barb and her gossip. Anne was a sort of hero to some of these people--or heroine--and now here you are. They don't know much of anything about you, where you came from or what you were doing before you came here. You don't have children and you're not Catholic and so you're a puzzle. A mystery. You're attractive and you appeared out of nowhere and you don't have a lot to say. They don't know what to make of you."

"What should I do?"

"They're good folks. Give them time and get to know them a little, and they'll come around. Just be yourself. The summer play group starts next week. Every week through the summer we get the kids together in the afternoon at the pool and let them have some fun. You could come to the pool. Or to park days if you like."

"So I should mingle more?"

Mary Celeste bent and brushed away a gnat which had settled on Jack's forehead. "Only if you want to. I could come by the house and take the children to park days, but I think it would be good if you showed up. Let the moms warm up to you."

Amanda's Old Owl had recently given her the same piece of advice, and a sudden thought occurred. "Did Father Krumpler ask you to watch out for me?"

Mary Celeste smiled. "That obvious, eh? All right--he put me up to it. He's quite the conniver."

Though she disliked the idea that Father Krumpler had spoken to Mary Celeste--she wondered exactly what he had told her--Amanda managed a wan smile. Having a guardian angel like Mary Celeste pleased her.

"Don't worry," Mary Celeste reassured her. "Father K's one of the good guys. He didn't tell me anything about you, just asked me to give you a hand if you needed one."

Her affirmation of Father Krumpler gave Amanda the courage to ask her about New Orleans. "Barb told me that he had trouble at Tulane with a student. A woman. She said the girl committed suicide and Father Krumpler had to resign."

Mary Celeste's pale Irish face darkened like a thunderhead, and she held one hand over her eyes against the sun and swept the picnic area. When she stopped, Amanda followed her gaze and saw her staring at Barb, who was chatting with Tom and Mr. Christopher. For one instant Amanda half-expected Mary Celeste to tear a branch from the pine tree, mount the small rise to the picnic tables, and thrash Barb Brinkman within an inch of her life. Then she dropped her hand from her brow and threw Amanda a look of utter disgust.

"She knows better. She knows what really happened, and she still spews the same old garbage out. What did she tell you? That Father K. got caught screwing some little undergraduate who ran away and hung herself?"

"Not in those words. It was more what she implied."

"Yes, Barb's the queen of implications."

"So she wasn't telling the truth?"

"Not even close. There was a student, and she did commit suicide-- she used her mother's sleeping pills and her father's liquor--and Father Krumpler was involved with her and he did leave the university after it happened. The girl's name was Abigail LaGarde. She'd grown up in Bay St. Louis in Mississippi--her parents had connections with New Orleans and the Garden District--and she lived in the apartment they owned there. When she was a sophomore, she was recruited into a sex group off-campus. It was one of those groups you can find in a lot of places these days--group sex, sadomasochism, pornography, and prostitution.

This group also practiced voodoo and some other weird things. Abigail LaGarde became an active member. After about six months or so, she sought out Father K and told him she was possessed. She came to him for an exorcism. Instead, he recommended counseling."

"How do you know all these things?"

"I looked it up online. It was a big story at the time--at least in New Orleans--if only because she came from an old family. New Orleans was pretty slimy then--this was pre-Katrina--but the case caused a stir. Anyway, the family never blamed Father K or the university. In fact, the mother and father both acknowledged he was trying to help their daughter."

"Then why did he leave?"

"He blamed himself. She had come to him seeking the rites of the Church, and he had offered her some sessions on a psychiatrist's couch. It was the right thing to do, incidentally. Only doing the right thing didn't take away his guilt."

"He told you all that?"

"Two years ago he gave a talk at church to the young adults' group about the reality of evil in the world, and he used the case as one of his examples. He talked about how we often don't even recognize evil anymore and how we cover it up with different labels."

Jack stirred in his stroller, puckering his lips and then frowning in his sleep. His tiny face was flushed, his cheeks and forehead soft and waxen with the heat. Mary Celeste smiled. "It's always amazing to me, no matter how many times I think about it, that we can grow from a creature like Jack there into the beings we are--a bundle of nerves and feelings and experiences. Life's messy, isn't it?"

Later, after they had strolled back up the hill, Amanda packed up the remains of the salsa and bean dip, and helped Mr. Christopher gather the children at the car. Mikey wanted to bring a plate filled with stones he had collected, which kept falling from the plate as he tottered across the parking lot, and Teresa, ever dramatic, sulked in her car seat as if in perpetual mourning at leaving her friends. The drive home was quiet; Mikey fell asleep before they left the parking lot, and the older children had worn themselves out playing and running in the heat. Even Mr. Christopher seemed content with silence.

Meanwhile, Amanda's mind worked overtime. The day had filled her with impressions and thoughts, each of which demanded some singular contemplation, but which all tumbled around and bumped together like marbles in a box. Within the space of the evening the halo she had given Father Krumpler had slipped and had then been righted again, glowing even more brightly; her conversation with Mary Celeste had brought her an ally and friend; she had successfully endured being introduced to a dozen strangers; she was not the anonymous figure she had assumed, but was a subject of speculation; the Wicked Witch of the West had daunted but not destroyed her; and Mr. Christopher had revealed a humorous side that had escaped her for the last eight weeks.

Hidden in those thickets of conversation was the day's final revelation, that Barb Brinkman and Mary Celeste Moore both thought she was pretty and wondered--in Barb's case, evidently wondered a great deal--whether she might become attracted to Mr. Christopher.

Which, Amanda realized with a shock, had already happened.

———————

Sometimes, Father Krumpler told Amanda, we are so unaware of ourselves and our motives--maybe even most of the time--that we require the casual comment of an outsider to open our eyes so that we can see where we are and what we are doing. Instinct and desire can work on us long before conscious thought.

In many ways Amanda had approached her position at the Christophers with the same sense of duty and diligence she had exhibited at Saxon and Henle. Her initial aims were simple enough: to manage the household, to keep the children clean and safe, to provide healthy meals, to teach them their lessons, to obey and to be obeyed. But the metallic resolve with which she had begun her post as governess had dissolved quickly in the acid test of reality. The children needed more than freshly-laundered socks, chicken casserole, times tables, and historical dates. They needed affection and tender care. And this need Amanda understood, for she needed affection and care as well, which the children heaped on her by the bushel-load. They took her to their hearts--not with gushy sentimentality, but in the way of children, straight-up and naturally.

That evening after the picnic, while Mr. Christopher bathed the children and settled them in bed, Amanda poured herself a glass of water, went to the back porch, and sat on the steps in the dark. The weeks since her arrival in Asheville had worked changes in her, most of them coming under the aegis of the children, who were so instrumental in shifting her attention outward, away from that cold stone which had been her heart. With his wise counsel, Father Krumpler was also chiseling away at this stone and helping her to reshape her life. Her recovery, such as it was, seemed to owe little to Mr. Christopher. He was her employer, her supervisor, her boss, and for Amanda the demarcation between employer and employee was clear and unmistakable, and should never be crossed. Romantic entanglements could be as ruinous to a professional relationship as incompetence or sloth. In her old life she had taken some pride in maintaining such standards.

So what had happened? Why did two women, so very different from each other in personality and outlook, suspect her of being attracted to Mr. Christopher? What had she done, how had she become so transparent, that others felt they might read her like a book?

Sitting there in the quiet darkness--the center of Asheville was only a few blocks away, yet even in summertime the neighborhood with its trees and wide yards built a wall of silence against the noise of the city--Amanda sorted through her behavior these last few weeks. She saw how with the approach of each supper hour she was more attentive than the children to the time when their father would arrive home. She would watch the clock, and the sound of the truck coming up the driveway brought a jolt of pleasure. She would trail the children to the door, watching as they dashed across the porch and down the walk to greet their father, finding her own delight in the smile on Mr. Christopher's face as he hugged the children. After suppers she had taken to lingering in the kitchen, sweeping a clean floor, wiping down for a second time the sink and counters, checking again a grocery list that she knew by heart, all in the hopes that he would appear in the kitchen to fetch Teresa a glass of water or to pour himself a glass of wine.

She had fooled herself. She had told herself that she was being thorough by leaving the kitchen ready for a white-glove inspection, that her anticipation of Mr. Christopher's arrival was the natural consequence of his trust in her and her admiration for him. But now, with a sickening shame, she saw herself as Barb and Mary Celeste, and probably most of the other parents, must have seen her--a tanned, lithe stranger whose intentions regarding Nathan Christopher revealed themselves in every inch of her face. She imagined how she must have looked seated at the picnic table, watching Mr. Christopher with open affection. The old Amanda Bell would have hidden her feelings behind a rampart of cool reserve, had such feelings arisen; but the new Amanda, the one being chipped, shaped, and reborn, had lowered the drawbridge of her fortress and walked out into the sun, revealing her emotions to all who had eyes to see them.

This recognition of her possible attraction to Nathan led her at once to consider its dangers. If she allowed these feelings to grow, or if she continued displaying them as openly as she apparently had at the picnic, they might well bring an end to her days as a governess. She must not allow such a thing to happen. More than anything else in the world, she needed to be here in this home, this safe and private refuge, not back on the open road or on the street, or even worse, in some office where intrusive employees dug into the business of their co-workers.

While considering this possibility, Amanda took a hefty gulp of water. She choked and was still brushing beads of water from her dress when the screen door swung open. "I thought I heard you out here, Miss Bell. Mind if I join you?"

"No, sir." Still coughing as if she'd come up from a bad dive into a pool, she scooted over to give him some room.

He settled himself beside her on the step. "Nice night."

"Yes, sir."

"I'll need to cut the grass sometime this week." He wrapped his arms about his knees. "I thought you might be reading in your room."

"No, sir." By now her coughing had abated, and she leaned one shoulder against the stair railing, pushing herself as far away from him as possible.

"I've seen some of your books. Dickens, Austen, James. Heavy-duty stuff."

After her mediation these last few minutes, she found she could hardly speak to him, yet his mention of literature gave her some ground for maneuver. "Do you read much yourself?"

"Suspense novels is about as far as I go in the fiction department. Robert Crais, James Lee Burke, Stephen Hunter. I'm partial to history and biographies. Right now I'm reading Michael Korda's book on Lawrence of Arabia. Do you know much about him?"

"About Lawrence?"

"Yes."

"When I was in high school my father rented the movie." Vaguely, Amanda remembered Peter O'Toole dressed in white robes like a sheik, surrounded by camels and desert sands.

"That's when I got interested in him, too, when I watched the movie. I read his *Seven Pillars of Wisdom* and his *Letters,* and even tried to plow my way through *The Mint,* which was terrible. He was an amazing man, a genius according to Korda, and tough as nails." He had turned toward Amanda while he was speaking, but she didn't dare return the gesture. "Speaking of tough, how did today go for you?"

"It was fine."

"I saw you talking to Mary Celeste quite a bit."

"We were comparing notes on the children," Amanda said, which was partially true, "and she was kind enough to introduce me to some of the other parents. Have you known her for a long time?"

"Oh gosh," he said, and finally looked away from her and into the dark yard. "Let me see. Eight years, I guess. Anne got to know her from church, and then Tom and I did some work together. She's like the sister I never had. She's a hoot, isn't she?"

Amanda nodded. "She's awfully fond of you."

"She makes me laugh. I hope the two of you can become friends. And it went well with the others?"

He put the question casually, but she detected anxiety in his voice. Had someone commented to him about her? Or had he seen her speaking with Barb Brinkman when she had hauled out her daggers? "Everything was fine, sir."

He sighed, and leaned back with his elbows on the steps. "I'm glad. By the way, Mary Celeste thought you might like to bring the children to the summer get-togethers. You know you can always use the van."

"I'll be glad to take them."

For a few moments they were quiet together. Crickets and tree toads made their night music, and from the house next door came the sounds of a window opening and murmuring voices. Someone else might have felt compelled by that silence to make small talk, yet Mr. Christopher seemed perfectly comfortable. "Everything's all right with you, isn't it?" he said, suddenly. "I mean, you're happy here?"

"Oh, yes sir," she said, and then did risk a glance at him, anxious to read his face even in the shadows, wanting him to know how highly she valued her position in his home. "I love the children and taking care of things. I haven't done anything wrong, have I?"

He gave a low laugh. "Wrong? Heavens, no. I was just checking to make sure you were happy enough. It's not easy taking care of four children and a house every day. It must be a very different life for you. Were you happy in Atlanta?"

Not since the interview had he asked Amanda a single question about her past. Until now, both of them had kept the door shut on all topics except those which had to do with the immediate: the children, the housekeeping, shopping. The other Amanda would have answered his question assertively in the affirmative, but she was not the other Amanda. Her old swift surety was gone, and now, trapped in the open, she felt caught off-guard.

"You don't have to answer. I was just wondering--"

"No, it's all right." She paused. "I thought I was happy then. I'm much happier now."

"Here?" He sounded so surprised that she laughed. "You know what I mean," he went on. "I think my kids are great, but they're still just kids, and you're around them all day. You aren't making much money-- you're surely making far less money than you made in Atlanta--and you're stuck in the house most of the time. It can't be much of a challenge."

"Oh, I don't know. I've learned how to teach subtraction and fractions simultaneously while holding a three-year-old in my lap and listening to his sister recite 'The Purple Cow.'"

He laughed softly. "I hadn't thought of it that way. I guess you have picked up quite a few skills. Next you'll be teaching them advanced sand-castle building. Which brings me to my next question."

"Sir?"

"You know, you don't have to call me sir. As a matter of fact, I wondered if we shouldn't dispense with formalities and call each other by our first names."

"Sir?" Amanda said automatically. Fortunately, the shadows hid her embarrassment.

"I wonder if we need to continue being quite so formal."

"We agreed at the beginning that formal address was for the best." Even as she spoke, she recoiled from her words--stiff, priggish, prim. How naturally his name would trip from her tongue--Nathan, Nathan Christopher sounded like music to her--yet to allow that shift in address would signal the picnic moms that she and Mr. Nathan Christopher had crossed one more line of familiarity. Besides, if she had trouble now keeping her affection for him from her face and eyes, how could she ever block that same affection from her voice, from saying his name?

"That's true. Still--"

"The children are accustomed to Miss Bell. Departing from that arrangement might confuse them."

"I just want you to be comfortable here."

Hoping to close this particular subject, Amanda reminded him of his original point. "You were going to say something about sand castles?"

"Sand castles?" He frowned, thinking, then said: "Yes, yes, that's right. In another three weeks, right after the Fourth, we're going to the beach. Every year we rent a house down on Emerald Isle for a week. We've been going since Tim was five. I wondered if you'd like to come along with us, Miss Bell."

She had won the name game, only to be confronted by this new challenge. Unless she sorted out her feelings, a week at the beach with Mr. Christopher as her only adult companion struck Amanda as singularly dangerous. There would be no prying eyes away from Asheville, but there would be plenty of gossip. Besides, she was uncertain how the invitation might interfere with her own attempts to disguise her affection.

"Just you and me and the children, sir?"

"Oh, no. We always go with the Moores. The house is huge, and we split the expenses. You'd have your own room, of course. You could help with the children, but it's a different schedule-- no school lessons, no getting up at any particular hour. The house is right on the beach. It's a low-key vacation. We don't really do much except enjoy the ocean and take life easy."

"Shouldn't you talk with the Moores first?"

"I already did. Today at the picnic. They thought it was a great idea. Mary Celeste said she could use some help keeping the rest of us in line." He chuckled. "I think she'd enjoy some adult female company."

"I wouldn't want to be in the way."

"You'd be a great help. The children would love having you come along. And it wouldn't be much work, if that's what you're thinking. You'd have lots of time for the beach" When she hesitated, he added: "I'd really like you to come with us."

A moth fluttered at her face, and she brushed it away, trying to think what would be best for everyone.

"Please," he said. "We want you to come."

To refuse made the most sense. His pull on her was strong and would only grow stronger as they spent more time together. Here they were separated by his hours at work. But at the beach they--

She was too late. He thrust himself up from the steps. "Silence gives consent."

"I thought I had a right to remain silent."

"Only in a court of law," he said. "And you've made a joke, Miss Bell. I'm impressed." He laughed quietly. "We'll go over some of the details when we get closer to the date. I guess I'll say good-night."

"Good night, sir."

"Sleep well, Miss Bell."

His voice smiled when he said her name, and she didn't need to see those quick dark eyes to know that he was laughing not in mockery, but with something that resembled friendship.

Chapter Ten

Amanda had never believed in true love--not the heart-stopping, catch-in-the-throat, can't-live-without-you love of popular songs and romance movies. Like others who deny as real what they cannot see, taste, touch, smell or hear, Amanda regarded the senses as the gateway to the brain and thought, and distrusted what lay beyond those senses.

To realize that she might be falling in love with Nathan Christopher therefore came as an immense shock.

Over the next few days, as she sifted through the thoughts and emotions roused by the picnic, Amanda acknowledged first that she had fallen in love--perhaps with Mr. Christopher, but certainly with his children. From the beginning, they had given her emotional succor, had become a means of recapturing broken bits of herself. Over the past two months, she had become acutely aware of how important it was to be needed, to offer to others care and compassion. She had driven the children to the Y, prepared their snacks of cinnamon graham crackers and milk, performed that myriad of tasks involved in raising the young. She had commenced her service as a job, but the children repaid her efforts a thousand-fold by their affections, inspiring her to work even harder, to the point that late evenings often found her with a pen and paper drawing up a detailed schedule for the next day. Father Krumpler's wisdom in placing her in this situation became clearer to her. By serving the children she had saved herself.

Like the children, the Christopher home worked a sort of magic on her. By tending the gardens, by sweeping and dusting the rooms, by washing the dishes, Amanda grew familiar with the peculiarities of the old house--the stain on the carpet where Tim had long ago spilled some tomato soup, the small sofa in the schoolroom which was a breeding ground for dust bunnies, the patch of grass in the yard where Teresa claimed "the fairies danced at night." This familiarity bred not contempt but love. The house enveloped her with its sweet wizardry of pleasures--the sprawling comforts of the sitting rooms, the squeaking of the back-porch screen door opening and closing, the feel of silverware and crockery that had known ten thousand meals. She felt safe here, so much so that one morning she woke and realized that for three nights running she had left the carving knife, the Cutco which she had once held in sleep like a lover, in its hiding place on the top shelf of her closet. She showered and dressed, then carried the knife into the kitchen, placed it in the cutlery drawer, and prepared breakfast.

But what of Nathan Christopher? Amanda could not pick a single moment when her affection for him, like some exotic flower, had first taken root. Examining her emotions in the days after the picnic, she counted dozens of small moments that might have drawn her to him: his evenings spent alone watching television or reading; his rumpled look in the morning when he came into the kitchen for coffee and the oatmeal she'd prepared for him (she had soon assumed the task of preparing his breakfast, since she made the children their breakfast as well); the patience in his voice when, bone-tired, he would read to the children before bedtime, or tell them stories of his boyhood, or answer their questions. But not then or afterwards could she put her finger on the moment in time when pity for him tipped into admiration, and then into desire.

Mr. Christopher himself gave no sign of sensing this affection, much less of returning it. He was always courteous, attentive, slightly formal.

He respected her privacy. With the exception of that Saturday evening when he had sat with her on the porch, he never sought to pry from her information about her past. As June melted into the heat of July, he did join her more frequently on the porch or in the back garden after putting the children to bed, but Amanda ascribed these appearances to a desire for some fresh air and greenery after a day's work. Sometimes they hardly exchanged a word on these warm evenings, yet their mutual silence was comforting and peaceful. When they did speak, she might think to tell him something about the day—a comment from one of the children, some small victory or disaster on their perambulations about town--or Mr. Christopher might share with her a particular difficulty he'd experienced at work, a customer who wanted to change the color of a house in the middle of the job, the trouble in finding good help.

Only once did he give Amanda cause to wonder whether he felt anything similar to the passion which she now kept under lock and key. It was late on a Saturday afternoon, the weekend before the Fourth, and she sat in the yard keeping a desultory eye on Teresa and Mikey while skimming Dodie Smith's *I Capture the Castle*, which she'd read before in her teens. Mr. Christopher was on a ladder, painting the eaves of the high corner of the house nearest the garden. He was wearing a baseball hat that advertised B.B. Barnes along with jeans and a paint-splotched blue shirt. At some point in years past Anne had installed a sandbox in one corner of the yard, and there Mikey and Teresa had played for the better part of an hour. Now Teresa had become bored. She first ran about the yard pretending to be an airplane while Mikey continued playing with his trucks, oblivious to her swooping dives above his head; she tried skipping rope; she rode her tricycle up and down the grass. Finally she darted across the lawn, her tiny legs moving like scissors, grabbed the base of the ladder, and shook it.

"Good Lord!" Mr. Christopher cried out. When Amanda looked up at him, he was gripping the ladder for dear life and glaring down in anger and astonishment at his daughter. "What are you doing?"

Teresa shook the ladder again. "Come and play."

"Stop that shaking! Don't ever shake a ladder! I—"

She shook the ladder again. "Come and play!"

"Did you not hear me? I said—"

Again she pushed and shoved against the ladder. "Daddy, I said—"

"Do you want me to come off this ladder, young lady?" he roared.

"Yes," Teresa said.

There was a long moment as Mr. Christopher regarded her, gape-mouthed. Then he lifted his head and looked at Amanda, who returned his stare with trepidation, fearing from the anger in his voice that he was about to explode. And he was—but not from rage. He gave a great burst of wild laughter, a laughter that proved so contagious that a split second later she was laughing with him, laughing so hard that within another moment she was dabbing her eyes and ducking her head for fear Teresa might think she was weeping.

Teresa herself still stood at the bottom of the ladder, mystified by their response to her, and undaunted in her request. "I want you to come down, Daddy."

He nodded to her. "I heard you, sweetie," he said, "and I'm coming down."

Carefully he brought down the brush and the bucket of paint with its clothes-hanger hook. He gave Amanda another look when he reached the base of the ladder, a glance lasting less than the space of a breath but which locked onto her eyes and connected deeply with her.

"Let me put the top on this paint can and wash out the brush," he said. Five minutes later, he had squirted water on the sandbox for Teresa and was helping her make a castle with a road around it for Mikey's cars.

———

Shortly after nine on Tuesday morning, when Amanda was still muddling about with all these feelings, the telephone rang. With Mikey and Teresa following her--Teresa, who was playing pirates that morning, carried a plastic sword and had decked Mikey out in a red bandana and fastened a large gold ring to his ear--she took the call in the kitchen. It was Father Krumpler who, once he had wished her well and inquired after what he called her "tribe of wild things," asked her to meet him at the Café Med in lieu of cooking supper at the rectory. "I'll be cooped up here all day with appointments and meetings. I need some air and elbow room. Supper's my treat, by the way."

"Are you sure? I don't mind cooking and washing dishes."

"Positively sure. I need some fresh air."

"You're more likely to get exhaust fumes at a sidewalk café."

"All right, then. I need some bright lights and strangers."

Before meeting Father Krumpler that evening, Amanda strolled down Haywood Street to Pritchard Park, where budding Bobby Fishchers took on all comers at the chess tables and street entertainers juggled balls or strummed guitars to earn their rent. Under a scraggly tree in the middle of the park a singer in a greasy red bandana plunked out some Bob Dylan numbers. On the edge of Wall Street, in front of the Flatiron Building, two young women were playing violins together, while on the opposite corner a woman dressed like a ballerina who had spray-painted herself silver stood absolutely motionless on a box, striking a new pose only when a spectator put money in the cookie tin at her feet. Beside her a young man in a Chicago Bears t-shirt rolled rubber balls across his shoulders, up and down his arms, and over his head.

The bars and restaurants of the streets were crowded with drinkers and diners, and the hazy air felt alive with the noise and movement of townspeople and tourists on the sidewalks. Amanda swung back around the square, past the Grove Arcade on Battery Park, past the cafes that spilled from the arcade onto the sidewalk in a messy profusion of chairs, tables, and patrons. Here outside the Café Med she found Father Krumpler sitting at a wrought-iron table, a glass of wine at his elbow.

He spotted her from a distance, rose, and waved. As she approached, several college-aged men, clearly from out of town, slowed as they passed, openly staring at her until they saw her hug a priest old enough to be her grandfather.

Father Krumpler, who had seen the young men leering, laughed. "My dear, you exude sex like a perfume."

"Why can't men ever learn that all women don't like being ogled?"

"Now there's a word I haven't heard in years." He pulled out a chair for her and then sat again himself.

"I'm the old-fashioned type. And I don't exude sex."

"I ordered wine for you," Father Krumpler said, pouring her a glass from a sweating half-carafe. "I also took the liberty of ordering supper for you. Lamb with roasted fennel. Delicious."

"You're even more old-fashioned than those boys, ordering for a woman without a word of consultation."

"I suppose I am." He breathed deeply, offered a smile to everyone within sight. "I can't tell you how good it feels to be out and about tonight. It was a long day--a long two days, for that matter--what with parish meetings and hospital visits and planning a funeral. Being anonymous is just the ticket for me tonight."

In his priest's collar and black shirt Father Krumpler was as anonymous as a movie star. The pedestrians passing their table kept pausing to look at him. One man, a sunburned barrel-chested fellow in an Izod shirt and baseball cap, drifted toward them as if to approach their table and speak with the priest, but then changed his mind and hurried down the sidewalk after his companions.

The waitress set the food before them, and after the blessing they ate. Father Krumpler's choice proved impeccable. The lamb and fennel on a bed of rice, accompanied by a medley of vegetables, were a delight, and Amanda was suddenly ravenous.

"Good?"

"Delicious."

"I've always been partial to lamb."

"I haven't eaten any in ages. In fact, I can't remember the last time I had it."

"So did you go to the picnic?"

"How did you know about the picnic?"

"It was in the church bulletin. I figured you might go."

"Well, you figured right."

She told him about the picnic while they ate, leaving out the encounter with Barb Brinkman.

"Agreeable, I take it?" Father Krumpler asked after they had tucked away a good portion of lamb and rice.

"Wonderful. It's also my first meal in weeks that I had no hand in cooking. Thank you so much."

"I thought you might enjoy getting out. Besides, it's a sort of celebration for me. Thursday is the anniversary of my ordination--forty-four years as a priest."

She raised her glass to him. "Congratulations." He returned her salute by clicking his glass against hers. A middle-aged lady at the next table threw them a quizzical look, and Amanda laughed aloud. "Were you a terror with the women forty years ago?" she asked, feeling light-hearted as a child. "Did you exude sex like a perfume?"

As he laughed along with her, she saw him as he must have appeared in his late twenties, freshly ordained, a handsome young priest--he was handsome still--surrounded by flocks of women, young and old, drawn to tempt and touch the untouchable. "There were women," he confessed, "and they often embarrassed me. I was too young to know how to handle them. I was not the suave, sophisticated specimen you see before you today."

She laughed again, and then surprised herself by breaking into tears. As she dabbed at her cheeks with her napkin, Father Krumpler watched her with his kind, discerning eyes. "Sorry," she said, blotting her cheeks. The woman who had been watching them stared gape-mouthed, too intrigued to look away, and her interest only made Amanda want to laugh and cry all the harder. "Sorry, sorry," she said. "Ignore me."

"Tough day?"

She shook her head, and took a sip of the wine to stop this latest descent into what she had once regarded as female emotionalism. Vaguely, she remembered her encounter with the young woman long ago in the airport and her contempt for the girl's tears.

"No," she said at length. "It was a good day. It was you. I imagined you being chased by scads of women down through the years, and it was funny, but now I've become one of them. I've fallen in love with you, Old Owl."

For once one of her admissions took the priest off-guard. His smile ran away, and he looked at her gravely, appearing more like an owl than ever.

"Oh, for heaven's sakes, I don't mean that kind of love. I don't want to drag you off the altar and into bed. I meant I love you as a--"

But the word wouldn't come. How long had it been since she had used it? Her college days? High school?

"As a friend," he said.

"Yes. As a friend. You saved my life." *And you have loved me*, she wanted to add, but even her increased capacity for revelation wouldn't allow that open admission.

"Not me," he said. "There's someone else doing the work."

"Well, I can't see him. I see only you. And now look at me--my one and only true friend in the world is a priest pledged to celibacy who's forty years older than I."

"Friends come wrapped in all sorts of packages. Even small ones. You've made quite an impression on the children. I've seen how they look at you, and I hear them talking to Nathan after Sunday Mass. They adore you, you know. You've made an enormous difference in their lives. And think what they've done for you. They've touched your heart, I think, with their hugs and kisses."

———

It was true. All day long they touched her--Mikey tugging at her fingers, Teresa throwing her arms around her neck, Bridget laying her hand on her shoulder while they read a story together, even Tim, who had reached that age of boyhood when hugs and kisses seem unmanly, embracing her from time to time. These physical touches were like the healing waters of some saint's spring, slowly transforming her, restoring her to health.

Considering these gifts, Amanda nearly leaked another stream of salty water, but Father Krumpler's next topic brought an end to that temptation.

"And Nathan? How are you feeling toward him these days?"

His question, which she should have anticipated, tore her from her reverie of the children. He had trapped her, perhaps unwittingly--she could never tell when the Old Owl used his innocence as a pry-bar--and though Amanda remembered the promise she'd made to herself to conceal her growing enchantment with Nathan, this priest was the man who had spent two months helping her to rip down her castle walls stone by stone, who was teaching her to face herself and others. He was not easily deceived.

"Mr. Christopher's my employer," she said, taking care while she spoke to look at the tables around them rather than into Father Krumpler's face--the middle-aged woman with the gimlet eye had departed, replaced by two men absorbed in their own conversation--and to keep her voice and face scrubbed clean of emotion.

But she had hesitated, and Father Krumpler put his elbows on the table and leaned toward her. "You talk with him daily," he persisted. "Surely the two of you have built some sort of rapport."

"Mostly we talk about the children. About meals and shopping and the house."

"Bridget told me you were going to the beach with them in three weeks."

The waiter came to their table and began collecting the plates. "Will there be anything else? Some dessert?"

"Another half-carafe of wine, please."

When the waiter left, she smiled at the priest. "In vino veritas?"

"In amicitia veritas. Do me a favor. Walk twenty-five paces down the sidewalk and then come back again."

"What's that?"

"Walk down the sidewalk--go to that lamppost--and then come back again."

"Why?"

"Just humor an old man."

Feeling foolish, Amanda pushed back her chair, walked down the sidewalk, passing two other cafes, touched the lamppost with her fingertips, and returned to their table.

"Happy?"

Father Krumpler looked smugly satisfied. "At the tables between us and that lamppost there are twenty-two men ranging in age, I would guess, from twenty to seventy. Eighteen of them noticed you. Fourteen of them followed you with their eyes. Three women did the same thing, but we'll leave them out of the equation."

"And your point is--"

"Nathan's a man. He's lonely. He has just spent a horrendous time dealing with death, remorse, and four motherless children. It seems impossible to me that a woman as beautiful as you doesn't make an impression."

"I don't feel beautiful."

"Those men think you are."

"I can't speak to that."

"All right." The waiter brought the wine, and Father Krumpler refilled their glasses. "All right. But you can speak for yourself. How are you feeling about him these days?"

Again she tried ducking behind a façade. "He's kind to me. He's generous. I never feel like a servant."

"You know what I'm asking."

The Old Owl wanted truth, yet the implications terrified her. Suppose she confessed to him that she had become smitten with Mr. Christopher, that she was falling in love, whatever that benighted phrase meant in the modern lexicon. What then? She and Nathan were living under the same roof, sharing meals, spending hours every evening and every weekend in each other's company. What would happen if she revealed her infatuation with her employer, the fact that he hovered all the time in the back of her mind, that she was already counting the minutes until her return to the house, wondering whether he would have the children in bed, whether he might be waiting to talk with her? Given this state of mind, wouldn't Father Krumpler tender the most obvious advice, that she must leave the household to avoid stirring up scandal? Or did he already suspect her affection? Had someone from the picnic, Barb Brinkman being the most likely candidate, spoken to him about her?

Despite these fears, she couldn't lie to him. This realization astonished her. If she lied to him, if she evaded his questions, then they were back where they had started in April, with portcullis and crenellated ramparts, with her soul hidden away in the castle keep. Only this time the separation would be even worse, for two months ago he had been a stranger rather than a friend.

"I have become attracted to him," she said, feeling as if her whispered declaration had thumped down on the table between them like a load of bricks.

"I thought as much. Was it so difficult saying that?"

"Yes, it was. It was difficult."

"What do you mean by attracted?"

"I think I may be in love with him. I think I'm falling in love with him. And I don't even know what that means, much less what to do about it."

He had a bag of tricks, this old owl, with which she had become all too familiar during their other meetings. One of these involved sitting back and staring at her with the inscrutability of a Buddha until she was forced to speak.

He sat back and stared.

"I know what you're doing."

No response.

"If you hadn't become a priest, you'd have made a fine interrogator for the CIA."

He grunted, smiling, but offered no response.

"You asked, and I've told you the truth. He's kind to me, and patient, and I love to hear him say my name. He's a wonderful father--you can't fake that--and he's intelligent and thoughtful. He's quiet, too, like me."

She paused, but he wouldn't take the bait.

"I know it's a cliché--the governess falling for the master of the house, the nanny and the widower. I've read a hundred novels with the exact same plot. All right, then-- I'm a walking cliché. I don't give a damn."

Not even a nibble.

"I know what you're thinking. You'll want me to go away now. You're afraid there will be some kind of scandal. I'll bet someone has already come to you and told you it's a scandal. Who was it? Mrs. Brinkman? I saw how some of them looked at me at the picnic. Like I was some sort of fortune-digging whore. Well, they're wrong. Nothing has happened. Mr. Christopher doesn't know anything."

———

The owl blinked. In the ensuing silence there came over Amanda one of those awful moments of heightened awareness she had some-times experienced during the previous winter when everything around her had taken on a sharp, painful reality: the warm odor of wine and the street, the gabble of conversations, the waiter standing by the doorway of the Café Med perspiring lightly in the evening heat, the lattice-work of the wrought-iron table beneath her fingertips. So acutely did she feel her surroundings that she might have been sitting in front of Mr. Henle again, mesmerized by a doom she was powerless to prevent. Only this time she had changed, she was a different person; this Amanda Bell was not the one who had sat glued to her chair beside a piano-playing sadist while having her life ripped apart. This Amanda Bell had acquired some small lesson in humility; she had learned to ask for mercy.

"Please don't tell me I have to leave them. Please. I promise you nothing will happen between us. I'll keep my distance. Mr. Christopher won't ever suspect anything of my feelings for him. You know how much this work means to me. You've said yourself how much I've changed, how much better I seem. I'll be good. There won't be any sort of scandal. I'll be good and keep my distance if you'll just--"

"Shhhh," the Old Owl spoke at last. "Pull yourself together, Amanda. No one's going to make you go away."

She stopped talking. Father Krumpler drew himself up and bent toward her across the table. "Dear girl, no one's going to make you go away," he repeated. "Drive that idea out of your head. Your leaving would devastate everyone--you, the children, and Nathan. What would be the good of that?"

"I just thought--"

"You thought what?" he asked when she broke off.

"Well, I know how the Church feels about sex, and I just thought--"

This time he interrupted her. "People who say they know what the Church feels about sex, even Catholics, almost never know what the Church teaches about sex."

"But I thought--"

He cut her off. "What's important right now isn't necessarily what you feel about Nathan, but whether you can acknowledge those feelings. You've spent your entire adult life suppressing your emotions--anger, love, grief, loneliness--shoving them into a corner so you could advance toward what you regarded as success. You carried these emotions with you, but it was like carrying a sack of bowling balls. Now look at yourself. The sack is much lighter. That you have suffered is plain to see. It's one reason all those heads swiveled round when you walked down the sidewalk just now--your past and your suffering are a part of your beauty. But you've gotten rid of a lot of weight. And you've added positive elements to your life. You've won the affections of the Christopher children, you seem capable of friendship judging what you've told me about Mary Celeste, you have work that is worthy and fulfilling. And now you've fallen in love--"

"I fail to see the good in that."

"There are dangers, of course, the chief being the scandal that you mentioned. Nathan moves in a tight community, and people are aware of those around them. By the way, Barb Brinkman wasn't the one who came to me."

"Who was?"

"Did I say anyone was?"

"You just implied it."

"Look," he said. "We're getting sidetracked. We were talking about your feelings for Nathan. Just the fact that you have them is good. He has all those qualities you mentioned. He's handsome and has money, and he--"

"I don't care about his money."

"Oh, for heaven's sakes. Will you be quiet and let me finish?"

Returning truculence for truculence, she said: "Go ahead and finish, but I'm not after his money."

"What I'm trying to say is that feeling affection for Nathan shouldn't surprise you. It certainly doesn't surprise me."

"Do you mean you knew I'd feel this way when you suggested working for him?"

"I didn't know anything at all. I did consider an attraction to him might be a possibility. But your feelings for him aren't unusual or strange. They're normal. That's the point I'm trying to make. Besides," he added casually, "as you've already said, a governess falling in love with the paterfamilias isn't unheard of. In those English novels you're so fond of, it's practically a tradition."

Exasperated as Amanda was by the priest's easy manner and his anticipation of her sentiments regarding Mr. Christopher--why on earth had he so strongly recommended her for the position if he foresaw such a development?--his reference to her old reading habits brought her up short. He was absolutely correct, of course; the Victorians had created a mystique around the governess and installed her in the romances and Gothic literature of the day. *Jane Eyre* highlighted the popular celebration of the governess as a possible mistress, a femme fatale, a woman trapped by her circumstances who lived in a twilight zone between her wealthy employers and the lower servants of the house. In *Vanity Fair*,

Rebecca Sharp played governess to the Crawly family, married a younger Crawly son, and literally became "crawly" herself, worming her way into society through lies and deceit. Even in *The French Lieutenant's Woman*, John Fowles had selected as his main female character the disgraced ex-governess Sarah Woodruff.

"Why did you do this?"

"Do what?"

"If you knew this would happen, why did you put me with him?"

"I didn't say I knew it. I simply considered it a possibility."

"But what do I do now? Can't you see how awful this could be? I can't snap my fingers and make my feelings go away. What am I supposed to do?"

"Why, you could do any number of things. You could run away. You could look for other work. You could confront Nathan with your feelings. But I think the best thing for you is to stay the course. Keep doing what you are doing--educating and taking care of the children, helping Nathan with the house and the children, and of course, cooking suppers for me."

"This isn't funny. What about me? Have you thought about what this could do to me?"

His eyes blinked at her behind his glasses. "Amanda," he said. "Amanda, Amanda, Amanda. Of course I thought of the consequences. Surely you know by now how I feel about you. But let's look back for just a moment at the last few months. You came to me for help in April, and you were so unlike the person I'd met on the flight to Atlanta that I didn't recognize you. You asked for help, and I did what I could do to help. From what you told me that first day--and I don't think either of us would change our opinion of your condition then--you were displaced. You weren't connected to your true self. The loss of your job, the utter destruction of your plans, and the rape were the catalysts to that displacement, but they weren't the causes. You had already removed yourself from most human contacts. Most harmfully to your own spiritual condition, you had removed yourself from the possibility of love.

"Now, I could have helped you find housing and gotten you a job at Wal-Mart or in some office as a secretary, but what might that accomplish? You would likely just fall back into the same rut as before. You would have recovered your old self and gone right back to where you were, with a few scars, of course, but without any real interior change. You'd be a half-person again, functioning yes, but like a machine that had been patched together. Only you aren't a machine. And sooner or later--and probably sooner--you'd break down again.

"So I suggested the Christophers. You needed to find some way to love and to be loved, which means you needed to discover someone outside yourself who required your help and attention. The Christophers were ideal for you--look at how far you've come since April, how much joy you've already experienced. Remember when you told me how you felt about your parents? How excluded from their lives you sometimes felt?"

"Yes."

They had spoken several times of her parents, of the wall the two of them had created between themselves and the rest of the world, including their daughter.

"You told me the affection of your parents for their friends and even for you always seemed somehow to have stopped short of real love. You said they put up a barrier between themselves and the rest of the world, and that you felt locked out. Some of that closeness felt by your parents was natural and good. Love and marriage are supposed to be that way, to an extent. Yet from what you've told me your mother and father took that good and twisted it into something different. They made themselves too exclusive. In some ways, they were just like what you had become before you landed in Asheville--they had built up a wall, possibly for protection, and without realizing it had cut themselves off from all others, including their own daughter."

"But I know they loved me. I just never felt included. Maybe I didn't let myself be included."

"Possibly. But it seems more likely, given that they were the adults and you were the child, that they set out the rules of the game. Remember when you told me you often felt you were the adult and they were children?"

"Yes."

"It's not supposed to be that way. Not when you're ten or eleven years old."

He held out his hand, palm up, and gestured toward the people around them.

"You and everyone else your age are the products of a confused time, a time when sex has become paramount and when love has become, for so many people, a terrifying word. It's strange, isn't it? A hundred years ago, people were more protective of the flesh and rarely discussed sex, but somehow they gave their hearts away more freely. Now the coin has flipped, and in many ways you and your generation are the product of that change. In terms of love--real love--our present age has brutalized both men and women. You're taught how to be independent but not how to love, how to have sex in every possible combination and style, but not how to give or receive real love. Love and commitment terrify many young people nowadays. We live in a cold hard world where it's easy to indulge in sexual pleasure and very difficult to find love."

"I never indulged in sex."

"True. But in a way you abstained because you didn't recognize the possibility of love. You saw the dishonesty behind sex these days--that physical satisfaction alone can bring you happiness, fulfillment, joy--and you took what you thought was appropriate action, but turning away from sex caused you to turn away from love, from friendship, from human tenderness. You locked yourself away from the gifts of friendship and love." He cleared his throat, took a drink of wine, and followed it with a chaser of water. "And now you've fallen in love with Nathan and you're terrified of the possible outcome. That's natural. We're meant to feel hesitation and even fear in the face of love--especially the sort of love you're experiencing. The uncertainty terrifies you, the way it terrifies most people. You're in the middle of a story and you can't predict the outcome. There are too many variables, too many possible endings. But that fear is a part of the story. It's why so many young people these days avoid love--or at least try and avoid love. It scares the hell out of them and they're afraid of being hurt. But you can't live as a fully human person and not risk being hurt."

Not everything he was saying was clear to Amanda. She would need to carry his observations back to her room and turn them over in her mind for quite a while to determine whether she understood him or even agreed with him. "All right," she said. "But what about now? How do I deal right now with Mr. Christopher and my feelings?"

"There's no quick and easy formula. You'll have to feel your way. Call it on the job training, if you like." His voice grew warmer and less clinical. "Amanda, you have this enormous ability to commit to work and to a cause. You proved that at Saxon and Henle. You've proven it helping out the Christophers. Right now I would suggest you take your feelings for Mr. Nathan and push them in another direction."

"I have no idea what you mean."

"You'll have to sublimate those feelings, channel them into some other aspect of your work and away from Nathan."

She was puzzled by his words. "Isn't that what I did before? Lock up my feelings? Try to protect myself?"

"No. Back then you put your feelings in a cage. You not only hid them from others, but more importantly--and it was a the major cause for your destruction, your way of reacting to your dismissal and your rape--you hid them from yourself. You wouldn't acknowledge them or claim them as your own. You kept your emotions locked away and didn't even know you were doing it. This time you're a different person. This time you can sublimate your feelings. Instead of locking away your affections, you can consciously grant them recognition while at the same time steering them in a different direction.".

"That doesn't make any sense to me. How do you steer feelings?"

"You've already taken the first step by acknowledging your love for Nathan. We'll leave aside the exact nature of that love for now. What's important is that you've shared those feelings with me and recognize them in yourself. You've allowed them to breathe, to be born. Now you have some choices to make. You could, for example, tell Nathan what you've told me."

That option horrified her. "Not a chance. No, I--"

He held up a hand. "I know you don't want to do that. You're afraid of risking your position, and you're also afraid, like everyone else who's ever fallen in love, of rejection. But you don't need to tell Nathan with words. Your hesitation in that regard is healthy. You're not ready to tell him anything. You need to wait a good while yet to see whether your affection is genuine. But you do have to find a place for the emotions stirring inside you. You know how you've handled this in the past, how you've taken those feelings, without even recognizing it, and tucked them away. You smothered them with work, with your ideas of advancement, with what you regarded as a necessity for your job as a manager.

"But there's another approach. You can take your feelings for Nathan, which this time you have recognized and openly acknowledged, and you can turn them toward a different objective. In this case, that objective might be the children or even Nathan. You might, for example, begin to think of yourself as a servant--not a nanny, not a governess, but a true servant of love, a human being engaged in the deeper service of love. To give of yourself as in fact you are already giving, to know you are serving something greater than yourself that is worthy of your love: this is the beginning of the sublime."

His ideas were like some of the legal documents that used to come across Amanda's desk at work. She caught their gist, but now must do some serious burrowing to ferret out and understand the details.

Father Krumpler must have understood her confusion, for he shrugged and gave a rueful smile. "Too much too fast too soon."

"No, no, it's not you. I just need time to absorb what you've said. But can't you give me some practical advice? What do I do tomorrow morning when I serve everyone breakfast? How do I face Nathan?"

"You can be yourself. You continue to do whatever it is you're doing, but always with love. Acknowledge openly within yourself all that you're feeling--your affection for the children, your affection for Nathan--but put those emotions into your actions. Offer your service out of love. When you put breakfast on the table tomorrow morning, do so knowing you are serving someone else and not yourself. You aren't making breakfast to impress Nathan; you're making it to bring order to the day and health to Nathan and his children. When you talk with Nathan in the evenings, don't talk with the idea of enhancing yourself in his eyes, or of seducing him, but with the goal of listening to him and sharing with him in order to make him feel better, to help him heal and grow stronger himself."

"I'll need to think about all this," she said. "I don't think I understand you at all."

"You will."

Twilight had colored the evening blue, had softened the lineaments of the buildings and muted the voices of the other diners. They sat in silence for a while, and then Amanda had a thought. She leaned forward, smiling mischievously. "Do you know," she said, "we're just gotten through a long conversation without your once having mentioned him."

"Who?"

"Your boss. God."

Father Krumpler returned her smile. "Good heavens, child, where have you been? We haven't talked of anything else for the last half hour."

Chapter Eleven

During her long and vinous session with Father Krumpler Amanda gained a vague awareness of what he was asking of her, a request which later became clearer when she reviewed their conversation while lying in bed awaiting sleep. He was instructing her to put aside her own desires and fears in favor of the children and Mr. Christopher, to look to their needs rather than worry over her own, to pour any romantic thoughts of Mr. Christopher into her duty toward him. Father Krumpler wasn't asking her to alter her service to the Christophers--her performance to that point would have scored high marks in anyone's eyes--but to draw more deeply from the well-springs of that service.

His advice seemed simple enough--to act with love in all she did, to fuse her attraction to Mr. Christopher to her daily duties--yet the practical execution of that advice proved difficult. The realities of her work as a governess--the squabble between Teresa and Bridget over a plastic tea set on Wednesday, the chicken and rice casserole burned in the oven on Thursday, the search for a missing shoe for Mikey on Friday just minutes before leaving for Mass, and a hundred other rough-and-tumble daily details--seemed comically far from the priest's idealism. His "service of love" brought to mind pictures of missionaries in Africa, teachers in a ghetto, Mother Teresa; Amanda served by mopping up Mikey's spilled milk or forcing Teresa to brush her teeth in the mornings.

Nor did this service of love quell her passions for Mr. Christopher. His arrival home from work still quickened her breath. A conversation left her wanting more of him. When he read stories to the children or talked with them before bed, she would linger nearby just to hear his voice. When she saw him pained by his grief, she wanted to touch him, to hold him and offer comfort. She fantasized about becoming a real part of his life, sharing the place in his heart now held by Anne.

Here was one factor in the equation of governess and master overlooked by Father Krumpler: the master's deceased or missing beloved wife. Unlike Jane Eyre's Mr. Rochester, a tormented man who had hidden his mad wife in the attic, Nathan Christopher had by all accounts cherished his wife. Even from the grave, she reigned over the hearts of her husband, children, and friends, a saint, as Mary Celeste had called her, who exercised a suzerainty with which Amanda could never compete. Death often burnishes the reputation of the deceased in the eyes of those left behind, polishing away defects, smoothing the creases of deformity, yet Amanda suspected that Anne had been the real thing, a woman who with extraordinary force had loved her god, her children, her husband, her family and friends.

Oddly enough, Anne's spirit of love touched Amanda as well. In the days following her conversation with Father Krumpler at the Café Med, when she was so awkwardly attempting to follow his advice, to sublimate passion with the astringent practices of fealty and service, Anne came often to Amanda's thoughts. Anne had once handled the plates which Amanda washed after supper; she had opened these same books which Amanda read to the children; she had sat in this same room in which Amanda sat talking to Mr. Christopher in the evenings. As she made her way through each new day, Amanda sensed the other woman's presence, watchful, approving even her frequent mistakes and missteps. Anne Christopher was too sweet, too wise a woman to make a vindictive ghost, too kind and gentle-hearted in Amanda's own mind to wish her anything but success. There was little sense of rivalry: Amanda recognized that to vie openly with this spirit for the love of her children and

Mr. Christopher would be fatal. Such a competition would be lost from the start: the children belonged to their mother: she herself had no friends, she believed in no god. From any such rivalry she would only emerge second-best.

One change which she did note in herself was the manner in which her days began and ended. For years Amanda had wakened with plans buzzing in her brain like a general on the day of battle, reminding herself to address a certain memo, to speak with a certain employee, to arrange a more efficient transfer of information between her legal staff and the accounting branch. During those same years she had fallen into sleep toting up the defeats and victories of the day while looking ahead at the terrain and battle lines of the coming dawn. She was a plotter of maps and graphs, a tactician drawing up a Maginot Line here, a run through the Lowlands there, and her bed was her central headquarters, her command post of dreams.

Since her talk with Father Krumpler, this habit, an examination of self and circumstances, had returned, but with a major difference. Whereas previously those few minutes each evening and each morning had gone into practical planning, she now lay on her cool sheets and gave herself over to contemplation and wonder. Frequently she marveled at her present life, grateful for her circumstances and for the good fortune which had brought her into this home. With this sensation of gratitude she felt a concomitant debt, but to whom or to what she might make payment on this debt was unclear. During these few minutes of morning and evening meditation Amanda also thought often of Anne, contemplating how the ghost might have endeavored to meet certain challenges and finding solace in the fact that Anne, too, must have lain abed just as she did, wondering how she might best meet the needs of her loved ones.

In addition to her blundering attempts to carry out what Father Krumpler had asked of her, two particular circumstances impeded Amanda's attempts at a service of love. The first had to do with Mr. Christopher. In the days leading up to their coastal excursion, he took more of an interest in Amanda than he had previously displayed. This interest was not in any way some sort of mucky flirtation, but constituted instead a heightened involvement in her life in the house. In the evenings, he carried dishes to the kitchen, swept the floor while she washed up, and asked whether he might help in any other way. Later, after tucking the children into bed, rather than sitting in the living room with his beer or wine, books, and television, he would seek her out, and finding her in the kitchen or on the porch outside, would discuss her plans with the children for the next day, their summer reading, the shopping.

Never at any time did he attempt any deeper intimacy. He addressed her always as Miss Bell and treated her with the greatest deference, clearly interested in what she had to say and in doing what he could to enhance the lives of his children while at the same time seeing to Amanda's happiness. It was as if they had both received the same advice from Father Krumpler, as if Mr. Christopher had gotten the same marching orders to serve more profoundly others outside of himself. Often he seemed as awkward around her as Amanda herself felt around him. He took more care, she thought, with his words, and almost consciously held himself a little more aloof than he had in the last two weeks.

Of course, his heightened concern for her work with the children, the chores about the house, and her well-being discomforted her efforts to guide her affection away from him. His propinquity became even more of an exquisite form of torture, in which each tiny gesture became laden with an import far beyond its outward sign. One evening, when he handed her a plate from the table for washing, his fingers brushed against hers, and that brief, simple touch affected Amanda more deeply than any kiss that had ever touched her lips. Whenever he looked directly into her eyes during some conversation about the children, she gathered a thousand implications from his glance, and would blush and stammer like some seventh-grader bumping into her secret valentine in a crowded school hallway.

——•——

The other ambush came from a different direction entirely. It was the Monday afternoon before the Fourth, and the children and Amanda were in the back yard. She had finished weeding the flower beds--she had dressed for outdoor work in shorts, sandals, and white t-shirt, but was nonetheless perspiring in the heat, her face damp and dirty--and had just begun clipping some roses for the supper table when Mikey suddenly let out a bloodcurdling screech. Amanda jumped up from the bed of roses near the porch, and saw Mikey and Teresa howling with fright and tearing across the yard toward her. Dark spots whirled round them in the sunlit air. Dropping her garden shears, she sprinted across the sidewalk and lawn, grabbed them both up by the waist, changed direction, and ran to the porch. A lone yellow jacket made a dive at her head, but she dodged again and ran up the steps onto the porch.

Teresa was sobbing and stuttering as she told Amanda what had happened. "A h-h-hole by the tree," she said. "We f-f-f-found a hole by the tree and poked it with a s-s-stick."

She was holding out her hand to show Amanda an angry red welt. Then Mikey screamed again and grabbed his thigh, and she tore his clothes from him, swatting away a bee from his waist. She stripped him naked, throwing his clothes to the side of the porch, and then pulled away at Teresa's shorts and blouse, yanking off her clothes so violently that the girl momentarily forgot her stings and gazed at Amanda in wonder and fear.

"Into the house," she said, snatching up Mikey and grabbing Teresa by the hand. "Into the kitchen," she directed again, and called out over her shoulder to Tim, who had come running down the stairs: "Are they allergic to bee stings?"

"I don't know."

"Call your father on the phone and then bring it to me." Holding Mikey against her side with one hand, she used her free hand to shake out a dish towel onto the counter, sat him on it, lifted Teresa, and placed her beside her brother. Teresa was crying in spasmodic gasps, but had recovered enough to pat her brother on his shoulder. Bridget hovered just inside the door. "Run upstairs and bring me some clothes for them," Amanda commanded her. In addition to the sting on his thigh, Mikey had two welts--one on his hand, the other just above his right knee--and Amanda was trying to remember what medication bee stings warranted when Tim brought back the phone. "He says Teresa's not allergic--he doesn't think any of us are--but Mikey's never been stung before."

"Help me hold them," Amanda said, taking the phone and shifting to one side so that Tim could stand in front of Teresa. "Mr. Christopher," she said, and realized only then how badly she was panting and how panicked she sounded, "we were out back and they found a hole with yellow jackets. Teresa was stung once, and I've counted three stings on Mikey, and I didn't know--I can't remember--what to put on the stings or if the children were allergic. I was gardening and they were just playing and then Mikey started screaming--"

"It's all right." His voice came to her calm and strong. In the background she could hear other voices and wondered dazedly if he was in some sort of meeting. "I don't think anyone's allergic. Above the medicine cabinet in my bathroom is a first aid box. Do you remember when you started work? I showed it to you then."

"Yes, sir," she answered, though at that moment she could scarcely remember her own name.

"You'll find some hydrocortisone cream there. Dab some of that on the stings." He said something over his shoulder to the others in the room, then was back with her. "Keep an eye on them for the next few minutes. Calm them down. Give them something cold to drink. If you see abnormal swelling, call me right away and I'll come home."

"I'm so sorry. I was out in the yard with them. I--"

"It's nobody's fault. Look--call me in fifteen minutes and let me know how they're doing."

"Yes sir."

When Amanda hung up the phone, Mikey was still sobbing as if he couldn't catch his breath, and she very nearly began crying with him, wanting to take away his pain, wishing that the bees had instead attacked her. "Shhh," she said, dabbing on the cream. "Shhhh. It's going to be all right."

Mikey's sobs settled into an out-of-breath gulping, and she rubbed his tiny back and shoulders, thinking with wonder how frail he was, how small. At her direction, Tim brought her a wet washcloth from the bathroom, and she cleaned his face and then Teresa's, sponging away the sweat and tears.

She had just finished this task and had sent Tim to soak the cloth in the sink again when the doorbell rang.

No one rang the bell during the weekdays except the UPS man. Amanda nearly ignored the caller, but then remembered that Mr. Christopher had asked her to keep an eye out for some building plans being delivered to the house. She pulled Teresa from her perch on the sink board, settled her on the floor, asked Bridget to wipe her sister's face with the cool cloth and to help her dress, then carried Mikey to the front door, with Tim following behind them.

Mr. Christopher had commanded her never to open the door without first looking out the peephole. The buzzer rang again just as Amanda reached the door; "One moment," she cried, and shifting Mikey on her hip--he had buried his face in her shoulder--she put her eye to the tiny hole, squinted, and saw Barb Brinkman.

Reluctantly she reversed the deadbolt and opened the door.

"Miss Bell," Barb Brinkman drawled, moving forward so quickly that Amanda had no choice but to step backwards and admit her to the foyer. By the time she had closed and locked the door behind her, Barb had swept past her and down the hallway, leaving a trail of perfume and calling over her shoulder, "I'll just put these in the kitchen."

Barb, Amanda realized, possessed a rare beauty--dark eyes, dark hair, the build and tan of a tennis player--and on this particular afternoon she looked especially striking. The pink blouse she wore softened the severity of her mouth, and the khaki shorts revealed long shapely legs that most women would envy. She glanced at the children as she entered the kitchen, put the aluminum foil package she was carrying on the table, paused for a long slow gaze at the fixtures and floor as if inspecting for dust, and then let her eyes settle on Amanda as if she had found a source of contamination.

Making Amanda feel small that afternoon was an easy task. Barb looked as if she'd stepped from the pages of *Glamour*, while she, holding a teary, naked three-year-old, had dirt on her hands and face from gardening, stains on her shirt, and sweat running down the back of her neck. Barb put one hand on her hip and gave her a cool smile. "Are you opening some sort of New Age commune?"

"Pardon me?"

"No clothes," she said, nodding to Mikey and then toward Teresa, who sat slumped forlorn and half-dressed on the floor, with Bridget working to pull up her shorts.

"They were stung by yellow jackets."

"You have to watch out for those." She made no move to examine the stings, but did ask Teresa, "You all right, honey?" After she nodded, Barb said to Bridget: "Are those her clothes?" When Bridget nodded, Barb said: "Why don't you and Tim take your sister into the living room and help her get dressed? We'll bring everyone something cool to drink."

———

After they left, Barb examined Mikey's stings. He seemed sleepy, and Amanda wondered aloud if that was a sign of an allergic reaction.

"No," Barb said. "He's just worn out by everything that's happened to him. Debbie has bee allergies. She swells up and has trouble breathing. I have to carry medicine in my purse for her. Here--let me help you get some underwear on him."

She pulled his feet one at a time through the openings, then scooted the underwear over his sting without touching it. Amanda thanked her for this small kindness, wondering whether she had misjudged Barb until the older woman stepped away and looked her in the eyes. Her smile was condescending, her eyes dark pools of disdain and malice. "So tell me," she said, "which is more difficult: watching children all day or managing a law office in Atlanta?"

Her soft words paralyzed Amanda. "How did you know I worked in Atlanta?"

"I was curious and looked you up online. I found your address and your workplace. Saxon and Henle looks like a prestigious firm. What happened? Why did you quit to come here?"

"I--I lost my job."

"To some guy named Joseph Grenier, I see."

Surely she had heard Barb wrong. Not Joseph. "Pardon me?"

"Some man named Joseph Grenier has replaced you. You're a University of Virginia graduate, class of 2004. You're also the subject of a gay man named Justin Hobbes on his blog. He has a site where gay men discuss gardening and night clubs. He posted three messages for you there. In the first he asks where you've gone. In the second he writes that he has stored your furniture and that Nutmeg--I assume from what he said that Nutmeg is his name for your landlady--has rented out your apartment. In the third, he asks you to please let him know where you are."

Despite her sneer, Barb's information about Justin touched Amanda deeply. Never had it occurred to her that her neighbor would have cared enough about her to leave such messages.

"--- seems quite the queen. I wonder what other sorts of friends you had down there in Atlanta."

A stronger person might have told Barb Brinkman to go to hell and to get out of the house. Yet her venom had done its work, and she was already casting her threads about Amanda, wrapping her so tightly that she could hardly think. "Why would you look me up online?"

"Investigate you, you mean?" Barb laughed with derision. "Because I have eyes. I can see how Nathan feels about you, but I'm willing to bet he doesn't know a thing about your past. I'm willing to bet you haven't told him about friends like Miss Nancy-Pansy." Barb took a step closer, and Amanda leaned backwards into the counter. "You're one of Father Krumpler's little projects, aren't you? One of those down-on-their luck people he's always taking in, like stray cats? Only this time you're a cat who can hurt someone. You're after Nathan--he's even invited you to the beach, hasn't he?--but I'm telling you right now, you're not going to get him. He doesn't belong to you."

She left off, clearly implying to whom Mr. Christopher belonged, and then reached past Amanda's head, opened the cabinet, and pulled out a small plate. She unwrapped the foil package which she had brought, selected four chocolate chip cookies, and arranged them on the plate. From the refrigerator she took the plastic gallon of milk and poured four small glasses.

"Teresa doesn't like milk."

"Let her try it again. It's good for her."

Barb had attacked on so many fronts that Amanda scarcely knew what to say. Once upon a time she had possessed the power to outflank such an assailant, to use her own willpower and force of personality to knock such an opponent's words back down her throat, but now she was a disheveled babysitter brought to task by a foe who could wield mockery and censure with a masterly touch.

"Mr. Christopher asked me to go to the beach to help watch the children."

"Please. There's no need to play coy with me, Amanda. Nathan asked you to the beach because you've thrown yourself at him and caught his interest. Anyone with eyes can see what you're doing. Nathan was alone and hurting, and you saw an opening and moved on it. I know all about women like you. That woman at work, that nurse, did the same thing to our family. She set her sights on Jim, his money and his looks, and didn't give a damn about anything or anyone else. She moved on him and took what she wanted."

"You don't have the right. You don't have the right to say these things about me. You don't even know me."

"No right?" She laughed at Amanda. "It goes beyond right. I have an obligation. Anne was a dear, sweet woman who loved her children and husband. Do you really think you can replace Anne? Do you really think that you can live up to--"

Tim entered the kitchen holding the phone aloft. "It's Dad," he said. "He wanted to make sure everything was okay."

With Barb's intrusion, Amanda had forgotten her promise to call him back. She was reaching for the phone, an apology already forming on her lips, when Barb handed Tim the plate of cookies and took the phone from him. "You go enjoy those with your sisters," she said. "I'll be right in with some milk," and then she began speaking into the phone. "Hello, Nathan. Barb Brinkman here...Yes, everything's fine...everything's under control now...No, I was just dropping off some treats for you and the children. I thought you could use some homemade cookies...She does? Well, I'm delighted to hear that. I worry about you so much...Yes, she's right here...That's not necessary--everything really is under control...All right. Goodbye then."

With smoldering eyes she handed Amanda the phone.

"I take it everything's all right," Mr. Christopher said.

"Yes, sir. Teresa seems fine, and Mikey's asleep in my arms right now."

"Poor little guy--a nap might do him good. And you're all right, Miss Bell?"

Whether it was imagination or reality, she was uncertain, but some note in his voice seemed intent on more than the children and yellow jacket stings. "Yes, sir, everything's fine."

"I'm sorry about this," he said, and once again there was that note, as if he was speaking of more than the children.

"Yes, sir."

"Hang in there, Miss Bell."

"I will, sir."

"Call me if you need me."

"Yes, sir."

She clicked off the receiver and laid the phone on the counter.

"'Sir,'" Barb Brinkman sneered. "And 'Mr. Christopher.' Come on now--do you really think you're fooling anyone? I know what you're plotting, and so do a lot of other people. It's not right what you're doing, living here with him, tempting him. People are starting to talk. They're wondering what is going on. It's not right, living under the same roof--not with the children here. People are starting to wonder--"

"Stop there," Amanda said, adjusting her grip on Mikey and holding up her free hand as if calling a dog to heel. The old Amanda Bell was back, the woman who could handle any mutinous employee with a hard stare and an algid word. "It's one thing to attack me. But not Mr. Christopher."

"I'm not attacking Nathan. I'm saying that--"

"You're attacking him by implication. He's my employer, and I won't have it. If you really think he would do as you're suggesting, and if you're talking about it with other people, then you're no friend of his. Certainly and clearly you're no friend of mine, and I can accept that. But we're under his roof with his children, and I'm not going to stand here and listen to you slander him. He's my boss."

Barb laughed. "Boss? Right."

"You need to leave."

Barb stood glaring at her with both hands on her hips. Amanda turned her back to the woman and started toward the door and the hallway. "I'll show you out," she said over her shoulder. She didn't look back--one must never look back after giving an order; to do so casts an immediate doubt on one's authority--but she could feel Barb following her down the hall and past the living room to the door. Amanda opened the door and stepped aside.

"I'm going to drop by from time to time," Barb said, stopping just outside the door.

"I can't prevent you."

"I've left a note on those cookies. I expect it to get to Nathan."

"Good-bye, Mrs. Brinkman," Amanda said, and closed the door in her face.

———

The children were sitting on the sofa. Three of the cookies had vanished from the plate.

"We saved a cookie for Mikey," Bridget said.

"I'm thirsty," Teresa said.

Carefully, Amanda sat Mikey on the sofa. The circles around the stings, each about the size of a quarter, had gone from red to white. As she released him, his eyes opened, and he stared a moment at her before sitting up and looking around the room in a daze. "Look Mikey," Bridget said, and handed him the cookie. He nibbled at it. "Thirsty," he said.

"I'll be right back," Amanda said, and went to the kitchen and put two of the three milks poured by Barb Brinkman on a tray. She filled a glass with water for Teresa and poured the fourth milk into a sippy cup for Mikey. Her hands were shaking as she lifted the tray. Blinking with tears, she managed to return to the living room without spilling any milk and slid the tray onto the coffee table. "Here we go," she said, aiming for enthusiasm but emitting a choked half-cry of anguish. She blinked hard, trying to force back the tears.

Bridget slipped from her chair, and stood beside her, patting her knee. "It's okay, Miss Bell."

"Mrs. Brinkman's mean," Tim said, handing the glass of water to Theresa.

"You heard us?" Amanda asked, horrified.

"No," Tim said. "But she's mean, and I could tell when you came out of the kitchen that she'd hurt your feelings. Don't let her bother you. She was mean to Mom once too."

"She was?"

"It was at church, right after Katie came to live with us. She told Mom that she would never let a stranger into her house and that Katie wouldn't bring anything but trouble. She said she wouldn't be surprised if Katie didn't have some kind of disease."

"What did your mom say?"

"She didn't say anything to Mrs. Brinkman, but when we got home she told us that Mrs. Brinkman was a sad person and we should pray for her."

"Ah," Amanda said, though at that moment the only prayer she could summon up for Mrs. Brinkman would have involved a boatman named Charon and a river in Hades. "What should we do now?" she asked, and then thought to add: "What would your mom do right now?"

"She'd tell us to pray for Mrs. Brinkman," Bridget said.

"And about the yellow jackets," Teresa added.

Before Amanda could say anything else, the three of them closed their eyes. Mikey sat beside her, holding the cookie, chocolate smeared moistly on his lips. When he took another bite, they opened their eyes.

"And now?" Amanda asked.

"We could go back outside," Tim suggested.

"I don't want to go outside," Teresa said. "Not yet."

"We could eat another cookie," Bridget said with a smile. "And you could have one with us, Miss Bell."

Amanda smiled back at her, took the plate into the kitchen, and got five cookies. Before returning to the living room, she pulled the taped envelope from the top of the package and placed it with the rest of the mail on the dining room table.

Once the children had gone to bed, the house was always quiet, as if noise itself had gone to sleep with them. Despite the fact that there was no air-conditioning to block exterior sounds--for most summer evenings the cool mountain air and the overhead fans in the rooms provided comfortable temperatures--Cumberland Avenue with its broad yards and family homes was on most nights as peaceful as if they were living in the country. That evening Amanda was sitting on the side porch before going to bed, listening to the chorus of tree frogs when the screen door opened and Mr. Christopher came outside carrying two glasses of wine.

"I thought you might enjoy some refreshment."

She had half-stood when the door opened, wondering if he needed her for some task. She took the wine and sat again.

"Mind if I join you?"

"That would be nice." After her last conversation with Father Krumpler, and perceiving that Nathan disliked being called "sir," she had made an effort to discontinue that particular form of address.

"I poured a cup of gasoline down the yellow jacket hole at dusk. You won't have to worry about them again, though I doubt the children will play in that corner of the yard anytime soon."

"I'm awfully sorry for what happened."

"It wasn't your fault." He rocked a moment longer in the chair. "It's funny, but in nearly every accident involving the children either Anne or I were standing only a few feet away. Once Bridget came running through the house, fell into a doorway, and split her head open. And another time--you know those balls with a paddle attached to them by a rubber band?"

"Yes."

"Well, Tim's rubber ball got caught under a radiator and he pulled it as hard as he could and the ball flew back and hit him right in the eye. He spent the next two weeks looking like a prizefighter. I was sitting two feet away reading a book."

"I'm just glad they're all right."

Mr. Christopher laughed softly. "Given all the possibilities, it's always amazing to me that any of us make it to age ten." He stretched, then covered a yawn.

"A long day?"

"Yes, but I'm not complaining. I'm grateful for the work. We have this one client from Florida who's building a second home here, and she's driving all of us--the electricians, the plumber, my own crew--crazy with changes from the plans."

He talked a few minutes more, describing his difficult day and the caprice of the woman for whom he had worked, a multi-millionaire who had apparently married and divorced four husbands, each wealthier than his predecessor, and who now had, it seemed, more money than was good for her. He had worked for her several years before when she had bought a cottage in Weaverville, which she had repaired and then sold for a tidy profit just before the housing crash.

"She's a demanding old pirate, but she pays on time and likes my work."

Amanda smiled at him. "I'd say a lot of people like your work."

"What do you mean?"

"You're busy. You've got a waiting list of clients. You've got three crews out on the job all the time. Given the state of the economy these days, that's an achievement."

"I suppose it is at that." There was a warm surprise in his voice, as if he himself hadn't considered all these factors. And perhaps he hadn't: most people, Amanda was discovering, caught up in the day-to-day swirl of living, forgot to raise their heads and look up and down the river they were traveling.

"In fact," Amanda said, remembering how she had felt at the end of the day when her problems at the office had seemed daunting and wanting to encourage him, "you're doing great."

He gave out a laugh of warm gratitude. "It's good to come home to a cheerleader."

"I'm only telling you the truth."

"You know, I once read somewhere that when an ancient Roman general won a great battle Rome would give him a triumphal parade. He would ride through the streets of Rome in a chariot with the spoils of war--captives, gold, trophies--processing ahead of him. Anyway, a slave would stand beside him in the chariot the whole time, whispering in his ear "All glory is fleeting" and "You are nothing but dust.""

She looked at him, trying to decipher where he was going with this story.

"Well," he said, "I'm the opposite of that general. I'm torn up by self-doubt half the time, and the rest of the time I'm running ragged. But instead of someone countering my successes, I have you to boost me."

In Atlanta Amanda had done little ego-building, delivering the vinegar of harsh criticism to her staff without ever adding honey. More and more, practicing the advice given by Father Krumpler, she had become aware of how little appreciation the world offers those who slog through the muck and mire of daily living.

"So now I'm your slave?"

He seemed shocked, saying "No, no, Miss Bell," when she laughed to let him know she was teasing him. He shook his head, said, "You got me that time," and then after another pause said, "Bridget told me you cried today."

Coming so swiftly on their shared laughter, his remark caught her off-balance. "I'm sorry if it upset her."

"She was concerned about you. She thinks the world of you, you know."

"The yellow jackets upset me," she said, not wanting to tell the entire truth.

"Bridget seemed to think it had something to do with Barb Brinkman's visit."

"Her visit surprised me. I was right in the middle of trying to treat the stings. And then when she came I forgot to call you back."

"You don't need to apologize for that. I'm sure things were pretty chaotic at that point. Barb didn't say anything to hurt your feelings?"

To tell a lie to him was unconscionable, but to spill out the details of the whole episode would be to compromise too many emotions. While she was sorting out her words, trying to discover a way through this difficult passage, he sensed her quandary and reached out to help her. "Barb was a great help to me after Anne died. She brought over a meal once or twice a week, she helped care for the children, she offered many times to listen to me if I needed someone. In the note she left with the cookies, she repeated that offer. She wrote that she thought you might be overwhelmed sometimes, having so little experience with the children, and wanted to help you if she could."

He mused a moment longer, then added: "She also wondered if I wanted to go with her to visit the Biltmore House. Someone gave her two passes, and knowing how much I liked building and architecture, she thought I might be interested in spending the day with her. It might be nice. The last time I went to the Biltmore was ten years ago with Anne."

Though she had not visited the Biltmore House during her days in Asheville--the tickets cost at least fifty dollars--Amanda knew it to be a splendid place, billed as America's largest residence, and she could see why the architecture would appeal to Mr. Christopher. "It sounds like fun."

"I know Barb can be abrasive. Especially to some women. Anne didn't care for her--she never said anything, but I could tell--and Mary Celeste makes no bones about disliking her. She thinks Barb has ulterior motives for everything she does. What do you think of her?"

"Of Mary Celeste?" Amanda asked, knowing whom he meant but stalling for time.

"No. Of Barb."

She offered him the obvious. "She's very attractive."

He waited for her to say more.

"And she makes great cookies."

He laughed. "I take it, then, that you're in the Mary Celeste camp."

"I don't really know her at all."

"She's had a rough time of it. When Jim--that was her husband--left her for another woman three years ago, it caused quite a scandal in our little circle of home schooling Catholics. She does have female friends there, and they rallied around her, at least as far as I could tell. She's gotten past that. You have to admire her for that much, at least."

"Yes."

"I think she's ready for marriage again." He hesitated again. "It's good for children to have two parents. You know, people who get divorced or are widowed often say they have to be both mother and father to their children. I'm not sure I really buy that. I know that I can't take Anne's place, and I'm certain she couldn't take mine. A husband and wife should be complementary when it comes to the children. Without one, there's a sizable gap." He looked at Amanda. "She's asked me to go with her this Saturday. It's the Fourth of July weekend, probably the worst of the year in terms of crowds, but she says in the note she'd still like to do it now. I'm thinking about going. I wondered--if I went, would you be willing to watch the children? I'm afraid I'll be gone all day and into the evening."

"I'll be happy to watch the children."

"I can make it up to you after the beach. I could even ask Barb to watch the children one Monday so you could have a three day weekend."

"You don't need to make it up. I'm happy to watch the children."

"It doesn't seem fair. I--"

"No," Amanda said, cutting him off. His face jerked toward her in surprise. "No. I really don't mind. I don't need a make-up day."

The truth was that she didn't want that woman watching the children, she didn't want Barb Brinkman taking her place, and she knew that the children didn't want her watching them either. They saw through her, just as she did, and to leave them with Barb Brinkman seemed deliberately wicked.

"All right then," he said. "Thank you."

———

That Saturday Amanda was thankful for the distractions of the children. Had she endured that day alone, knowing that Mr. Christopher was with Barb Brinkman, she would doubtless have been eaten up by jealousy. This was another new emotion, this gnawing, powerless speculation crowding her head with a thousand scrambled scenarios, each a pinprick of pain, yet the children provided her some escape. The weather was lovely--not too hot, blue skies, a wind from the west--and they spent much of the day in the yard, where Teresa and Bridget built a fort under Tim's direction, the location of which, Amanda noticed, was on the opposite side of the yard from the nest of the deceased yellow jackets. For most of the time she weeded flower beds, clipped some of the grass growing onto the sidewalk, and read from the second volume of *Kristin Lavransdatter*. The book was hardly a distraction--Kristin herself seemed as mixed up in regard to her own love life as was Amanda--but it comforted her to read a book once held by Anne, a book, judging by its wear, she had apparently treasured.

Supper was light fare: crusty French bread, cheese, carrots and apples, watermelon for dessert. Later, after the children had bathed, Amanda made popcorn and they sat in the living room and watched *The Voyage of the Dawn Treader*. By nine o'clock both Mikey and Teresa were falling asleep on the sofa, and Tim and Bridget wore the heavy-lidded look of slumber on their own faces. After promising them they could finish the movie the next day with some fresh popcorn, Amanda picked up Teresa, Tim lifted Mikey, and they went upstairs, where she put them to bed. This was the first time she had performed this task alone--she had several times helped Mr. Christopher ready them for sleep--but they knew their routine, and it went like clockwork. After helping Mikey and Teresa brush their teeth, and after gathering in the girls' room for a decade of the rosary, which Tim led, she tucked Mikey into his bed, where he instantly rolled to one side and closed his eyes. Returning to the girls' room, she found Bridget had already gotten Teresa to bed and was beneath the sheets herself.

"It's a little warm in here. Would you like the fan?"

"Yes, please," Bridget said, and Amanda switched on the overhead fan. She gave Theresa a kiss on the forehead--she had already drifted close to sleep, but smiled at her--and then went to Bridget's bed to do the same. When Amanda bent to kiss her, the girl reached out beneath the sheets, put her arms around Amanda's shoulders, and hugged her. "I love you, Miss Bell."

Those simple words, words so stale and abused, yet so replete with meaning that they terrify modern men and women, nearly brought Amanda to tears. She could not recollect the last time someone had said those words to her. Certainly she had not heard them since the death of her parents. To have them spoken with such purity of heart, to know that Bridget meant them, brought from her such a rush of emotion that it was all she could do to murmur back, "I love you too, Bridget," and then tuck the sheets beneath her chin.

Bridget lay looking up at her with her large eyes, and Amanda could see in that eight-year-old face the woman Bridget would someday become: beautiful, caring, honest, quiet. "You're going to stay with us, aren't you, Miss Bell?"

"For as long as you need me."

"Always, then," Bridget said, and rolled to her side.

Chapter Twelve

That week at the beach was all Nathan had promised-- it was a vacation, Amanda's first real vacation in many years. The children largely entertained themselves. Possessed of Mary Celeste's habit of command, Erin Moore delighted in the creation of games and activities that kept the others busy for hours each day: building enormous sandcastles, devising inner-tube and float trains in the gentle surf, packing up a picnic for a hike up the beach, constructing an enormous fort of blankets, pillows, chairs, and suitcases in the room she shared with her two sisters.

The seven bedroom house sat on a part of Emerald Isle so narrow that they could easily see both the ocean and the sound from the decks of the second floor. It felt almost at times as if they were in a ship rather than a house, especially at night when they sat on the upper deck and the wind from the ocean blew hard and the planks rocked slightly beneath their feet. In the dining and living area on the second floor, where the Christophers and Amanda had their bedrooms, there were sofas and chairs scattered around the large room, a large case crammed with paperbacks and best-sellers left by previous occupants, a flat-screen television, and a cabinet filled with board games and tattered magazines. The children shared a room with two bunk beds. Nathan took the adjacent master bedroom, whose chief claim to that title came from an

JEFF MINICK

attached bath, while Amanda stayed on the other side of the living area in a room with a queen-sized iron bed painted white and spread with a cover decorated by blue and white sailboats. The Moores took up their berth on the first floor, where there was an extra bedroom and a sitting room joined to a small kitchen. They used this lower kitchen only as a place for storing baby bottles and extra groceries, for the two families ate all meals in common upstairs.

They arrived on a Saturday, and by Monday--on Sunday, both families had gone to Saint Mildred's in Swansboro for the morning mass--their days assumed a routine that lasted until their departure the following Saturday. Because of the children, the household rose early, ate a leisurely breakfast, and were down on the beach by nine, where they remained until lunchtime. Until three o'clock they stayed inside the house, letting the little ones nap and avoiding the scorching heat of the day. Another excursion to the beach brought them to the supper hour, before which Mary Celeste and Amanda would drink a glass of wine while Tom and Mr. Christopher consumed martinis. The evenings brought walks on the beach, games, conversations, and reading. Tom Moore and Mr. Christopher liked to watch the news, offering loud comments about the fallen state of the world, the debt crisis, and the fallout of the explosions in the Middle East. On several nights the older children were given the treat of watching movies which the families had brought from home. Once the toddlers were asleep, the four adults sat outside on the upper deck, watching the ocean tumble its waves to the shore, enjoying another drink, and conversing.

In the evenings both families also prayed the rosary together in the common room. Though Amanda did not join these prayers--both Erin and Tom Junior, pink and languorous from their first day on the beach, glanced at her when she took up a chair slightly apart from everyone else--the repetitions of the Our Fathers and Hail Marys were soothing even for a non-believer such as herself, the prayers as rhythmic and sonorous as the beat of the surf on the shore. All the children except the toddlers, Jack and Mikey, knew their beads, and the thin, piping voices

242

of Theresa and the two Moores closest to her age, David and Maggie, touched Amanda's heart with their devotion and innocence.

Food preparation also assumed a natural rhythm and division of labor. Tom Moore enjoyed making large breakfasts--omelets, waffles, sausage-and-egg pie--and Mr. Christopher put together sandwiches, chips, and fruit for lunch. Suppers fell to Mary Celeste and Amanda. Here Amanda served mainly to assist Mary Celeste, grilling out hamburgers, concocting a seafood platter, marinating shrimp and serving it up with risotto and a hearty salad.

After Mary Celeste and Amanda had finished cleaning the kitchen on Sunday evening--they had prepared a crab and broccoli quiche with loaves of French bread and watermelon for dessert--Mary Celeste gave the sink and counters a last wipe, and then ordered Mr. Christopher and Tom to watch the children. "Amanda and I have slaved at the stove," she said. "Time for a break. We'll be back in half an hour. Grab some sandals, Amanda, and let's make a break for it while the getting's good."

"A break?" Tom said. "What about us?"

Both men were sprawled on the chairs in the common area, watching the sports channel while the children read or played around them.

Mary Celeste snorted. "If you looked any more relaxed, I'd have to peel you out of those chairs with a spatula."

"No rest for the weary," Mr. Christopher said.

"Work, work, work," Tom added.

Mary Celeste was already marching Amanda to the door. "I'd like to avoid trips to the hospital this week, so please try to stay awake," she commanded them over her shoulder. "Come on, Amanda--time to make our get-away."

On reaching the end of the boardwalk, they kicked off their sandals and strolled along the edge of the surf on the hard brown sand, letting the water roll over their feet, drifting higher onto the beach whenever a larger wave threatened to wet them. A pair of gulls followed until it became obvious the two women had no food, and then flew out over the ocean with harsh cries. To the west the setting sun brought colors to the sky like a rose-colored palette.

"Red sky at night," Mary Celeste said. "According to the weather reports, we're in for a good week of sunshine." She was wearing cut-off jeans, a white t-shirt, and a crumpled fisherman's hat pulled low over her eyes. Despite liberal applications of tanning oil, the day on the beach had tinted her fair skin a reddish hue identical to the colors of the sky. With her lively brown eyes, her red hair, and her slender build--how, Amanda had wondered in amazement earlier that day when Mary Celeste appeared on the beach in a jaunty green two-piece, could she look so shapely after giving birth to five children?-- she was one of those women who was attractive whether wearing an evening dress or swim-suit. "Twenty minutes of freedom. I hope you didn't mind me dragging you along?"

"It feels great." The pull of the Atlantic, the warm water, and their slow, easy pace worked far greater wonders of relaxation than the spa Amanda used to visit in Atlanta, paying a hundred dollars a session for a hot tub and a quick massage.

"For two or three years, I'd come here with Tom and the children, and just when I'd begun to relax a little, it was time to go home. Now I say to myself as soon as I arrive, "You're on vacation," and it starts right then. Right from the first."

"I haven't vacationed at the beach since I was a girl."

"Where did you go instead?"

"I worked most of the time I was in college. And after that, when I took a week of vacation, I stayed at home and read and relaxed."

She didn't tell Mary Celeste she had stayed home because she had no one with whom to share a vacation. Mary Celeste sighed and then said: "That sounds wonderful. A whole week alone, doing whatever you wanted. Sleeping late, watching television, reading books. Not that I'm much of a reader. Nathan says you're a book-lover. What kind of books do you like?"

Briefly, Amanda told her about her love for the Victorians, for the English novel and poetry. "I've seen *Pride and Prejudice*," Mary Celeste said. "That shorter one--not the BBC version. Erin loved that movie. She's the reader in our family. Even Tom liked that one, though I think he liked looking at the actress who played Elizabeth." She laughed. "I don't have much time for reading, but even if I did, I'm afraid you'd find me reading best-sellers and love stories."

"This summer I've moved more toward the Americans. Right now I'm reading *O Pioneers!*" Two weeks earlier, she had gone to the Mr. K's used bookstore at the River Ridge Mall, where she had browsed for two hours, lost in the stacks, delighted as usual by the texture and odor of print and paper. She'd found a copy of Willa Cather's novels in the Library of America edition for only seven dollars, and had just begun the previous evening reading Cather's account of immigrant life on the frontier.

"I've never heard of that book," Mary Celeste said. "Not that it means much. I'm not what you would call well-read."

"What do you like to do?"

"I love cooking. Now that I think about it, I like reading cookbooks. It's funny, because I don't really enjoy eating that much. I don't have any particular desire to go to fancy restaurants or to eat French food. But I love trying new recipes. Some of them don't work--I've probably made lifelong Francophobes of my children from my cooking. And Tom, too, though he's a pretty good sport about it." She squinted at Amanda. "Let's see--what else? I like movies--we never go to the theater, that costs a fortune--but we have Netflix. I like crafts. Long ago I took some courses in jewelry making at Haywood Community College, and Erin and I have done some projects together. Mostly, though, I spend my days playing referee and teaching the tribe the basics of math and reading. Speaking of which--" She pulled her cell phone from her pocket and checked the time. "I suppose we should head back before the boys go into a major panic."

They walked in silence. The waves broke around their feet and the wind off the ocean stirred the sea oats on the dunes. Down the beach

Amanda could see the blue-and-green tarp which Tom and Mr. Christopher had set up as their headquarters on the sand. "They'll need to take that down tonight," Mary Celeste said. "In case the wind comes up."

"Yes."

"Rumor has it that Nathan went out last Saturday with Barb Roberts."

"Yes, he did. They went to the Biltmore for the day."

"How did that go?"

"I'm not sure."

"He didn't say anything to you?"

"Only that he enjoyed the day. He did say that he took pleasure in seeing Gustafino's tile work at the Biltmore House."

Raphael Gustafino, Mr. Christopher had explained to her, was the architect who had designed the Basilica. He was buried inside the wall at the front of the church opposite the Marian Chapel--Tim and Bridget had once taken great delight in swinging open the heavy metal door of the tomb and showing Amanda the Latin inscription on his tomb. Gustafino had come to Asheville at the behest of the Vanderbilts to help with the design of the house, and Nathan had enjoyed seeing the architect's signature use of tile at the house. To Barb Brinkman, however, he made no reference except to say that he had "enjoyed" himself.

"What time did he come home?"

"Before eleven, I think."

"Well, that's a good sign anyway." She veered to their left, walking into the water to her knees, sinking a little as the receding tide pulled the sand from beneath her feet. "I know Barb helped him after Anne died--we all did--but marriage with her would be a disaster. Barb is a manipulative, conniving woman, and when she doesn't like someone she's all knives and razor blades. She doesn't like me very much, and I hate to tell you this, but she doesn't like you much either."

"No, she doesn't," Amanda said, and then told her of Barb Brinkman's visit to the house, of what she had said and how her caustic insults had forced Amanda to ask her to leave.

"You did the right thing."

"I wish she could like me."

"She's talked about you with some of the other moms. Most of them don't pay any attention to her, but she has her little clique. You understand now, don't you, that she wants Nathan for herself and thinks that you're after him as well?"

They had slowed as they approached the house, and came to a stand-still by the edge of the water. Mary Celeste stood watching the lighted house, her hands on her hips, like a general getting ready to take command once again of the troops. She turned her head to look at Amanda and smiled mischievously, reminding Amanda of an Irish sprite she had once seen on a Saint Patrick's Day card. "So are you?"

"Am I what?"

"Are you interested in Nathan?"

"No," she said, so shocked by the other woman's impetuosity that her voice croaked out its answer. "No," she said again, more firmly.

She didn't like hiding her attraction to Mr. Christopher from Mary Celeste. All of her feelings for him pushed against one another within her, and she strongly felt the impulse to share them with Mary Celeste. Amanda had watched her these past twenty-four hours at the house, and knew her to be above all things both just and compassionate, as well as direct, but her own confusion prevented her from telling the truth. She lacked the words to convey the mess in which her emotions wallowed.

Mary Celeste's patience in awaiting some elaboration, however, forced her to say something more. "I work for Mr. Christopher," she said, "and I try to keep my personal feelings out of that work." She then tried to steer Mary Celeste back to the safer topic of Barb Brinkman. "But you're right about Mrs. Brinkman. She isn't the right person for Mr. Christopher. She doesn't like the children very much, and she thinks more of herself than she does of Mr. Christopher and what he needs."

Mary Celeste whooped, sending peals of laughter so far down the beach that the two men surf-fishing nearby raised their heads from their bait bucket and looked at them. "If you were in a beauty contest, they'd give you the reward for discretion," she said. "You sound just like Anne. Give her a sour apple, and she'd tell you how pretty it was."

Amanda blushed at her remark, not at the compliment but at the comparison.

"Come on," Mary Celeste said. "Time to descend again into chaos."

Together they walked to the plank walkway, retrieved their sandals, washed the sand from their feet beneath the spigot beside the outdoor shower, and went back into the air-conditioned house, where Tom and Nathan greeted them with unadulterated relief, though the children were playing quietly in the bedrooms below. As Amanda watched Mary Celeste for the remainder of that evening, readying her brood for bed, then sitting on the deck with a glass of wine, she realized that for the first time in her adult life she had the opportunity to make a true female friend. Already she admired Mary Celeste for her abilities as a wife and a mother, for her imperturbable humor, her sisterly rapport with Nathan. She sensed Mary Celeste enjoyed her company as well. She might become a woman in whom Amanda could confide without fear of belittlement or shunning, a confidante to whom she could tell the truth about anything and have her remain a steadfast friend.

That evening on the beach, however, when Mary Celeste asked about Mr. Christopher's return from his date with Barb Brinkman, Amanda hadn't told the whole truth about that Saturday evening. She hadn't told Mary Celeste what she had found on the bookshelf in the living room while Mr. Christopher and Barb Brinkman were across town dining at the Deerfield.

———————

After getting the children to bed that night, and still basking in Bridget's embrace, she had gone to the living room. There she had wandered around the room, looking at the photographs of the family, touching some of the books on their shelves, trying to discover how the room had felt when Anne had lived here, some clue to her personality beyond what she knew from the children and her friends. Without obsessing about order as Amanda once had, Anne had clearly valued harmony--the books on the shelves, though not alphabetized, were arranged by subject: history, biography, novels, poetry, and the large collection of religious literature, catechisms and prayer books, saints' lives and conversion stories. Before these volumes Amanda had paused on this particular evening, drawn by the slips of paper emanating from many of the books, markers of passages or sentences special to Anne. The notes written in her hand on these pieces of paper, and sometimes beside the text itself, were mundane observations for the most part--"How true!" "I'll need to think this over," and frequently, "?", but these jottings told Amanda that this collection of spiritual writings had figured centrally in Anne's life.

Sitting on the floor of that large, quiet room, she pulled out a marker-littered book, *Catholic Christianity* by Peter Kreeft. For a long time she examined the text of the book. Anne had heavily annotated the pages in a variety of inks and pencil, with some pages dog-eared and others marked by sticky notes on which she had inscribed various comments, mostly reminders to herself to remember what the author had written. According to the publisher's blurb, the book was a commentary on the *Catechism of the Catholic Church*, a fat green volume sitting on the same shelf.

Having decided to examine Kreeft's book further--she didn't think Mr. Christopher would mind--Amanda was rearranging the other books so that they might stand together again when her fingers touched a book which had gotten pushed behind its shelf-mates. Pulling it out to stand with the others, she found no ordinary book but a black leather volume with gilt-edged paper and a raised cross on its front. Opening the book to its first page, Amanda saw inscribed: "No more scraps of paper or schoolroom notebooks! Here's a journal worthy of your thoughts. With love on this Christmas of 2008, Nathan."

The writing beyond this note belonged to Anne. Amanda recognized her hand immediately, having seen it on the margins of books, on recipe cards, and on those scraps of paper Mr. Christopher had mentioned. Anne had kept a journal, with each entry carefully dated, running from the day after Christmas until the middle of March, the month of her murder. Amanda read the first page, which described the coming of Katie and her baby into their lives, and then guiltily closed the book. Anne had clearly hidden the book--Mr. Christopher rarely read these books on faith, and the children had several times called these volumes "Mommy's books." Amanda was just as clearly an intruder, an interloper into Anne's past. Rising with *Catholic Christianity* and the journal in hand, she moved to the sofa, switched on the lamp, and sat with the two books on her lap. Part of her wanted to open the journal, to begin reading at once, to discover something more about the woman who had once loved the man with whom she was falling in love, the woman who had raised such fine children, who had walked about this room, who haunted her mind like a song. Yet some cautionary voice warned Amanda that the journal might well be a Pandora's box, that she not only lacked any right to view what Anne had written, but that reading it might portend unforeseeable consequences, some dark outcome beyond her ken.

She was still sitting in her state of indecision when she became aware of footsteps in the hall. Without even thinking about it, she slipped the journal beneath the Kreeft book just as Mr. Christopher entered the room.

"Everything go okay here?" he asked, and after she'd given him a brief report of the events of the day, he nodded toward the book. "That was always one of Anne's favorites. She bought it when she began home schooling the children. She was always reading to herself from it."

"I can tell," Amanda said, turning to the shelf of books and then back to him. "I hope it's all right if I take a look at it."

"Of course, of course." He smiled, clearly remembering something about Anne. "She always felt she didn't have the knowledge of cradle Catholics, though the truth is she knew more about the Faith than ninety-nine percent of the rest of us. A lot of converts are like that--they have the fire for learning and study."

He told her then of some of the architectural points he'd enjoyed seeing at the Biltmore, and without mentioning Barb Brinkman, bade Amanda good-night. As he went upstairs, she switched off the lamp and the overhead light, and went to her room and closed the door.

Another woman, stronger of will, might have resisted all temptation to read what Anne had written; another woman might have given the journal to Nathan Christopher as soon as he had entered the room that evening; another woman might have returned the journal to its sanctuary on the bookcase to be discovered by someone else at a later time.

Amanda was not that woman.

Thanks in part to Anne's fine penmanship--she had the looping hand of a well-trained schoolgirl--and in part to the brevity of some of the entries, Amanda finished reading the journal in less than an hour. The first six weeks of entries recorded the activities of the children and the impact of Katie and her baby on the household. Here Amanda learned how each day had drawn the runaway girl closer to the Christophers, how Anne had finally persuaded Katie to contact her parents in Richmond, Virginia, how the writer John Scully, who was present at the Christmas Eve birth of the baby, began his courtship of the young mother. Anne described this courtship with humor and grace, accurately foretelling that the two of them, despite the disparity in their ages--Scully was apparently in his late twenties--would one day be wedded.

Each page also revealed Anne's love of her faith. She headed her entries with the feast days of saints and referred to saints, Mary, Christ, and God as matter-of-factly as another diarist might have recorded the weather or the particulars of a meal. She frequently mentioned her prayer life and her readings from the Bible and various books of religion. There was no guile or false piety in her records; she wrote of faith as if it was as natural as air. Alone with blank paper and her own thoughts, she appeared in the journals as she did in the memory of her friends: kind, charitable, wise in the ways of the human heart.

Only when Amanda had read three-quarters of the way through the journal did it dawn on her that Anne had rarely mentioned Mr.

Christopher. Her portraits of her children, of Katie and Scully, Mary Celeste and Father Krumpler--Amanda smiled over Anne's affection for the old priest-- were vivid, sincere or humorous depending on the circumstances. When Nathan appeared, however, he seemed flat, his entrances on the page made in a perfunctory manner, as if he was more a part of the background of events than the central figure in her life.

Then this note:

February 17 Ash Wednesday
 Nathan went back to the office tonight. Tim was quiet but I could tell he was upset. Another broken date for chess.

This was followed by several entries concerning Nathan:

February 20 St. Elizabeth of Mantua
 The same dream. The third time since Christmas. I am standing outside on the porch looking into the living room. It feels like winter-- the trees have lost their leaves--but I'm not cold. Inside the house I can see Nathan with the children. He is in his chair and they are sitting on the sofa. Tim is holding Mikey, and Bridget and Teresa are crying, crying and crying, but Nathan doesn't help them. He just sits there, removed. I rap at the glass with my knuckles, but they can't hear me. I shout at the frosted glass. Nathan just sits there and doesn't help the children. Can't he see them? Then I feel myself being pulled away, and they fade out, and I wake up.
St. Elizabeth predicted her own death. Am I sending myself signals?
 What would he do if I was dead? I know he doesn't connect with them. What would he do?
 And now another baby on the way. I need to tell him soon. Will he be angry again this time?

February 22 St. Margaret of Corona

His touch brings me alive. It would be so easy to do as he wishes, to simply shut out everything else--the children, our friends--and love each other. The mirror in which we admire ourselves: the beloved. Cut out the world and live for each other. A heaven made hell.

February 23 St. Polycarp

A cool silence through most of the meal this evening. He is worried about business. He lost another contract today. The owner of the property couldn't get his loan and so Nathan doesn't get to build. But more than that, too. He loves the children. He would lay down his life for them without thinking about it. But does he like them? Certain politicians speak of their love for "the people," but they can't stand the people except in the abstract. I don't know if Nathan loves the reality of the children--their mess, their noise, their needs. After supper he sat in the living room watching basketball and keeping to himself until they had gone to bed. Then--then--he wants me.

March 1 St. Albinus

Nathan was nearly an hour late for Tim's birthday party. Mom and Katie and I kept the children amused with games and a pre-meal treat of ice cream. When he finally did come home, he was awkward and distant. Why can't he connect with them? What will it take? He becomes defensive whenever I try and talk with him about it. There is a coldness growing in him toward them. He seems to regard them as nuisances, as obstacles between us, rather than as the living evidence of our love for each other.

March 8 St. John of God

Soon. He'll surely notice the change in me soon. I have to tell him about the baby. He'll be upset. He loves me--I know this each time he touches me--but he doesn't like sharing me. Sometimes I wonder if he ever wanted children at all.

The dream again. I think I will die soon. Writing that sounds silly. But what if? What would he do? What would happen to our children? Or is that part of the plan?

Please, God. Let me live. He's not made to be mother and father. Not even father.

If something should ever happen to me, please, please watch over Nathan and the children.

The journal ended a week later, two days before her death.

Anne's remarks about the children and their relationship with Mr. Christopher shocked Amanda. How could Anne have been so blind, so mistaken? Mr. Christopher was the best of fathers, present in the lives of his children, diligent for their welfare, concerned at all times for their wants and needs. Didn't he spend every evening at home with them, playing games, going over their schoolwork, seeing to their baths, saying prayers with them and tucking them into bed? In all other observations of her friends and the children, Anne had seemed so insightful, so astute and loving in her evaluations. How could she have so grossly misjudged her own husband?

Or had Anne judged him rightly? What if he had changed? Perhaps when Anne was living he was uninvolved with the children, resentful of them. And those dreams which had led Anne to believe she might die soon--she wrote as if more concerned with how her death would affect Mr. Christopher as a father than with her own welfare. What sort of person harbored those thoughts?

And what would Mr. Christopher think when he read these comments? How would he feel learning his beloved wife had so strongly faulted him as a father? His love for her, still so bright and shining that he could scarcely speak of her without a catch in his voice, would suffer a heavy blow from these revelations. His dead wife's words would burst over him like some black storm of guilt, painful accusations shading every thought of her, shadows tainting his love and his memories.

These questions brought a web of complications for Amanda. Having now read the journal, she couldn't blithely hand it over. Mr. Christopher would ask if she had read it, and even had she wished to deceive him, she knew she would fail. He would realize she had read the journal, and prevarication might irreparably damage her own relationship with him. She thought of returning the black book to its hiding-place on the shelf, but was afraid of its eventual discovery and the pain it would bring to him. Of course, she could destroy the journal, drop it in a trash can uptown, but that alternative seemed a sacrilege, an erasure of the past mocking Anne's death.

And so Amanda had vacillated, concealing the journal in the bottom of a drawer beneath her socks and t-shirts until she could see a way out of her dilemma.

———

The happy chaos of the household and the natural rhythms of the coast--they counted the hours by the sun rather than by any clock--brought several small gifts to Amanda. The fresh air, the tides, and the tangy smell of the marshlands behind the house ignited in her a deeper appreciation of her physical self. For the first time in years she became aware of the pleasures of the body: the heat baking into her skin on the sand, the perfume of oil and sun on her flesh by day's end, the taste of crab and shrimp, the murmur of waves breaking on the sand, the cry of the gulls, the laughter and voices of the children at play. In addition to her evening walks with Mary Celeste, she began her mornings by jogging a good distance down the beach.

At supper on Tuesday evening, after they had finished eating and the big table was a litter of paper plates covered with shrimp tails, bits of broccoli, and stray kernels of rice, Mr. Christopher brought up the idea of an evening out for Mary Celeste and Tom. On past excursions to the beach, each couple had apparently gone out on a "date night," while the other couple took command of the children. "You should go out tomorrow," he said. "Amanda, Erin, Tim, and I can handle this bunch of scamps."

"Go, go," several of the Moore children urged at once, joined by Mikey. Erin said, "We'll be fine, Mom." To be left without the supervision of their parents was clearly high adventure for them. Tom Moore sprawled lazily in his wicker chair, looking around the table and grinning. "I don't know," he said. "The troops look ripe for revolution. We might come back from supper and find Teresa queen of the castle with David as her king."

Teresa blushed and giggled. She had developed a crush on David, who at eight was a year her senior, and had taken to following him everywhere on the beach and staying at his side in the evenings during the rosary and the board games. David frequently scowled at her, but the dark look was perfunctory. Before supper he had brought her three pink shells he'd found on the beach that day, along with a sun-bleached Coke bottle.

"How about it?" Mr. Christopher asked. "There's a new restaurant back in the village. You could go there. Or there's that seafood café you always liked up the beach."

"I don't know," Tom said, pointing at Teresa, who wiggled with delight at being the center of his attention. "I see a lean and hungry look in that young lady."

"We just ate supper," Teresa said.

"Hush," Mary Celeste said, and the table quieted at once. She glared at Tom. Only her eyes hinted at her teasing. "We're going. And I want that restaurant near the bay over in Swansboro--the one with candlelight and tablecloths."

"Good Lord, woman," Tom said. "Do you know what that place costs?"

"And I want my dream date. A rich and handsome man who listens to every word I say and who thinks I'm the most beautiful woman on the planet."

Tom looked at Mr. Christopher. "Do you know someone like that around here?" He smiled then at Mary Celeste. "Who is this mystery man--one of the neighbors? Were you flirting again on the beach?"

Though she usually rose to such taunt with some crushing rejoinder of her own, Mary Celeste ignored him, instead fixing her attention on Mr. Christopher. "Tom and I will go out tomorrow. And on Thursday I want you and Amanda to have your own evening out."

This pronouncement fell like a bomb at the table. Though the children instantly began chanting--"Go! Go! Go!"--" with Mikey banging the table with his spoon, Amanda felt pushed off-balance. She flushed with embarrassment at the commotion, and tried to laugh the proposal away, saying "No, no." Though she was looking at Mary Celeste, she could feel that Mr. Christopher was equally disconcerted. He was laughing at the din made by the children, but the laughter sounded hollow. "Really, Mary Celeste," he said. "I--"

"Hush," Mary Celeste said again, and the children hushed. She leaned on the table toward Nathan, then pointed toward Amanda. "This poor girl has spent the last three evenings helping make supper for you two men and a platoon of children. On top of that, she has endured listening to you and Tom discuss sports and politics. She's entitled to an evening out, and so are you."

"But--"

"But nothing," Mary Celeste said. "If Tom and I have our evening out, then so should you. And so should Amanda."

"You haven't even asked Amanda if she wants to get away for an evening."

Every head at the table swiveled toward her. Being the focus of those attentive faces flustered her--Mary's Celeste's unexpected proposal had so numbed Amanda that her tongue felt locked in place--but then she looked to her immediate left and saw Bridget smiling and nodding. The girl put her hand on Amanda's shoulder--Amanda could feel that touch for days afterward, the gentle squeeze--and said, "You should go and have some fun, Miss Bell."

Amanda nodded back at her and said, returning her smile, "All right--I'd love to go."

The children clapped, and both Erin and Tim pumped the air with their fists.

"I'm clearly the victim of a conspiracy," Mr. Christopher said to Tom, then noticed that he too was applauding. "Et tu, Brute?"

"Oh, for heaven sakes," Mary Celeste said. "It's supper together, not a death sentence."

———

After supper, when they were walking on the beach, the sand wet and cool beneath their feet, Amanda asked Mary Celeste why she had brought up the idea of an evening out with Mr. Christopher.

"Lots of reasons." She stopped, letting the water slosh around her ankles and then moving inland a few feet at the next big wave. The few days of sunshine had grown freckles on her face, and with her red hair blowing in the wind she looked more like a female pirate than a mother of five. "First, it seemed only fair. Why should Tom and I go out for an evening of fun--and we always have a great time when we go out, no matter how much he pretends to complain about it--while you and Nathan spend the entire week with the children?"

"It's my job. Besides, I'm having a wonderful time."

"It's also a vacation. And even back home you aren't with the children round the clock the way you are here. You'll see--it will do you good to get away for an evening. And it will be good for Nathan too. He really wants to go."

"He does?"

"Of course he does. Couldn't you tell?"

"No, and I don't want him to feel that he has to go to supper with me. I really don't mind not going--I wasn't expecting it at all--and I don't want him to feel some sort of obligation."

Mary Celeste laughed then, that wild merry laughter which by now Amanda recognized as one of her trademarks, so filled with sheer joy that anyone hearing it had to smile. But this time Amanda looked at her without smiling, trying to find the cause for her hilarity. Mary Celeste's laughter died away at that look, and she smiled tenderly.

"Let me tell you something," she said. "After Anne's death, Nathan changed. For a long time he was deeply depressed, of course, but everyone understood that. He had lost a woman he truly loved. No one expected him to be sunshine and roses. People who didn't know him the way I do thought the children would take up his attention, and they did in a way. And I have to say his relationship with the children changed after Anne died. I knew Nathan pretty well, Amanda, and he was no great shakes as a father. He was there, naturally, but it was Anne who did most of the parenting. Nathan wasn't really engaged with them. He didn't really connect with them, you know? When it comes to our commitments, there is a natural order of love--God, spouse, family, work. With Nathan none of that mattered. He put Anne above everything, and work was next, and then the rest. Anne never said much, but I know she would have liked him to be more involved. After she died, I worried less about him than I did about the children. They'd lost their mother, and they had never really had Nathan as a father.

·"But he came around. That summer he began spending more and more time with them. He made the connection, somehow, and gave them all the affection and love they needed. It made me happy just watching them together. He had Katie to help, and even though she was hardly more than a child herself and had a newborn, he could have left everything to her. But he didn't. He somehow found the right priorities, the right order of things, and became a good father."

Anne's journal came to mind, and Amanda wondered if Anne had spoken to Mary Celeste about her concerns for Mr. Christopher, but she didn't ask. Mary Celeste took her silence as a signal to continue.

"But Nathan was still severely depressed. It just didn't show on the outside anymore. Even Tom wondered if Nathan shouldn't see someone--a therapist, you know, or a priest--and for Tom to say that is going a long way. He considers counseling, a lot of it anyway, just a cut above voodoo. Anyway, Nathan couldn't shake off his depression. He didn't have much to say around his friends, even with Tom, and he didn't laugh the way he had when we were together. And then you came along."

She seemed on the verge of saying more, but turned away and began drifting down the beach. Amanda followed at her side, thinking again of the journal and wondering what Mary Celeste had intended to tell her. They walked in silence a good five minutes, drifting rather than setting their usual fast pace, and their conversation seemed at an end when Mary Celeste stopped again, digging a trench with her toes in the sand and watching while the next lapping wave filled it with water and foam.

"And then you came along," she said, "and Nathan changed. He smiles more, and he jokes around with Tom the way he did when Anne was alive. There's happiness in him again, and you can see it reflected in the children. You may not see it, because you weren't here to see him earlier, but it's there. A lot of people have noticed the change."

"Like Barb Brinkman?"

"Like Barb," Mary Celeste affirmed. "She's crazy with fear because she can see the good you've done Nathan. And some of the others--they think you're chasing after Nathan. Others are worried about your intentions because they care for Nathan. They don't want to see him get hurt. A few of them, Barb's friends, just like to gossip. They're the ones you've got to watch out for. I've seen them rip up a few other people, including a priest once who came to the basilica. He was young and a little effeminate, and they couldn't chatter enough about him. He left after a year and went back to Charlotte, and those back-stabbing harpies were the reason he left."

Eight months earlier, Amanda would have dismissed such gossip, feeling its sting but letting it run past her. To get the job done was what had counted then, and the arrows of those who had hated her at work couldn't penetrate the thick armor of her ambitions. Now, however, with that armor removed, torn away by all that had happened to her, Amanda felt open and naked, vulnerable to attack. Father Krumpler's charge to her to serve the Christophers while putting aside her own desires might work to tame her own affection for Nathan, but she lacked the power to withstand the slander of others.

"Mary Celeste," she asked again, "why did you suggest I go to dinner with Mr. Christopher?"

"I told you," she said.

"Were those the real reasons?"

"Those were real reasons," she said, but then smiled. "Well, maybe not the real reason."

"Why then?"

"Maybe I just wanted to give the two of you a little nudge." Her eyes flashed at Amanda, teasing her. "Mary Celeste Moore--a living, walking, breathing Matchdotcom."

Her teasing and humor were irresistible. "You are wicked."

"'As wicked as wicked can be.'" she said, quoting the poem about a pirate she'd read earlier that day to the children. "And you are Mary Poppins. You probably didn't use an umbrella, but you floated down from somewhere and did your magic and helped heal a family."

"I'm not Mary Poppins."

"Maybe not. But you're a mystery. And luckily for you, I'm a woman who happens to like mystery enough to let it keep its secrets."

———

On the drive to the Front Street Grill that Thursday evening Mr. Christopher described his favorite fish markets. They passed five or six of these, and he had patronized all of them over the years. He even pointed out the parking lot where, he said, a man sold only shrimp daily from noon until suppertime. His favorite place was a dumpy, faded building near the boats and docks of Beaufort. "It looks trashy on the outside, but it's got the best fish on the island," he said. "And they'll filet the fish for you in about ten seconds flat."

Riding alone with him in the car, leaving the children for an evening out, felt strange, and Mr. Christopher was talking, Amanda suspected, because he felt nervous himself, especially in the face of her own self-conscious silence. Crossing the causeway from Emerald Isle to

Swansboro, he asked if she was chilly--the blast of air-conditioning made her feel like one big goose bump--and her "Yes" was the first word she'd spoken since they had left the house. He turned off the air, rolled down the windows, and let the sweet, brackish smell of the bay fill the car.

At the table with its fresh flowers and crisp linens he suddenly lost this rush of words, and they sat without speaking after placing their order, looking out the window at Beaufort Inlet. Boats bobbed on their moorings, shining with the setting sun, and all around them diners chatted and clattered their silverware, but Amanda was only vaguely aware of these pleasures. Her insides felt twisted up from nerves, and she was thankful when the waiter returned with their drinks--she had ordered a glass of the house white wine, Nathan a martini--if for no other reason than having at hand some physical object on which to focus her attention. She was just beginning to descend into full-panic mode, certain that the evening was turning into an utter disaster, when Nathan pushed his drink aside and leaned toward her across the table. "This is awkward, isn't it?"

She nodded. "Yes, sir."

He smiled at her gaffe. "Maybe we should be a little less formal. Just for this one evening."

"All right."

"I can call you Amanda, then?"

"Yes."

"And you'll call me Nathan?"

"Yes," she said, and tried it out: "Nathan."

"You have a pickle in your mouth." It was the expression he used with the children when they were cross or upset.

"Nathan."

"Better. A sweet pickle."

He laughed then, and though she joined him, Amanda felt stiff as a cadet. Other than a swimming suit, shorts, and a few t-shirts, she had brought only a few articles of clothing on the trip. For their supper together she had chosen a sleeveless salmon-colored blouse which accented her tan and her one white skirt. Nathan was wearing khaki trousers and the white shirt he'd worn to Mass on Sunday. She wondered if men selected clothing or worried about their apparel with the same attention as women. Certainly Nathan looked handsome in that simple attire, brown as a sailor, clean, impeccable, radiant with that healthy glow which the beach gives to most of its visitors. She wondered if he saw her as she saw herself: awkward, ill-at-ease, silenced by her very affection for him.

"Well," he drawled jokingly, "that's settled anyway." He lifted his glass and proposed a toast: "To you, Amanda."

She clicked her glass against his and took another sip of wine. "We could play twenty questions," she said.

"Twenty questions?"

"Favorite movie. Worst moment ever." She smiled. "What we want to be when we grow up."

"All right. You go first. Amanda." He hesitated using her name.

"All right. Favorite movie?"

"That's a tough one, but I'll say *Gladiator*."

"I heard somewhere that most men choose *The Godfather*."

"It's a great film, but people get so caught up in the romance of the Corleone Family that they forget it's about crime and corruption. I like Russell Crowe as Maximus better. Do you know a lot of men?"

"Is that one of the questions?"

"I guess it is."

"Not in the way you might mean it. I think I read something about men and *The Godfather*."

"What exactly did you do at work?"

"It's my turn," Amanda said.

"So it is. Go ahead."

"You're stuck for a year on a desert island. Other than people, what would you miss the most?"

"Shaving," he said promptly. "All that sun and salt would make for a scratchy beard. My turn now?"

"Yes."

"All right." He thought a moment. "You're sent on a mission into space for a year. Which Hollywood film star would you want with you?"

"That's good." She considered a few options, then smiled. "Jimmy Stewart."

"Jimmy Stewart?"

"He was a pilot."

"Ahhh."

"He was also one of the few movie stars who was happily married and loyal to his wife."

Marriage and wife threatened to bring a small cloud to the conversation, and Amanda hurried on: "Plus, I always liked the way he talked." She leaned toward Nathan, imitating Stewart. "Well, Amanda, you just say the word and I'll lasso the moon for you."

"*It's A Wonderful Life*. That's a good imitation. Can you do anyone else?"

"He's the only one. And that was your next question."

"I can see I'll need to be more careful. Your turn, then."

"When you were Tim's age, what did you want to be when you grew up?"

"I wish I could tell you something exciting or romantic--a cowboy, a pirate, a soldier. But even then I wanted to be a builder. I wanted to make buildings--houses, offices--that people would love. You've seen the Grove Arcade?" He added quickly: "That doesn't count as one of my questions, by the way."

"I went there with Father Krumpler last week again. For supper," she said, thinking suddenly that she had found a way out of her dilemma with the journal. She would ask Father Krumpler what she must do. He would know.

"I loved that place as a kid. My granddad would take me there--this was before it became a shopping arcade, but the architecture is the same--and I loved the way it felt with the gargoyles and the iron gating inside. It made me glad just to walk inside the place. I guess I wanted to give that same joy to other people."

"So you grew up in Asheville?"

"One too many questions," Nathan said. "It was my turn."

As they went on playing the game, laughing together as each question became more ridiculous than its predecessor, the barrier of discomfort between them dissolved. For the first time in months, with the exception of the children, Father Krumpler, and Mary Celeste, Amanda felt comfortable in the presence of another human being, and she couldn't even remember, excluding Father Krumpler, when she'd felt so at ease in the comfort of another man. Even the interruption of the waiter bringing their food--Nathan had ordered the grilled yellow fin tuna with a colorful cucumber-tomato salad while Amanda had the seared crab cake with red peppers and jasmine rice--did not dissolve the harmony between them.

"Do you mind if we pray?" Nathan asked.

He made the sign of the cross, and Amanda bowed her head. Other than with Father Krumpler, this was the first time she had ever participated, even cursorily, in public prayer, but the sensation was as natural as if they were sitting at the table at home.

"Good?" Nathan asked after she had taken her first bite of the crab.

"Delicious. Yours?"

"Excellent. The next question's yours, by the way."

She could see that he mirrored her own trepidation at the loss of their newfound conversational momentum. She wiped her lips with the white napkin and asked: "What does being Catholic feel like?"

He chewed slowly, thinking, and swallowed. "This one might take a while."

"I don't mind. I'm truly curious. Were you raised Catholic?"

He took a sip of his martini. "I'm a hybrid. My mother was Catholic, my father a sort of lapsed Baptist agnostic. They met in school down in Raleigh. My dad went to State, just like my grandfather and just like me, and my mom was a student at Meredith College. When they were raising us, we went to Mass every Sunday, and my mother said prayers at mealtime and before bed when we were little, but it was all pretty pro-forma.

When I went away to school, I quit going to Mass unless I was home on vacation, and then I quit going altogether after my mom died."

"What brought you back?"

"Anne." He paused at the memory, smiling. "After we decided to marry, she told me that she wanted a church wedding. Part of it had to do with girlhood dreams--the white dress, the church, the walk down the aisle--but there was something else, too. I didn't know what it was then, and I don't think she knew either."

"What was it?"

"I think that somehow God was calling to her. Or at least that she wanted God. Her own family never went to church. Anyway, once she'd made up her mind to have a church wedding, she went to see a priest." He chuckled at the memory. "I don't think she knew what she was getting into. The priest told her that if there was to be a wedding in the church, then I needed to start coming to Mass. He invited her to come, too, and then explained we'd both have to attend the marriage preparation course in the parish. He also said we'd have to wait six months before getting married. Most people would have given up at that point and gone somewhere else, but instead Anne began asking questions. One question led to another, and before she'd left the church that morning she had signed us up for the marriage classes and the adult catechism class."

"Was it Father Krumpler?"

"Oh, no. He wasn't here yet. It was Father Bill Bianco, a little Italian priest only a few years out of seminary. A very blunt man who always looked as if he needed a shave. He has a parish somewhere down in Charlotte, I think. He came up for Anne's funeral and was one of the priests on the altar. My turn?"

"You still haven't answered the question. What's it like being Catholic?"

"It depends, I suppose, on what kind of Catholic you are."

"What's it like for you, then?"

"Hard." He inserted another forkful of tuna into his mouth, chewed, swallowed, and said: "There's comfort in believing and in practicing the faith, but the rules are tough. If you're devout like Anne, I think it might be easier, but even then it can be a struggle. People nowadays don't like rules, they don't like someone or something telling them how to live. Even when you understand that the teachings of the Church--all the teachings about sex and contraception, about caring for your neighbor even if that neighbor hates you, all the moral guidelines--even when you understand these teachings are meant to bring you closer to Christ, even then it's still hard."

His words again put Amanda in mind of Anne's journal and her many prayers for assistance in her daily living. "But there are consolations?"

"Yes, but they can seem pretty thin compared to the demands. Anne got a lot of strength out of the Church. I'm not as strong in my faith as she was. Her faith made her see the world and every day in it as an adventure. She told me once that becoming Catholic changed the way she saw things. She said the Church gave her new eyes--like someone who puts on a pair of glasses for the first time. But even people like me--people with a weaker faith--see the world a little differently. Faith, even a questioning faith, gives a purpose to life that doesn't exist otherwise. Anne used to say her faith added joy to joy and comfort to sorrow. My turn now. What's it like not being Catholic? Not believing in God?"

"I never said I didn't believe."

"Do you?"

He was smiling when he asked his question, but his eyes were intent and serious, and Amanda dropped her gaze and picked at the remains of the crab cake. "I don't know. I think I might believe."

"You don't need to explain. As I say, I lived that way for my early twenties. I can remember how the world felt to me then. Darker. Colder." He hesitated. "I don't mean you feel that way, of course."

The mood might have turned pensive again, but Nathan was too alert to allow for that possibility. "You've asked a lot of questions. I'll give you one more and then it's my turn."

A hundred questions about his faith, ranging from the sublime to the ridiculous, rushed through Amanda's head. Why did Catholics have to go weekly to Mass? Why did they go to confession? What was the point of the rosary? Why did they dip their fingers into water when entering and leaving the church? Why did they listen to the pope? What was a saint? Was Anne in heaven? What was heaven?

This line of questioning, however, she decided to abandon: she could follow it up during her next session with Father Krumpler. This evening had presented her with a golden opportunity to find out more about Nathan, and so she peppered him with half-a-dozen more questions, discovering in the process that he had worked his college summers as a carpenter's assistant; that he loved both snow and sunshine but that rainy days left him feeling as gray as the weather; that he had once, on a dare in college, rappelled from the fourth floor of his dormitory; that he loved the smells of fresh earth, newly cut wood, and babies' heads. This last confession made Amanda laugh so hard that Nathan reddened with embarrassment. "What?" he said, in a defense which only made her laugh harder. "There's something wrong with that? Have you ever smelled a baby's head?"

————

After supper they ordered coffee. The restaurant was clearing out by then, and they took the coffee on the outside deck, beyond which the sound shimmered black as velvet, displaying a jeweler's case of lights from the homes on the surrounding shore. By now they had moved from their game into a natural mode of conversation, sitting closer together while enjoying the sight of the night-darkened water. Here their occasional silences no longer gave rise to anxiety or awkwardness, but were marks of punctuation between their murmured thoughts. Later the next day Amanda remembered few of the remarks they traded back and forth on that shadowy porch but found instead it was the sound of Nathan's voice--soft, intimate, interested in all she said--that remained most with her.

Only once did he touch her. As they sat there on the deck, and later on the ride back to the house beside the ocean, which seemed much shorter than the drive out, Amanda felt as if Nathan wanted to hold her hand--it was that sensation of earlier years and clumsy dates, when the boy in the theater can't quite figure out how to put his arm around the girl beside him--but he made no such move. When they rose to leave the restaurant, however, and he opened the door for Amanda to re-enter the interior dining room, he placed his hand on her elbow, guiding her toward the exit. That one simple gesture, his fingers on her flesh, sent a tiny jolt of electricity tingling along her nerves.

It was on this evening, and specifically with that touch, that she came with certainty to recognize the depths of her attraction to him.

PART IV

Chapter Thirteen

July rolled into August, that month of heat and harvest, and Amanda found herself gathering crops of her own. Her curiosity about the Church, its creed, its principles and practices, its quarrels with the world and within its own walls: all these subjects and others led her to Anne's bookshelf. The saints in particular fascinated her, as they had Anne. She marveled at their variety--soldiers, housewives, monks, nuns, merchants, artists, they were as pixilated a band of souls as had ever existed-- but she felt disconnected from their one common bond: their faith. Why did so many human creatures, different from one another as snowflakes, sacrifice so much, sometimes their very lives, for an unseen being? Why did they give up the visible for the invisible, the tangible for the intangible? How did a woman like Anne Christopher believe in such things?

Anne's presence haunted that old brick house like a sachet, and the heart of that presence lay in these dog-eared books with their marked passages, penned comments, and slips of paper. It was Anne and her small library as well as Father Krumpler, with whom Amanda continued to meet, that satisfied some of her many questions about the Christopher family's faith. Yet she was frustrated too, for each answer brought another dozen questions, each new revelation led her through yet another door into another room where still more conundrums sat waiting explication.

JEFF MINICK

Often, lying in her bed and reading from those books, Amanda would bask in the familiar presence of the house, comfortable and familiar as an old quilt. Here in this place she had found what she had not known since the death of her parents, a place to call home. Whenever she returned to the house, even after a short while, coming back from an excursion to town, from a run around the neighborhood or a walk with Mary Celeste--after the vacation, they got together two or three times a week for a stroll around Montford, their friendship freshening with each step--each time the house met her like an embrace. Her first thought on her return, which she often spoke aloud if one of the children or Nathan were present, was: "It's good to be home." Those in the world who have always possessed the good fortune to call a place a home, however humble, cannot know the pleasure and security that word brings to those who dwell only in a house or an apartment. This particular home with its fourth generation of Christophers, filled with children and haunted by Anne's gentle spirit, drew Amanda ever closer by its enchantments and mysteries.

Love is to a home what nails are to a house, and that August and early fall Amanda's affection for the Christopher children deepened and became more real with each passing day. Father Krumpler's advice regarding service had taken such firm hold that Amanda no longer thought about the act of service, but instead simply served, bringing to every task a compound of affection and discipline. Not only had she become more and more a part of Christophers' lives, but they also become an ever greater part of her own. Even in the early evenings, when Nathan took charge of them, the children occupied her time. She wrote out lists of activities for them, planned syllabi for their fall lessons, reviewed curricula from the catalogs collected by Anne.

As for Nathan--she remained in a state of warm confusion. Since their supper at the restaurant, they had grown easy with each other in their confidences and friendly affection. In the late evenings he would sit with her on the porch or in the living room, and listen to her accounts of the children, and relate the joys and discouragements of his day. Sometimes they would read silently together, comfortable in the stillness of the house, occasionally sharing with the other some particular passage from the book at hand. They were still "Miss Bell" and "Mr. Christopher" in the presence of the children, but alone they had become Amanda and Nathan.

The thought, muddled at first, then with increasing clarity, occurred to Amanda that her growing affection for Nathan, and the mode of its expression, had more in common with her treasured Victorian books than with the mood of her own culture and age. Each gesture, each word from Nathan, bore more weight than if they had become modern lovers tumbling quickly and dutifully into bed. The twenty-first century, it appeared to her, set great store by sex, but had diminished love; it had mechanized sex, with many giving themselves over to sex thera-pists and pornographers, gaining the flesh but losing their hearts. It was ironic: her fellow moderns mocked the Victorians for their modesty and outward sexual decorum, their rigid rules of courtship, their stifled and stilted sexuality, yet modernity, or so it seemed to Amanda, had destroyed romantic love itself: the slow unfolding of secrets, the delicate disclosures, the importance of a word, a smile, a glance.

She and Nathan, it seemed to her, were dancing a waltz, while the rest of the world pounded away in a rave of savage music and slamming bodies.

Nathan, Amanda was reasonably certain, knew of their waltz. When he addressed her as "Miss Bell," he did so with a twinkle in his eye. Several times, when she was tidying her room or writing in the journal as recommended by Father Krumpler, he knocked lightly at her door and asked if she cared to join him on the back porch, as he put it, "to watch the stars come out." At the end of each day, he seemed as delighted to see her as she was him, walking briskly toward her across the back yard from the car, the children all around him, waving to her and calling out "I see you've survived another day, Miss Bell," a congratulations which invariably made Bridget slap him on the arm. Several times after Sunday Mass, which Amanda began attending on their return from the beach, Mary Celeste teased him about his appearance and demeanor. "Nathan," she would say, "you've got the lilt of an Irishman in your voice today" or "Nathan, you look like that old song 'Walkin' On Sunshine.' What's up with that?" He would offer a retort, but his defenses and counter-charges failed to hide his felicitous mood.

As for Anne's journal, Amanda decided to return it to its hiding place on the shelf. She saw no need to hurt Nathan with the journal's revelations. Someday he would find it himself, and be wounded, no doubt, but this way the responsibility lay with fate and not with her. Occasionally, whenever the routine of her duties needed Anne's inspiration, when reading her prayers and thoughts offered Amanda special comfort, she would secretively withdraw the volume from the dust and shadows, and read for a few minutes. More and more, both in reading Anne's words and in sensing her continued presence in the house, Amanda found herself comforted by the woman who had so fervently loved Nathan, who had born and loved these children, who had striven so mightily to make a home for all of them.

———

Waving his gin-and-tonic toward the rose bushes around the statue of Mary, Father Krumpler said: "Quite the horticulturalist, isn't he? He keeps these things and the ones out front in full-bloom until November every year."

They had just finished a discussion of the holy family, and for an instant Amanda thought he was referring to Saint Joseph. "He's a fine johnny-on-the-spot," Father Krumpler continued. "Good with plumbing, a wonderful painter, even tinkers around with some of the minor electrical problems."

She realized then that he had referenced the Basilica's sacristan, Nick, whom she had met when she had first come to the church.

"I have always loved roses."

"You were a lit major--I think that's a requirement. Do you remember reading about the meaning of the rose in the Middle Ages and Renaissance?"

"I do indeed. I had a professor who spent three class periods discussing roses and their place in literature. We talked about the complexity of the flower, the thorns, its sheer beauty, the association of all these things with the human heart."

The sticky air of this early September evening was redolent with the odor of these particular roses. After eating supper--in a nod to the heat, Amanda had prepared a large salad with an oil and vinegar dressing accompanied by crackers and slices of cheese--Father Krumpler had suggested taking what he called "beach chairs" to this patch of lawn behind the church. "I'm tired of air-conditioning," he said. "Let's sweat a bit."

For half an hour or more, while he sipped at his gin and Amanda her iced water, she had peppered him with more questions, issues about the faith that had risen from their reading that week. They had spent some time during supper on the meaning for humankind of the hypostatic union--Christ's nature as the god-man--and had somehow gotten from that prickly subject to the concept of the communion of saints and why Catholics prayed for the dead.

"You know, Amanda," Father Krumpler said now, "I wonder if you shouldn't begin formal instruction in the Faith. The classes begin this next week."

"How does that work?"

"You'd attend classes here at the basilica every week. You'd be what is called a catechumen. You'd come to Mass, too, but right before the Creed you'd go off with the other catechumens for class as well."

"You mean I'd leave during the middle of Mass?"

"Well, yes. For the Eucharistic part of the celebration."

"But I like sitting with Nathan and the children."

"You could rejoin them right after Mass."

"Couldn't I sit with them for the first part of Mass?"

"Deborah likes the catechumens to sit in the front of the church for the first prayers and readings."

"Who's Deborah?"

"Deborah Shannihan. Our director of religious education." He squinted, whether from the sun or from displeasure Amanda could not tell.

"Please," she said, realizing how pathetic she sounded even as she spoke. "I can't see that it makes much difference where I sit."

"No, it doesn't, does it? I'll have a word with her, if you decide to participate."

"What happens after the classes?"

"At Easter, on the Vigil, you join the Church if you feel so inclined."

Easter seemed safe, far-away, remote. "But I can still see you, can't I? And talk to you?"

"Heavens, of course you can. In fact, it might be for the best. Deborah isn't always the safest guide. She's sometimes a little fuzzy in her theology."

Amanda knew Father Krumpler well enough by now to interpret the meaning of his remarks: Deborah Shannihan was an incompetent nincompoop.

"Why do you put up with her then? Why do you let her teach?"

"It's not up to me. Keep in mind I'm an old dog who's officially retired. I'm just here to help. Father Reed runs this place."

Father Reed, whom Amanda knew only by sight, frequently presided at Mass. He was a pale, corpulent man, a stirring homilist who apparently deemed racial prejudice and immigration laws the chief stumbling blocks to entry into heaven and who off the altar was surrounded by adoring older women. Though Amanda had attended Sunday Masses since their return from the beach, she noticed that Nathan often scowled during Father Reed's sermons. She made a mental note to ask Nathan later that evening what he thought of Father Reed. He would be more direct than Father Krumpler in his judgments.

"All right," she said. "I'll take the classes."

Father Krumpler swirled the ice in his glass. He was wearing civvies this particular evening: a short-sleeved yellow shirt, tan trousers, a pair of brown shoes. Looking older and somewhat less imposing in these clothes, he might have appeared to a casual passerby a grandfather with one of his progeny, settled here on the grass to impart a lesson in wisdom. Listening to him, and remembering how he had rescued her and what he had meant to her these last six months, Amanda felt her eyes blur with affection. To distract herself, and to prevent him from seeing her tears, she turned away and stared as if with some newfound fascination at the hazy, green hills rising from the horizon beyond Montford.

Six weeks had passed since the vacation at the beach, and Amanda's sessions with Father Krumpler had undergone a subtle change. He remained her counselor, a guide who listened to her and helped her sort out the push-and-pull of the past as these tides washed against the shores of her present life, yet he had also become more a friend than a counselor. On some of their evenings together she asked him questions about his own life, learning that he was born in Maryland, an infant who came into a world of war and the clash of ideologies, and that growing up in the fifties his chief aspiration was to play short-stop for the Orioles. At Gonzaga High School he found himself more given to history and philosophy than to a baseball diamond, and his matriculation at Catholic University in 1962 had stirred in him a love for theology as well, to the point that, despite the earthquake of Vatican II which had shaken the Church that year and whose aftershocks had ceased only in the last twenty years, he had decided on the priesthood as his proper vocation. "The tug on the heart," he told her with a self-conscious laugh, and that tug pulled him into both a doctoral program of medieval studies at Johns Hopkins and a seminary in Maryland. His degrees took him as a teacher to several Catholic universities, with the last being Tulane in New Orleans. Retirement from his teaching duties had brought him to the mountains of North Carolina, where the diocese hired him as an auxiliary priest and where he entertained hopes of spending more time with his books and writing. "Of course," he added in describing his present position, "it didn't quite work out that way. Pastoral duties take up most of my time."

"Helping people like me, you mean?"

"Oh, no. There aren't too many like you," he'd said innocently, and when they had finished laughing, he went on: "It's more just helping people with their lives. They mostly need someone who will listen to them. I mean really listen--someone who hears them without some ulterior motive or cause."

Now he pushed up his glasses, which had ridden down his nose in a sheen of perspiration, and turned those sharp, inquisitive eyes in her direction. "And how about you and Nathan these days?"

"About the same. We talk in the evenings quite a bit more."

"You're becoming more real." He had a gift, rare among men, Amanda thought, for reading women as easily as he read his breviary or some philosophical tract, and she had learned to listen carefully to even his most casual comments.

"How do you mean?"

"In many of his books, C.S. Lewis discusses the varieties of love--what the ancients called the Ladder of Love. It once struck me how in several of his books Lewis showed that the higher we climb this ladder, the more real our love becomes. In *The Great Divorce*, for example, he describes how the inhabitants of hell can visit heaven. There they find heaven so real compared to the shadows they've left behind that even the grass hurts their feet. It's too hard, too real. In *The Last Battle*--did you ever read that one?"

"No."

"It's the last volume of the Narnia series. As the characters in this book come closer to heaven, everything takes on an added luster--colors and smells. And in *Till We Have Faces*, which is one of his novels so many people miss, and one of the best pieces of writing he ever did, Lewis retells the myth of Cupid and Psyche, and shows how Psyche become more and more real as she searches for Cupid, the god who loved her. If we can handle the journey, we become more real when we search through all our pain and suffering for love."

"Like *The Velveteen Rabbit?*" Amanda asked, which sounded silly even as she opened her mouth.

But Father Krumpler surprised her. "Yes, yes, yes. That's an excellent analogy. We become real by loving and being loved, and by all the suffering that comes with love, just like the Velveteen Rabbit."

Was there anything he hadn't read? "How do you know that book?"

"I've done a good bit of baby-sitting in my time. And I have to tell you--that's one story I can't get through without tearing up. It's an awful thing to be reading to a four-year-old and have tears running down your face. Scares them half to death." He laughed at some memory of such an occasion. "But you, dear Amanda--you've become more real. Do you know that?"

"Yes, Father. But it scares me. I keep thinking what might happen."

"Between you and Nathan?"

"And the children, too." Twisting in the lawn chair, putting her empty glass onto the grass, she pulled her knees beneath her chin and wrapped her arms about her legs. "I keep wondering what's going to happen to me. Where will I be at Christmas? Next spring? A year from now? I used to look ahead at my future and see it clear as a picture, but now it's all muddled up. Sometimes I think I know how I want it to turn out, but it's not the same as before. Back then I knew how it would turn out--I'd advance at work, I'd earn more money and more power, and someday I'd marry and have children and be a modern working mother and wife. It all seemed based on hard reality. Now the future seems like a dream, a wish that could disappear with a snap of the fingers. The possibilities terrify me, especially the worst possibility of all."

"That your dream will end where you started, alone and without a home."

"Yes," Amanda said, and nearly began crying herself. "What if Nathan doesn't love me? What if he finds someone else? I know I can't be a nanny the rest of my life, but what if I didn't have the children in my life? Where would I go from here? What would I do with myself? What if I fall apart again? I don't think I could stand that--not that awful craziness again. It would be even worse this time, because this time I would know that I'd gone crazy. I would know what was happening to me. And why would Nathan love me anyway? He doesn't know what happened to me last winter or what I became for three months. If he knew that, if he knew that I'd gone mad for a while, he might want me out of the house tomorrow. Who wants a crazy woman looking after children?"

Rather than answer, Father Krumpler said: "I could do with a quick walk. Would you like to come with me?"

———

Twice before they had taken an after-supper stroll through the downtown. Father Krumpler enjoyed the summer crowds--the busy coffee bars and cafes, the street performers, the tourists and artists--and tonight they ambled from the church to Pack Square and back again. Though it was a Tuesday, and the tourist season was passing, the avenues were crowded, and every block brought some new entertainment--a guitar player outside Malaprops Bookstore, two violinists beside the Flatiron Building, the chess players in Pritchard Park. The silver-painted ballerina was there, standing atop a milk crate perfectly still until some pedestrian tossed a few coins in the box at her feet, whereupon she would offer a short graceful dance, then bow and become frozen again.

Despite the absence of his priestly garb, several people recognized Father Krumpler. One florid-faced man, all bones and dirty clothes, begged money for a bus ticket to get home to Alabama. Father Krumpler gave the man a dollar, but then said "Get a new story, Jack," to which the man, startled to be called by name, replied: "Oh, I didn't recognize you without the collar, Father." Two young women, both brown from the summer, both as lovely as models, and both wearing an identical rose tattoo on their bare shoulders, said "Good evening, Father Krumpler," as they passed, and when Amanda shot a quizzical look at him, Father Krumpler merely shrugged. "They came to the rectory for some advice last month."

"You run in a lot of different circles, Old Owl."

On reaching Pack Square, they turned down Lexington Avenue with its string of restaurants and thrift shops, stopping now and again to look into the windows, conversing on half-a-dozen topics ranging from the spices in Indian cooking to the life of F. Scott Fitzgerald--the writer had spent a good deal of time in Asheville during Zelda's treatment for schizophrenia at Highlands Hospital, and she had died in Highlands in a fire after Fitzgerald's own death. When they returned to the rectory, they entered the church for a few minutes of prayer and then emerged again onto the patch of lawn and the statue of Mary, where Father Krumpler folded up the chairs and took them to the door. Amanda followed him with their empty glasses, which he took from her and stood on the ledge of the breezeway while he dug his keys from his pocket.

"Would you care to come up?"

"I'd better be getting back," she said, thinking she might spend an hour or so talking with Nathan.

Father Krumpler clearly guessed her motives, and smiled. "You're a pleasure to an old man. I'm really not sure which of us is helping the other."

"I'm afraid you have the permanent role of counselor."

"Really?" He had put the chairs against the wall inside the door and took up the glasses. She gave him a hug, said "Good-bye," and turned toward the stairs when he called her. "Amanda!"

"Yes, Father?"

"You know that Nathan loves you, don't you? You know he's fallen in love with you?"

"I'm afraid I don't know much of anything. Why would you say that?"

"I've seen the way he looks at you on Sundays when I celebrate Mass."

Her heart jumped at these words, but she tried to make a joke. "That means you're not paying attention to Mass." Then the question, unspoken these weeks since the beach vacation, came again to her lips: "But what do I do with that? I don't really know what I'm supposed to do."

"Be patient," he said. "Do what you are doing and be patient. Give love the time to work its magic. Remember always that a human being is a mystery as deep as the ocean. And don't worry about your future. I see a great life for you ahead."

And with those words he stepped inside the door and left her to the evening.

———

Shorter than Amanda, thin, pale, Deborah Shannihan stood before their eight-member class wearing a brown print dress and sandals. With her black hair tight in a bun at the back of her head and her glasses perched on her nose, she seemed the perfect picture of an old-time school teacher. On the small desk at her side was a stack of papers, a Bible, a *Catechism of the Catholic Church*, a stack of books which she would later distribute to her catechumens, a candle, and a box of matches. Amanda and the other catechumens sat in a semi-circle around this desk in this room in the bottom of the rectory, a place cluttered with chairs and odd bits of furniture. In the corner opposite Amanda was a sort of throne, a chair such as a priest might have used at Mass, alongside of which was an ancient plastic-and-steel high chair for toddlers. The green colored walls and carpeting offered an amalgam of odors: mildew, babies, sweat, coffee.

Mrs. Shannihan's voice would be an acquired taste, ill-matched as it was to her schoolmarm image. Though she was in her late thirties, her voice retained trebling echoes of girlhood, a falsetto squeak punctuated by nervous, trilling giggles.

After welcoming them to the class, she distributed the forms on her desk together with pencils and clipboards, and they spent a quarter of an hour filling in their personal information. In a box marked "Religion," Amanda wrote "None." In another box which asked the question "How did you hear about these classes?" she wrote "Through a friend." When Mrs. Shannihan had collected the forms, she arranged them on the desk, then declared that they would pray.

"First, we light the candle," she said, and struck a match. "This flame represents the flame within each of us gathered here this evening. It is the flame which lives inside of us, the light in our darkness, the light that searches for truth and a way to live. Let's pray."

She made the sign of the cross and offered a prayer of gratitude for the gathering and several petitions asking that the catechumens might find their own inner light. With the end of the prayer, she blew out the candle, explained that at this first meeting she would address some broad questions about the Catholic Church, and invited them to ask questions. She posed a question of her own to start them on what she called "your journey."

"Most of you probably know more than you think you know about the Catholic Church," she said. "For example, who founded the Church?"

The question was an easy one--Amanda had heard the answer repeated by the children a dozen times from their catechism lessons, and had confirmed the answer from both Scripture and the Catechism--and she raised her hand. "Jesus Christ founded the Catholic Church."

"In a way, I suppose that's true," Mrs. Shannihan said. "But it's Saint Peter who founded the Church."

"I thought Christ gave Peter the keys to the Church."

"Well, he did," she said, a bit more slowly. "But it's Peter who founded the Church."

"But didn't Christ also say that Peter was the rock on which he would build His Church?"

"Yes, but he meant all Christian churches."

"Then wouldn't Protestants have to recognize the primacy of Peter?"

Deborah Shannihan looked at Amanda as if the question had never occurred to her. "That's a complicated question, and we'll tackle it later. Okay? Now let's move along. During our time together we'll look at all sorts of Church teachings. Some of these teachings may seem strange to you at first. From the Church's doctrines about Mary to issues like abortion and contraception and homosexuality--we'll look at all these things. Sometimes people who don't know better get all mixed up about the Church's position, particularly when it comes to sex. Take the issue of homosexuality. Here the Church gets a bad press. Does anyone know what the Church teaches?"

"That homosexual desire isn't necessarily evil," Amanda said, "but that homosexual acts are intrinsically evil."

She was quoting words from the Catechism. Amanda had thought of Justin Hobbes and his friends when she'd read this teaching, and had wondered how he might react to it. People got excited about the wording of that passage, but what everyone seemed to forget was that the Church regarded all sexual intercourse outside of marriage as sinful. She didn't exactly understand this point of abstinence herself--it seemed what the Church called a "hard teaching"--but she was too embarrassed to ask either Nathan or Father Krumpler, or even Mary Celeste. Here in the anonymity of strangers she hoped to discuss the issue of sex and the Church.

But now clearly was not the time. A strained look appeared on Mrs. Shannihan's broad face. She seemed to Amanda to be grinding her teeth. "To commit a sin, the act must actually be sinful. The person must be aware that it is a sin and consent to it."

Now, Amanda thought with some excitement, they were speaking the same language. "That's what I read," she said, glad to be seeing eye-to-eye with her.

"But even a gay person who's aware it's a sin may not be culpable. He may not be able to help himself. The same holds true for straight people as well. They may not be able to control themselves."

"So only the people who can control themselves really commit sins?"

"That's right," Mrs. Shannihan said, and the lines around her mouth eased. She even smiled at Amanda.

"But wouldn't that make everyone want to lose control of themselves?"

"Pardon me?"

"Well, if I knew that sleeping with someone when I wasn't married was a grave sin, but I wanted to do it anyway, wouldn't that tend to make me want to lose control of myself? Wouldn't it encourage me to lower my willpower?"

"We're talking about people who can't help themselves."

"That's what I mean," Amanda said, smiling back at her, certain now that they were looking in the same direction. "If we become convinced we can't help ourselves, then couldn't we go ahead and sleep with someone and not commit a sin?"

"We can't do that." The lines around the thin lips were set in place like deep cuts. "Only people who can't control themselves can."

"But I don't understand," Amanda said, thinking now not of gay men and women, nor of other fornicators, but of herself. "Couldn't I just tell myself that I didn't have control anymore and then go ahead and sleep with someone?"

"Of course you can't."

"But then--"

Deborah Shannihan held up one of the registration forms and peered at it down her nose. "Ms. Bell?"

"Yes."

Recognition showed in the teacher's face. "You're an acquaintance of Barb Brinkman's, aren't you?"

Amanda was too stunned to offer a nod. Mrs. Shannihan smiled again at her, though this time the smile had become a barrier of barbed wire and watch towers. "She knows you, I think. Your name came up at our teachers' meeting."

With those few words, she had cordoned Amanda off from the group as effectively as if she had placed her in a prison. For the next hour she remained silent, her eyes fixed on the floor, her stomach tight as a knot, while Deborah Shannihan introduced them to her version of the Church and the ancient faith of which it was the guardian.

———

In addition to the phone calls which she made to Nathan in the evenings, the little notes which she sent him through the mail, and the letters which Amanda assumed she emailed, throughout August Barb

Brinkman had continued to drop by the house two or three times a week during the hours when she knew that Nathan was at work. She had Amanda trussed and knotted; she knew that Amanda could not order her to desist from these visits, for she was not truly the mistress of the household. She knew too that Amanda wouldn't dare complain to Nathan, for such a complaint would then demand explanations on her part which Amanda was unprepared to give. Barb Brinkman was one of those predators who could spot and use the weaknesses of her prey, a huntress expert at reading the bent twig, the dim footprint left in the damp grass. On one level Amanda could understand Barb Brinkman's talent for stalking prey, for she had once operated by the same set of instincts regarding human nature, though she had gone a step farther into such wickedness by justifying her own insights as professional and managerial.

On these visits Barb always found something to criticize in the house--the children's dress, the kitchen floor in need of a broom and a dustpan, Amanda's own appearance. She never directly critiqued Amanda--she fancied herself too much a lady for frank remonstrance--but always offered her opinions as backhanded compliments. "Oh," she would say, "you must have missed those little weeds by the front walk," though Amanda had planned outdoor work for the afternoon, or "I'm sure it's hard to maintain your appearance when you aren't used to all this responsibility," if Amanda appeared at the door in jeans and a t-shirt. In the same fashion, Barb Brinkman undoubtedly passed these comments along to Nathan, giving Amanda failing report cards made under the guise of innocent comments, in the hope that he would soon detect her shortcomings and rid himself of her.

Children, Amanda was learning, are the most sapient of the race when it comes to matters of human nature; they have not yet begun to second-guess the motives of those around them, and so quickly and accurately take the straight path to the interior while adults follow the zigzag paths of their own speculations. None of the Christopher children ventured beyond the barebones rules of etiquette when Barb Brinkman visited the house. Teresa, so lively in the company of other adults, positively wilted in her presence, shrinking into herself like a pupil before a tyrannical head-mistress and fleeing at the first opportunity into the yard or the far reaches of the house. Tim, as usual, kept his thoughts to himself after one of these visits, and Bridget would only sigh and then offer to help Amanda with whatever task engaged her.

On this particular Thursday, the day after Amanda's first catechism class, Barb stopped by with Mark and Debbie. The Christopher children, who had never learned the Biblical adage of the sins of the fathers, did not apply this injunction to mothers either; they took Mark and Debbie upstairs, and within a minute Amanda could hear the clatter of blocks as they engaged in building some castle or city. "We were on our way to the Mall, and I just wanted to say hello," Barb said. Today she was wearing a simple russet dress whose color accented her dark hair and low black heels whose slight formality gave her the advantage of both height and style over Amanda. "I hear you're taking catechism classes now."

"Word travels fast."

For once, Barb Brinkman blushed, correctly taking Amanda's comment as a jab at her as a gossip.

"Deborah Shannihan is a friend. I needed to call her about the faith formation program and she mentioned your name."

Although her thorns of criticism and her unexpected visits still pricked Amanda, one consequence unforeseen by Barb in her war of attrition was how well Amanda had come to anticipate her maneuvers. No longer did her animosity completely fluster Amanda, and though Barb still possessed the power to wound her by her words, even there Amanda's immunity to her insults was growing stronger.

"Deborah said you made some interesting comments."

"She had some interesting answers."

They were standing in the living room near the fireplace, where two hours earlier Tim and Bridget were reading while Mikey and Teresa shaped play-dough into tables and chairs.

"You must be awfully busy these days with the startup of school and fall activities," Barb said, flicking her eyes at the mess on the coffee table.

"We manage to stagger through the day," Amanda said, though the truth was that life had indeed become a whirlwind. In addition to the increased hours of schooling, Tim had Scouts and soccer practices, Bridget and Teresa went to dance twice a week, and the home school play group now met every other Friday afternoon. Either Nathan or she spent four or five evenings each week taking the children to one of these activities while the other remained at home to clean up the supper dishes and ready the other children for bed. In spite of the extra work--Nathan had raised her salary another hundred dollars per week--Amanda found herself enjoying the change of pace and watching the children bring home from their activities some new tale of triumph or failure.

"I was surprised to hear you were going to the catechism classes. You don't strike me as the type."

"Really? What type am I?"

"Oh, I didn't mean anything by it," Barb said carelessly. "I just meant you didn't seem at all religious."

"How do I seem?"

"I don't mean anything," Barb repeated, though she was clearly picking every word with the greatest of care. "You know, it's awfully hard being a Catholic. If you really practice your faith, that is."

"Father Krumpler once said that he thought it was harder not being a Catholic."

"How is Father Krumpler these days?"

"He's fine, as far as I know."

"You two have become friends, haven't you?"

"Yes, I suppose we have." Thinking of Father Krumpler, Amanda let down her guard. "He's one of the kindest men I've ever known."

"Yes, he's kind. Sometimes too kind."

"What do you mean?"

"Oh, you know," Barb said, making her words a double-edged sword. "He's always taking troubled people under his wing. I hear he knows

every drunk and homeless person from the church all the way to Biltmore Village. Someday that could get him into real trouble."

"What sort of trouble?"

Amanda had learned the dangers of asking Barb such a question,
but in her moment of reverie she had let her defenses down and had
forgotten her tactical manual.

"He'll take anybody in. Anybody at all. Someday he'll help someone
out, someone with a hidden past, who will end up really hurting him."

Now Amanda was back in her defensive position, though a little late.
"Father Krumpler strikes me as a man who can take care of himself."

"I'm not so sure. He gives so much of himself away. Someday one
of his little projects might come back to hurt him. How is Nathan these
days anyway?" she asked, shooting off another arrow from her inexhaust-
ible quiver while Amanda had yet to dodge the last one.

"Nathan?"

"What happened to 'Mr. Christopher?'"

Another arrow struck home.

"Surely you talk to him. Maybe on those nights after the children
have gone to bed."

"We do talk sometimes."

Barb was patting one hand against her thigh, like a metronome
keeping time. When Amanda didn't offer any other details, the hand
stopped. "He seems brighter these days. Happier. When my husband left
me I lived under a dark cloud for months and months. And then one day
the cloud lifted and I felt myself again. Life started to feel good again, a
little bit at a time, and I thought about him less and less. I wondered if
Nathan had reached that stage, that place where he knew he could go
on living again."

In her greed for Nathan, Barb had unintentionally opened a window
on her past. Through that window Amanda could see this woman as she
must have appeared three years ago: alone, scared to death, depressed.
Clearly her abandonment had shocked her, had demolished the world
as she'd known it. *Why, she's suffered just like you*, Amanda thought for

the first time. All of Barb Brinkman's dreams, all that she had believed about her future, had disappeared in the fire and smoke of her divorce. No wonder she was so angry, so savage about Amanda's unexpected appearance in the picture and the part she had taken in Nathan's life. She had imagined a future involving Nathan and had set to work building this new dream, only now, too, it had caught fire.

A wave of sympathy for Barb washed through Amanda. For just a second she even fantasized they might be friends, two women who had both faced raw ugly violations. Then came another arrow.

"You love him too, don't you?" Barb Brinkman said in a whisper, and all the masks were off: she stood before Amanda revealed in all her desire and tortured misery. She cocked her head, as if listening for the children, and then delivered a full frontal assault: "You've been after him from the first. And just look at yourself. You're a nothing who came from nowhere--no one knows a thing about you, and your little queer friend in Atlanta isn't saying anything. For all anyone knows, you've slept with a hundred men, and then you got into some sort of trouble and ran away. Why did you run anyway? Were you screwing the boss and his wife found out about it? I can tell just by looking at you you're no good. Look at how you're dressed, that t-shirt and jeans--anyone can see you're trying to tempt him. And now you want to join the Church? What a joke. And do you really think you can be a mother to his children? You? You don't have a clue about being a mother. Or a wife. Why do you want Nathan, anyway? Is it because he can look after you? Take care of you? You're such a bitch. I'll bet all you know how to do is --"

Amanda swung and slapped Barb Brinkman across the face, knocking her sideways. She twisted with the blow, and nearly fell, but then swung in turn and hit Amanda across the neck and cheek with her cloth purse. Something hard in the purse landed like a punch against Amanda's jaw, and she tasted blood in her mouth. Barb was swinging the purse backhanded, aiming for a second blow, when Amanda stepped forward and pushed her by the shoulders, shoving her backwards. She stumbled and fell, bouncing onto the sofa. She glared at Amanda like some cornered animal, her left cheek bright red.

"Get out!" Amanda said, whispering too now, less from fear of alarming the children than from what she might say or do to this woman. "Get out of here and don't ever come back!"

"You have no right!" Barb laughed contemptuously. "You're nothing but a nanny! You can't keep me out of here."

"I'll beat the hell out of you if you ever come back here," Amanda said, fighting to catch her breath. "I'll use a belt or a frying pan or your own purse, but you'll never make it past the front door. Now get out of here."

Still glaring at Amanda, her eyes savage and implacable, Barb awkwardly rose to her feet. She walked stiff-legged to the stairwell and called out, stifling the rage in her voice: "Children! We're going home now."

Faces appeared at the top of the stairwell. "I want to stay," Debbie said. She was holding Teresa's American Girl doll. "We're playing house. Can't we stay?"

"No," Barb said. "Come downstairs now. Bring Mark with you." By now the shock of what Amanda had done had pinned down her anger: her stomach was all twisted up, and yet if Barb had said another word, she was still afraid of what more she might do or say to her.

But Barb didn't speak, didn't even look in her direction. She walked with the same stiff-legged gait to the front door, standing inside the screen and looking outside into the bright-lit yard until the children reached her. Once she raised her hand and touched her cheek. When she turned, holding the door open and scooting the children onto the front porch, she had fixed her face into a smile.

"Goodbye, Mrs. Brinkman," Tim said. He was the only one who had followed her children down the stairs.

"Goodbye, Tim," she said, pleasantly, and then looked at Amanda, letting her see her hatred through that grimace of a smile, and closed the door.

———

The girls and Mikey continued playing upstairs. Tim asked if he could go outside for a while, and after reminding him that he still had half an hour's reading due from the morning, Amanda walked into the kitchen, cracked ice cubes into a plastic bag, held it to the side of her face, and went to the bathroom. In the mirror she saw that Barb Brinkman's purse had left a red welt on her cheekbone, though it didn't look bad enough to develop into a bruise. Holding the ice to her cheek, she looked at herself in the mirror--really looked at herself. Except for her evening out with Nathan, she had for months put on her makeup, brushed her hair, trimmed her eyebrows without really looking beyond those applications; she had not looked at the woman she had become.

Now she stared at the face in the mirror, the angular cheeks still thin from the time on the road, the mouth that seemed more inclined toward a frown than a smile, the wide, uncertain, and worried eyes, the bangs that needed trimming, the hair from behind her ears falling across her face. All her self-doubts, all her doubts about Nathan, swam in that face in the mirror. Who was she kidding, to think that Nathan might love her, that anyone could love her? What was there to love in this bundle of apprehension, fear, and self-reproach? And what had she done now? She had assaulted a mother of three, a woman who was at least willing to acknowledge openly her love, however twisted by her own turmoil and despair, for Nathan.

For the first time in her adult life Amanda Bell prayed. She had said the daily prayers with the children, bowed her head at meals with Nathan, and had even, usually holding Anne's journal in her hands, tried to pray alone, but these were husks, words emptied of nourishment or real hope, aspirations to prayer rather than prayer itself. Now, looking into the mirror, she prayed. She prayed that God would give her a sign that Nathan truly cared for her, that he wanted her in some capacity other than as a governess and a guardian for his children, that they had some possibility of a future together. *Please*, she said in the silence of her heart, *please give me a sign that he wants me. Please show me that he loves me and that I might give him the love he deserves. Just some small sign that I am not deluding myself, that he somehow wants me in his life.*

———————

Supper that evening was for Amanda a miserable affair. The throbbing in her cheek was gone, but Barb's words marched across the back of her brain like accusatory witnesses, all pointing their fingers at her deluded hopes. She tried feigning good-cheer with Nathan and the children, but knew that she was coming across as wooden. After supper Nathan gave each of the children one of Barb's brownies and then read the note which she had as usual attached to the top of the plastic container, his face as impassive as if he were perusing an advertisement from Wal-Mart. When he had finished, he folded the letter and slipped it into his shirt pocket.

Throughout the rest of the evening Amanda contemplated telling him what had happened that day and how she had slapped Barb Brinkman. Barb would surely relate the details, twisted to cast herself in the best light, to her friends, and Amanda feared that these half-lies would find their way back to Nathan.

But she couldn't bring herself to speak to him. When he came down to the living room around nine, having gotten Tim and Bridget into bed, she didn't join him for a visit, but decided instead to keep to her room and revel in her self-pity. Certain that he would take her absence as a desire for privacy, she was slumped down in the chair before the window when he knocked for her. She opened the door, and he took a step back, smiling.

"I wondered if you were coming out tonight."

"I might go to bed early this evening."

"Something wrong?"

"I--it's been a long day."

"You seemed distant at supper. Did anything happen?" He paused, and before she could answer he said, "Something happened with Barb Brinkman, didn't it?"

"Why do you ask that?" She wondered if he'd gotten a phone call.

"What else could it be? Besides, I can always tell when she's been here by the way you are at supper." Now she noticed that his smile wore a mischievous glitter, and his eyes sparkled with some inner joke. "You shouldn't pay too much attention to her, you know. I don't."

"She and I don't get along very well, I'm afraid."

He laughed then. "No, I'm sure you don't. Water and oil, I would think. She does make a wicked brownie, though. Would a brownie and a glass of milk coax you from your lair?"

"I'm not in the mood for brownies, thank you."

But he was not to be dissuaded. "A glass of wine, then? I bought some of that white merlot you like." When he saw her hesitate, his smile faded into earnest sobriety. "Please," he said. "I'd like to ask you something."

Wondering why he couldn't ask her right there, she reluctantly followed him into the kitchen. As he uncorked the wine and poured two glasses, he regained his roguish humor. "You know, Barb isn't just a whiz at brownies. She also keeps a very accurate calendar." He handed Amanda a glass, touched his glass to hers, said "Cheers," and tapped his shirt pocket wherein lay the letter. "She reminded me of the fall dance for home school parents."

"The one at the Basilica in Laurentine Hall?" She had heard several of the mothers discussing the dance at the last park day, but hadn't paid much attention.

"They have one every fall. It's nice, really. A wine bar. Some great hors d'oeuvres. I didn't go last year."

"And she'd like you to go?"

"That suggestion was made. She didn't want me to feel left out and offered to escort me. But it looks as though I'll have to turn her down."

"Why's that?" He was still smiling, and between that smile and the wine--the white merlot was a blend, and cheap, but Amanda loved the sweet, light taste--she was beginning to catch his off-beat mood. "Some other prospects beating down the door to your heart?"

"You are perceptive. You have nailed it precisely." He gestured toward her with his glass. "I'd like to take a certain Miss Amanda Bell to the dance."

She had asked for a sign. Here it was.

An automatic refusal was on her lips when she realized that she wanted nothing more in the world than to go with him to this dance--or any dance, for that matter. Only one small difficulty remained.

"I'm flattered," she said, maintaining their easy mood, "but I'm afraid I don't dance very well."

"You aren't Baptist, are you?"

"Baptist?"

"Some Baptists don't believe in dancing."

"No," Amanda said, and he looked so worried that she laughed. "I mean, I don't dance. I haven't danced since college, and even then it was fast dancing. I was awful."

With his concerns over her theological background allayed, Nathan relaxed back into his good humor. "One minute," he said, and put down his wine glass and left the room. In just a few seconds he returned with a CD, clicked it into the player which sat on the counter beside the microwave, and pushed the "On" button. Andy Williams began singing "Moon River," and Nathan moved toward her. Before Amanda could protest, he had taken away her wine glass, put it on the counter alongside his own, grasped her right hand firmly in his left, placed his other hand in the small of her back, and began slow dancing in a box-step in the wide space between the refrigerator and the doorway. Within another thirty seconds, he said, "Now a slow waltz," and switched his step, crooked his right arm upward, and glided with her up and down the kitchen floor through the rest of the song.

He was a fantastic dancer. He led firmly, was light on his feet and conservative in style, and moved with a natural rhythm to the beat of the music.

As for Amanda, she found herself a lump of lead transformed into gossamer, an uncoordinated goose made into a swan. Her feet followed his lead, and the pressure of his fingers on her fingers and on her back made her feel as if she had danced this way all her life. Effortlessly he guided her up and down that floor, coming within inches of the stove, cutting away from the door, carrying her past cabinets, coffee pot, and dishwasher. When the music played out, he dropped his hand from her back and spun her in a slow twirl, then stood holding her hand.

"I'd say you dance reasonably well."

Amanda was dazzled by his performance. The room still moved, the music played within her chest, she was panting slightly, a blush infused her face. He had touched a place buried deep within her. To mask her physical response to him, she asked: "Where did you learn to dance so well?"

"You're looking at the product of five years of cotillion classes with the infamous Mrs. Richardson, who until her death lived just three blocks from here and conducted dance classes in the living room of her house." He smiled at the far wall and Anne's picture. "And Anne loved to dance--all the old dances to the old tunes--so I had lots of practice over the years."

She was still stunned that this man could so easily make her a dancer. Rod Stewart was singing something about moonlight and roses, and Nathan pulled her closer to dance again, but Amanda stepped back, but kept her hold on his hands. "I'm not sure this is a good idea."

"Dancing?"

"Not just dancing." Being so close to him and feeling his body moving against her had aroused both her sexual instincts and her sense of danger. Reluctantly she released his hands. "I'm not sure if it's a good idea if I go to the dance with you."

"Why not?"

"It might send the wrong signals."

His face and quick response told Amanda that he had already considered that idea. "If I go with Barb Brinkman, I will definitely be sending the wrong signals."

"What will people think?"

"People will think whatever they think."

"What about the children? What will they think?"

"The children think it's a great idea. In fact, we can teach them to dance. Anne used to give Bridget and Tim lessons three times a week."

"You told them?"

"Actually, it was partly their idea. Bridget's at least. She wanted to know what Mrs. Brinkman had said in the letter, and when I told her she said that I should ask you to the dance."

Still searching for some objection to put him off, Amanda shook her head. "I have nothing to wear."

"We'll buy you a dress."

"Nathan, I work for you. You can't just buy me a dress."

"We'll call it a bonus. I don't pay you enough anyway."

"I won't be comfortable with those people."

"You've met nearly everyone. Mary Celeste and Tom will be there. And me." He was still smiling. "I'm afraid you're hooked."

"It's going to change how people look at us. Some of them aren't going to like it. Some of them don't like it already."

"Don't like what?" he asked, and then said: "I'm not a fool. I know what some of them think. You aren't going to make me beg, are you?"

"What will you tell Mrs. Brinkman?"

"I'll tell Barb the truth. That I appreciate her offer, but that I have a date."

"I'm afraid. I don't want to see you or the children hurt."

Amanda meant what she said, but the fact of the matter was that she had already given him her answer, and Nathan knew it. They were still standing close, and the dancing and talking and his touch had only left her wanting more of him. He sensed her attraction, the way she stood in front of him, not moving away, and laughed with such boyish triumph that she could only smile back at him.

"Swing dance?" he said, still laughing around the words. He took her hand and squeezed. "I do a wicked dip."

Chapter Fourteen

Amanda had her sign. She knew how Nathan felt about her, and she about him; they both knew, and over the next few days that knowledge pushed at them like a fast, hard current. Nathan made no further physical advances other than the touch of his hand when they practiced dancing in the evenings, and neither of them spoke of their feelings, but the mutual attraction lay between them, a bridge across a chasm wanting only the ceremony of a cut ribbon and a first tentative footfall.

In all of Amanda's previous experience of boys and men, the ladder of love was a short, blunt stepping stool whose top rung was coitus, carnality, fornication, sex. The society that had constructed this ladder now struck her as so emotionally crippled that the men and women shaped by its sculpting--its music, its art, its films, its television--were, in spite of their sexual freedoms, growing more and more distant from one another, more and more remote from real passion. In the last fifty years men and women had shaken loose the sexual shackles of the past, had become walking how-to manuals of sexual technique, but they had lost the deeper passions of their ancestors. "What's love got to do with it? Who needs a heart when a heart can be broken?": these lyrics from a popular song constituted, Amanda thought, the anthem of their liberation.

But she and Nathan were living in a different time--older, softer, warmer. Whether by dint of their circumstances, their respect for the other, or the dictates of faith, Amanda realized that together they were experiencing romance, the ecstasies of the heart found in *Le Morte d'Arthur*, in the sonnets of Shakespeare and the lyric poetry of the Cavalier poets, in Austen and the Bronte sisters, in Tennyson, Rossetti, and all the other poets and writers who had approached the sexual act not as a laboratory experiment or a piece of machinery, but as the coupling of nerve and blood, lust and passion, of desires heightened and checked by solicitude and charity. In her courtship with Nathan implication ruled: a murmur contained a world of meaning, a smile brightened a room.

In the late evenings they danced. They waltzed on the big back porch, they box-stepped in the kitchen, they did the swing on the concrete patio behind the house. Some saint once said "Pray all the time. If necessary, use words," and this same precept applied to Nathan's teaching. He spoke only a little, showing Amanda instead how to move, teaching her by guiding her through the steps. They laughed at their missteps, mostly Amanda's, and joked about becoming Astaire and Rogers, but at the same time they held each other delicately, lightly, as if what they were making might be easily broken.

"Dancing?" Father Krumpler said. "And you're going to a dance as well. Splendid, splendid."

"What do you mean 'splendid, splendid?'" Amanda asked. "Are you not listening to me?"

"Well, let's see. Nathan has asked you to a dance. You are practicing dancing with him in the evenings. And you're in love with each other. Does that about sum it up?"

"I like him," Amanda said. "I never said I loved him."

"Of course you didn't. Your entire generation is as terrified of using the word love as your grandfathers were of the word 'poorhouse.' Love scares you all to death."

"I see you're feeling fat and sassy after that meal."

Amanda had deep-fried two dozen chicken wings, then baked them with spicy sauce, and served them up with coleslaw and a loaf of warm French bread. Father Krumpler had told her that wings were his downfall, that they were terrible for his cholesterol but were, in his own words, "the food of the gods" in terms of taste. He had eaten half-a-dozen wings himself, licking his fingers and consuming a small pile of napkins, and now sat drinking a glass of chardonnay, happy that another pile of cooked wings awaited him in the refrigerator.

"Fat and sassy is exactly how I feel," he said. "Sassy enough at any rate to encourage honest language. Why can't you say you're in love with Nathan?"

"People don't say that anymore."

"Sure they do. At least, the wise ones do." He licked once more at his fingers. "Do you know that dancing is one of the ways human beings court each other? Like birds. Or certain insects. Was it George Bernard Shaw who quipped that dancing is the vertical expression of a horizontal desire legalized by music?"

"I don't know who said it, but I do know someone who wolfed down too many chicken wings tonight."

"Chicken wings are the ambrosia, the sauce, the nectar of the Olympus. And yours are as good as any I've ever tasted. All right, then--we'll skip love. Do you like Nathan?"

"Yes."

"And he likes you?" He was still smiling, playing with her.

"Yes, for heaven's sakes. And now I'm sorry I told you."

"No, you're not. You're not sorry at all. People in love can hardly contain themselves. I suspect you want to burst out with song and throw flowers at everyone you meet."

Amanda choked back another rebuttal, mostly because the Old Owl was absolutely right. She had floated through these last few days, a feather in the warm September air, and Father Krumpler was the first to hear her news. His delight had lifted her even higher, and she had spent fifteen minutes talking non-stop about her evenings with Nathan. Bread, coleslaw, and an uneaten wing still lay on her cold plate.

Father Krumpler sang, loudly:

"You're as corny as Kansas in August,

You're as high as the Fourth of July,

If you'll excuse the expression I use,

You're in love with a wonderful guy."

Amanda was thankful they weren't sitting outside the Grove Arcade where she would now be the center of attention of a dozen other diners. "Apologies to Rodgers and Hammerstein, I assume?"

"Once upon a time I loved musicals. Do you know I saw Mary Martin in the original Broadway production?"

"My mom loved show tunes. *South Pacific* was one of her favorites."

"Artificial contrivances, of course. A product of a more innocent time. Still, the music has held up. Do you want to hear more?"

"Thank you, no. Do chicken wings always have this effect on you?"

"No, not the wings. But watching two people fall in love sends my spirits soaring, especially when I know and love the two people myself. The world's a dark place and it's heartening to the rest of us to see a candle in that darkness."

"It's not heartening to everyone."

The Old Owl's hair wanted cutting; it stuck up, tufted and tangled, on the top of his head and jutted out beneath the spectacles about his ears. By her comment Amanda had sought some injunction or warning about Barb, but Father Krumpler sat smiling at her without saying a word. Losing patience, she said directly: "No advice?"

"Do you need advice?"

"Anything might help."

He feigned a sigh.

"Don't be a naughty old owl."

He drew himself upright, raised his right hand as if he meant to bless her, but then lifted his forefinger and counted: "One, trust your heart. You're ready." Up came the middle finger: "Two, avoid eating poisoned apples. Run as fast as you can from wickedness." Then the ring finger: "Three, take the glass slipper if it comes your way. Let some magic into your life." And then the little finger: "And four, Amanda Bell, allow yourself the possibility of joy."

———

There was still the matter of the dress.

"What do the other women wear?" Amanda asked Mary Celeste. She had driven over that evening for a hike through Montford and was striding beside Amanda at a fast clip. The evening was warm enough to do without a sweater, and they had walked down Cumberland, around Montford Park, and were making their way up Montford Avenue when Amanda told her that Nathan had asked her to the dance. Mary Celeste stopped and did a little dance of her own on the sidewalk, delighted by the news. "It's about time. I knew he would ask you, but he really dragged his feet."

She sympathized with Amanda's fears regarding gossip and Barb Brinkman and her comrades. "Stare straight at them. Confront them. Refuse them permission to make you feel small or bad about yourself."

"I don't want them to hate me. I don't want them to think poorly of me or of Nathan. Or of the children, for that matter."

Here Mary Celeste agreed with Nathan's disdainful comment. "They'll think what they think. Your job is to know the truth and then go ahead."

They were passing the convenience store on Montford when Amanda asked about attire.

"Most of the men wear coats and ties, though not all. And the women wear dresses or skirts. People dress, but it's not too formal. What were you thinking of wearing?"

"I don't have any good dresses here. I left them in Atlanta." That city and her life there seemed far away, dream and nightmare meshed together, unreal. Mentally she sorted through the clothing Justin had packed away. "There were the clothes I wore for work--a blue sleeveless dress, lots of white blouses and different skirts. Mostly black and red. Three or four business outfits, mostly grey with white or pink blouses. One obligatory little black dress. A rust-colored outfit that I never liked much. I don't know why I wore that one...."

"Whoa," Mary Celeste said. "Back up. How did that black dress look on you?"

"All right, I guess." Amanda had bought clothes in those days to intimidate or impress, and had worn the black dress at some office parties, Chamber of Commerce functions, and catered meetings.

"Go for the black dress. If you're going to cause an explosion, it might as well be a big one." Her eyes glowed playfully at the thought, and Amanda was certain she was imagining the face of Barb Brinkman. "Yes, a little black dress would be just the thing."

"But I don't want to cause an explosion."

"Too late."

"Why? What happened?"

"Nothing happened. But everyone knows you and Nathan are going to the dance together. Some of them--his true friends--are happy to see Nathan take an interest in life again. Some of them couldn't care less. Some of them, for whatever reason, hate you for it."

There was no point in pursing that last point. The previous Friday afternoon at the park Amanda had felt scrutinized by a few of the women. She had followed Mikey around as usual, helping him climb up the yellow plastic sliding board, pushing him in the swing, filling his plastic bucket in the sandbox. Barb hadn't shown up that day, which struck Amanda as strange, for she had not missed, to the best of Amanda's recollection, a park day. Even though she remained away from the mothers who had gathered round the picnic tables, the prickling at the back of her neck told her she was the recipient of some intense examination.

"I wish I was invisible."

"Well, you're hardly that." They turned down Elizabeth Street toward Cumberland and the house. "Look here--tomorrow evening after supper you and I will go shopping. No, wait--that's too late in the day. Tomorrow afternoon I'll bring my crew over to the house and Erin can watch the children while you and I go shopping. We'll look at dresses. I know several good places."

"I have to budget my money."

"We'll start with the Goodwill store and work our way up. We'll look at all sorts of dresses and see which one best suits you." She squinted at Amanda, a look of appraisal, and laughed that inimitable laugh. "But my money's on the little black dress."

———

"Kismet," Mary Celeste said.

They were in the women's aisle of the Goodwill Store on Patton Avenue, the first store to which they had gone, and the black dress was hanging on display at the end of a rack of six dollar skirts and dresses--a Mac and Jac number soft as silk. With her eyes dancing in triumph, Mary Celeste took the dress from the rack and held it up in front of Amanda. "What size are you?"

"I'm a six."

She looked at the tag and laughed. "It's a six. Kismet again."

"I didn't know Catholics believed in fate."

"In this case, it's more than fate. It's a miracle. A dress like this that fits you for seven dollars, you must be living right."

"You don't think it's too--" she couldn't find the right word--"too flashy?"

"Not flashy, no. But it's sexy as all get-out. Try it on."

In the dressing room with its garish yellow lights Amanda slipped out of her slacks and blouse, and shimmied into the dress. It felt light as air on her hips and shoulders. The hem broke just above her knees, the sleeves fell an inch below her shoulders. The V-shaped neckline plunged to a point between her breasts. The shimmering material clung to her in all the right places. Amanda ran her fingers over the dress, trying to imagine how it might feel to Nathan.

"You're beautiful," Mary Celeste said when she stepped outside. "Turn around."

Amanda pirouetted slowly, blushing with embarrassment. The last time she had shopped for clothing with a companion she was seventeen years old and her mother had helped choose a dress for that year's prom.

"It's perfect."

"You don't think it's too much? I don't want to offend anyone."

Amanda had stopped turning, and Mary Celeste was examining the dress carefully for marks or tears. "How would you offend anyone?"

"I want to dress like the others. I don't want to look--" Amanda didn't need to search for the word, but felt awkward saying it. As usual, Mary Celeste had no trouble blurting it out.

"Too loaded for bear? Too hot to handle?" She touched the strap of the dress and made a sizzling sound. "Ouch!"

Amanda turned from her and examined the dress in the mirror on the door of the dressing-room. It fit as if designed especially for her. The last of her summer tan appeared warm and golden against the black material, and her hair, which had deepened in color the past year, was golden too. This time last year no second thoughts would have troubled her so--she would have bought the dress because it fit her so well and precisely because it made her look sexy and powerful--but now she wanted most of all to please Nathan without calling too much attention to herself. In the mirror Amanda saw Mary Celeste eyeing her critically.

"Amanda, you could be wearing sackcloth and ashes," she said, "and some woman would still hate you for your beauty. You can't let the Barb Brinkmans of the world decide what you can or can't wear."

Amanda ran her hands down her hips, feeling the material melt away beneath the tips of her fingers. Mary Celeste grinned, that wild, daring, trademark smile.

"We'll need some accessories," she said. "Some jewelry--nothing expensive--and some shoes."

"I have a pair of shoes that should match the dress."

Mary Celeste shook her head. "New dress, new shoes. I think it's some kind of a law."

———

A mirror is never a woman's best friend. That Saturday evening, as she stood before her own bedroom mirror, the image in the glass mocked her judgment. The black low-heeled pumps, which cost five times as much as the dress; the black shawl which she had picked up a week earlier at a thrift store on Lexington; the plain gold necklace and gold earrings which Mary Celeste had lent her: everything complimented the dress but her. She truly could not tell how she would appear to others, whether she looked as if she were trying too hard or whether she was too pointedly sexual. Was the hemline too long? It broke just above her knees. Too short, then? Did the neckline plunge too far between her breasts? She told herself to remember not to lean forward too much when seated. After so many months, she felt ill-at-ease in formal wear. She had compensated by wearing only a little make-up and a faint slash of rose-colored lipstick. She had pulled her hair back into a tiny bun at the back of her head. Everything was in place, yet still she felt ungainly, a cinder-sweep pretending to be a princess.

But her time was up. She squared her shoulders, picked up the tiny black handbag which had come from the same shop as the shawl, and touched Anne's journal which lay on her nightstand. She had borrowed the leather book from the shelf not to read but to serve as a talisman. What would Anne, the loving spirit who haunted this house, who had shaped Nathan and born and shaped his four children, think of her? Father Krumpler had once explained that the communion of saints was the bond between the living and the dead who were in heaven and purgatory, and as Amanda's fingers brushed the journal she asked Anne to watch over her this evening and to bring honor to herself and to Nathan. Then she opened the door of her room and stepped into the hallway.

In the living room Nathan stood with his hands behind his back. Behind him the children sat lined up on the sofa, their overnight bags at their feet. They were spending the night at the Moore house, where Mary Celeste had arranged for Erin and her best friend, Amelia Cardoza, to watch the children along with Erin's siblings. When they heard the click of the door latch, their heads swiveled as one in her direction. She walked toward them.

Bridget jumped to her feet. "Miss Bell," she said, and then stopped, staring.

Nathan came behind her, slim and handsome in his dark suit. Like Bridget, he seemed in a state of shock. Then he smiled. "You look absolutely beautiful."

"Like Aubrey Hepburn," Teresa said, running to Amanda. She had watched *Roman Holiday* that week. "Only with golden hair." She hugged Amanda around the waist before she could bend to her, and then pulled away and pinched the dress between her fingers. "It's so soft."

Then they were all around her, even Mikey who said "You smell like flowers," and they went out to the car with their bags and drove to the Moore's house. Teresa and Bridget sat on either side of Amanda in the back seat. Both of them kept looking up at her, their faces pale and solemn in the shadows, and she put her arms around them and gave them each a kiss on the forehead. "You'll be good for Erin tonight, won't you?" They nodded, and Teresa said, "She's going to teach me to play Monopoly, and I get to sleep with Maggie."

Bridget patted her fingers against Amanda's thigh. "Is it silk?"

"No, but it's soft, isn't it?"

"Did it cost a whole lot?"

"I bought it at Goodwill."

Bridget nodded approvingly. Her mother, Amanda knew from past conversations, had taken them shopping there many times. Bridget pulled herself erect and whispered in her ear, "You make daddy happy."

Amanda looked at her. "He used to be sad all the time, and now he's happier." She wiggled against her seatbelt and raised her face and kissed Amanda's cheek. "I love you, Miss Bell."

"And I love you," Amanda said, squeezing the girl's shoulder. And it was true, as real as the night itself. More than anything else in the world, she loved these four children and the man driving the car. More than anywhere else in the world, this was the place she had longed for in her heart for so many years. Had Bridget said anything else, tears might have ruined Amanda's face, but the girl turned toward the front of the car and rested her head again on Amanda's shoulder.

———

On the ride to the dance, the knot in Amanda's stomach tightened. Droplets of rain sprinkled across the windshield when they hit the bypass--Amanda had checked the weather that afternoon, wanting to leave nothing to chance about the evening--and after all her careful planning she realized that she had forgotten an umbrella. "There's one in the trunk," Nathan said when she asked. He smiled at her. "It's black, so it should go with that dress. You look great tonight. Have I told you that already?" He laughed. He had already complimented her several times, though his finest tributes came from the glances he threw her way. "I'm almost afraid to dance with you. You're like one of those desserts that looks so pretty no one wants to touch it."

Amanda smiled and tried to banter back, but apprehension had dulled her wits. Her mouth was dry, and a vise of nerves pinched her throat.

"You all right?" Nathan asked kindly.

"Yes," Amanda replied. Her voice was high and shrill, and Nathan looked at her, and then they both laughed. "I'm all right," Amanda said, in a voice that no longer sounded like Minnie Mouse. "I'm a little nervous."

"Me too, if that helps any."

"Why are you nervous?"

"It's the first time I've gone to anything like this since Anne died. I've done picnics with this group, and a few parties, but no dances. Or maybe I'm just naturally nervous around women who look like movie stars when they wear black dresses."

He started to say something else about the dress, a joke no doubt to ease her fears, but instead lifted his hand from the steering-wheel and touched the back of his fingers to her cheek. "It's going to be all right, Miss Bell. We're going to be the hit of the party, the mystery couple, the dynamic duo, the pair in black who set all tongues wagging."

A shiver ran through her, and for comfort she reached for his hand and held it in her lap. Outside of dancing, they had never held hands, and their interlaced fingers brought her strength and calmed her alarm. He stroked her fingers, and she lay her other hand on their twined fingers, feeling the heat rise within her. His touch was the most natural thing in the world.

He squeezed her hand. "Just follow my lead. Like dancing."

If I keep holding his hand, Amanda told herself, nothing bad can happen.

———

Laurentine Hall, which sat beneath the hundred-year-old basilica, was an architectural gem in its own right. To the right of the entrance were a small kitchen and the restrooms, while to the left was the hall itself, a medieval-looking place with brick walls and a large brick column in the center of the room. Here were more of Gustafino's signature tiled ceilings. Miniature copies of the tiled dome in the church above, these ceilings captured and amplified all sounds made beneath them.

On this stormy evening--Nathan and Amanda had seen sheet lightning in the mountains beyond the church as they walked down the short hill to the entrance--the church hall resembled a castle great-room set up for a night of feasting. At the far end of the hall were two tables draped in green cloth and laden with wine bottles and two tubs of beer in ice. Halfway down the wall toward the kitchen was a table with musical equipment and a DJ, an older man with his gray hair knotted into a ponytail. Along the same wall nearer the kitchen were several tables covered with food. Amanda took the key lime yogurt pies she had prepared earlier that day to the dessert table.

"Chin up," Nathan had joked as they entered the hall. "Eyes front." Yet the first three people they encountered--a dark-haired woman on a cell phone at the coat racks and two men engaged in conversation at the top of the short flight of steps leading to the hall--were complete strangers, at least to Amanda, and it was not until they had turned from the dessert table that she remembered Mary Celeste telling her that homeschooling Catholic parents from Hendersonville had also been invited to the dance.

As she and Nathan searched for their seats among the tables between the bar and the music, Suzanne Gordon spotted Amanda and waved her over. She had five-year-old twin boys and a two-year-old girl, and had just joined the organization in September. She was a year younger than Amanda and shared her affinity for Jane Austen.

"It's so nice to see you, Amanda."

Suzanne was one of those women who can bear a child and three months later look as if she was ready to run a 5-K race. Tonight she wore a shimmering blue dress and a turquoise pendant around her neck, and looked no older than a teenager. "I hardly know anyone here. Your table's right this way. I hope you don't mind, but I had them switch some seating cards so we could sit together. I was nervous about seeing everyone." They reached the table, set for six, and Suzanne introduced herself to Nathan. "I've heard lots about you from some of the other moms."

"I'm not nearly in need of confession as they say."

Suzanne laughed. "Actually, from all I've heard about you, I was expecting a cross between Heathcliff and Mr. Darcy."

Nathan looked at her with puzzled eyes.

"You'll have to forgive him," Amanda said. "He's not a fan."

"Don't feel bad," Suzanne said to Nathan. "Neither is Jonathan. His tastes in literature run to golf magazines and political biographies. Here he is now."

A man, tall, gangly, and bluff with weather, appeared at her elbow carrying two glasses of white wine. Suzanne made the introductions. "Jonathan's with the forestry service," she said. "I'm lucky he's here. He collects data on forest fires, and this time of year often takes him out of town, but there aren't any fires anywhere tonight."

Nathan shook Jonathan's hand and asked him what exactly it was he did with the service. Suzanne rested one hand on her husband's shoulder and asked where Mary Celeste was. Amanda explained the shared babysitting arrangement.

"She and Tom should be here soon." Amanda pointed to the two remaining chairs at the table, one of which contained a large brown purse. "Who else is sharing our table?"

"The Tortinellis. One of the Hendersonville crew. Tess told me that they had tried to mix up the tables so we could all get to know one other." Tess, a tall woman with a slight stoop who was one of Barb Brinkman's close friends, had recently taken to treating Amanda with silent contempt. "That's them over there at the hors d'oeuvres table." She indicated a dark-haired man and a heavy-set woman with beautiful long black hair. "He does something with computers and they have four children. They're nice."

"Would you like a glass of wine?" Nathan asked Amanda.

"Yes, please."

"Chardonnay?"

"That would be wonderful."

As soon as he left, weaving his way among the tables and chairs toward the bar, stopping to say hello to different acquaintances, Amanda felt vulnerable and alone. Probably it was a trick of the imagination, or outright paranoia, but she couldn't rid herself of the feeling that some of the others were watching her. Suzanne chattered on about a kindergarten program she was using for the twins, and Amanda made an effort to pay attention to her, grateful that Suzanne was either ignorant of how some in the group felt about her relationship with Nathan or that she had decided to ignore their slanders.

"There's Mary Celeste and Tom," Suzanne said, breaking off, somewhat breathless. From the other side of the tables near the door Mary Celeste waved, no doubt relieved she had found Amanda with Suzanne rather than Barb or some of the others.

"She's nice," Suzanne said. "You're friends, aren't you?"

"Yes."

"Someone said you were."

Those simple words, the tone with which she spoke them, told Amanda that Suzanne was cognizant of the gossip, aware of the rumors surrounding her, and that she had decided to take the charitable route and ignore them. She smiled at Amanda now, looking young and fresh, still a girl in many ways, and Amanda wanted to hug her from sheer gratitude for her charity. The hall suddenly seemed brighter, the lights warmer, the company of strangers and familiars more welcoming.

Looking past Suzanne, Amanda saw that Tom and Mary Celeste had stopped to talk to a couple she didn't know, more guests from Hendersonville, but Mary Celeste was frowning in her direction.

"Hello there," said Barb Brinkman.

She had come up behind Amanda while she was talking with Suzanne. At her side was a tall man wearing glasses and with hair graying at the temples. He had a strong angular face, bright and alert, and intelligent brown eyes.

"Amanda, Suzanne, I'd like you to meet Dr. Frederick Healy," Barb said. "Frederick, this is Amanda Bell and Suzanne Gordon."

Politely he inclined his head. "Most people call me Fred."

"Frederick is a radiologist at Mission," Barb said, ignoring his comment.

"Hello, Fred," Nathan said, joining them. He handed Amanda her wine, smiling as if he hadn't a care in the world. "And Barb--it's good to see you too."

"You know Frederick?" Barb asked in surprise.

"I put up a barn on his property four years ago. All timber-framing and native stone, and built as solidly as any house."

"More than any house," Fred added. "My horses sleep better than I do."

"It's probably the only barn in Western North Carolina with a game room and a wet bar," Nathan said.

"This guy is the best," Fred said. "With a little care, that barn will be there long after the house is gone."

"So you know Barb?" Nathan asked.

"We met at a medical meeting," Barb said, and turned to Amanda before any other questions could be asked. "You look stunning tonight, Amanda. Very much ready to dance."

Amanda understood Barb's code and what she meant by "dance." But Nathan took her remark as an opportunity. "Speaking of dancing," he said, "I'm ready for the floor. Amanda?" He took the glass of wine from Amanda's hand, placed it on the table alongside his own, and took her hand. "We'll break the ice."

———

Breaking the ice for Amanda meant falling into dark, cold water. The dance floor, scarcely more spacious than the living room where they had practiced, loomed before her large and empty. But the DJ brightened when he saw they intended to dance, called "What'll it be?" and when Nathan called back "Anything you want," the DJ hit a few buttons and announced "Zoot Suit Riot."

It was swing music all the way, an easy number for dancing, and Nathan led Amanda through the steps as if they were back home, but with an added charge of excitement now running through his hands and his movements. Amanda was conscious of the eyes on them--when he spun her around, she saw Barb watching with cool brittle eyes from the tables--but then the music took her up, and as others joined them on the floor, her self-awareness dropped away and she simply danced. When the music stopped, the DJ called out "We're off and dancing!" and played another fast swing number. Other couples came to the floor, including Mary Celeste and Tom, and they danced more tightly together, bumping together at times and laughing. Then he played Natalie Cole singing "Unforgettable" and Nathan, who at home had slow-danced in a formal way, now pulled Amanda closer to him, their faces almost touching.

"It's all right?"

"We'd look strange otherwise," Nathan said. "Look around you." The other couples swayed together, all close. Mary Celeste had buried her head against Tom's shoulder, looking like a girl in love at her first formal. "Unless you mind."

"I'd hate to look strange."

He chuckled. "A joke and the night is young. Miss Bell, I do believe you're loosening up." He squeezed her hand. "Sometimes I wonder what's become of my prim and starchy governess."

"I left her hanging in the closet back home."

Nathan pulled her to him. The Drifters began singing "Up On The Roof." Amanda closed her eyes, rested her head against his chest and shoulder, and let the music carry her, breathing in his scent, feeling the heat and strength of his body. Here was another stepping-stone toward each other, this dance in public where their feelings, always hidden behind words, concealed by what he called her prim governess and his own formal demeanor, were revealed, not only to those watching them, but more importantly, to each other. Since the beach they had communicated in code, letting others see them one way while they practiced their private cryptography, deciphering signals and messages sent through words and eyes. Now, for the first time, they had dispensed with the code.

They danced through several more songs, then Nathan took her hand and led her to the buffet. Here were shrimp and quiche, seafood and chicken casseroles, and a medley of side dishes and breads.

Carrying their plates, they returned to their table and found Tom and Mary Celeste seated at the table next to them.

"You looked great dancing out there," Mary Celeste said. "Nathan, I'd forgotten about all those dance lessons you took as a kid."

"Mrs. Richardson is doubtless smiling down from heaven," he replied, then added as an afterthought: "Though I have trouble seeing her with a smile on her face."

Mary Celeste leaned closer to Amanda. "You look lovely tonight. Any attacks from the Barb brigade?"

"None so far."

Suzanne returned with her own plate of food, followed by Jonathan. "How'd you learn to dance that way?"

"I had a good teacher." Amanda nodded toward Nathan.

"You're kidding me. You, Nathan? I would never have taken you for a dancer. You seems so quiet and shy. Of course, I've only just met you. Anyway, the two of you looked great out there. This is such fun. Hi, Mary Celeste," she said, leaning past Amanda. "Hey, I'd like to talk to you sometime about the Seton curriculum. When you have a chance, I mean."

For the next half hour or so, eating and chatting, Amanda felt safe, so protected that protection soon ceased to be of any concern. Suzanne and Nathan sat on either side of her, and Amanda could turn to chat with Mary Celeste whenever she wished. She enjoyed getting to know Suzanne. She was bright with innocence, charitable in her opinions, as playful in spirit as a puppy.

She and Nathan danced again, and drank wine, and as Tom Moore put it, "grazed the buffet." Lisa Tortinelli, the dark woman from Hendersonville sharing the table, was reserved, but her husband Anthony, a systems analyst and computer trouble-shooter with the Henderson County government, was a gregarious bear of a man. He had left the Army four years earlier, having fulfilled his ROTC commitment, and swapped stories about military life with Tom. Several times Nathan left the table to say hello to other friends, but Amanda scarcely noticed. She no longer felt the need of remaining at his side.

The thunder-clouds outside had burst over the basilica shortly after their arrival, illuminating the windows with lightning and once causing the lights to flicker, but Amanda could see by the windows near the buffet that the storm had settled into a steady rain. The hall which was so gloomy in the daytime had come alive now with the glow of the table candles, the music, and the conversation, cloaking her, Amanda thought, in anonymity, making her no different than any of the others. Even when she and Nathan danced, the floor was crowded with other couples.

The room was too small to avoid Barb Brinkman altogether-- Amanda saw her several times stealing a glance in her direction, stolid-faced, and heard her odd, false laughter--but she kept her distance. All Amanda's apprehensions that Barb might create a scene, that she might do or say something to damage Amanda or Nathan in front of everyone, appeared misplaced. On this night at least, there was to be no lit match, no fuse, no keg of powder, no explosion. Barb seemed happy enough being with her Dr. Healy, and her affection for the man made Amanda wonder whether she hadn't changed the object of her interests from architecture to medicine.

———

Around ten o'clock, the DJ announced a short break from the music and turned his microphone over to Karen Gorman. Karen was a thin, short woman with close-cropped, frost-tipped hair, narrow brown eyes, and a Jersey accent. Though she had introduced herself to Amanda on the playground during the early summer, she had since avoided her. Amanda couldn't be sure, but suspected Karen was one of the women who had bought into Barb's calumnies.

When Karen stood in the light beside a small table holding several packages and envelopes, the buzz of conversation in the room slowly faded. "Welcome again, everybody, to the fall dance," she said. "We still have two hours until our evening together ends. I hope you're all having a grand time. How about a round of applause for Barb Brinkman and the decoration committee?"

The brick and tile room rang with loud applause.

"We have something special for the ladies tonight," Karen continued. "I have five gifts wrapped up here on the table. Three of them are gag gifts, and two will make you happy you came here tonight. We've put your names in the basket. The first five names win the gifts."

She reached into the basket and drew out a slip of paper. "Alicia Munez wins the first gift. Alicia is visiting us from Hendersonville. Come on up, Alicia."

Alicia, a petite woman in her forties with long, black, braided hair, went to the front of the room and opened the gift which Karen handed her. Everyone clapped when she held up a piece of paper and Karen announced, "A family pass to the Arboretum."

After Alicia sat down, Karen pulled another slip from the bowl. "Andrea O'Connor gets prize number two."

Prize number two was an old black iron. Andrea, one of the older mothers who was quiet but who had always gone out of her way to include Amanda in conversations when she was present, laughed after she had unwrapped this gift, then mimed using it as a dumbbell. Someone near the front called out, "A door stop for a door prize," and Andrea laughed again, looked at it, and said, "I'm not sure what I'll use it for--my husband and children can tell you what I think of ironing-- but I'll figure out something and let you know."

Again Karen ran her hand through the names in the bowl. This time she seemed to take just a few seconds longer. She held up the paper and read, "Amanda Bell."

Hearing her name in that room shocked Amanda, for she was not an official member of the organization. With Nathan smiling encouragement, she got to her feet and walked toward Karen, feeling smaller and more vulnerable with each step. When she got to the microphone, Karen handed her a blue gift bag topped with crumpled white paper. Amanda took the bag and started for her seat.

"Open it up," Karen said.

Amanda pulled out the wrapping paper, put the paper on the table, and drew from the bag a bundle of black cloth. After placing the bag on the table, she shook out the flimsy cloth and held it with both hands. There was a small gasp from some of those near her when they saw the fishnet teddy. Then someone laughed.

"A Sheer Lace Teddy with a pink bow from Victoria's Secret," Karen said, capitalizing the words with her voice. She had turned to look at Amanda as she spoke, which meant that Amanda was the only one in the room who could see the mix of mockery and triumph hiding in the woman's eyes. "The second gag gift of the evening. Or maybe not a gag gift after all. Amanda, that little outfit matches your dress nicely." Some people laughed while a few, men and women, whooped at the black undergarment. Seemingly encouraged by their reaction, Karen plucked the flimsy undergarment from Amanda's fingers, stood to one side, and held it up in front of Amanda. "It fits you," she declared. "Some fishnet stockings and scarlet garters, and you'll have the perfect outfit."

She handed the teddy to Amanda, and as she hugged her, she whispered in her ear, "How appropriate." Turning back to the microphone, she said, "Let's have a hand for a good sport."

She couldn't let it end this way. She fixed her eyes on Barb Brinkman, bumped Karen from the microphone with her hip, and held up the teddy between two fingers. She forced a smile to her face. "Well," she said, "I don't think it will work as a doorstop."

As the others broke into loud applause, she blindly stuffed the shimmering garment into its bag and made her way to her seat, unable to look at anyone, the smile plastered on her face. Karen's whisper told her what she had instantly suspected, that the gift was part of plot, that Karen and Barb and perhaps some of the others had deliberately aimed this gift at her. A great rage rose up in her alongside the pain they had caused, yet she could do or say nothing but return to her table smiling like a fool.

———

When Amanda sat, dropping the bag beside her chair, the others around her were laughing and making good-natured jokes. "Thank heavens I didn't win that prize," Suzanne said to Amanda. "You were great, but I would have died from embarrassment."

Only Mary Celeste seemed to understand what had happened. She touched Amanda's shoulder, pulled her closer, and squeezed. "Good job," she whispered. "Don't let those bitches see how you feel."

Close to tears, Amanda nodded. The smile on her face hurt. Mechanically, she lifted the glass of wine to her lips. She didn't hear the next two names called by Karen Gorman, or the applause, and never saw what two remaining gifts were bestowed on others in the room. The fury and pain inside her sucked down all other perceptions as though into a dark whirlpool. Nathan leaned to her and said something, but his words seemed faraway and void of meaning.

And yet slowly, within the next few minutes the pain abated, and the room ceased to be a blur. The music was playing, and the voices around her became real again. "Where's Suzanne?" she asked.

"She took some of the dishes to the kitchen," Nathan said. "Said she wanted to give us some elbow room on the table. Would you like to dance again?"

His face wore such an undisguised affection that Amanda shivered. Whether he understood what had just taken place at the microphone was hidden away. All that showed was his love for her.

"Let me give Suzanne a hand first," she said, touching Nathan on the shoulder and thinking to herself how the others--Barb and her crew of magpies--would never hurt him, that they couldn't touch him, that he loved her and would evade forever their fangs and claws. She wanted to kiss him simply for the tenderness showing in his face, but said instead, "I'll be right back."

Scooping up a pile of plates, napkins, and utensils, she walked around the clutter of tables and people, staying in the shadows, skirting the dance floor, and descended the three steps leading to the kitchen. She had reached the last step when she heard her name.

"But I don't think Amanda's that way at all," Suzanne was saying. "She's nice. She--"

"--she's brought scandal to our group," someone said, and Amanda recognized the voice that had whispered so hatefully in her ear. "You know what she's doing in that house. Think of the children. Do you think it's right--"

A clatter of dishes hid her next words.

"--won't believe that," Suzanne was saying. "The children seem perfectly all right to me, and I know they love Amanda. I've watched them at Mass and on the playground. You're all wrong, and you should stop right now. There's clearly nothing--"

"There's clearly everything," Barb Brinkman said. "Open your eyes and look at her. Look at what she's wearing tonight. That dress. Look at how she dances with him, how she looks at him. And look at how she throws herself at him. She's got him all bollixed up. Nathan's lonely and then she moves in and starts sneaking into his life."

"It's not our business," Suzanne said, furiously. "None of you have the right to do this to her."

"It's clear what's going on," said another voice, one Amanda didn't recognize. "Did you know that the children are sleeping over at the Moore's house? That leaves her and Nathan together for the rest of the night. What do you think they'll do? Go home and dance off to separate bedrooms?"

"I don't know what they'll do." Amanda pictured Suzanne backed against a wall, cut off from any exit, trapped. "It's not my business to know what they'll do. Or yours either."

"It is our business," Barb cut in. "We all knew Anne. The woman was a saint. Do you think she'd approve of someone like Amanda moving in and raising her children and corrupting her husband? Amanda Bell is a nobody who came out of nowhere who sees what Nathan has and wants it for herself."

"But he has four little children. I don't know too many woman who would be willing--"

By now Amanda was walking backwards up the steps, the plates clutched in hands, her breath caught in her throat. She had to get away; she had to find some escape; she couldn't stand here and listen to them anymore.

"She's two-faced," Karen said. "She's like one of those step-mothers in the fairy tales, all sweetness and light until she marries Nathan, and then she'll be a dictator. She knows he'd never agree to a divorce. Once they're married and she has him in her claws, she can--"

Amanda swiveled toward the dance floor, toward the tables beyond, and smashed into a body coming down the stairs, a man, upending the plates with their remnants of red shrimp sauce, bits of fruit, and gobs of rice casserole into her chest. The plates fell from her hands, clattering and breaking on the tiled floor, spattering her legs with more food.

"Good grief! Amanda!" Jonathan Gordon had stepped backwards and was regarding her with horror and regret on his face at the mess they'd made. "I'm sorry. I was just looking for Suzanne. I--"

But Amanda was already past him, half-running toward the door just beyond the pillar, slipping toward the night, an escape, solitude.

Chapter Fifteen

She had forgotten the rain.

The thunder and lightning had gone, but the rain fell in a steady downpour on the streets and pavements. Amanda was wet before she had gone twenty feet from the door, still half-running, and by the time she had crossed the bridge into Montford her dress was soaked, clinging cold and wet to her skin. A car approached her as she reached the other end of Flint Street, its lights cutting across her arms and breasts, and she caught a glimpse of the driver's startled face as he passed her. She slowed to a fast walk, folding her arms across her chest, aware of the cold and the smell of wet earth from the yards and gardens of the houses. The shadows deepened as she left the bridge, and she lengthened her stride, shivering, pushing herself to walk faster, thinking that if she could only reach the house, she could throw her belongings into a duffel, dump the bag into car, and escape before Nathan even knew she was gone. If she could just make the house, she might have a chance to disappear back into herself.

She had put the church three blocks behind her when she remembered she had left her house keys in her purse on the table beside the dance floor.

She'd break a window. She'd take one of the bricks from the garden path and smash the window of the back door, turn the lock, assemble her belongings, and go to her car. She kept a spare key for the car in the nightstand beside her bed. She would pack a few things, get the key, start her car, and drive away, drive somewhere, anywhere, before Nathan could find her or before she could be hurt anymore. She would call Father Krumpler and see if he might give her shelter from the night and all those hideous half-truths. If she couldn't reach him, she would just go away, away from all the lies, poison, and hate. She had done it once. She could do it again.

Another car came from behind her, splashing her with light, and she pulled her arms more tightly together and hurried on. She was shivering now in the cold and the rain, and the big trees along the street afforded little protection. Rainwater ran down her face and hair; her soaked dress clung to her thighs and breasts; her feet squished inside her shoes.

The car passed her, then cut into the opposite lane and swung up against the curb. Blinking from the rain, Amanda saw the driver's door open, and Nathan stepped out.

"Get in the car, Amanda."

"I don't want to." Her teeth were chattering. She brushed the water from her eyes. "Leave me alone."

"Please," he said. "Get in the car."

She started to walk past him, but he stepped in front of her, the car running, the door open. "You're soaked. Get in the car and we'll talk."

She tried again going round him, but again he sidestepped her, blocking the pavement, close enough to touch her. She couldn't see his eyes in the shadows. He shrugged out of his coat and put it around her shoulders. She tried to take it off, but he held it in place. "Please," he said. He left his hands on her shoulders, holding her there with the rain soaking through his shirt, and then steered her toward the passenger's side of the car. "Please get in. We're both getting drenched out here. Look--you're shivering. Come on now. Come on. I'll drive you home. Jonathan told me about the dress. He was really sorry. He didn't--"

"It wasn't the dress." She halted again, standing in the rain though he had opened the door. "It wasn't the dress."

"I know." Gently he pushed at her shoulder, and she ducked her head and sat on the seat. "I know what happened," he said, and closed the door.

He moved quickly to the other side of the car, as if he thought she might run, and ducked inside and closed the door. On the console between them were her purse and shawl; he had remembered to get them before coming after her. His shirt was splotched with drops of rain. She sat beside him shivering, her face averted, looking out the side window at the wet, black night. She didn't want him to see her this way, not tonight, not ever, not this way, not defeated and running away, and she began crying, no longer caring about her makeup. The runnels of rainwater had ruined her face anyway.

"I know what happened," he said, "and now I'm going to drive you home where you can be warm and dry."

"You don't know." Her lips and mouth wouldn't work properly, the words broken by emotion and by her shivering.

"I do know," he said, and pulled the car from the curb and drove them the remaining four blocks to the house in silence, gliding into the back lot, cutting the lights and switching off the engine. He popped open the door, heaved himself from the seat into the rain, came around the car, and opened her door, drawing her out and putting his arm around her shoulder. He hurried them across the back yard. On the porch he unlocked the door, pushed it open, and guided her into the kitchen but without turning on the light, sensing, Amanda realized, that she wasn't ready for light just yet. He stopped by the stove, ran water into the tea kettle from the tap, and put it to boil on the stove.

"No," she said. "Not tea. Something else. A drink."

"Wine?"

"No. Something else. Something you drink when you're...when you're...."

"We'll stick with wine," he said, firmly, and flicked off the stove. "But we need to get you dry first."

He gave her his hand, warm and firm, and led her from the kitchen down the hall. Here again he didn't turn on the light, but she could make out the lineaments of her room from the street light shining through the window. "You'll need to get out of those wet clothes," he said, taking his coat from her shoulders. "Dry off and put on a robe."

"I don't have a robe."

"Pajamas then."

"I don't have those either." She was still shaking, though not as hard. "Only sweats and a t-shirt."

"Those will do. How about a towel?"

"It's in the bathroom."

He returned with the towel. Briskly he wiped her arms and throat, and dabbed at her face. "You finish drying off and change out of the dress," he said, "and I'll get the wine--I bought a bottle of that Cardinal's Crest you like so much, the red, I thought we could share it later on this evening--and then we'll talk."

"I'm so sorry, sir." She hardly knew what she was saying. She held one end of the towel and let it droop to the floor.

He ignored her reversion to formality. "Sorry for what?"

"For embarrassing you tonight."

"There are some tonight who should be embarrassed--who are having the hell embarrassed out of them right now, if I know Mary Celeste--but I'm not one of them. And you aren't either."

"I was running away." The shock of what she had done, of what she had intended, settled on her like a dull ache.

Ignoring her self-recrimination, Nathan took the towel from her and dried her shoulders. "You need to change. You're ice cold. Why don't you--"

"I was doing it again. I was going to do it again."

"Doing what?"

"I was running away."

"You weren't running away. You were running home. Home. And who could blame you? Suzanne told me what they were saying. She was giving them hell when I left. I would never have known she had it in her."

"They hate me and they'll never change."

"You overheard them, didn't you? When they had Suzanne cornered in the kitchen?"

"They think--they think I--they were saying all these things--"

He moved closer, pulling her to him. She could feel his warmth through his shirt. "You'll get wet," she said. "And I'm a mess. I--"

"Shhhh." He was holding her close, his arms around her, his cheek against her forehead, warm and comforting, and she could feel him smile. "I'm already wet. Listen--I've seen how Barb is. I've seen how she's treated you. What she's done to you. But I didn't know what to do. When they gave you that thing tonight--I saw right away it was planned, that it was no accident--all I could think was how brave you were up there. You were beautiful and strong compared to Karen and Barb and all the rest of that crew. You were great. And I thought then what I've thought for a long time. I thought how much I loved you."

He kissed her hair. When she looked up at him, he bent and kissed her mouth. His lips were soft and warm, and she kissed him back. She could taste salt in her mouth from the tears. It was their first kiss, and she was wet and shaky, splattered with shrimp sauce and grease, water dripping from her nose and chin, and she had never felt so fine or wonderful in her entire life. He touched her face with his fingers, then cupped her cheeks with both hands and kissed her again, harder this time. When they broke apart, she felt disoriented, standing there dripping wet in the dark. "Nathan, I--" But she couldn't say the words he'd said to her, even though they were true, even though she wanted more than anything else in the world to tell him how much she loved him. If she spoke those three little words, she thought he would somehow realize what a mess she was, what she had once been and what had happened to her and how much she wanted him. She no longer knew why she wanted him, whether it was for himself alone or for him and the children and the way they were together, or whether it was for his house and the security it offered her. She wanted her love for him to be pure, to be purely and solely for him, the love she'd read about in books when she was a girl, but she loved all the other parts of his life, too.

He kissed her again, touching her bare shoulders and neck with his fingers, warming them by his touch so that her cool skin prickled. Without willing a response, without thinking about it, she felt herself opening to him in that kiss, certain that he could taste the heat behind her tears. She don't know how long they stood there kissing, warming each other with their bodies, swaying together until he slowly pulled away, still holding her but looking at her again, his face inches from her own.

"I'd forgotten how that feels."

"I've never felt this. Not this way."

"I'd like to hold you. I'd like to take you to bed and make love to you. Right or wrong, that's what I'd like to do." He was staring hard at her. They had stood so long in the dark shadows that they were visible to each other now, and she could see his eyes reading her face. "But you want to say something first, don't you?"

"How did you know that?"

"Didn't I tell you? In addition to building houses, I read minds." She looked at him seriously. "All right," he said. "I've lived with you for six months. I've watched you when you weren't aware of it. You have a look that you get sometimes, as if you're happy but that you're afraid all your happiness is going to run away from you like water through your fingers. You had that look in your eyes right now."

"I have some things to tell you."

"I'll listen. But I'm going to want to kiss you the whole time you're talking."

"Not if you could really see me. I'm soaking wet and have shrimp sauce down the front of my dress. I've probably ruined your shirt."

"I've always been partial to shrimp sauce."

"There's more. You don't know who I am. What I was."

He pulled her close again and kissed her lips, lightly, softly, showing her that he didn't care about the sauce or the wet clothes. Then he felt her hesitation and fear, and pulled away, still holding her shoulders. "All right. I'll get the wine and change my clothes and meet you in the living room in five minutes."

Before she could say anything else, he turned and left her room.

———

In the bathroom she took off the dress, rinsed it in the tub, then submerged it in several inches of water. She washed her face and hung the rest of her wet clothes from the shower rod. Back in her room, she switched on the lamp on the nightstand, wiped herself dry, then pulled on white socks, her gray sweat pants, and a turquoise-colored t-shirt.

After washing the make-up from her face, she avoided looking in a mirror. She was too ashamed to look at herself. This evening which had meant so much to Nathan--and to her as well--was ruined, and some of the blame for that ruination lay with her. Had she not reacted so hysterically to those ugly words coming from the kitchen, had she simply backed away from the door and gone back to Nathan, she might have gotten through the rest of the evening without making such a fool of herself. By running away she had allowed them a victory, and now, with Nathan having pursued her, they all knew how much he cared for her. Whatever Suzanne or Mary Celeste said to them, those who despised her would take that knowledge and add it to their suspicions, and would make certain everyone in their tiny circle knew as well. They would brand her as a money-chasing whore. Even Mary Celeste wouldn't be able to disabuse them of that notion.

———

Nathan interrupted these thoughts by knocking at the door. "Amanda?" he said, and his low voice made a song of her name. She opened the door and found Nathan dressed as she was in a t-shirt--his was a dark military green--and sweat pants. The hallway was still dark, but a glow of yellow light shone from the living room.

"I ruined your shirt, didn't I?"

"I'll treasure every last little red dot. Besides, fair is fair. You wear sweats, I'll wear sweats." He held himself away from her, shy and diffident. "I've brought the wine to the living room and fired up the gas logs. I thought we could talk there."

He held out his hand, and she took it and followed him down the hall and into the living room. The open bottle of wine sat on a silver tray on one of the ottomans along with two large glasses. "We can move the couch closer to the fire if you like, or we can sit on the floor."

"The floor," Amanda said, and they sank down on the thick rug in front of the fireplace. The heat from the gas logs was already knocking the chill and damp from the air, and Nathan poured wine into the glasses and handed one to her. "To us," he said, and they touched their glasses together and drank. The wine cleared the tears from her throat. Nathan put his glass on the brick hearth and moved close to her until their knees were touching and took her hand. He kissed her on the lips, then said, "There, now. I'm ready for whatever you throw at me, as long as you don't tell me that you're a murderess or that you prefer rich old men."

"None of the above." She squeezed his fingers. "First, I want to tell you again how sorry I am about tonight. I made a fool of myself."

"No, you didn't. I'm as responsible for what happened as anyone. I should have seen what was coming. I knew Barb was jealous, but I thought it was just her. And then when they gave you that gift--that's when I knew. That's when I understood. I'm ashamed of myself for not seeing how some people were treating you."

"I felt ashamed, too, when I was up there in front of everyone."

"You handled it well. No one else knew except Mary Celeste and me. I saw what they were doing and how you stood up to them. That took a lot of courage and strength."

"What else could I do?"

"You could have thrown it back in their faces. You could have laughed it off, made a crude joke, joined them in their stupid charade. You could have burst into tears. Instead, you just stood there and faced them down. Your dignity made them all look about six inches tall. It's probably why they cornered Suzanne in the kitchen. You'd made them little and they were trying to look big again."

She hadn't intended to look dignified. She had only wanted that moment to end, had wanted to fall through the floor, and now she was silenced by his observation. She had seen him offer some piece of wisdom to the children, explanations of what had happened to them during their day, but the level of this insight when applied to her was new. She put her hand on his knee and squeezed out a thank you.

"If you think about it, that bunch has insulted me as much as you. They think we're sleeping together. They're telling people we're sinning against chastity."

His use of this old-fashioned word startled her. "Do you believe in chastity?"

"I'm afraid I do."

"I didn't think anyone believed that anymore."

"It's a pretty small club. And I wasn't always a member." He put his hand on top of hers. "But that can wait until later. You wanted to say something else, didn't you?"

"'Want' is probably not the right word."

"Need, then. Or obliged. Pressured? Possessed by necessity?" He bumped playfully against her knee. "You can stop me anytime. Otherwise, I'll need a thesaurus."

"Obliged, then," she said, and she started talking before he could say anything else or before her last bits of courage finally blew away. Unable to look at him--she stared instead into the steady gold-and-blue flames of the fireplace--she told him about the Amanda she used to be, how she had bossed and bullied her employees, how she had dominated them, how she had met Father Krumpler at the airport, how Mr. Henle had fired her and why she had deserved it. She told him about leaving her apartment and belongings, and wandering blindly across the country, and how for so long she had hated and feared other people, and how she had finally remembered Father Krumpler, who had saved her from self-destruction and who had brought her to this home, the place and means of her salvation.

The old clock whose clicks and chimes she knew so well sounded as she finished. It was only a quarter past eleven; the dance was still in progress unless Mary Celeste had ended it with a punch to Barb Brinkman's nose. Little more than an hour had passed since she had fled the church.

"'The 'Ice Queen.' I have trouble seeing that."

"It's what I was. Sometimes I still feel her inside me."

"And that was all?"

"Isn't it enough?"

"Yes." With his free hand he took a drink of wine. "I just thought there might be something else."

Now she did look at him. "All right," she said, wondering again how he could read her thoughts and her past, certain that Father Krumpler would never have revealed anything to him, and certain, too, that Barb Brinkman knew nothing about the rape. Clearly, Nathan had studied her and could read her so well that he had guessed there was more to her story. "All right. That same day when I was fired I went back to my apartment. There were two men. They were stealing things."

The rest wouldn't come. She lowered her head, looking now at his hand, the fine strong fingers on top of her own.

"Did the men take everything?"

"Everything I had left inside of me."

"Did they hurt you?"

"They beat me. And they did things to me. I was afraid they were going to kill me when they finished."

"And you didn't tell anyone?"

"Only Father Krumpler."

They sat silently with the fire lapping at their faces. Nathan never moved his hand or lessened the steady pressure of his fingers. He took another drink, put down his glass, and handed Amanda her own glass. The wine was thick and heavy on her tongue.

"I'm so sorry, Nathan."

"You have to stop saying that. You have nothing to be sorry for."

"There was no one before that, but I'd understand if you didn't want me. I'd--"

"Don't say that." He lifted her chin with his fingers and kissed her on the lips. "Right now I want you more than anything else in the world. I'm sorry for what happened to you. To tell you the truth, I thought you were going to tell me you were married and had run away from a husband. So you were never married?"

Remembering how she used to be and trying to reconcile that memory with marriage made Amanda smile for the first time since she had left the church hall. "No, I've never been married. When I said there was no one before you, I meant it."

"You mean--"

"No one in my heart. And before the break-in…those two men were the first…." It made her sick remembering them. She asked, incongruously, "Do you think Anne would have liked me?"

"She would have loved you the way you are now." He thought a moment. "She would have loved you however you were. Anne had this incredible gift for people, one I never had."

"Would she like me with the children?"

"She would want the children happy. She wants the children happy."

"You feel her too then? Here in the house?"

"Sometimes."

"It's a good feeling."

"Yes."

He stroked her knee. She could feel the strength of his fingers through the cotton fabric.

"What do we do now?"

"Right now?"

"Yes."

"This is where I take you by the hand and lead you to bed."

"What about chastity?"

"Oh, we'll be chaste. But we can still be affectionate. I'd like to spend the next hundred years or so holding you and touching you and listening to your voice."

"'Had we but world enough and time.'"

He laughed softly. "I'm guessing that's another one of your writers. Do you know how often these past months you've made me smile or even laugh out loud when I think of something you've said? I love you and I will be, I promise you, one of your better students." Then he stood and offered her his hand. "Unfortunately, we don't have a world of time. We're due to pick up the kids by noon tomorrow."

———

He led her to her bedroom. He had hesitated a moment at the bottom of the stairs, and she thought he might lead her upstairs to his room, and wasn't sure if she was ready to lie down with him in the same bed Anne had shared with him. Besides, she wanted the familiarity and ease of her own room. As if reading her mind, Nathan moved past the stairs, gliding in the darkness lit only by the glow of the fire behind them, and led her through the doorway. He shut the door, and then stopped beside the bed and kissed her again, slowly, before flicking on the lamp on the night-stand. "Too much light," he said, and flicked the lamp off. But then he turned the switch again, throwing light into the room.

"What's this?"

Amanda was already pulling down the comforter and looked at him and then at the night-stand.

"This looks like the journal I gave to Anne."

He was staring at the leather journal on the night-stand, its black cover glinting in the light, right where Amanda had left it after getting ready for the dance.

"I once gave her a journal that looked exactly like this one." He took the journal in his hands and flipped it open. His face went blank when he saw the writing inside. He turned the pages, slowly, holding the book open, and then looked at her.

"You have Anne's journal?" His voice was unbelieving, as if he were hallucinating, and his stunned dark eyes hardened. "Where did you get this?"

"I can explain," Amanda said, realizing as soon as she spoke how awful that sounded, how all the explanations from this moment until doomsday would not suffice. "I found it behind her books in the living room. I--"

"And you've been reading it?"

"Yes, but what happened was that I found the journal in July and started reading it and it helped me to get to know her and then tonight I just wanted to--"

"And you never told me?" He wasn't even listening. Disbelieving, he looked from her to the journal and back again. "You've had it all this time--"

"I didn't have it. I put it back on the shelf."

"But you knew about it and you didn't tell me."

"I can explain," she repeated. "I was going to give it to you, but I was afraid for you. I didn't want to see you hurt. I--"

"You knew about this"-- He shook the journal at her--"and didn't show it to me? What were you thinking?"

"I was going to tell you, Nathan. And I kept putting it back on the shelf after I read it. Anne helped me, what she wrote helped me, but I was afraid you'd be hurt. I--"

"Hurt doesn't begin to describe it." He moved back around the foot of the bed and toward the door. She reached out and touched his arm, but he yanked away.

"Please don't go. Let me explain. Let me tell you--"

"We'll talk in the morning," he said, his voice cold and dead. He stopped just outside the doorway to give her a last furious glare. "The 'Ice Queen,' right? Maybe that fits after all."

He closed the door and was gone.

———

She had made a mistake, and that mistake had inflicted pain.

This time Amanda didn't even think of running, of pulling her duffel from beneath the bed and loading it with clothes and toiletries and sneaking from the house to her car. She couldn't leave Nathan, not now, and she couldn't keep running for the rest of her life from pain or mistakes. He might have need of her. If nothing else, maybe she could serve as the focal point of his own pain once he'd read what Anne had written about him, to deflect in some small way the agony he was likely to feel from Anne's words.

She wanted to rest, but the bed had become a cold and lonely place. Instead, she dragged the big chair in which she had spent so many hours reading to the window. She switched off the lamp on the night-stand, pulled the comforter from the bed, and curled up under it in the chair. In a few minutes, when her eyes were accustomed to the darkness, she could make out the trees and shrubs of the side yard outside the window. The rain had stopped, but water was dripping from the leaves of the trees and the eaves of the house, playing a sort of listless music in the night.

For a long time Amanda thought of Nathan upstairs reading the journal. She kept listening for him, his footsteps, his tread upon the stairs, a creaking floorboard that might signal a return to her, but the house remained wrapped in deep, black silence. After a while she closed her eyes and began praying for him. She was still unaccustomed to prayer, unsure of what to say or whether anyone was really listening or whether anyone was even there to listen, but she prayed anyway, asking the powers she so little comprehended or even recognized as real to intercede with Nathan, to let him read the journal with a heart open to Anne's own sense of loneliness and pain, to let him understand, if he could understand, why she had not given him access to those words.

Who was this being to whom she spoke in her heart? Many claimed this god was love itself, a supreme deity who had sent a part of his very essence to live as a man among men and women, a man who was himself love incarnate, yet it seemed to Amanda that love was so messy a process, so agonizing even in its beauty and joy, that a god of love was as much a curse as a blessing. People could lose their faith for any number of reasons: the death of a child, the horrors of wars and holocausts, the ordeal of endless pain. But what about the awful misery wrought by love? What about the anguish caused by love? If God was love, and love itself brought heartache, despair, and pain, then what was so grand about such a god? Why would anyone want a god of love?

Everything she had done that evening she had done from love, yet everything she had done had ended in failure. Because she loved Nathan, she agreed to go to the dance. Because she loved Nathan and wanted to attract him, she had bought the black dress. Because she loved Nathan, she was scorned and hated by others, and was now humiliated as well. Because she had loved Nathan and didn't want to see him hurt, she had kept Anne's journal from him. If God was Love, and if she had acted from love, and if all this love had produced was more mess and more wretched emotions, then what did that make God? If this was love, then was not God some demon in disguise, the progenitor of all the torments of the human heart, all the blood and tears and mess of shattered dreams and failed longing?

The minutes dripped past her like the water from the trees outside. The last time she looked at the clock on the bureau it was half past one. Several times she was aware of the chimes from the clock in the living room. Whenever she closed her eyes, the room, the house, and the night took on that sort of nightmarish distortion when sleeping and wakefulness merge into a surreal borderland, when dream and reality become so confused that separating the two becomes impossible. Snippets of the evening, both real and imagined--Karen's whisper in her ear, Suzanne's kind eyes, Mary Celeste dancing with Tom--flickered in Amanda's mind, muddled, grotesque flashes of the real and the unreal.

Finally, though, she slept.

———

When she woke, her muscles and joints were knotted; her neck had crimped from the tilt of the chair; her knees ached, and her fingers were painfully stiff. She stretched, thrust out her arms, and whacked her fist straight in someone's face. Surprised, she cried out, lurched sideways, and nearly overturned the chair.

"Wow," Nathan said. He was sitting like a shadow on the floor beside her, holding one hand to his face while gripping the arm of the chair with his other. "You throw a wicked left."

"What are you doing here?"

"I came in about an hour ago or so. You were sleeping and I sat down to watch you, and then I guess I dozed off myself."

"What time is it?"

He fumbled around on the floor and flicked open his cell phone. The light illuminated his face, and she could see from his reddened nose that she had socked him hard. "It's a little before five."

"I didn't mean to hit you. I was stretching."

"It's okay. I deserved a good punch in the nose." He shifted his weight to see her more directly, and groaned. "I don't think I've ever fallen asleep before sitting by a chair. I'm all cramped up."

She noticed he was wearing a white shirt and dark pants. "You've changed clothes again. Were you going out?"

He shook his head, but answered indirectly. "I did a lot of thinking upstairs, and I want to apologize for last night. I had no right to treat you that way. You were protecting me--I see that now. I was a fool."

"You were upset."

"Will you forgive me for what I said to you?"

"Yes." She touched his face. "Of course I do."

"Everything Anne wrote was true. I was away most of the time. More than I really needed to be away. And I put her and the children and even God himself after my work. I didn't mean to hurt her. I wanted the opposite. But what she wrote in the journal is how it was. I wanted her more than I wanted the children. I was blind. I didn't understand how it was supposed to work."

"And now you see."

"Too late, but yes. Now I see."

"I'm sure Anne knows that."

"Where did you say you found it?"

"She'd hidden it behind her books in the living room."

"You said you'd read the journal before. I don't get it. Why read it again?"

"I've read it several times. Or parts of it. Her words, all that she wrote about the children and you and everything else--the house, prayer, God--what she had to say helped me. She was whole in a way that most people aren't. Everything that was happening, from life in the Church to Tim's scraped knee to the menu for supper, seemed holy to her in some way. I wanted to be more like her."

"I think Anne would tell you that you should be you. The best you can be." He pushed himself awkwardly to his feet and rotated his torso back and forth, working out the kinks from his nap on the floor. "What a strange evening."

"It didn't work out as planned."

"Maybe it still could. Let's try it and see." He held out his hand and helped her from the chair. They bumped together in the gray light of the room, and then he led her back to the living room where the fireplace gave out its light and warmth, and settled her on the sofa. Here the dawn was more pronounced, the light stronger, and she could see the fatigue in Nathan's eyes and face. But another emotion played there as well. He was smiling, standing tall and straight before the fireplace, his eyes cleared of sleep, glinting and mischievous.

"This room is one of my favorite places in all the world," he said, gesturing around him. "I played here growing up as a boy. I spent hours and hours here with Anne after we were first married. When I think of the children, I nearly always picture them in this room. Everyone and everything I have ever loved in the world is in some way a part of this room." He knelt beside Amanda on one knee, his back to the fire, holding himself erect so that even kneeling their eyes met levelly. "In the last six months you have become a part of our lives, mine and the children. In my mind you have become a part of this room and of our world. I don't want to live in this room anymore without you in it."

He was staring into her eyes, still smiling but with something new behind the smile, something fierce and protective and intense. "In those six months you have become a part of our lives. You came to love the children, and they fell in love with you. I can't explain why they were so attracted to you. Maybe because you all had gone through a storm and found comfort together. But I saw how they loved you. And the thing is, Amanda, I fell in love with you too."

She had spent the last two months, the days from the beach onwards, when she had fallen so deeply in love herself that she had avoided contact with those eyes, certain that if he looked at her this way he would see to the very bottom of her emotions. Now, however, she couldn't tear her gaze away from his. He held her like a hypnotist.

"I wanted to tell you how I felt about you so many times, but I was afraid you didn't feel the same way. There were so many questions. What if you left me? What if you weren't here anymore? What would happen if you didn't love me? And then last night I nearly lost you through my own blindness and stupidity. When I was upstairs last night, when I had finished reading what Anne had written about me--and it was all true, more than true, she was being charitable--I realized how badly I had misjudged you. I had jumped to conclusions. And I thought too that you must hate me after reading her words. But I'm not that man in the journal anymore. I'm not the same man."

"I understand," Amanda said. "You had to change to survive."

She knew about survival and change.

Nathan broke off his stare, looking down at the carpet beneath his knee, and was silent for so long that she wondered whether he had finished, but then he raised his head and his eyes came back to her.

"I know I have no right after last night to ask you this," he said. "I went off half-cocked, and I have to tell you that I'll likely do it again. It's part of the package. But I want to ask you to stay on here."

"I'll stay. I was already planning to stay."

"No, I don't mean it that way. I want to ask you--" He reached out and took her hand. His fingers were trembling. "Would you marry me, Amanda?"

The room faded around her. He became the core of all her attentions. A vein throbbed lightly in his neck. His hair was slightly rumpled on one side of his head from sleeping against the bedroom chair. His dark eyes held her face as gently as his fingers held her hand.

"Marry you?"

He might have laughed at the dazed wonderment on her face, but he was already plunging forward. "Marry me, Amanda. As in 'to have and to hold, in sickness and in health, for richer or for poorer, until death us do part.' That kind of marriage. I want you to be my wife."

"Why?"

"I love you," he said, simply. "I've loved you for a long time now."

"I love you too."

He smiled. "You make it sound pretty awful."

"I'm not used to saying that to people." She remembered the children, and added: "Not to adults, anyway."

"I'm more than willing to let you practice all you want on me."

"I'm afraid, Nathan."

"Of Barb?"

"No, not Barb. She can't do anything else to us."

"Is it Anne?"

"No, not Anne. It could never be Anne. Thinking of her--and I do think of her, Nathan, I do--is a comfort to me."

"What then?"

He was still kneeling before her, holding her hand, looking into her eyes, and she slid off the sofa and knelt with him, to speak directly to him. "I'm afraid for us. I do love you and I've thought of marriage. But I'm afraid of what might happen to us. I'm afraid of letting you down, making mistakes, failing you."

The last reaction Amanda expected from him was the laughter that followed her confession. Had it contained even a trace of mockery, that laughter might have offended her, but he was laughing with sheer delight at her words.

"Me too," he said after a moment. "I'm afraid of all those things. And they're going to happen, you know. I can guarantee you I'll make mistakes all the time. Sometimes I'll hurt you or make you angry, and sometimes you'll do the same to me. But that's what marriage is. It's falling down all the time. What I need is someone who will help me get up again, dust me off, and set me straight. And I see that person in you. I love you, Amanda."

His words, which no man had ever said to her, stiffened her courage like medals pinned to the blouse of a wounded soldier. "I love you so much."

"Is that a yes?"

"To have and to hold. For better or for worse."

"For falling down and picking up." He kissed her again, a soft kiss this time, one that barely touched her lips.

"I love you."

"You're sounding better about it already. But keep practicing."

"What do we do now?"

"It's nearly six. We have six hours until we get the children. I would suggest sleeping."

"Is it all right if we fall asleep together?"

———

This time he led her up the stairs and down the hall to his bedroom. It was darker here from the shadows cast by the oak outside, and he guided her by the hand to the bed through the shadows which moved in the room as the wind outside shook the leaves of the oak. Beside the bed he kissed her again, a slow kiss of reassurance, and then bent beside her and pulled back the covers of the bed. She lay on the sheets while he pushed off his shoes with his feet. Watching him move in the darkness, Amanda smiled at the thought that he had changed his clothing to propose to her, and then he was beside her, pulling the covers over the two of them and settling his head on the pillow.

"We can go slow, can't we?" she asked. "Not just tonight but for a long time?"

"Slow," he said. "And with plenty of stop signs."

For a long time afterwards they didn't speak. They kissed and then touched each other as if they were new creatures, fragile as glass, fearfully and wonderfully made. His fingers were gentle, and in the pale light of the new day spilling through the windows he caressed her face and throat as if afraid that she might vanish at any moment. His touch was like a poultice, draining away her fear, her terror that her rape might have ruined touch and intimacy forever. Once she cried a little with relief and happiness at simply being so near him, closing her eyes so that he wouldn't see her tears and stop his caresses.

They drifted toward sleep holding each other, their faces nearly touching on the pillow. "Are you all right?"

"What do you mean?"

"I thought men needed--." She couldn't find the word she wanted. "You know what I mean."

She could feel him smiling at her. "It's not a requirement," he said, "though I have to admit it's not easy." He paused. "We'll feel better about ourselves waiting. And we have the rest of our lives together."

"My knight in shining armor."

"The armor's a bit dented, but I am at your service, my lady."

"When shall we be married, do you think?"

"I looked at a calendar today. Would New Year's Eve do? It's a Saturday this year."

Amanda liked the fact that he had an answer to her question, that he had already thought about the date. "New Year's would be magical. The old giving way to the new."

"I won't forget our anniversary that way either."

She punched him lightly on the arm.

"We'll need to do the marriage preparation with the Church."

"What's marriage preparation?"

"We'd meet with Father Krumpler. There are marriage preparation classes, and I think we're supposed to wait six months, but I'm sure he'll give us a pass on the time requirements if you speak to him about it."

"Why me?"

"He likes you, in case you haven't noticed. He tells me so every Wednesday."

"Wednesday?"

"I've been seeing him for a while now. Right after the noon Mass on Wednesdays for half an hour or so."

Amanda jerked up on one elbow. "You've been seeing Father Krumpler about me?"

"Since before the beach. I need his advice. He's pretty good, you know. Anne used to go see him."

"You went to him about us?"

"There's no reason to get angry. He was very encouraging. He told me to do everything I could to serve you. He said to forget myself and think of you. He said--"

He stopped talking when Amanda flung herself with a cry onto the pillow and held her hands over her face. Within seconds she was shaking so that her ribs and stomach hurt, and she had trouble catching her breath. Nathan was above her, sitting up on his knees, stroking her hair. "Shhh. Shhhh. It's okay. Don't cry. I wasn't going behind your back. It was more about me than you. I had to sort out a lot of things. I--"

Amanda seized his wrist with one hand. It took her a long moment even to speak. "I'm not crying," she said finally. "I'm laughing. I don't think I've ever laughed that hard in my life. That wicked wicked man." She gulped another deep breath. "He was seeing me and giving me the same advice on Tuesdays."

"He what?"

"You know how I've cooked supper for him on Tuesdays?"

"Yes."

"He was counseling me. At first he helped me look at my past. Then after a while we mostly talked about you and me. He told me to make my love for you a service. To give myself to you without revealing how I truly felt."

Nathan sat back on his feet. "That old fox," he said, astonished. "He gave me the same advice."

"Old Owl is more like it." She was still laughing. "I don't know whether to hit him or kiss him."

"A priest for a matchmaker."

"And fairy godmother, though I don't suppose that really fits."

"Unbelievable."

"I love that old man."

"That word just gets easier and easier, doesn't it?" He cupped her cheek with his hand and kissed her. "Have you ever told him that you loved him?"

"Yes, but not enough."

"You can practice on him too."

"Oh, that felt so good to laugh that way."

They were so close together that she could feel his breath on her cheek. "I'd like a small wedding."

"Small sounds good. If that's what you want."

"You and the children and the Moores. Maybe Suzanne and her family. And anyone else you care to invite."

"Whatever you want."

"Small is what I want. And I want Father Krumpler to marry us."

"I'm sure he'll be absolutely delighted. He can float to the altar on that big swollen head we're about to give him."

"Oh, so wicked. I still can't believe it." She laughed again with sheer delight. "I might join the Church, too. Can I do it by the wedding?"

"You'd need to pass a test first and learn the secret handshake."

She snuggled more tightly against him, and yawned. Sleep was creeping into both of them. "You can teach me."

"I bet you could pass already. Let's see. Who made you?" he asked her, taking the first question from Teresa's catechism.

"God made me," Amanda answered verbatim, the answer drilled into her memory by a hundred repetitions with the children.

"Who is God?"

"God is the supreme being who created all things."

"Why did God make you?"

"To know, love, and serve him in this world, and to be happy with him in the next."

Nathan chuckled. "You'll pass with flying colors."

"I'm not sure I can believe like Anne."

"You're not Anne. You're Amanda."

"Nathan, I have to tell you. I'm not sure how much faith I truly have."

"Sometimes I wonder if anyone is sure of that." He pulled her closer. "Maybe faith is like everything else. Maybe the more we practice it, the better we believe."

They were murmuring now, letting sleep tiptoe closer.

"Should we take a honeymoon?"

"Wherever you want to go." He rolled onto his back so that Amanda lay with her head nestled against his shoulder and chest. "How about a trip to England? You could visit all those places you've read so much about."

"Could we really do that?

"We could."

"Would you like that?"

"I'd like to go wherever you'll be happiest."

"England sounds nice. But I'm happiest here."

"I love you, Miss Bell."

"And I love you, Mr. Christopher."

He held her so tightly against his chest that she could hear his heart beating. "You're a brave woman, Amanda, taking on me, four children, and a rambling old house."

"I'll get the job done," Amanda said, carefully choosing her old mantra, recognizing the truth of the words even as she smiled with gentle mockery at the woman who had once uttered them, the woman who had lived all those years behind a moat and in a high tower, that woman who had known so much and understood so little about the true value of the things of this world.

She was still smiling as they drifted into sleep, smiling at them both, Nathan the knight of scars and dented armor, she the lady of thorns and castle walls, embracing each other, tugged by the passing minutes into that future whose triumphs and tragedies, when faced together with a beloved, wise chroniclers had once described as "living happily ever after."

About The Author

In addition to writing essays, reviews, poetry, and short stories--he is a book critic for the Smoky Mountain News, and his work appears regularly in Chronicles Magazine--Jeff Minick tutors home-educated students in Latin, history, and English literature. He has lived in the Asheville area for thirty years. Readers who wish to contact the author may visit his Facebook page, Minick Online, or email him at saintsbookco@aol.com.

Made in the USA
Middletown, DE
02 November 2023

41758301R00203